I0635937

TOMLIN

TOMLIN TAKAHASHI DUET BOOK #1

THE CAÑON SERIES BOOK #1

GIGI MEIER

GiGi Meier

Cover Design by Just write. Creations

Editing by Revision Division LLC

Author Photograph by Tara L. Grundemeier

ISBN: 979-8-9877336-0-8 (e)

ISBN: 979-8-9877336-1-5 (pb)

GiGi Meier Media LLC

DEDICATION

To those who build a fortress around their heart to protect it.

TOMLIN

PROLOGUE

I hate Denver.

This city killed my dad. Medically airlifted here and left to die. This fucking city is dead to me, like him.

"What do you want?" he demands, rude as hell.

His face appears on a screen mounted next to the doorbell.

Irritated, my fingers curl over the edge of the box holding his belongings. It's all the crap he left at my best friend's house, which I offered to burn in a barrel behind my garage. She couldn't do it, or rather wouldn't let me do it. Now I'm here, in Denver, two hours from my home, returning all his shit.

"Open the door."

I try the handle, not afraid to barge into his steel and glass museum of a house, but the door's locked. Figures. I bang on it with my fist, intending on making as much racket as possible to get his ass down here to open the damn thing.

"No solicitors," he barks and points into the screen.

My gaze flickers to an engraved gold sign mounted beneath the doorbell. I don't give a shit. I know why I'm here, and soliciting isn't it.

"Open the door, or I'll carve my name on it."

I fish out my keys, giving him about two seconds to do it before I etch a line down the expensive wood.

"Oh, this is nice. Very smooth."

"What are you doing?" he yells.

The screen goes blank as footsteps thunder toward the door. It flies open when I start on the curved line of the *D*. The first letter of my name.

His dark brown eyes are blown out. His mouth gapes, showing off his perfect white teeth, and astonishment coats his face while his finger traces the deep grooves. Taking advantage of his temporary lapse in judgment, I brush past him to enter the glass house.

"You should get that fixed," I toss over my shoulder because I'm certain he has a butler or handyman that will sand out my initial with no problem.

My eyeballs can't decide what to look at first. It's all super modern, with white furniture everywhere.

Some crazy-looking statues are stuffed into cutouts in the wall, and weird abstract art hangs in enormous displays beside each other.

"What's that supposed to be?"

I tilt my head as I gaze at one. A child could have done better finger paintings.

"Who are you? And why are you in my house?"

He stands in front of me, blocking the view of the rest of his house and forcing me to analyze him instead. I get what she saw in him.

Without a shirt, he's impossibly fit. The sculpted caps of his shoulders connect to bulky muscles, making a straight line to the top of his neck.

His round pectoral muscles sit an inch beyond his eighteen-pack abdominals, and his wide lats taper down to a tiny waist. The gray joggers drape dangerously low from his hips, with a faint happy trail disappearing underneath. Even his feet are nice. Rare for a guy.

"If you're done ogling me, please answer my questions."

He's handsome, with a square jaw, cut chin, and almond-shaped eyes under thick black hair, intentionally gelled to stick up.

"You wish. You're way too pale for me."

I snort, shoving the box into his chiseled chest and leaving a burn mark near his nipple.

"Kylie wanted me to give you this box of crap."

"I don't want it. Let her keep them as mementos to remember me by."

He glances inside the open box with disdain before deserting me in his art exhibit living room. They're his clothes and shit. Why wouldn't he want them back? They probably cost a pretty penny. Tempting, I could resell them online if I had the time and cared.

I follow, watching his back muscles shift while he walks into the kitchen to pour a thick green slug from the blender into a frosted glass.

Unceremoniously, I dump the contents of the box on his kitchen island, which is bigger than my mattress. Then I drop-kick the box across the room, narrowly missing him. Damn shame. I wish it would hit him even though it wouldn't hurt with all the muscles.

His eyebrow pops up, unamused.

"I don't care. She doesn't want your shit, so here ya go."

With my job done, I spin on my heel, causing my Converse to squeak on his gleaming marble floor. He trails after me when I remember the pale pink card stuck in my back pocket.

She made me swear I would give it to him. She even sprayed it with perfume. Pathetic.

"Oh, she said to give you this."

I whirl around to give it to him. His hand is outstretched,

waiting when I decide he's an asshole and not worth her sappy words. Nope, he's not getting this. I rip it into pieces and toss it in the air, much to his surprise and my satisfaction.

"Yep, I knew I had it somewhere." I beam when I look at the confetti mess marring his white floor, and his eyes follow. "My part is done. Bye, asshole."

He doesn't say a word when I yank open his door and walk outside. I head to my truck when curiosity gets the better of me. I glance back to see him watching from his floor-to-ceiling windows with absolutely no shame.

Loser.

Unlocking the driver's door, I notice a new dent in the front quarter panel that I don't recall being there before. Squatting to examine the dent, there are three black streaks. I know I didn't hit anything to cause it. This is intentional.

"Son of a bitch."

It had to have happened while I was inside with the asshole. I stand to flip him off, and he moves closer to the window, pointing while drinking his green sludge.

Distracted and annoyed, I don't see the three hoodlums walking down the street until they're almost on me. Two stand at the front of my truck, while the other stands at my driver's side tire, which is entirely too close to me.

"Pop the hood," the one with a filthy wife beater says.

I assume he's the ringleader.

Bro better walk the fuck away because I'm not staying in this shithole city. These guys are a perfect example of why.

"Get the fuck out of my way."

I step off the curb, my keys dangling from my index finger when I glimpse a tire iron in the bald guy's hand at the front grill of my truck.

"You do this?"

I point to the dent, the one perfectly shaped like the end of the iron.

"Didn't do nothing," he leers, then smashes the front headlight with the iron.

He trades looks with the dickwad beside him, and I charge forward, only to be held back by the ringleader.

"What you going to do about it, girlie?" he taunts, breathing against my ear like a freight train.

Are they after me or my hot rod?

Either way, I go berserk. Stomping my foot into the center of his and ramming my pointy elbow into his ribs with a hearty thud. He groans and bear hugs me as I fight to get away. Wrestling my hand loose, I haul back and punch him square in the nose. I'm rewarded with a satisfying snap.

He howls in pain, instantly releasing me, with blood pouring down his lips and chin. Pain from my knuckles shoots up my arm and I shake my hand for it to stop.

"You broke my nose!" he shrieks, lunging toward me. His filthy nails scrape across my skin before I kick him in the balls.

"I know, dickwad."

He collapses to his knees, one hand cupping his nose, the other holding his dick. I fucking love that weak spot on men. Hearing a commotion behind me, I whirl around, readying my fists for a counterattack.

The asshole does a roundhouse kick into the tire iron guy's chest. It sends him hurling into his grimy friend and they collapse to the pavement.

While the thug clutches his wife beater undershirt, the tire iron clangs against the concrete. As he struggles to breathe, the veins on his neck bulge, and his face turns red. The grimy dude shoves his buddy off to go after the asshole, but he straight up kicks the guy in the stomach. The dude doubles over, grabbing his midsection and collapsing near his friend.

The asshole whips into a fighting stance over the pile of men, waiting for another attempt, but the hyperventilating wife-beater-wearing thug waves him off.

They're done. No match for Mr. Karate Moves.

My mouth dries at the ease and skill with which he handles them.

The grimy guy hunches over the curb, heaving into the asshole's green grass. The ringleader is holding his nose and running sideways to ensure the asshole doesn't come after him.

"You're welcome," that arrogant asshole says while smoothing back a lock of onyx hair that fell over his forehead. The waist of those damn sweatpants is even lower than before, and I'm salivating at how muscularly perfect his body is.

"I had it handled."

He's arrogant as hell.

If he wasn't so damn hot, I'd wonder how Kylie dated this dude?

"Didn't look like it to me," he says, walking away from the thuds trying to get off the ground and out of present danger.

"You got a pen?"

His switch-up surprises me. I indulge him by opening the driver's door and sinking behind the wheel to reach for a pen in my glove box.

"Here."

"And paper."

"Why didn't you say both at the same time?"

I'm tempted to give him a bloody nose for his bossiness.

"Because I didn't. Paper?" he says, snapping his fingers.

I pause, trying to hold myself back from punching that smug look off his face. "You're an asshole, you know that?"

"You've made that clear. Paper?"

He plants his hands on his hips. It gaps the front of the waistband, confirming he's going commando.

Damn my eyes for staring at the long outline of his dick now at eye level with me. I pluck a gas receipt off the floorboard and hand it to him with a scowl. He swiftly scribbles on it and then gives it to me. It's a bunch of numbers.

"What's this?" I ask since there are no dashes. The way it's written looks like a social security number with spaces in between.

"My number. Use it some time."

He tucks my pen behind his ear.

Is he seriously hitting on me after breaking my friend's heart?

Asshole.

"Right, I forgot to give you something else."

I shred the paper and throw it in the air to sprinkle over the curb. He smiles, and it's heart-stopping. Perfectly symmetrical shiny teeth made by a dentist and not his parents. I can see why she's crying over him. He's genetically perfect. But nope, assholes aren't my kind. Hell, dating, in general, isn't my kind.

I get out of the car to pick up the free tire iron, compliments of the dickwads. The thugs are hobbling down the street, pride forcing them to go. They deserved that beat down for what they did to my baby.

Inspecting the headlight, the thug scraped the top of the cover and busted the light. That fucker. I'll need to order the part today, so I don't get pulled over for a missing headlamp. The dent I can pound out when I get back to the shop.

"What?" I scowl because the asshole is still standing there watching me.

"What's with this old jalopy?"

"I'll have you know, this is a classic 1968 Chevrolet El Camino. It's the most valuable year. Figures someone as dumb as you wouldn't know," I explain, driving the tire iron into the palm of my hand a few times, imagining it's his face.

"Looks like a soda can."

"Shut up. I'm saving up for my paint job. Now move so I can go."

"Let me see your phone."

"Nope, I'm a one-trick pony, and that pen and paper bit was it for me. Bye, asshole."

He moves to the sidewalk with an amused smile while I slide behind the wheel and bring that beautiful engine to a roar.

I drop the iron on the floorboard and look up as he's making a circular motion to roll down the window. We're done here. I flip him off as I pull away from the curb. When I glance in my rearview mirror, he's standing where I left him.

Another reason I hate Denver.

It's packed with thugs and assholes.

1

CAÑON CITY

(THREE MONTHS LATER)

"Hey Carl, whatcha got for me?" I fasten the hair holder around my right pigtail and glance in the mirror to ensure the bands are even with one another.

"Morning Dani, we've got a new client. He's shipping in a car that sat outside for a couple of decades," Carl says from behind the newspaper.

He's the only guy I know that still gets the thing and reads it cover to cover.

"Sounds like my kind of job."

I tie a pink bandanna over the crown of my hair to protect it from the oil job I have planned for today before strolling past him to the box of doughnuts on the back counter that is calling my name.

"Yup, I know you love a challenge, and from the looks of the pictures, you're in for one."

He folds the newspaper and adds it to the pile against the wall that we are supposed to use on messy jobs to keep his floor clean. His old office chair whines when he leans forward to turn on his dusty computer.

I shove half a doughnut down my gullet before pouring a cup of coffee.

"That's from yesterday," he mumbles, hammering on the keyboard as he hunts and pecks for the letters.

"Dammit, Carl, you know it's the one thing I need to get me going in the morning."

I pour the coffee back into the pot, grab the handle, and walk to the small kitchenette by the bathroom to dump it out. After soaping and rinsing it, I head to the machine to start a fresh pot.

"You'd think you'd know better after all these years."

"Yeah, well."

No sense in arguing with Carl. He's too old to change. I finish my doughnut while flipping through my customer charts to see the status of each job and what parts I'm still awaiting.

"You working on the Hernandez Buick? You're behind. It needs to be out in two weeks," he chides, not looking up from the big box computer from a decade ago.

He's too much of a cheapskate to replace it. The keyboard is new from all the pounding he's done on the last four he killed.

"If you'd let me hire another person, I wouldn't be behind," I state the obvious, although he never agrees with my statements.

"Job security. Kids these days don't appreciate such a thing but, in my day—"

"Yeah, yeah, in your day, man invented the wheel, got it. I'm out of here." I pour my cup of coffee and sneak another doughnut before heading to the garage.

"When's the new client coming in?" I pause, with my back resting on the glass door.

"Car arrives in an hour, depending on the transport driver's motivation to make his bonus. Client shortly after. I'll come to get you when he arrives."

He frowns at my pigtails. It makes him uneasy when people

think he's employing a minor. Don't stop some of his old geezer customers from looking at my full rack.

"Ten-four."

I push through the door, breathing in the smell of grease and motor oil, which is as enticing as perfume on a hooker. I walk over to my little slice of heaven at the far end of the garage.

Pulling out a few paper towels to lie on my workbench, I set my doughnut and coffee down to survey my tools to make sure they're all in place and that Judd didn't use any of them.

The shop is quiet today.

Other than Carl inside the office, I'm the only one here. Enjoying the solitude before Judd arrives to ruin it, I open my locker and drag out my coveralls. Depending on how hot it gets today, I may ditch them later.

For now, I'm hunting down a brake fluid leak and adding motor oil, and prefer not to get it on my clothes or in my hair. The last time that happened, it took about five vigorous scrubs of my clarifying shampoo to get my hair back to its natural light blond color.

I tug my covers over my Converse and cutoff shorts, leaving them unzipped at the waist with my tank top peeking out. It's cooler for now. I'll zip up when I get under the car to see what I'm dealing with.

With Judd not here, my playlist dominates the garage. It's a race between us to get here early, and he sulks when he has to listen to all my cheesy pop music. He's into that heavy metal crap where dudes throw their heads around.

When I have to listen to that shit, I want to throw my head against the wall. Carl doesn't care what we play as long as we keep working.

I wolf down the doughnut and chase it with a few slugs of coffee before scrolling through my playlists.

Once the girl squad starts up, I belt out the words to the

song, using my wrench as a microphone. Singing and dancing around the Buick, I pull out the tools I need and deposit them on the floor.

When I have everything, I lie down on my creeper, zip up my covers, and slide under. After some time checking the line and the connection to the master cylinder, I find the culprit.

"Morning, Dani."

"Hey, Judd. How'd it go last night?" I shout over my music.

"She wouldn't leave this morning, and now I have to listen to this girl crap. Today blows already," he whines, and I grin while working the line coming off the cylinder.

"Did you tell her up front it was a quick bang? Girls tend to hang around expecting breakfast if not told otherwise."

"I always tell them the deal. Some are too stupid or too clingy to believe me."

I don't feel one bit sorry for him. The dude is a manwhore.

"Go to their place instead? Then you can come and run. Get it?" I grin, tightening the bolt and humming to my music.

"You tell me that all the time and I never listen. Can I come over tonight?" he asks, turning down my song, which causes me to frown.

"Hey, I love that song, and hell no. You're not getting in these pants, lover boy. I don't have any STDs, and I'd prefer to keep it that way," I holler from under the car, but he doesn't reply, nor does he turn my music back on.

"Judd?"

"Dani, there's a guy here for you."

Judd's voice sounds tight. I glance to my left, and a pair of gleaming black dress shoes are standing between the cars.

Fancy. Who's that?

"Give me a sec."

I finish connecting the line, knowing I'll have to check it later and slide out to see who this mystery guest is. The second

I lay eyes on him, I flash back to that day, three months ago, when he hit on me.

Twice.

What the hell is he doing here? Does he have a box of her junk too? I need to stop being the middleman in her disasters.

"Why are you here?"

I sit up on the creeper, not intending to stand and give him the time of day. Who cares if he hovers over me and cast glares at Judd?

"Looking for you. It took me forever to find you."

He's all gussied up in a fancy black suit and tie and looking very out of place here. His dress shoes clack on the concrete floors when he walks closer.

"Funny, I wasn't lost, so it's no wonder it took you forever. That still doesn't answer my question. What do you want?" I repeat, a silent Judd milling about his station over the asshole's shoulder.

"You."

"Not happening."

I lie down and roll under the car, continuing to work when his shoes shuffle toward the front tire. My mind is racing down the details of that day because I'm pretty sure I turned him down. Made it crystal clear what I thought of him.

"You didn't let me finish." His frustrated voice amuses me, but I hold back my laughter.

"Spit it out then."

"I want you to restore my car."

His car?

He's the new client? How can that be?

No, this isn't happening. I'm not hitching my wheel to this fancy-ass wagon. That's for damn sure.

"Again, not happening."

"Why?" He sounds bewildered and more frustrated. I love it.

"Cuz you're the asshole that broke my friend's heart and was an asshole again when I dropped off your shit. And again, when you hit on me. That, kid, in baseball is what we call three strikes, and you're out." I drop the wrench, which clangs against my ear.

"Fuck."

He squats, his pants so tight, I wonder if they're going to rip. "Are you okay?"

The concern in his voice is expected from a novice that knows nothing about cars. I've dropped, spilled, and burned many places on my body. It's an occupational hazard.

"I'm fine. It slipped."

Because of the excess fluid soaking my fingers. Good thing my bandanna is on.

"If I recall, I saved you that day. Where's the gratitude for that?" His concern clears faster than the gratitude he's looking for.

"Hand me that rag over there?"

I point to it resting by his foot, knowing I can reach it myself, but I hate him, so I'll make him work a little.

"I didn't need your help. I had it covered."

He picks it up with two fingers and tosses it into my general area. The fussy little thing can't get his fingers dirty.

I roll my eyes as I wipe the fluids from my hands and gather my tools.

"You didn't have it covered. One guy already had you. I'd hate to think about what would have happened if I wasn't there. You're welcome, for what it's worth."

I roll out, tossing the rag into the wash can, and lean over to get up from the creeper without busting my ass like I did last time.

"They were after my car. No big deal."

I walk to my station to wipe down my tools before hanging them on the wall. I don't need his dirty dick hands tainting the pretty pink handles. Pink paint on every last one of them so he can't steal or borrow them and lie about it later.

"You're naïve if you think that," he huffs, his dark brown eyes intense as they follow my every move.

This shop isn't big enough for that.

"Then good thing you were there," I concede, planting my hands on my hips to square up with him.

"You want a good job sticker or something?"

"I want you to fix my car. You owe me that."

"I don't owe you shit. Now move. I got things to do."

I sidestep him, trying to get over to the driver's door when he blocks my way. Judd's trying hard not to listen, but this shop is too small not to hear everything.

He takes the tiniest step over, unwilling to give more. I'm not the skinniest girl in the world, but I shimmy past, hoping the brake fluid on my covers gets on his designer duds. I yank the driver's door open to test my repairs.

"You going to a funeral or a wedding?"

With the driver's door propped open, he inconveniently leans against it. The throaty engine gurgles.

Not a good sign.

"Excuse me?"

He raises his voice over the car's sputtering. I have a fair bit of fine-tuning to do to get that perfect purr.

"You're wearing a suit when it's the dead of summer and going to be in the nineties today. I figure you're either going to a funeral or a wedding. Why else would you be wearing it?"

Not that I don't love Colorado summers, but the unusually high temps heat the garage and make it an inferno. Carl's tiny mounted fans in the corners of the garage are like a gentle breeze when I'm wanting a hurricane.

"There are other reasons besides those two." He lowers his voice when I cut the engine off.

I cast him a suspicious look.

"Interview? That's not really your house, is it? You live with your parents, right? I knew that place was too clean for a dude."

Poser.

I know what I need to do next. Two things actually. Get rid of him and continue working.

"I'm gainfully employed," he replies, resting his hands on the frame of the door and trapping me in place.

I think this guy loves power moves because he keeps using them all over this garage.

"Who says that? Gainfully employed. It sounds like you're a senator or a census worker."

I yank on the doorframe to get his ass off it before slamming it shut.

"It would to a high school dropout."

I whirl around to tell him to fuck off when Carl comes waddling through the door. His curious gaze falls on us and I snap my mouth shut.

"Good, I see you two have met," he says. The asshole's head flies around to meet the old man's eyes.

"Yeah, something like that," I mumble, debating if I should tell Carl how I know him.

"Good. Mr. Takahashi, lead the way."

Carl sweeps a hand toward the lobby door. The asshole looks at me for a second, nods, and then strides toward it without another word.

Mr. Takahashi?

Interesting.

I follow the men through the lobby, out the back door to a parked trailer, unloading a rust bucket behind the fence at the far end of the property. I stop as they continue toward it. This isn't happening over my dead, rotting-in-the-hot-sun body.

"Dani, come up here," Carl hollers over his shoulder.

I can't stop my feet from dragging on the concrete leading to the car. It makes enough noise for them to turn and watch me drag them the last ten feet. When I finally stand beside them, the rust bucket lurches inward as if giving up. It should, I have.

"This your hunk of junk dying in our lot?" I ask while we all stare at it.

"Er, yes. That's, um, him."

I laugh. This is priceless.

"Him."

The asshole called himself gay, and he didn't even realize it.

"Dani," Carl warns, and I rein it in for his sake, only for his sake. Not the asshole's.

"What's so funny?"

"You called this heap of crap a guy, which makes you gay. I love it," I blurt out, disregarding Carl's disapproving look.

"Is that not how it goes? You call yours her, so I thought it follows gender lines," he explains politely.

I know that shit's an act, for Carl's sake.

"Yeah, cuz she is. It's okay. You're gay, so stick with him."

I pat his back and Carl shifts with unease at the mention of sexuality.

I don't think he cares, gay or straight or whatever. He's not one to talk so openly about it. It's a generational thing.

"Well, what do you want to be done to, er, him?" Carl asks, and this gets better and better. I cross my ankle over the other and wait patiently as both of them fidget.

"Fix it up, like new again."

I chuckle when he reverts from 'him' to 'it'. Carl leans back to flash me a warning look behind the asshole's back.

I cover my mouth and prop my arm under my elbow as if I'm deep in thought.

"Original or reproduction parts?" Carl asks, and his eyes slide to mine.

"What do you recommend?" the asshole asks me. My lip snarls at the helpless sight of his rust bucket. "You don't like it? It's a muscle car and a good year."

The car should go back to where he found it, pushing up daisies.

"I'm not a fan of cars from the seventies but to each his own." I shrug, avoiding the question since I won't be taking on this project.

"Do you know what it is?" the asshole challenges, causing my blood pressure to rise.

"Yeah, before someone tortured it slowly over the course of many, many years and finally murdered it, it was a 1972 Ford Gran Torino Sport 351 Cobra Jet V8. But now? It's a rusted-out soup can. Good luck."

I pat his back and start to turn away.

"Dani."

Curse you, Carl.

"Can you restore it?" the asshole asks with a hint of sincerity.

I wipe the sweat from my forehead, knowing I can restore it, but I won't.

"She can restore anything. She's our best preservationist," Carl brags.

I roll my eyes, and the asshole raises an eyebrow. The best preservationist out of two is a step above winning a participation trophy in school.

"Preservationist, huh? Then she's perfect for the job. When can you start?"

"Half past never. Carl, I need to get back on the Hernandez car. I'm behind, after all. Bye, Mr. Takahashi."

I take two steps back, planning to run on my third step.

"I'll pay thirty percent more."

He does the unthinkable. He appeals to Carl's business sense.

"You don't even know what it's going to cost to resurrect this thing from the dead," I say, cupping my hand over my eyes to block the morning sun. "Doesn't matter, anyway. I get paid the same if I work on him or the other five cars in front of yours. As I said before, good luck."

"Dani, I decide around here, not you. Now Mr. Takahashi —" Carl starts.

"Call me Tomlin, both of you, please."

He smiles at both of us, genuinely at Carl, and for effect at me.

I'm partial to asshole, but Carl won't let me call a potential client that.

"Tomlin, what Dani's trying to say is that she already has commitments for other clients. Perhaps we could get someone else to work on it. Judd has more experience than Dani and is ahead of schedule, unlike some people."

His parental eyes flash his disapproval, and I glance away when the asshole catches the look.

"With all due respect, you said she is the best and has a waiting list. Does this Judd person have a list of clients waiting for his work?"

"No, but I can assure you that his work—"

"What's the difference, then?" Tomlin presses.

I remain silent as they go back and forth as if I'm not standing right here.

"Dani's a little too much of a perfectionist. She doesn't meet deadlines because she's meticulous with her work. It borders on obsessive and, at times, disruptive to the other clients. But she's earned a reputation for herself, so I can't move clients away from her. Even if she took your project, she wouldn't meet whatever deadline you set for her. She barely listens to me, and I own the place."

They both chuckle at my expense, and I take another two steps back. On three, I'll run for real this time.

"I tend to be a bit of a perfectionist myself, so I understand the trap we put ourselves in. I'll wait then for her schedule to clear. In the meantime, can it remain here?"

He can't park that heap here for the next year because that's how long it will take me to get through my waitlist.

"Sure, let's work up the paperwork inside."

Carl claps the asshole's back like they're long-lost friends, and I must stop this.

"This perfectionist didn't agree with it. Looks like you're on Judd's schedule. That's a shame. See ya around."

I drop my hand, let out a small wave, and speed walk toward the garage.

"Dani, don't be rude to our client. Get back here," Carl calls to my back.

I grit my teeth and turn to face them as they walk toward me. The asshole's smirk pisses me off.

"I think what Dani means to say is she needs the right motivation to take on my, what did you call it again?" Asshole mocks, and I easily rattle off the insults.

"A rusted soup can, a hunk of junk, and a heap of crap. Any will do."

"Very clever. To take on my preservation. A little incentive, perhaps, to move it up in her schedule, so I don't have to lurk around here, waiting for months."

A year, actually.

Shit. An entire year of him lurking before I start.

I could set aside my perfectionist ways to move through the cars quicker. I hardly think it's fair that he gets to jump the line. That's not happening.

Whom am I kidding?

I can't not be a perfectionist. It's in my DNA. Dad was a perfectionist. He'd never let me cheat or cut corners on a restoration. He taught me everything I know.

"Nope, there's nothing I need. Where's Judd? Judd? Come out, come out wherever you are," I scream across the parking lot toward the garage.

When I don't hear a response, I turn back to the guys.

"He's probably working. That Judd is a stickler for detail."

I walk toward the open bay and flat-out run when I round the corner.

"Yo, Judd!"

He's scrolling through Tinder, ogling girls at his station, when I tap him on the shoulder.

"Dude, didn't you hear me calling your name?"

"I blocked it out."

He keeps scrolling, staring at one bikini-clad girl after another.

"Hey jerk, this is serious. I gotta car for you. Come meet the guy. You'll love him. He's all fit and shit like you. It will be great."

I tug on his coveralls, knowing they will be in the garage at any moment, and I still have a deal to seal.

"I'm not gay."

"Duh, I know. I meant you can bro it up, lift weights, spot each other, talk shit, and whatnot. Come on. You're wasting time. He's right out here."

"It's all settled. Dani will start—"

"No! Judd agreed to do it, so I'll leave you to it."

My song and dance better work because the last time I owed Judd a favor, I had to work in a bikini all day. Let's say oil is harder to get out of crevices than coveralls.

"Nice try. Judd, go back to work."

Carl gives me the eye again, three times in ten minutes. It's an omen of a bad day.

"Dani, come with us."

Judd scowls at me before picking up his phone to scroll again. I follow behind, dragging my feet again, but no one cares enough to comment.

Carl pushes through the glass door. The asshole holds it open for me in fake chivalry as he touches my pigtail when I pass. I swat his hand, trying not to punch him as we walk down the hall to Carl's office.

"Let's all have a seat and discuss the project. First, why don't you tell Dani what the incentive is? I think she'd like to know," Carl says, trying to bait me as he shuffles around the desk piled high with crap to plop his ass behind it.

"No incentive necessary. Who wouldn't love to work on a rusted-out soup can? I know I would."

I lay my hand against my chest for effect and perch against the short bookshelf stuffed with papers and other knickknack junk to avoid sitting in the chair next to the asshole.

He laughs, Carl frowns, and I look away.

"A custom paint job," the asshole says, and I return his gaze.

"You want a custom job? That's fine. We got a talented guy that does a sick pinstripe if you like that sort of thing. No worries, though, because that's a long way off. You still gotta source the parts if you're going replica."

"No, you finish ahead of schedule. I'll pay for the custom job you want."

He smiles like the devil, and now I'm the one laughing.

"Joke's on you because I'll have that paint job done and paid for by the time your tin can rolls around."

I dig my fingernail into my ear to check for wax, completely disinterested in anything else that comes out of his pie hole.

"Dani," Carl warns, pointing a pencil at me before digging around his desk for his schedule book.

"He's agreed to pay for it and the thirty percent increase if his car is next after the Buick."

That sneaky shit.

I scowl at the gall of buying his way to the front of the line. He arches his eyebrow, challenging me to decline, and I'll take that challenge. I flick the wax from under my nail before I start.

"That's an awfully nice proposal, Carl. But how will you explain to the other customers ahead of him that he gets to jump the line? Some have been waiting three months already. They will not be happy to know some guy saunters in here offering a ridiculous amount of money he thinks of paying to spite me."

I glare at both.

"Dani, that's enough. Your attitude would anger your father. Since he's not here, do I need to turn you over my knee as he would?"

I hate that he's known me my whole life. Otherwise, this would be harassment, and I could file a claim somewhere in the government.

"No, Carl."

"Let me handle the clients. You worry about getting that car done and finding parts," he says, acting all tough and blowhard.

It takes everything in me not to roll my eyes, so instead, I stare at the peeling wood-paneled wall behind his head.

"Yes, Carl."

"Stop patronizing me. And apologize to Mr. Takahashi."

I gasp, my eyes meeting the asshole's gaze and watching a smirk play at his lips.

"I'm not saying sorry to him. Did he tell you he's interviewing?"

I throw out my arm, my finger pointing to the asshole as I glare into the old man's beat red face.

"He doesn't even have the money to pay for the restore, much less thirty percent on top. Thirty percent on top of nothing is still nothing. Tell him. Tell him what you told me about the suit and stuff in the garage. Go on, tell him about the interview today."

"Dani, what has gotten into you? Of course, he has the money. He contacted me a month ago when he was arranging for the car you see outside. Things like this don't happen overnight. He's already paid for six months of storage fees in advance."

My arm drops as I look suspiciously at the asshole, trying to detect if he's lying. His facial expression is soft and unguarded. He's the best damn actor I've ever met.

"Did he tell you he broke my best friend's heart?"

That gets his face to tighten, swallowing up the sincerity to revert into a stony mask.

"See, did you see what he just did right there? He knows I'm right." My gaze volleys between the men, settling on the asshole's icky brown eyes.

"Yeah, you didn't think I'd say it. Well, I did."

I bow up feeling like a badass, and the room goes silent. This guy's an asshole and Carl deserves to know.

He stands, catching us both off guard, and takes calculated steps to the door.

"I believe I've worn out my welcome. I'll part ways and have the shipper take my 'heap of junk' to another preservationist. I'll expect a refund of all expenses incurred by the end of the week. Good day," he vomits his threats before leaving the small office.

Carl scrambles to his feet, wobbling a bit and knocking some papers to the floor as he shuffles past his desk to scurry after the asshole.

A blink of guilt comes over me. I may have taken it too far.

Meh, good riddance.

Smiling, I tiptoe to the door and peek around the corner. Their heads are lowered, as are their voices when they walk toward the customer lobby. Once the hollow bell rings at the top of the front door, I know the coast is clear for me to bolt back to my station.

2

"What's that all about?" Judd's practically on top of me when I brush past him to turn the music back on. Pivoting to answer his question, I lean against my station to put some respectable distance between us, even though he's already intruding in my space.

"Just some asshole that broke my friend's heart asking me to fix his car. Get this, he offered Carl thirty percent more to jump the line. The asshole thinks he can buy Carl like that." I shake my head in disgust. "And he even offered to pay for my paint job if I finished early."

Judd laughs, getting the hint and stepping out of my personal space. It helps because I was one second from shoving him.

"That's impossible. You can't even finish your coffee the same day you pour it. Everything in your life is half-finished."

Judd gestures to the stained coffee cup from Friday with coffee still in it.

"Shut up," I hiss, hating that it's true and making a mental note to dump it out later.

"If Carl didn't ride your ass like a donkey, nothing would get done."

"I said, shut up."

My hands roll into fists. It wouldn't be the first time I launched myself at him.

"How's the GED coming?"

The smug bastard knows precisely how it's going. It's not.

"Fuck you, Judd," I spit through clenched teeth, trying to not lose a day's work over a fistfight again.

Deciding he's not worth it, I turn away, thinking about what's left to do to get that Buick out of here and prove all these jerks wrong.

Judd presses his chest into my back, the hardness of his body pushing me against the cold metal counter. I try to elbow his ribs when he plants his palms flat on the steel, pinning my elbows to my waist. His mouth drifts toward my ear. His breath is heavy against my skin as his cheap cologne seeps into my pores.

"Get your nut brush off me," I seethe, as this isn't the first time he's harassed me like this.

Most days, I endure it to make it end sooner, but today, I'd rip his pornstache off and claw his eyes out, especially after how frustrating this morning has been.

"Womb broom. And you love my mustache. Think of how it will feel against that tight little body of yours."

His hard-on digs into my back. I wrestle to get him off me, but there's no escaping him.

"Act like your hairline and back the fuck up."

I lean forward to ram my upper body into his, but he barely moves.

Why can't Carl waddle in and see this? I swear that old man has the worst timing.

"I like it when my girls put up a little fight," he says,

exhaling across my neck and thoroughly grossing me out with his bad breath.

I'm about to ram the back of my head into his nose when the clack of dress shoes catches us both by surprise.

"The lady said get off her, and I'm inclined to agree."

The asshole's anger travels across the garage like a fast and deadly bullet. I turn my head in the direction of his command, but Judd's big-ass head is blocking my view.

"It's cool, man. We're just talking." Judd's voice rises. His manhood threatened as he lifts off me.

I spin around, eager to see him get his ass kicked when Judd raises his hands in surrender. The asshole, on the other hand, is quick to charge forward to grab Judd by the collar of his covers. His face is placid, with a fire in his eyes and a throbbing jaw muscle. Interesting.

I grab my coffee and rest my elbow on my station to watch the show. Judd hates tough guys because he thinks he's his own form of badass. He doesn't know what the asshole is capable of, but I do. This should be fun.

"I'm going to be around here a lot now that Dani agreed to do the work."

My mouth opens to protest, and he shoots me a murderous look that has me taking a swig of my coffee. Yuck, cold. I set it down, mentally reminding myself to dump it out as well.

"If I see that shit again, I won't hesitate to take you outside."

He shakes Judd with his final words, but I know what's coming.

"Let's go, tough guy," Judd sneers, jutting his chin up but coming up about four inches shorter than Tomlin's height.

Yep, challenge accepted.

Judd never backs down.

He loves to fight and has come in here too many times with a busted lip or black eyes to prove it. I've never actually seen him fight, but from all the bragging he does, he seems to hold his own. I wish there was a way to place bets and make a little green off this fight. I'd go all in on the asshole.

Damn shame.

The asshole sneers or smiles. I can't decide which, but he looks satisfied to fight Judd either way. If taking down two guys in a matter of seconds is any sign, he'll easily win this. If we were at a bar, I could get an over-under started.

Damn shame again.

They stride toward the open bay, passing glares when Carl pops around the corner. He's all smiles with his new customer paying extra.

I look away, grumbling, "Bullshit."

"There you are. Did you get it squared away?" Carl's chipper tone fails to read the room.

It's amusing when they stand in front of each other, acting as if they weren't about to go to blows. Judd's eyes glance from the asshole to Carl, waiting for him to admit what's about to go down. Bunch of overgrown toddlers.

Grabbing my ratchet set, I squat down on my creeper and slide under the car. Their deep voices rise in anger. I simply shake my head and start tightening the supply line. This should make Carl happy. I could have stood around and gawked, but I continued working.

I'm proud of myself.

His dress shoes appear by the tire while I whistle, letting him know I'm not interested in talking to him.

"Dani, a word?"

He stoops down, and if he wants to make eye contact, he will have to lie on the filthy floor for that.

"Busy, asshole," I say loud enough to not be heard by Carl.

"Danielle Louise Winters, get out here," Carl hollering my full name as Dad used to isn't a good sign.

I'm going to nunchuck that asshole the second we're out of

Carl's sight. I let my socket clang to the concrete floor in a juvenile protest but roll out to glare at both.

"What now? Can't you see I'm trying to work here? You know, get caught up. Finish the car."

I know it's a weak excuse, but it's the only one I got.

"You're taking the job. Get up and get the specifics so you can start on the parts today," Carl orders while the asshole towers over him.

He doesn't seem satisfied that he won, which is weird because if I got my way, I'd be twerking.

"Back to work, Judd."

I groan as I drag my ass off the creeper. Carl ignores me by walking away. Judd looks murderously at the asshole, and I stomp toward the open bay, needing a break from all the testosterone in here.

I'd never admit it to him, but I'm a little giddy over his car. It's in the worst shape I've ever started from, but if I can pull this off, she'd be a beaut. I practically skip to his heap of crap for a closer inspection when the asshole strides my way.

The floorboard is gone, along with a hole in the roof from years of climate damage. The body is in terrible shape, and a smile passes over my lips. I'm in for a rigorous workout to get this steel hammered out.

"What do you think?" he mutters, trailing beside me and stopping when I do. "Can you restore it?"

My fingers brush a rusted-out hole in the trunk and throw large chunks into the storage lot grass. I don't answer him right away. Choosing to survey the driver's side, which seemed to have been resting beside a tree with the amount of sticky sap coating the driver's window.

"Did you pick this thing out?"

I don't even bother looking at him when I continue my trek around the engine. The roof has a horizontal dent in it, probably from a fallen tree branch. The front end has so much damage it looks like it was in a head-on collision. Once I pry the crumpled hood off, I'll have a better idea of the shape of the engine.

"Yeah, why?"

I cup my hand over my eyes again when I look at him.

"No reason. Why me?"

"You're the best," he says with a tilt of his head.

"Don't bullshit a bullshitter. Give me the real reason."

He joins me at the front of the car, the breeze picking up the edges of his black hair, giving him a more carefree look.

"Does he always do that to you?"

He ignores my question for his own.

"Who? Judd? He means nothing by it." I toss my thumb over my shoulder toward the garage. "I had it under control."

"Didn't look like it to me. You realize that's twice I have saved you."

I gaze at him, trying to figure out if he's being sarcastic or not.

"I'm no damsel in distress, asshole, so back off. I'll handle my shit, and you handle yours. Which right now is me and this soup can you call a classic."

I drop my hand, setting this conversation aside to kneel and look under the engine. It's not leaking anything. It probably dried out years ago, which means replacing a hell of a lot of parts. That's going to be tricky. He does realize I might need to sub in some replica parts.

"It is Tomlin, not asshole."

I don't care what his name is. He'll always be an asshole to me.

"Don't care."

I pick at some corrosion as I inspect the rest of the engine from this angle.

"Are you always this difficult?"

He shifts, leaning against the car, and it groans under his

weight. His carelessness surges it toward me. I jump back to land on my ass, and it narrowly misses trapping me underneath.

"Are you fucking crazy? Never, ever, touch a car when someone's under it. Are you fucking stupid? It could have decapitated me!" I scream at him.

The look of realization on his face, followed by horror, says it all. He did not know. It wasn't intentional.

Fucking idiot.

"Dani, I'm so sorry. Are you okay?"

He's squatting in my face, and the closeness is that of an intimate lover. It catches me off guard, and before I know it, he's tugging me into his arms for an unnecessary hug.

I'm not big on compassion or people comforting me. After growing up with a dad that never did it, random hugs make me uneasy. No one touches me except Judd. He's constantly doling out unwanted sexual advances, but I've grown thick alligator skin to it after all the years.

"If anything happened to you because of me—"

Guilt, not compassion. Third damn shame today, and it's not even noon.

"All right, all right, already, get off. I know you made a mistake, but let's not make this more than it is," I hiss, struggling to untangle myself from him.

He immediately releases me and stands up, putting a good amount of distance between us. Far more than necessary, but judging by his actions, I think his reaction surprised him too.

Pushing myself up from the ground, I dust off my already filthy coveralls and straighten my bandanna. He shoves his hands in his pockets, punishing them for reaching out without thought. Good, let that be a lesson to him.

"That little stunt might have cost you more money, seeing as how hard it hit the concrete. It may have broken a piece that I could have salvaged."

He nods, seeming to retract into himself. Interesting. Someone gets withdrawn when scolded. I'll have to remember that since we'll be working together over the next several months.

"I'll try to source original parts, but it might be hard because back in the day, they didn't put as many in production as they do now. From what my dad used to tell me, they used cars from this decade in the demolition derbies, up to one hundred cars a night."

"What does that mean?" he asks, keeping his distance and looking more uncomfortable.

"Original versus restored, age-old debate among purists."

He looks even more lost, and I find myself intrigued why he even started this little project in the first place.

"Are you keeping or flipping her?"

"Flipping?"

I shake my head. This is too much handholding for me, and we haven't even started.

"From the top then. There are wildly differing opinions on what makes up original and restored. Typically, purists want to keep it completely original with numbers matching, so it's basically what they call a survivor. Regardless of the condition, the failing original parts are removed and rebuilt exactly as original, but the exterior remains untouched or, in your case, rusted with holes. And I believe you looked at my sweet ride with disgust when you called it a jalopy because it was waiting for my sick paint job."

He looks bored or angry. I can't tell which. Possibly mad at himself for making such a dumb purchase.

That's on him.

He should've educated himself before he pulled this shit can out of the front yard it died in.

"And the other opinions?" he inquires, raising a curious eyebrow.

"Okay, then you get to another school of thought that if you can't live with the existing condition of the car or it's not safe to drive, you replace failing original parts with rebuilt replacements such as the carburetors, alternators, etc. Obviously, the numbers don't match, but the engine compartment and undercarriage are cleaned but untouched. You still get the exterior restored, but it's not original anymore. Then again, look at her."

His eyes follow mine before traveling back to me.

"She's far from original in this condition. It would be a hybrid where the factory integrity is retained but no custom paint, non-original gauges, or other modifications. You still with me, Chief?"

"Yes. Go on."

I take a big breath before launching into his last choice.

"We could restomod her. Meaning updating many of the car's components, again numbers not matching, but the overall appearance is close to stock. You could go with aftermarket tires, a modified engine compartment, and update the interior. It's not original, but it's fairly restored with new parts and usually cheaper."

"Price is not a factor," is all he says, staying unusually quiet through my whole diatribe of car restoration.

"Well, fancy pants, we could over-restore it to private museum quality where we dismantle her completely and restore or replace every part with a new-old-stock part. It's far from original since the worker, me, wasn't even born when this baby rolled off the assembly line, so you're rebuilding it with non-original hands. But it would be hand-built, and hopefully, if I care enough about your shit can, it will far exceed the delivery condition from the original factory it came from."

He nods, and then that gorgeous smile he used to trap my best friend slowly spreads across his face. The last one, he likes the idea of having a show pony.

Figures.

"The last one. How long?"

"Shouldn't you be asking how much? It's the most expensive, and then with your ridiculous upcharge added to it, not to mention my paint job, which you still don't know the cost of, you'll be paying more than she's worth."

I step closer to him, watching the smile fade. Exactly what I thought, cheapskate doesn't want to pay because his gainfully employed ass is a door-to-door salesman by the looks of his suit.

"I already told you money is not a factor. How long will it take you?"

"Right, we all have a money fairy running around throwing fistfuls of it in the air," I answer with my usual sarcasm, but it doesn't elicit a response. "Ten to twelve months, give or take a month."

"Four."

"Four? As in months?"

"Yeah, you want that paint job? Do it in four months."

I glare at him, standing in his shadow to ensure he sees my full scowl.

"I've got to finish the Buick first, then break yours down, rebuild the parts if I can hammer them out, and that's not including finding them if I can't. You're ignorant. You don't even know what you're asking. Four months, my ass!"

"Seems like you need a push, and I'll be that for you."

Anger bubbles within me.

"You're unreasonable and irrational. Get Judd to do it. He's open. Otherwise, ten to twelve months, give or take a month."

I look at the sky, inhale a deep breath, and try not to lose my shit on him.

"You. Four months or no paint job."

He offers his hand like we're spit-shaking on an agreed-upon deal.

"Well, good luck with Judd. I'll see ya around."

I step back and to the side, about to stride away, when he captures the back of my coveralls.

"Let go."

I rotate to slug him, but he dodges my fist like the freaking karate master he is.

"What would Carl say if you blew this deal for him?" he challenges.

I debate on crushing his ballsack with my knee. It would make me really fucking happy but would also make Carl really fucking mad.

"He'd bitch and moan like a girl, but that's nothing unusual," I reply, wrestling my collar out of his grasp.

I straighten my covers in a huff and start walking toward the garage. I've lost enough precious time teaching him Classic Cars 101.

"Your dad raised you to be a quitter?"

No. He. Didn't.

No one, and I mean no one, talks shit about Dad.

I whirl around and cover the short distance between us. My finger goes into his face as a compromise for not punching it.

"Don't you dare talk shit about my dad. Or so help you, I'll lay your ass out right here and now."

Fury has my heart racing in my chest and adrenaline pumping through my veins.

Yeah, let's go, motherfucker.

"I'm scared, daddy's girl."

That fucking asshole. I rocket my arm back, ready to hear a satisfying nose crack when he catches it in his hand. His long fingers close around my fist, clenching it in midair. I'm not a southpaw, but I become one when it launches, still eager to break his fucking face. He captures it as well. We look a spectacle with his hands engulfing my fists.

"Too predictable, Dani. You should know your competition before you take them on. It will save you from getting beat."

"Let go, asshole," I sneer through clenched teeth and bound hands.

"Tomlin, not asshole. Say it." His bored look from earlier is now one of amusement. It pisses me off even more. "Say my name, and I'll release your hands."

"Hell no, asshole. Now let go, motherfucker." I drop my chin to head butt him, but he's too damn strong and holds me back.

"You have a sailor's mouth. You get that from your daddy, too?" he taunts, and it's all I can take.

"He's dead, asshole."

It comes out harsher than I intend, but the cold reality is that he's gone. Even though I wanted to crawl into the grave with him when he died, I couldn't and nothing I say will bring him back.

My words hit him like my fists are intending to, and he immediately releases me. My chest heaves in anger and hurt, and I can't even meet his eyes.

It's not that I'm ashamed of losing my dad. He was a great man. It's just that the hole in my heart has yet to repair itself. If it were a car, I'd pound out the damage and make it look new again, where you couldn't even tell it was damaged, to begin with. But I'm not an inanimate object.

Life's cruelties have created a mountain of hard feelings in me. I don't sit around and whine about it because it does no good. I can't change the fact that he's gone, and I miss the hell out of him.

"I'm sorry for your loss. I didn't know, Dani."

"Yeah, well."

I shrug, looking at the straight edge of his pocket square. Who, under the age of eighty, wears a pocket square in their suit? Unless they're dead, lying in a casket. Damn, even my thoughts are depressing me now.

"Ten to twelve months, you said?"

I don't miss the hopefulness in his voice when my eyes fly up to meet his icky brown ones.

"Oh, now you're agreeing to my timeline after pitying me. Fuck you, asshole."

I thrust my chin up, challenging him because I don't take anyone's pity.

"Can you stop? You're acting like a pissed-off porcupine, throwing needles at everything that makes you bristle."

"Very poetic. You write sad songs too?"

"Forget it."

3

His head shakes as strides past me straight to the garage. I wait till he's almost out of sight before I jog back to see what he's up to. Staying out of sight, I peek around the corner to see him approach Judd.

Is he?

They talk back and forth in a somewhat civilized manner and end up shaking hands. He did. Judd catches my eye and smirks. The asshole gave him the job, and somehow it makes me even angrier that my leverage over both guys slipped. I hate men.

"I'll be out of town for the next couple of weeks, but I'll check in on the progress when I return. Thank you again for doing what Dani obviously can't."

Asshole being an asshole.

"No problem, Tomlin," Judd replies with a shit-eating grin.

Two can play that game, boys.

"Bye, asshole," I say, walking past him into the garage to my station.

"Always a pleasure, Danielle Louise Winters," he calls out to my back.

My full name.

No, he didn't. No one calls me by my full name, except Dad and Carl, and only when I'm in trouble. He's so getting his ass kicked the next time he saunters in here.

Waiting until the asshole leaves the garage, I ask Judd, "What was that all about?"

Even though I already know the answer.

"Wouldn't you like to know?"

His chest swells with arrogance as the screeching of the asshole's tires reverberates through the open bay doors.

"Shove it up your ass, Judd."

I stomp over to shut off his crap music and start my angry music this time. My mood is pissy. I need a little Green Day in my life, where we rage together.

"Not that crap. You walked out. My pick," Judd protests, walking toward my station.

I know exactly what to say to get my way.

"Let me have this, especially since I lost my rad paint job and that project. Carl will be super pissed at me, too, so let me sulk with my music."

I sound as pathetic and disheartened as possible before looking out the open bay.

"Fine, but only today. Tomorrow, it's who gets here first," he says, running a hand through his sandy blond hair as if he has some sort of authority over me.

Sucker. He falls for that line every time.

I'm very glad I don't have to waste ten to twelve months of my life, give, or take a month, tied to that asshole. Fucker crossed the line talking about Dad. He will drive Judd up the wall if he micromanages him the way he tried to do with me. I almost feel sorry for Judd.

Almost.

Feeling both angry at how crappy my morning has gone and grateful I don't have to deal with her ex, I text Kylie to see if she wants to grab a beer after work since it's been a while.

Then, like a woman on a mission, I bust out a crap ton of work. Angry music always motivates me to push myself.

Judd, being smugly satisfied by today's events, even has his trap shut and focused on his work.

Carl wanders in midday, muttering something about having ordered pizza when we want to take a break, but I push through with a cold Mountain Dew. I'll eat a piece later before stuffing my face with wings and beer tonight.

That reminds me. I need to check my phone to see if she's in.

I wipe my hands on a rag, stuff it in my pocket, and hit my phone screen. It lights up to her text message, agreeing to our usual bar.

The drinks at Murdocks are cheap or free, depending on which locals are frequenting the place and thinking they'll get a piece of ass off her or me. Never.

I had a one-night stand after too many rounds, and when I woke up in a strange motel by the highway, it scared the living shit out of me. I swore off them ever since. That was before I secured my fuck buddy, Zach. We knock boots with a simple texted emoji. It's always at his place because it's fifty times cleaner than mine and not above a garage.

Plus, we are compatible in the sack. Out of it, we're not friends. We don't date each other, and I rarely run into him around town. It's perfect. No commitment, no feelings, just a few condoms, and orgasms, and I'm out of there. Damn, I should have texted him first. I'm horny as hell. I'll text him later and see if he's up for it.

What am I saying? He's yet to turn me down. That sounds like a nice evening. Beer, wings, and getting drilled into his mattress. I text him, and it doesn't take a second before he texts back a simple nine. Meaning, be there at nine o'clock tonight.

My anger burns off, and my gratitude rises. This day just got better. I wind up singing at the top of my lungs with every song on my playlist, forgetting I'm supposed to be sad, for Judd's sake.

Screw it. I don't care. I'm getting laid.

It's been too long. Why I have waited almost two weeks to see Zach is beyond me. I hope he puts me through the paces. I need it.

Mmm, if he does those things like last time, well, damn, it's good dick.

"Dani, turn that music down. It's vibrating the waiting room glass. Now, what's this I hear about you losing the Takahashi deal?" Carl yells.

I pop my head out from under the Buick's hood to glare at Judd for outing me so quickly. The bastard didn't even wait a day before tattling on my ass. I should have been more surprised that Carl didn't know when he walked in and offered us pizza for lunch.

I mash the pause button on the music to answer him.

"Judd tell you?"

"Yeah, something about being museum quality and beyond your capacity or something like that?"

Carl plants his ass on the stool that I sometimes eat my lunch on.

Interesting.

The asshole's going with my recommendation. More interesting is that lying dick, Judd, making up bullshit stories about him being better than me.

Meh, what the hell do I care? I know the truth.

"Yeah, we talked through the options, and I balked. As you said, Judd has more experience than me. He should take it."

I shrug, glancing at Judd to see him turn away with a gloating look. Dickhead.

"Next time, I decide. Not my employees."

Carl's eyes narrow at me, not even looking at Judd before he scoots off the stool and waddles back inside. I know he does not believe it, but he won't make a stink in front of Judd about it. He'll wait till Judd's gone and confront me privately about dumping it off on him.

I walk back to the car, ducking under the hood and sneaking glances at Judd. He's cleaning his tools, which means it's quitting time. He's my built-in alarm clock, doing the same thing at the same time every day.

I like it because it saves me from glancing at the clock all day. Plus, I need to quit at about the same time to grab a shower and get up to the bar.

"You staying late?"

Judd walks over to lean against the fender and ogles my tits. It's too hot in the garage to keep my coveralls on all the time.

"Yep, Carl's on my ass because I'm behind, so staying late to catch up," I mutter, tightening the head gasket and wishing him away.

"Lucky Carl."

I pause and look at him.

"Get out of here before I wrap this wrench around your skull."

He chuckles, moving his hip off the car to stand over me.

"You're over tightening it."

The smell of his sweat makes me want to gag, and I shift over to get some room between us.

"Don't you need to find your next cling-on?"

"Right-O Dani-O, there's a pair of tits out there that need motor boating. Doors up or down?"

He walks away, and I breathe freely. Some dudes just have a bad pH and he's one of them. I don't know how he gets laid so much despite it.

"Down. Don't want any sleazebuckets named Judd slipping in here to watch me work."

42

"Funny. See ya in the morning."

I keep working until the heavy doors clang against the concrete floor. Then I give it another five minutes before his crotch rocket fires up and blasts off.

Once the sound fades in the distance, I clean my tools and place them back on the wall. I text Kylie my status and see I have about an hour to degrease and get ready.

"I'm leaving too. Lock up, will ya?" Carl shouts through the lobby window and I throw him a thumbs-up.

I'm for damn sure going to lock all the entry points. He thinks it's protecting the cars. I'm more concerned about my safety, not insured cars that can be replaced.

4

The bar is sparse. Then again, it's Monday. The only people are the usual alcoholics, married men avoiding going home to their families, and us.

"Hey bitch, it's been forever since I last saw you. I thought you hated me or something after the fiftieth decline."

Kylie's the better looking of the two of us, with large light brown eyes that she calls hazelnut, high cheekbones, and full lips that all the guys stare at.

Her long chocolate hair is piled on the top of her head in some style she must have seen on Instagram, and her business attire tells me she came straight from work.

She reaches for the peanuts I always warn her are full of piss.

"It hasn't been fifty."

I sigh, expecting this comment. She knows I work my ass off and always gives me grief for it.

"At least three," she says, crossing her legs and causing her skirt to hike up her tanned thighs. She's advertising for free drinks. Got to love her subtlety.

"Carl's been on my ass about this car because the owner's

been riding him. Shit rolls downhill, so I've been putting in a lot of time to finish it. It's going in this show in California."

"Seriously?" She shakes her head.

Classic cars have never been her thing, so she doesn't understand how blowhard these guys get about them. Now, a new expensive car with a hot owner, that's right up her alley.

"Old men care more about their toys than their adult kids. It's good for business, and that's good for me. Puts food on the table, a roof over my head, and all that crap."

I signal to the bartender to order my wings because I need to set my taste buds on fire with some sriracha-covered chicken.

"Speaking of boys and toys, are you still seeing Zach?"

Her voice peaks when saying his name, as if implying more.

"Not seeing, fucking. And yes, tonight, in fact," I mutter as the bartender approaches. "Can I get the fire-in-the-hole wings and another beer? And whatever she wants."

I toss my head in Kylie's direction, and she orders some salad. It's a dangerous choice in a bar like this. There's no telling what little field mouse died in the lettuce waiting for someone to order a salad.

"You got to be kidding me."

"What?" Her eyes are wide with curiosity.

"Who orders a salad in a dump like this? You should order greasy bar food and stop eating the piss peanuts."

I push the bowl toward the leering drunk on the other side of her. He digs his grimy fingers into it almost immediately.

"I'm on a diet."

"Why? You're fit, almost fitter than me," I say because working on cars and pounding out the metal keeps me in top shape.

"Thanks for the compliment, but I got a new guy."

She beams, tugging that stupid bowl away from the grumbling drunk to grab a handful.

"So?" I say, missing her point.

"He hasn't seen me naked yet, and I want to look fantastic when he does."

She tosses the nuts in her mouth, casting a glare at the drunk trying to share them with her.

"That's dumb. You look great, and I'd do you if I swung that way."

"Thanks, babe, but I'm trying to do it right this time," she explains, chasing the nuts with a long drink of her beer.

"Why?"

I'm dumbfounded that she would worry about impressing a guy. They're all knuckle-dragging Neanderthals and not worth the effort.

"He's different, conservative, and sweet."

"Uh-oh. Sounds boring. Run while you still can."

What on Earth makes her crazy ass think she won't get bored with normal? I mean, I'm relatively boring, and even I need a little flair in my life, hence Zach.

"Dani, I'm going to be twenty-five in a few months, and I'm not getting anywhere dating the same douchebags, one after the other. So, when Ryan asked me out at the grocery store, I said yes."

I choke on my drink, and she pounds on my back a few times.

"Ryan Mulvaney? The kid that had crossed eyes throughout school?" I question, trying to catch my breath.

"He got that fixed before high school, and you know that."

"Yeah, but Ryan Mulvaney?"

"For the ladies, from the gentlemen at the table over there."

The bartender shoves two fresh beers in front of us, and we turn to raise our glasses in appreciation. Her legs always do the trick.

We'll be sandwiched between them in half a minute, and that's when we bitch about babies and dirty diapers. Instant pest repellent.

The guys are decent enough if a little too old. We've been coming here long enough to get hit on by all kinds, young, old, male, and female, but it's the same story every time.

"Hello," the taller and lankier dude says, sliding into our conversation.

Yep, time to pretend she has spit up on her shoulder.

"Is that baby formula on your shoulder?" I ask, glancing over at the short, balding one while pointing at the imaginary spot.

"That baby, if he's not shitting, he's spitting," she says in a fake southern drawl.

That's her part of the fun, picking different accents that she thinks best fit the guys hitting on us. She licks her thumb and wipes her shoulder before shoving the same hand out to make introductions.

"Sorry about that. I'm Darla, and this is Charlene."

The tall one hesitates to shake her hand for fear of getting her spit or baby vomit on it. He tips his imaginary hat instead. She acts offended, shooting daggers at him while wiping her hand down the front of her shirt.

The bald frumpy one wrinkles his nose and looks like he wants to escape. I've seen this many times before. Poor guy. He needs more practice on how to get out of sticky situations.

"I'm Jake, and this is Chad. Did you say, baby?"

The tall one is brave for asking a follow-up question. Most don't or will fake some lame excuse about mistaking us for someone else. Most are smoother than these two.

"Yeah, little John Christopher. He's a bugger. But whatcha going to do when the condom breaks? I can't give them back. Bless their hearts," she drawls.

I hide my smile in the frothy foam of my fresh beer.

"Them? How many you got?" The bald one speaks for the first time, trepidation in his voice.

"Only four. Why? You got a problem with kids?" Her eyes

narrow like she's angry and about to start something with him. He takes a step back, which surprises both of us.

Seeing a window of opportunity open, she takes it by sliding off the barstool and jabbing her finger into his pudgy chest.

"Listen here, mister, if I weren't lactating and needing to pump this breast milk in the bathroom, I'd knock you upside your head until all you saw were stars. So best stop judging me."

Wow, she's gone all out this time. I'm even getting grossed out.

"No offense. I thought you could use a drink. We better be going. We got that thing. Right, Chad?" The tall one lies, needing the dad body to cover for him.

"Um, yes, that thing," Chad says, his gaze flickering toward the exit.

"Thanks for the beer," I say, holding it up in a gracious salute. They bolt when she steps closer, and I laugh at how outlandish her story is this time. "Can you drink beer and breastfeed?"

"Bye, boys." She lays on the southern charm, and they don't even turn around to acknowledge her. "I don't think so. I'll be back. I seriously must pee, and I want to call Ryan. Maybe tonight's the night. If you know what I mean."

She winks and tugs her skirt down. The entire bar knows what she means by how loud she is.

"It's implied, but be my guest."

I smile, turning to face the bartender as he places my wings in front of me. Perfect timing. I'm knuckle-deep in sauce with a burning fire circling my mouth when a presence looms over me.

Please, not again. I'm her wingman, not the other way around. The whole kid spit-up thing only works with two people. Dammit to hell, I'll have to wing it, literally.

"Danielle Louise Winters, what's a crappy girl like you doing in a nice bar like this?"

You've got to be kidding.

What karma gods did I piss off to get him again? I turn to see the asshole lounging his long, fit body against the sticky bar top.

"Don't you have that the other way around?" I mutter before unceremoniously licking the sauce from my fingers as he watches.

I'm not wasting good sauce on being a lady with manners. He knows what I do for a living, and it's far from ladylike.

He cups his chin as if thinking and taps the air with every word he says.

"Crappy girl, nice bar. Nope. I got it right."

"You're such an asshole."

"Yes, you've covered that. Many times. You have a little something right here."

He motions to my entire face, and I shrug, not bothering to clean up. I don't give a shit.

"What are you doing here? Did you follow me to beg me for a second chance at fixing your heap of crap?" I ask, taking a drink and picking up another wing.

"Hmm, wouldn't that be interesting if it were true? May I?" he asks, pointing to my stack of wings and plopping down on Kylie's barstool.

"No, moneybags, get your own."

He smiles that arrogant heart-stopping one and snatches a wing away before I can slap his hand.

"Got to be faster than that, Dani. Didn't I already tell you that?" he chides, seeming to enjoy pissing me off.

"Well, I hope you like hot wings because that's what they are."

I hope he can't handle them and starts tearing up like a little bitch.

"To answer your question, no. Judd took the deal, and I never go back. No second chances. You'll do well to remember that."

He grabs another wing, and I smack his hand—obviously fast enough this time.

"Get your own and stop spewing more useless shit I don't need to know." I rip into my wing, imagining it's his hand.

"Can you say one sentence without cussing?" he asks, tearing into his wing like it's no problem.

His icky brown eyes study me as if genuinely interested in knowing. My cussing isn't that bad.

"Yeah, leave, asshole. See, I just did."

"No, you didn't, you said asshole," he says, neatly wiping the extra sauce on a bar napkin.

"That's not cussing. That's your name. I can't help but call you what you are."

I chew with my mouth open, hoping to gross him out enough for him to bail.

He puts his bones on my discard pile and takes a napkin to clean his fingers again, which are barely dirty by the freakishly neat way he eats. Unfortunately, he's taking the heat from these things better than I thought.

Dammit, I wanted to see him cry.

I look around for Kylie, wishing she wasn't calling Ryan so she can bitch slap him into next week for what he did to her.

"Hey, that's my beer!"

I try to snatch it from his hand, but he leans away, chugging the entire thing. Now my mouth is an inferno with no beer to cool it.

"Technically, it's not. That guy bought it, so it doesn't belong to either of us. It's the free space," he justifies before grabbing another wing.

"You saw that? Were you spying on us? That's fucking creepy."

"Not spying, observing. And yes, that was a pretty interesting story you two cooked up." He inhales the wing and reaches for another.

"Seriously, stop taking my wings."

I wrap my hands around my pile to guard them when he laughs. It's deep and husky, coming so easily as if he doesn't have a care in the world.

Damn, it's nice.

Where's she? Taking a dump? I glance over my shoulder at the bathrooms. No sign of her.

"Are you always this stingy?" he asks, motioning to the bartender with two fingers.

"Yes, I'm stingy, crappy, I cuss a lot, I drive a jalopy, and I have a sailor's mouth. Any other insults you feel like hurling at me?" I snap, and the humor slides from his handsome face.

When you ball up all the shit someone's thrown at you, they tend to forget how many insults they've hurled until you call them out. His head dips, while he traces the wood grain of the bar top until the bartender slides two beers in front of us.

"Thanks, man."

He throws down a twenty, and the guy walks off with it. The awkward silence grows between us until that savior I'm waiting for finally gets her ass off the toilet.

"Tomlin?" Her surprised voice matches his face when he turns around.

Oh shit.

It's going down now.

As much as I thought I wanted her to save me, I want to see this messy scene unfold. Anticipation coats my sriracha-covered insides.

"Kylie, how are you?"

He stands, going in for a hug, and it's awkward as fuck between the two of them. I half expect her to slap him across the face, but she didn't.

She hugs him and pats his back like a grandma at church. I grab my beer to douse the flames in my mouth, never taking my eyes off the action, so I don't miss something good.

"I'm good. Great, actually."

She smiles when the hug ends. Not a fake one, but a real one, and he does the same.

What's happening?

"Good, I was concerned. You know, with how things ended."

He seems nervous or shy, I can't tell which one. It's doubly weird since he's only been an asshole to me. Or maybe I have been to him. Hell, if I know, or care.

"Oh, it wasn't the best, but I've had worse."

She nervously giggles, and I reach for a wing, unable to tear my eyeballs away.

"So, you're okay? With everything?" He grips the back of his neck, squeezing the muscles before letting go.

What did he expect would happen? Did he think she left town or something, and he wouldn't ever run into her?

"Yeah, Tomlin, I'm fine. Actually, I'm better than that. I'm happy. I'm sort of seeing a guy, and he's different but good. Good for me and good to me. If we kept hurting each other like we were, I might have missed out on him. So yeah."

She stumbles through her speech with a happy gleam about her. Good for her. Maybe dull is what she needs, after all, to balance herself out.

"That's great. I'm thrilled for you." The words leave his mouth, but they're missing the inflection in them.

As the awkwardness continues, I'm content to munch away on my wings while holding my beer and watching how this plays out. Hell, this is better than Netflix.

"How about you? Are you seeing anyone?" she asks, and his eyes slide to me.

I throw my bones on the pile and take a longer-than-necessary drink when her eyes move to mine.

Why are they looking at me?

"No, I'm still single. I have not seen anyone since we ended things."

His gaze returns to her as he clears his throat, obviously uncomfortable talking about his love life.

"Did you get your stuff back? You dropped it off, Dani, didn't you? I know how you procrastinate things," she says, and I frown. I don't need her adding another flaw to the ever-growing list the asshole is keeping.

"She did. She was sure that I got everything, right Dani?" His deep voice pulls me into their conversation, and I nod.

Thank goodness I have at least ten more wings to go because I'm using every single one as an excuse not to contribute to this conversation.

"Did you get my card?" she asks, looking at me and then at him.

Our eyes connect as guilty partners in crime.

"Card? Nope, I don't recall a card," he says, and just when I think we're in the clear, he throws me under the bus. "Dani, did you see a card?"

I shake my head, saying, "No, it must have fallen out or gotten lost in my apartment."

We look at her in unison, sealing the deal on our imaginary spit handshake to deny the truth to my best friend. She lets out another nervous laugh, and we both kind of smile along with her, if you call a curled lip from me a smile.

"That's a relief because I said some things that would be embarrassing now."

I nod, and his eyebrows rise.

"Good thing," I murmur.

"Well, that's one time your crap hole of an apartment finally paid off. When you find it in all that mess, do me a favor and throw it away."

Add another insult to the list. I'm messy too.

"Sure, of course."

Having my best friend take potshots against me isn't cool, especially in front of him. I slump against the bar top, no longer wanting to get laid by Zach. I want to be babied by someone that will rub my hair and tell me it's okay to feel insulted. Zach doesn't do that sort of stuff.

I don't even want to finish my wings or beer, which is a crime against humanity because both are delicious, and after skipping free pizza this afternoon, I wanted to double down on dinner.

"Look, I'm going to push off and let you two finish catching up."

I stand, digging into my back pocket for some cash. With his stupid fast reflexes, the asshole reaches out to throw more money on the bar to cover my tab, and it pisses me off. I don't take charity.

"Ooh, going to see Zach, are you?" She practically sings, and the asshole's dark orbs flash to mine.

"Who is Zach? Your boyfriend?" he quizzes, even though it's none of his damn business.

"Take your money back. I'm paying my bill."

I throw his cash toward his untouched drink, but he doesn't move to accept it. I put my money down on the tab and flag the bartender helping a regular at the other end.

He nods, and I'm good to go.

"Zach's NOT boyfriend material, if you know what I mean," Kylie answers with a wink.

Once again, everyone in the bar knows what she means. Saying she's subtle is like saying I don't cuss, and we all know neither is true.

"Have a good night," I say to both without looking at either when I tap the bar top with my palm.

I give Kylie the briefest of hugs before she turns to the asshole and chats him up. I'm almost out the door when I round the corner to glance back. He's looking downright angry now.

Good.

Payback.

As I approach the parking lot, the neon light of the bar sign flickers overhead, and I debate on texting Zach now or when I get home. Later, I need a believable excuse. I fish my keys out and unlock the car door before dropping in and starting her.

I don't even have my truck in drive when I catch the asshole striding out of the bar to his car parked in the shadows. He seems in a hurry and doesn't even notice blowing past my vehicle to exit the parking lot. Good thing I didn't start backing out, or else he would have nailed my truck bed.

His car fishtails on the street and then races away like the cops are after him. By the time I pull out of the parking lot, I can't even see his taillights.

Good riddance.

5

The following two weeks are a continuous cycle of working to the bone and falling into bed nearly unconscious, only to start again. Aside from Judd's usual harassment, the bitching about deadlines from Carl, and Kylie's voice mails about how great Ryan is, I can't even remember what day of the week it is.

I've worked through both weekends to make that Buick purr like a cat and roar like a lion. It's off to paint once the customer comes in today, but my part is finished.

I couldn't be prouder of my work.

Inside the office, pouring my third cup of coffee of the morning, I'm convinced I'm driving myself to an early grave with my bad habits.

Oh well, I'll sleep when I'm dead.

The bell above the door chimes. I spin around, expecting to see Mr. Hernandez so we can go over his car before I release it to paint when I'm sorely disappointed.

"You look like hell."

The first thing out of his mouth is an insult.

"I must be in hell because Satan just walked in."

I round the counter with a glazed doughnut in one hand and a coffee in the other when he follows me.

"I'll get Judd for you."

I take a step back when he plucks the sugary goodness from my hand and stuffs it in his mouth.

"Bro, stop eating my food. First my wings and now my doughnut."

He tries to reach for my coffee when I slide it away.

"Yo Judd, your customer's here," I yell as loud as I can and smile when he flinches.

"Did you miss me, Dani?"

He gives me that shit-eating grin of his and I swear it makes me want to throttle him.

"Hell no."

I didn't realize the last two weeks have been heavenly without him here annoying me. If heavenly is hundred-hour work weeks in an old garage with sugar and caffeine as a slow intravenous drip.

He laughs, and I forget how gorgeous he looks doing it. I hate how good-looking he is. I thought I had lost my mind when I went home from the bar rather than getting laid. Zach was cool like he always is and even believed my lie about getting a batch of bad wings. But I couldn't bring myself to text him to reschedule. Every time I tried, I thought of this asshole.

Why? I have no idea.

"Charming as ever. You probably belch and scratch your balls simultaneously," he says, with amusement rimming his brown eyes.

"Wouldn't you like to see?"

I move behind the counter to grab another doughnut from the box when he plants his elbows on the countertop.

"Give me a bite," he demands.

I fall against the cabinetry lining the back wall to obscenely eat it.

"Get your own, freeloader," I mumble, with chunks of sugary dough hanging from my mouth.

Taking me at my word, he walks around the counter and pats my side to move over.

"Excellent customer service would be to offer your client one, not stuff your face with them."

"Well, when my client, Mr. Hernandez, arrives, I'll be sure to offer him one," I say, drinking my coffee and chewing.

He mixes a fussy cup of coffee with whatever crap Carl buys to turn it into a sugar bomb.

"Is this all you have?"

He sneers, sticking a red swizzle stick in the cup.

"Yeah, Starbucks, what you see is what you get. Are you always so pretentious?"

I move farther down the cabinetry when the back of his hand bumps my hip again. He's opening and shutting drawers and doors. For what, I have no clue, but he's miffed when he comes up empty-handed. He's still banging shit around when it finally gets the best of me.

"What are you looking for?"

"Napkins, everyone has to have them," he huffs, looking mystified.

"Right here, idiot."

I grab the wad of brown paper towels I pulled out of the women's bathroom yesterday and wave them in his face.

"You don't use those," he says, appalled. "How disgusting."

I slam them on the counter in frustration.

"Are you for real? What does it matter?"

He stops and looks at me in disbelief.

"It's uncanny. I look at you and see a pretty girl, then you open that sailor's mouth, stuff junk food in it, or use these in place of napkins."

He grabs the pile of towels to shake in my face. "It's like you're a guy."

"Judd," I scream at the top of my lungs, and the asshole covers his ears, still clasping the damn things.

"Yo, Judd, the asshole's here."

I push past him, intentionally ramming my shoulder into his arm. He's on his own. Not my client, not my responsibility. Passing Judd, he makes a comment I don't quite catch as I wolf down the rest of my doughnut and finish my coffee.

Getting to my station, I pull off the yellow bandanna wrapped around my piggy tails and fix my flyaway hair in the small mirror bonded to the cinder block wall.

Carl hates when I wear my rag in front of clients and likes to call me Lucy in his Ricardo's voice. He thinks he's hilarious. I get him back by asking if that's the one with the genie and the astronaut or the one with the witch and her idiot husband.

He hates when I take the wind out of his sails by making him feel old. But what can I say? He is old. I've seen the show he's referring to in old Nick At Nite reruns and think she's funny as hell, but he'll never know.

When I catch the asshole watching me in the mirror, I flip him off. Then turn both middle fingers to Judd when he looks too. It's completely childish, but strangely, it makes me feel better. Deciding my hair's decent enough to meet Mr. Hernandez, I saunter past the boys and out the open bay door.

The overcast sky threatens to rain buckets at any moment. I hope Mr. Hernandez gets here before the storm starts. If he doesn't, I'll load the Buick into the trailer to protect the exterior from the elements while I show him the final product. I hope he doesn't mind standing in the back of a hot eighteen-wheeler to discuss his car.

Crossing the yard, I pull the cover off Mr. Johnson's 1967 Shelby GT500 to reacquaint myself with the work that needs to be done.

She's a beauty.

Her factory paint has worn in prominent spots, and her

once blue upholstered seats with white piping are torn and faded. Her dashboard is cracked, as are all the controls. Mr. Johnson said someone took a bat to her. Punk kids, but nothing I can't fix.

I snag the latch to pop the hood and inspect underneath. The engine is dried out, and corrosion cakes the battery and cables leading from it.

I've seen worse, much worse. After a thorough cleaning, I'll get a better idea of the condition of her parts. She'll rumble that gorgeous engine in no time and make for a happy owner.

6

————

"Dani," Carl hollers across the lot. I glance over my shoulder, hoping it's not about the asshole, and am relieved to see my client standing beside Carl.

I wave in acknowledgment before putting the hood down. Once it clicks, I grab the tarp to cover her from the impending storm, so I won't have to dry her out again.

With the cover arranged the way I want, I jog across the lot and into the customer lobby to a beaming client and a smiling Carl.

Why are they so happy?

"Hi, Mr. Hernandez." I thrust my hand as a greeting when he crushes me into a hug.

What the hell?

I squeeze my shoulders upward, trying to get out of his grasp because this is very unexpected and uncomfortable. He gets the picture when he releases me. The asshole looks intrigued as he gazes through the lobby window at us.

"Dani, you're a genius. Carl showed her to me and she's perfect." He clasps his hands together, taming them from hugging me again, and I'm grateful for that. "It's the same engine I heard when I was a little boy, and my father would take me for ice cream."

Ah, the smile and hug make sense. These cars are linked to their past. I've heard many stories over the years. First dates, losing their virginity in the back seat, a childhood car, and a whole gamut of other reasons. The latter is the case for Mr. Hernandez.

It took him three years to track down the car from his childhood, and when he saw it, he cried. Literally, at the dilapidated condition she was in, abandoned in an old junkyard with her VIN still intact.

The elements had done more damage to her than I initially estimated, and at every turn, I called him to decide how to proceed. He told me to call him Raul a dozen times. I never felt comfortable with that, seeing as he's in his early sixties, and it feels disrespectful.

"I'm glad you're happy, sir. She was a tough case, but so worth it. Are you ready for paint to pick her up?"

Carl's plump body pushes past our client to address me.

"Raul wants to drive the car to the paint shop. I canceled the trailer."

"But Carl, it's about to pour buckets—"

"Dani, it's the client's choice. If he wants to drive it, then he can drive it," Carl grits out, getting all blowhard on me.

A complete dick move.

"I understand that, but—" I start again, knowing this will be a showdown because I don't want it to get wet before it gets painted, and they have to let her dry again.

I didn't kill myself working fourteen days straight to meet my deadline for Carl to ruin it.

"Dani."

Oh, his threatening voice.

Screw him, I haven't had a day off, and one is coming. I turn away from Carl to appeal to my client. He has to see it my way.

"Mr. Hernandez, I know you're eager, like a kid at Christmas, right?"

"Yes, that's a good way to put it." He smiles fondly while Carl's heavy breathing grates on my nerves.

"If you worked night and day for six months and saved every dime to spend on a new toy, would you leave it lying in the mud on the very first day you got it? No, you wouldn't. It's no different with her. She drives beautifully, and I know you're excited to have her home again. But her paint job will be delayed if you drive her out in the coming storm. Worse yet, if the roads are slick and a car comes careening toward her, she'd be damaged, and we'd be back at square one. Let me call the scheduler back and have her trailer to the shop. I promise she'll be inside the trailer, protected from the weather and in safe hands the entire time," I'm practically begging.

Carl's angry breathing makes me about ready to choke him when Mr. Hernandez hugs me again.

"This is why I love you, Dani, always thinking of the cars as if they're your own."

He lets go, and this is entirely too many hugs in one day. Too many in a week. I know people get emotional, but this is ridiculous.

"Carl, she's right. I'd be beside myself if something happened to my Buick. Can you arrange the transportation again?"

I smirk.

Carl mutters a passable, "yeah" before waddling to his office. When Mr. Hernandez turns to follow Carl, the asshole is standing in the doorway.

"What do you want?"

"You call me poetic? What was that?"

He kicks off the doorframe and ambles toward me. I glance at his narrow waist, a fleeting inquiry of how he stays so fit when he eats all the same food that I do. Not fit, absolutely ripped to shreds when I think back to the first time we met.

"Honesty. You wouldn't recognize it if it ran your ass over, put it in reverse, and drove over you again," I say, dragging a hand down my exhausted face.

"Car analogy. I should have figured that's all you can relate to working in this place."

He stands in front of me, not smiling, not frowning, just being. I should punch the shit out of him.

"Look, you already have Judd dismantling that bomb of a car, so let's agree to stay out of each other's way."

I'm so taking the rest of the day off since I met my deadline. The customer is happy, and I'm dead on my feet. He touches one of my low piggy tails, and I slap his hand.

"These are cute, quite the opposite of that sailor's mouth. Maybe that's the appeal. Perhaps that's why he hugged you twice, but you didn't like it. Not in a creepy kind of way. You don't like to be hugged, do you? You bristled when I did it, concerned for your safety, and again when a happy, grateful man did it. Why?"

His imploring brown eyes stare into mine as if trying to figure me out. Well, good luck because I can't figure myself out.

"That's enough psychobabble for one day. Keep your hands off my hair. I don't want your oily hands on it." I dart around him to stomp toward Carl's office. "I'm taking the rest of the day off, Carl."

"No, you're not. Miller has parts that need to be picked up, and I told him you would since you have an open window before you start the Shelby," Carl commands with the phone dangling from his ear while Mr. Hernandez is content to watch us.

"You're killing me, old man. One day. I want one day to lie in my filth, eat in bed, and sleep in the crumbs."

I bang my head on the doorframe of his wood-paneled office, which still smells like the cigarettes he smoked years ago.

"That's vile," the asshole mutters behind me. I bang my head again.

"Send Judd," I beg, my eyes stinging with fatigue as I rest my forehead against the plastic wood.

"He's working on Mr. Takahashi's car right now. I'm handling the trailer, so that leaves you. Go pick them up, grab lunch, and that can be your break. Now get out of here." He waves a dismissive hand and pulls the receiver in line with his mouth. "Yeah, I'm still here."

I pull myself from the door and drag my feet in defiance of being ordered around for the millionth time today. Why can't that cheapskate pay someone to deliver the parts? Every fucking time, I have to go because my El Camino has a truck bed.

Pack of lazy bastards, he and Judd are.

"I'll take you," the asshole offers, following me toward the back of the shop to the private stairway leading to my humble abode.

"Get lost."

I climb the steps, footsteps pounding behind me, and I turn to face him.

"What do you think you're doing?"

I block the narrow stairway with my body, loving the fact that I'm towering over him from several steps above.

"Going with you, of course."

"No, you're not. Get lost before I scissor-kick your ass down the steps and walk over your crippled body when I get to the bottom."

I'm in a bad mood and would enjoy beating his ass right now. He's part of the problem. His stupid, breathtaking smile takes over, and I look away to avoid being entranced.

"You do know that's not a real defense move. It's an exercise fat women to do to convince themselves they can lose weight."

He steps up, the old wood creaking under his weight as he draws closer to me. I take a step up also because I like the distance between us, and he doesn't need to get any closer.

"Body shaming? What an asshole thing to say. No wonder you're single if you walk around saying shit like that."

"What? I like fit girls, not fat ones."

He shrugs, taking another step, and I refuse to move.

"What did Kylie ever see in you?"

My sneer is met with a smirk.

"Not what she saw, Dani, what she felt. You could feel it too, in about two more steps. I'll even let you keep the pigtails in. They would make great handles."

He's a fucking dead man.

I flash him the same sweet smile his grandma would when I take the last couple of steps down. Our bodies are inches apart when I tug on the zipper of my coveralls.

His icky brown eyes travel the length of my zipper until they stop at the abundant cleavage I've always hated. Hated because men like him treat me like a piece of ass.

Being an early bloomer at fourteen, as Dad called it, sucked because boys would talk to my boobs and never my face.

When I have his full attention, I place the palm of my hands on his chest and notice how solid his muscles are. Damn, harder than they look.

"That's it, babe."

Babe?

He's beyond dead now.

That babe comment gives my knee extra thrusting power when it connects with his pride and joy. He groans and immediately doubles over, losing his footing to tumble down a few steps before catching himself.

His watery eyes look up at me, and this 'babe' gives him her own breathtaking smile.

"Fuck off, asshole. And if you ever call me babe again, I'll finish what I started."

I turn and jog the rest of the stairs to the landing outside my apartment door. His groans fill the stairwell as I dash inside and lock the door behind me. My cheeks hurt from smiling so hard. Kylie may have forgiven him for being an asshole, but I sure won't.

Once an asshole, always an asshole.

I unzip the rest of my coveralls and strip down to take a hot shower. As I step into the bathtub and tug the curtain closed, his angry banging starts on my door.

I smile wider. Too bad I can't hear him over the water.

My shower is long and hot, shaving every overdue part of my body since I'll be showing a lot of skin down in the yard today. The more I show, the more help I get from the boys loading Carl's orders into the truck bed.

Shutting off the water, utter silence awaits me, and I chuckle.

Bye, asshole. Have a good day.

I rub lotion all over my skin, twist my wet hair into a loose bun on the top of my head, and smear on enough makeup to avoid looking like a hooker.

My denim shorts are entirely too short, with part of my ass hanging out, but that's the point of this little outing. The last time I ran over in my coveralls, I loaded all the shit myself, including a set of tires. Sexist bastards, the lot of them.

I debate about wearing a bra. My camisole has one built-in, but let's be honest, that shit doesn't support these huge jugs. They're next. After my paint job, I'm saving for a breast reduction because this pound of flesh is damn near too much.

Heck, live a little, no bra it is. Who cares if I headlight all day? Dudes look anyway. I might as well give the boys a peek at what they lust after. Once I have my pink camisole on with matching flip-flops, I grab my purse to head out.

I twist the lock on my door and almost run into Tomlin sitting at the top of the staircase. He looks up and mutters, "Christ" when I step around him.

I envisioned this happening at the bottom of the stairs, not the top. Either way, stepping over him is equally satisfying.

"Why aren't you gone?" I say as I stomp down the steps and then turn to glare at him.

"How about an apology?"

That fool has lost his mind if he thinks I'm in the wrong.

"If anyone owes anyone an apology, it's you to me. Calling me babe and suggesting I should take it. You're sick, talking to me about your sex life with my best friend, of all people. Where's my apology, asshole?"

I swear this guy makes me go from zero to thermonuclear in under two seconds. He stands with a grimace that disappears quickly as he tries to hide the extent of his discomfort. Good, I hope I broke his baby maker. He walks stiffly downstairs to join me by the back door.

"I'm not used to my opponent getting the better of me," he admits.

I snort my amusement. A guy his size with those karate moves. I bet they don't.

"Then it's character-building for you. Glad I could help. See ya around."

I push through the exit with him in tow.

"Dani, I'm leaving again," he mutters. "Longer this time."

Good, the fewest number of annoying people in my life, the better. I continue walking toward my truck. But this time, he's not following me like an eager puppy. Intrigued, I turn to see why.

"So?"

I jangle my keys, half wanting to get rid of him and half

wanting to know why he cares to tell me. He didn't before, so why now?

"I wanted you to know that I won't be bugging you anymore."

He shoves his hands in his dress pockets, giving a casual appearance. His tone is anything but.

With the dark storm clouds threatening to rage behind him, it paints a beautiful picture of a very handsome man standing against a backdrop of nature's fury. Magazine worthy if I were generous.

"Good."

I want to say I'm not the slightest bit bothered by his news. I want to say it, but I can't. I'm irritated, even though I have no right to be. He's not a friend. He's nothing to me, yet he thinks it's my business to know. Why?

"Right, this is goodbye."

He lingers, his shoulders slumping, and his leg bent from where I racked him.

"Bye, asshole."

The look on his face says it all, bothered. Then I feel like a guilty motherfucker for being a complete asshole to him, but it's not entirely my fault. It's his fault that he brings out the worst in me.

"It's Tomlin," he mumbles before hobbling inside.

The glass door swings closed behind him, with a reflection of me in the blackout film.

How can a knee to the dick humble a man? I can work it out physically, but mentally, I'm stumped. I try to make sense of our little exchange, but I can't. It makes no sense.

The crack of thunder, followed by a jagged bolt of lightning, makes me jump, and I hustle to my car before the sky opens. When I start my truck and pull around to the front, he's gone.

Maybe I could have been less offensive and maybe called him asshole less. I mean, I can't use his name because that's weird, but perhaps one less insult would have been better. Honestly, it's his fault for hitting on me again, calling me babe, and telling me to take it.

Oh well, I don't need any distractions—especially a handsome one that takes as good as he dishes out. I know I'm not for everyone. I get told that regularly. I hate to admit this, but it's kind of intriguing to go toe-to-toe with someone that takes my bullshit and throws it back at me.

Whatever.

My life is good. I got a new car to start tomorrow, a waiting list at least six months out, my little apartment, and one good friend. What more could I want?

Nothing.

I got it all.

7

Four weeks. It's been four weeks and one day if I'm truly counting on a calendar, which I'm not. He said he'd be gone longer, but not for how long.

The days are lost to nights, turning into weeks, until my irritation is at a boiling point and I'm ready to explode on someone.

"What's up your ass today?" Judd yells over the music. "You got your bitchy music on, and it's only 8:30 a.m."

I don't even bother answering.

Carl already made me turn it down. He said my music was vibrating the waiting room window. I smarted off, saying to invest in thicker windows. He waddled over to try to snatch my phone, so I complied by turning the volume down a fraction.

Lying under the Shelby, I scrutinize the coils and ask myself the same question.

"What *is* up my ass? Not just today, but in general."

Zach had put me through the paces last night, three times, in fact. Usually, that works because I leave vibrating, with a calm mind and sore lady parts. I only had two of the three last night.

My mind has been scrambled with bits of the asshole and our last conversation tormenting me these last few weeks, especially the look on his face before he left. He wanted to say more, and the longer he stays away, the more I mull it over. If only I gave him five more minutes, what would he have said? My curiosity is driving me crazy, and it's annoying as hell.

Every time he crosses my mind, I distract myself with work, which is easy to do with so much to be done. I enjoy getting my frustrations out by pounding on the bodywork a little too much. To the point that Judd asks whom I'm trying to kill.

I can't lie in that I envision his head under the hammer a time or two. Then it swirls to the asshole, and I hammer so hard my hand hurts from the vibrations. I should talk to Kylie about this, but not say the asshole directly. I'll substitute Zach's name instead. She obsesses over men. She'll know what to do. Screw it. I'll text her for a beer tonight.

Rolling out the creeper, I catch the edge to stand and twist my body in both directions to crack my back. Judd's quietly working on the asshole's car. I'm curious if he's staying in touch with him about the progress. I'm also curious if he asked about me.

Who am I kidding?

I'd have heard if Judd called him, as small as the shop is. Something about that doesn't sit right with me. Surely, he's encountered some problems by now that the asshole should have to decide on.

"What?"

His racket stops twisting when he catches me staring at him. I know that look. It's his don't-ask-any-questions look, piquing my suspicions.

"You're doing it wrong," I say. His hand is deep between the cylinder head and engine block while the other is fiddling with a gasket.

"Wait, that's the wrong part."

I shove against his shoulder and adjust the light dangling from the underside of the hood to get a better view.

"No, it's not." He shoves back, and I ignore him, wedging my hand down the space to meet his. "Get out of my engine."

"Dude, that's not an original. You're subbing parts."

I'm shocked that he's cutting corners with the asshole's car, which I'm fairly certain is against his wishes. Our eyes align when I grab the gasket out of his oily hand and yank it up to the light.

Sure as shit, it's a brand-new part. I get he might not salvage the originals, but he could have had Miller hunt for an original from a parts car.

"Did you call the client about this?"

He snatches it back.

"It's none of your business."

"The hell it isn't. If you're cutting corners and cheating your client on the price, Carl will have your head on a stake."

His face is a mask of fury because I'm challenging him.

"Carl doesn't know a head gasket from a spark plug. And since you hate my client, you will not tell him, so I have nothing to worry about."

He smirks, removing his hand from the engine block to wipe on a rag.

I stare at him in disbelief.

"This is wrong. You know that. It will blow, the car will over-heat, not to mention leak oil everywhere, and he'll be back in here with more problems."

I grab the light from the hook and shine it over the engine to look for more shortcuts.

"Where else have you cheated? Huh, Judd?"

I lower the light and hunch over for a better look.

"You're jealous because he picked me over your slow, incompetent ass. You know my skills are far better than yours. I got years on you," he sneers, trying to snatch the light from my hands, but I ram my elbow into his side.

He grunts to my satisfaction, and I think I spot another problem with the engine block.

"You're a wannabe, like your old man. Carl kept him around because he had a kid in tow. Felt sorry for him."

The light clatters to the engine, and I swing on Judd, ready to rip his pornstache off his face.

"You motherfucker."

He ducks.

When he recovers, I uppercut him. His teeth clack together when my fist connects with his chin. Before I know it, he whirls me around, pinning me to the front of the car with my arms trapped under his.

"Get your pin dick out of my ass before I rack it into a mangina." I clench my teeth, struggling to get his nasty body off me. A whiff of his body odor makes me nauseated.

"Or what?" He chuckles, skyrocketing my rage. "You act so tough, but look at you now. Just a weak, helpless woman."

His disgusting tongue slithers up my neck, fanned by his stinky breath on my skin. That's fucking it.

"I'm going to fucking kill you."

I'm heaving with revenge. Ready to unleash my fury, I drop my chin and slam my head against his nose in one beautifully coordinated move. The grotesque snap echoes in my ears, and warm liquid saturates my scalp. I'm pleased.

He lets go instantly.

"You crazy bitch. You broke my fucking nose."

I spin around to see blood racing between his filthy hands and dotting the floor. He shrieks over the music, creating such a ruckus that Carl waddles in faster than I have ever seen.

The back of my head hurts like a motherfucker. I must have hit a tooth or two because my hand is drenched in blood when I pull it away from my hair.

"What the hell is going on here?" Carl glares from Judd to me, expecting an answer as he plants his stubby hands on his thick waist.

"That crazy bitch broke my nose," Judd yells, grabbing a couple of rags to wrap around his thumbs as he lines them up on both sides of his nose to snap it back into place. "Son of a bitch, that hurts."

He shakes his head, sending blood flying into the air. I wipe his blood on the front of my coveralls since the stack of rags is over by Judd's station.

"Is this true?" Carl demands, and it pisses me off how he instantly takes Judd's side.

"Yeah, I did, Carl. Do you know why? I'm tired of being felt up, grabbed, licked, and propositioned. I'm sure you're both violating some laws somewhere."

I've been silent and putting up with this shit for far too long. Judd has been getting away with it, and Carl keeps turning a blind fucking eye to it.

I'm sick of these fuckers.

"Now Dani—" Carl starts with Judd standing behind him, two against one. Oh, I see how it is.

"No, Carl, you turn right around and ask Judd, not me. Ask him." I cross my arms over my chest, crinkling the rough fabric of my coveralls. "Go ahead."

Dick prick raises a taunting eyebrow. His nose is red and swollen, with blood smeared across his cheekbone and over his lips. I hate his fucking guts.

Dad wasn't a wannabe. He was the real deal.

"Dani, I can't have you going around breaking people's noses. He could press charges against you. Sue me. How would that look?"

The muscles in my jaw cramp from clenching my teeth.

"Un-fucking-believable," I scream, swiping the wrench

lying on top of the asshole's engine and launching it at the waiting room window.

To my satisfaction and Carl's horror, it shatters into a bazillion pieces in the customer lobby.

"Danielle Louise Winters, get the hell out of my garage!" Carl yells, and I double-flip them off before gathering my phone, cutting the music, and storming out the bay door.

8

I'm mad as hell. My mind runs through all the heinous ways those two can die. My favorite is burning the garage down, but my apartment would go up in flames. I can't do that to all the memories I have growing up with Dad there.

Stomping to my truck parked in the back of the lot, I strip out of my coveralls and yank open the door with such force that she squeaks in protest. I shouldn't take my fury out on my sweet ride. It's not her fault those assholes are assholes. I ball up my coveralls and chunk them on the passenger floorboard before getting in.

I rev my engine, making an obscene amount of noise before I peel out of the lot, leaving tire tracks on his old concrete. I hope it takes Carl forever to get those rubber marks off.

With my stomach rumbling and my purse upstairs in the very place I was just kicked out of, I speed toward the truck stop at the edge of town where I can get a cheap coffee and dough-nuts. The long drive will give me time to think about my next move as I race away from that fucking place.

This would have never happened to Dad. Carl always

respected him, but not me. I think it's resentment for being saddled with me after Dad died.

Not that he was my legal guardian, but he was obligated not to kick me out when I had to drop out of school during my senior year to support myself.

Dad had saved a little bit of money, but that went fast with rent, utilities, and food. I knew I could do the work that Dad did. Hell, I spent practically most of my life downstairs in that garage right alongside him, helping wherever I could and learning everything I know today.

Carl was reluctant to give me a chance until I fixed up the El Camino to prove it to him. The first year started fine, with learning and growing in my craft. But the second year, when I turned eighteen, Judd started up with his nonsense. It was occasional at first and has been growing ever since.

Today has been a long time coming.

Always having to scrape and save money for my tools, fight to build my client list, and put up with his harassment at the same time wasn't easy. Carl didn't make it easy, either.

I learned real quick that I had to protect myself because no one else is going to do it. And with no diploma, my options are limited. It's why I've put up with the bullshit for as long as I have. Now, I'm back to the question I've asked myself a hundred times.

What are my options?

None.

Barreling down the highway, with my music blaring, I don't see old sparky tucked in a cluster of trees until it's too late. He peels out, creating a dust devil behind him, and I murmur a string of cuss words.

"Fuck, add getting a damn ticket onto this already shitty day."

Letting my foot off the gas, I turn off my music, flip on my signal, and ease over to the shoulder. This highway is busy and loud, and it sucks to be pulled over.

"Oh well, tits don't fail me now."

I glance in the rearview mirror, seeing him take his sweet-ass time getting out of the car. It gives me a few minutes to adjust my bra and yank down my tank top to reveal an eyeful of cleavage.

I grab the end of my pigtail, split it in two to push the hair holder higher, and try to hide Judd's blood on the back of my head. By the time he reaches my door, I'm ready to pull a Kylie.

"Hi, sugar," I say in the sweetest, most drawn-out southern accent I can remember Kylie doing.

He's tall. His hat blocks the sun from my face, which I appreciate, and his sunglasses reflect my great-looking assets.

"Lucky me! Whatever did I do to get you?" I happily clap my hands together before beaming at him.

"Well, ma'am—"

"Call me Louise, hon. My full name is Danielle Louise Winters. Danielle after my daddy, Danny, but Momma calls me Louise. Momma always said Daddy was a scoundrel, so she didn't want a reminder of that two-timing bastard. She thought Louise fit better, don't you?"

I have to admit, my southern charm was better than I thought. I might have to do this at the bar next time.

"Yes, Louise is nice. However, do you know why I pulled you over?"

He takes off his sunglasses and tucks them into his neckline. His eyes are the prettiest green I've ever seen on a dude.

He's way cuter than I thought, with a boxy jawline and a dimple that cuts into his cheek when he frowns. If I weren't playing southern belle, I'd switch to horny hooker.

I scoot over to cross my legs, giving him a double show since I don't know if he's a boob guy or a leg guy.

"I don't, sir," I say, widening my baby blue eyes before blinking slowly.

"Speeding. You were going fifty-five miles per hour in a forty mile per hour speed zone," he says, glancing down.

At my boobs or legs, I can't tell.

"Oh, my goodness," I drawl. "I didn't even realize. I'm so sorry." I slide one leg up to the other, pretending to shift out of the sun. "I get so turned around with all these different roads."

"You're not from around here, are you?"

His hand falls to the window frame, and I coyly look at him before putting both hands up.

"Guilty as charged." Then I give him my most dazzling smile, with a few more slow blinks. "I hope you don't mind me being so forward but are all the officers in Colorado as handsome as you?"

Dicey. This may be taking it too far.

He smiles, the tip of his hat bobbing down, and our eyes meet.

One second. Two seconds. Almost three.

"Look, I'm not supposed to do this, but you seem a nice enough gal, so I'm going to let you off with a warning. Slow down and watch for the road signs. They will tell you the speed."

"Sugar, you made my day," I murmur, twirling my pigtail between my fingers. He watches for a moment, then pulls a card out of his breast pocket to hand to me.

"Whatever is this?" I flip the card over and see his name. "Alexander Hamilton? Oh, like the president."

"Yes, like the president," he says flatly. He's probably heard that his whole life and has grown to hate it. "It's my card. Call me if you need anything while you're in town."

"That's a mighty fine name for a mighty fine officer. And I will."

I wave the card at him before tucking it into the bra, knowing he's watching every second.

"Well, bless your heart, Officer Hamilton."

I can't decide if he's hitting on me or genuinely being nice. He pats the car before straightening back up.

"Have a good day, ma'am."

His fingers brush the brim of his hat, tilting it enough to show his blond buzz cut above his ears.

To really hit it home, I lean out my window and holler at his retreating back.

"Thank you, sugar."

Then wave like a lunatic at him. He glances over his shoulder, smiles, and slides his sunglasses on before opening his car door to slip inside. I turn around, roll up my window, and sigh in relief. That worked like a charm. Maybe there are a few decent guys left in the world.

After removing the card from my bra, I reach over to deposit it in my glove box. Who knows if this southern belle might need the officer for something in the future?

Glancing in my rearview mirror, he must be waiting for me to pull out. But I can't see the oncoming cars and don't want to risk getting hit. After a few more seconds of watching him, his patrol car reverses and eases back onto the road. I wave my hand off, really selling it, and chuckling at my ridiculousness.

Once he's out of sight, I get back on the highway and mind my speed until the exit for the truck stop appears on my right. Forgoing music since I'm about to get out, I veer off the road and pull into the closest spot to the front door.

Seeing as how this truck stop is on the interstate, it's jam-packed with passenger vehicles in the front of the building and two rows of semi-trucks in the back. I stuff my phone in my back pocket and grab the three bucks in change from my cupholder.

I'm careful not to scrape the car next to me with my long

doors when I get out. I push past a cluster of tourists asking for directions at the front of the store to make my way over to the hot beverage station.

While pouring coffee into a Styrofoam cup, a shrilly voice rings out to my left. It's a chick who looks strung out, wearing clothes too skimpy for daylight, smeared lipstick, and raccoon eyes for makeup.

Her blue and black dyed hair is pulled into a messy bun, and she's teetering on heels too high to walk in.

"Hey, watch it," a dude next to me says when I'm about to pour hot coffee all over his part of the coffee station. I jump, the hot liquid sloshing over the side of my cup to burn my hand.

"Motherfucker," I hiss, dumping the cup on the counter and grabbing a wad of napkins to smother my fingers.

That's going to leave a mark. The burn stings as I clean up the mess and place the lid on the cup. By the time I get it all cleaned up, she's disappeared into the crowd of people.

Whatever.

Walking through the aisles of various junk food and sweet treats, I spot the powdered sugar doughnuts I'm looking for when she appears again.

This time, she's walking like a show pony, her heels clicking and clacking on the slick floor while she half-jogs next to this guy twice her size. She's pulling on his arm, pleading for something, and he ignores her as he carries his snacks to the counter. I boogie through the swarms of people to get in line behind them, curious about what's going on.

Her cheap perfume wraps around me like an unwanted blanket, causing me to take a couple of steps back to fan the air between us. I want to pinch my nose to block the odor, but even for me, that's incredibly rude.

Leaning forward to eavesdrop, she's begging him for a tank top they sell on the opposite side of the store. The thin ones, branded with Colorado and a mountain scene across the front of it. Too cringy for my taste.

Annoyed by her begging and pulling on his arm, he yanks it out of her grasp, sending her out of control and flying back to me. I barely catch her while holding my coffee and not burning myself again.

"I . . . sorry," she stammers, looking ashamed while trying to regain her balance on her stilt shoes.

She's very young, far too young to be caked in all that makeup. I mistook her age when I saw her across the convenience store. Bruises dot her arms. She quickly tries to hide them by tucking her arms across her slight frame.

"How old are you?" I ask, looking from her coal-crusted brown eyes to the back of the nutsack that pushed her. I can't help the attitude building in me, but I soften my tone when I continue, "Are you legal? For that?"

I point to him. Her face is panic-stricken before he yanks her to his side.

"Mind your own damn business," he demands, spitting into his scraggly beard.

As if that will stop me. I move right up on them.

"The hell I will. You can't toss her around like a rag doll and expect me to mind my own damn business."

I tilt my head to the side, my pigtail caresses my cheek.

"Are you okay?" I ask her, ignoring the threats coming from the nutsack next to her.

Her eyes are wide, not from drugs but straight-up fear. Her cheeks are chubby, her skin has a bit of acne, and I realize she's a minor. And this disgustingly old man is the furthest thing from being a minor. It doesn't take a genius to know she's being abused by this monster.

Venom is flowing through my veins now. I'm pretty sure she's not with him of her own free will. And this nutsack uses his loud voice and enormous size to intimidate her into submission.

"Don't talk to her," he yells at the poor girl that looks like she's going to burst into tears at any moment.

He shoves her behind him and tries to intimidate me with his size. His long hair is greasy, sticking to the side of his sweaty neck, and his belly protrudes from the hem of his T-shirt.

"And you, get the fuck away from us."

He thrusts a fat digit in my face and if my hands weren't already full, I would break it off.

"What if I don't? You see this?"

I flip my head to show the back of my bloody hair. She peeks around his arm to look as well, her eyes widening at the sight of it.

"I already broke one nose today. Do we need to make it two?"

I'm no match for him, but causing a scene is my thing if it will help this girl somehow.

I shift toward her, asking, "Is he your dad or boyfriend?"

Both beat up innocent girls.

"Um."

She nervously glances from me to him, her hands twisting the lace strings of her bralette while tears collect at her lower lids.

"Collette, get in the truck," he barks, causing her to jump. His fat hands shove her toward the truck driver's exit at the back of the store.

The frightened girl shrinks in fright, for fear of being hit, and then tries to scurry away on those ridiculous heels.

"You're gonna wish you stayed out of my fucking business."

He throws his snacks on the shelves by the register and then pops his knuckles as an impending threat. I place my coffee and pack of doughnuts on the shelf beside his.

"Is that a threat? You think you're going to hurt me as you

hurt her?"

I toss my thumb in the direction she escaped and see we are garnering some attention from other people in line. Good, because this wrinkly old man isn't her dad and definitely not her brother.

Sick bastard.

"She's none of your fucking business," he roars, his hands lunging for my neck.

As they brush my skin, I ram my foot so hard and fast into his junk that he doubles over.

"You like them young, huh? Well, I like them soft," I spit out as his hands claw down my body.

Fury sweeps over me, way more than I had for Judd this morning, and my knee connects with his nose. The hideous snap is loud. His blood pours out of his nose, all over my white Converse to pool on the linoleum floor. I'm angry as hell, but a sense of satisfaction settles in deep as he is writhing in pain.

"You bitch!"

He struggles to stand upright while holding his nose.

Second time today that I have been called a bitch and broken a nose. When those sausage fingers lunge at me, I jump back. My heart pounds against my ribcage and my body heats, knowing he could seriously hurt me if he catches me.

"That's for abusing little girls, you sicko!" I scream because I need reinforcements to help me not get killed by this raging beast.

Thankfully, two burly men from another line dive to my defense by wrestling him away.

"Get off me!"

He rolls his shoulder, dislodging one guy's grip that causes him to lose his footing on the pool of blood.

My relief is temporary when the beast uses this sudden advantage to slam his fist into my temple. My head ricochets back, knocking me off my feet and into the family behind me.

"Fuck," I groan.

The husband catches me under my armpits and drags me away from the beast to sit on the floor.

Hot, searing pain flashes across my face and pierces my eye socket, forcing immediate tears to flood down my cheeks. I cradle my face in my hands when black specks cloud my vision.

The guy is roaring to get at me again when that familiar voice cuts through the chaos.

Well, shit.

"What's going on here?"

Of course, it would be him.

I raise my head, meeting Hamilton's gaze while two more guys wrestle the beast to the ground.

Hamilton stands between us.

"She fucking attacked me." His face is inches from the filthy floor as blood drips in a puddle below his nose. "Pull it up on the cameras. You'll see."

Two patrolmen flank the Good Samaritans, trying to catch the beast's hands as he lies on his stomach. He's a big guy and raging like a bull in their grasp. They struggle to get him to cooperate. It takes four men holding him down to tug his arms behind his back to handcuff him.

"Louise?"

I knew that was coming.

"Hey, Hamilton."

I drop the southern accent because I'm in real trouble now. The husband remains standing over me, a protective measure from the bull spewing threats at me. The mom already ushered her kids away from the scene. I can't blame her. I would do the same.

"It's Officer Hamilton. Wait, that was an act?"

His eyes narrow under the brim of his hat. I shrug, kind of proud of myself for fooling him so well.

"Tell me what happened?" he says, ignoring my lying

infraction.

"There's a minor named Collette, and that's her abuser. She's in one of those hundred trucks out back."

My hand falls away from my temple so Hamilton can see the swelling pushing against my eye.

"He lunged at me, so I racked him, then broke his nose when he threatened me."

His eyes linger on my shiner.

"Okay, let's get everyone up and outside."

The nice husband helps me to my feet, and I thank him. They shouldn't have seen this. Tourists are here to see the Gorge and Colorado's red rocks, not the gritty side of truck stop life.

"Thank you, sir. Tell your wife and kids I'm sorry they had to see that," I mutter before Hamilton hauls me out of the store by my arm.

Once we are at the hood of his car, I lean against it and start working my jaw to diffuse the pain.

"Looks like you took quite a hit," he says, pulling out a pad of paper and pen.

"Yup. You should see the other guy," I joke, and he doesn't laugh. "Ba-dum bum."

I play the air drums for my bad joke.

"I'll get the medic to check you out in a minute."

His eyes slide to the right, where the beast is struggling with the cops and screaming at me as they walk him over to the ambulance.

Big baby. Just snap that shit into place, like Judd did.

"From the top, tell me what happened."

"Don't you need to read me my rights or something?" I ask, still doing my face exercises.

"Do I have reason to?" he implores, cocking his head to one side.

"Look, you've got to find that girl. She looks older from a

distance because of the pound of makeup she has on, but I promise you she's not of age, and that isn't her dad. I saw bruises on her arm, and the way he threatened me, I think he's used to beating on women."

"Stay here," is all he says before striding across the parking lot to the ambulance.

I can't distinguish the words, but it's an angry shouting match. The beast is yanking his head away from the tiny female medic. The two officers are still holding him by a handcuffed arm.

Hamilton is standing directly in front of the guy, probably wanting to beat his ass from the looks of it. After a couple more minutes of arguing, Hamilton turns to grab his shoulder radio to talk into it. He looks murderous by the time he walks back to me.

"He denies it. Says he's traveling alone."

I sprint toward the abuser.

"You lying, motherfucker. Where's she?" I scream when Hamilton's arm circles my waist before I reach the guy. "You fucking piece of shit!"

"Calm down. I didn't say I believed him. I called the department that handles this sort of stuff. They're sending a unit out," he explains, forcibly walking me toward the back parking lot.

"You can let go." He's reluctant to, and I get it. I'm unpredictable, but at least he believes me. "Seriously."

I wait for him to stop touching me so I can fix my top, which got all twisted and is showing way too much boob, even for my liking.

"Now what?" I ask, looking up to see his eyes plastered to my chest as I adjust the straps.

Clearing his throat, he says, "That's a lot of trucks."

"Yeah. Is someone looking at the cameras? We could see when they came in and go from there," I volunteer, stepping into the shade of the building, to avoid squinting my hurt eye.

"We? You're not looking for her," he says calmly. "I still need to get your statement, and you need medical—"

"What if she jumps trucks? I thought she was strung out when I saw her inside, but she's scared as hell. I want to help if I can."

I feel sorry for her. The haunted look in her eyes spoke to me.

"Arrest me after we find her, but let me help. I owe you that much, ya know, from before, with the whole accent thing."

"Yes, we'll be circling back to that."

A voice crackles through his shoulder radio, and his hand presses a button, asking them to repeat it.

"Copy that. It's a blue truck with naked women silhouettes on the mud flaps."

"Of course." I roll my eyes. Men are pigs. "Did they say what color blue? There are all kinds out there."

I wave my hands at the row of trucks, seeing three different color blues on the first row alone.

"Nope, they were lucky to get that out of him."

"Why? Where's he at that they can't get more?" I ask, wondering if they booked him on anything yet. I should worry if they're going to book me on anything.

"In the back of the squad car. He's claiming self-defense." I blow out a big breath. "They're also collecting witness statements." He throws in. I suppose to make myself feel better. "The unit should be here in ten minutes, so let's go."

We walk into the sunshine. The heat makes me feel a little nauseated when it hits my throbbing head.

"You take this row. I'll take the back," he says, and I nod. "Don't approach it. Just call my name when you are within a few trucks of it, okay?"

"Okay," I mutter to his receding back, his gun belt rustling as he walks away.

9

_____

Figuring it would be easier to find the blue ones first and then walk down the side to check the mud flaps, I start at the beginning of the row. I'm about eight trucks in when I spot a fancy royal blue one with a double sleeping cab and a small white cross under the door handles.

This is probably not the abuser's truck. Taking no chances, I walk between the two cabs to check the mud flaps. More crosses. Definitely not his truck. Looking down the parking lot between the rows of trucks, Hamilton is farther ahead of me, and much faster at this.

Duh, this is police work, and he's a policeman. I'm about to walk back to the top of my row when movement in the windshield in front of me catches my eye.

Collette.

There she is.

Not in a blue cab, that lying bastard. It's a black cab with red and orange flames licking up the sides of the engine block. I'd appreciate the quality paint job if it didn't belong to a mother-fucking abuser.

I raise my hand and smile. When her curious face pops

back into the window, I wave. She eyes me. One second becomes five before there's a slight raise of her hand.

"Wait," I say and dig my phone out of my back pocket.

Unfortunately, there are several missed calls from Carl and texts from Judd. All of it makes me frown.

Shoving my phone in the air for us to talk on it, she shakes her head, indicating she doesn't have a phone with her finger wagging at me. I point to the passenger side door, then look both ways to see if the coast is clear of Hamilton before giving her a thumbs-up. She shakes her head again and disappears from the window.

I get it.

She's terrified.

How do I convince her to talk to me? If she's terrified of me, the police are going to send her into convulsions.

When she pops back into view with a pad of paper pressed to the windshield, I stretch taller to read it. She's asking what I want. I open and close my hand to show that I want to talk.

I point to the side door again, moving my hand in a circular motion to roll down the window. She slowly removes the pad from the windshield, and I dart between the trucks to wait. It takes everything in me not to climb up there with her. I know that would be too aggressive for this timid girl.

Thankfully, she has the keys to the rig because the window slides halfway down before her tear-stained face appears. The raccoon eyes from before are now red and puffy, with mascara streaking down her cheeks. I didn't see it inside, but she has a fading shiner, hidden by the makeup and coal-lined lids.

"Are you okay?" I ask, over the hum of the engine, two trucks down.

"Where's Rick?"

So that's the fucker's name.

"He's inside."

Half true.

"Did he do that to you?" she asks, tapping the window at my swollen eye.

It's not completely shut, thankfully, since his fist landed more on my temple than my eye socket.

"Yeah."

She shrinks back into the dark cab, so only her eyes were showing.

"But I racked him and broke his nose," I say, and that brings her entire face back to the window.

"He's going to be mad. He's going to take it out on me."

"Yeah, he was mad at me. He's getting cleaned up and calmed down right now." Another half-truth which she doesn't believe by the way she nibbles on her nails. "Trust me, he will not take it out on you. Is he family?"

She shakes her head, and a look of complete humiliation washes over her.

"Okay, I get it. I'm not here to judge. I'm here to help."

Second attempt at assuring her.

"Sometimes we get mixed up with the wrong type of people, Collette. I have been there. It's not fucking pretty. I know you feel bad, but there are people here to help. That want to help you."

I lean against the truck behind me, angling to see the inside of the cab. With the way it's tucked between two other semis with no interior lights on, it's impossible to see beyond the blackness surrounding her face.

"Isla. My name is Isla, not Collette."

Trust.

It's a start.

I smile at her.

"Nice to meet you, Isla. I'm Dani."

She gives me a small smile, and I have to ask the tough question now.

"How old are you?"

Her bottom lip quivers. As much as she's fighting those tears, they rise and fall over the coal edge in seconds.

"Fifteen."

Shit.

"Well, I'm twenty-one. Not much older than you. I've seen some shit in my life. I'm sure you have too."

I sympathize with this girl. What happened to her to get here? Especially at her age. When I was fifteen, I was in the garage handing Dad tools while he worked.

She bawls, sobbing into a paper towel. I want to walk around to the front of the truck stop, cut his dick off, and feed it to him. Hamilton spots me in between the trucks. I motion for him to be quiet while he walks down the passenger side.

"Isla, I want to get you some help. I'm not qualified or anything, but I have a sympathetic friend named Alexander Hamilton. Ya know, like the president on the twenty-dollar bill? He let me off without a ticket after I lied to him. I know it's hard to believe because men are a bunch of motherfuckers, but he's one of the good guys. I promise."

She cries, gripping the roll to rip off more, and I continue, "He's right here, looking all fancy in his uniform that his momma pressed."

Her face darts up, and her eyes are wide as an owl. Hamilton removes his hat and stands beside me, clearing his throat.

"Isla, this is Officer Hamilton. You can trust him because his parents named him after our president." I slide over to allow him more room as I make introductions to her.

"Hello, Isla," he says softly while lifting his hat as a sort of wave, then turns to me. "You know, Alexander Hamilton was never a president. I went along with it back there on the highway."

"Of course, he was a president. He's on the twenty-dollar bill." I roll my eyes while she watches us. "Duh."

"Again, that's not correct. That's Andrew Jackson, our seventh president on the twenty-dollar bill." His eyes move to Isla. "Did you know that, Isla? Is she right, or am I?"

Ah, trying to gain trust too. I like it.

I make a big gesture of looking at him with wide eyes and up at her, shrugging my shoulders. After a few long moments, she points at him.

"Well, I'll be damned. See how nice he is? Giving me history lessons in the middle of the parking lot. Do you think you can come out and meet him in person?" I ask, pressing harder than I'd like since two more officers are coming down the aisle that Isla can't see.

She shakes her head, withdrawing back to the darkness.

"She's fifteen," I mutter to Hamilton.

"Not good," he hums back.

"Isla, I have some other friends that I would like you to meet. They're here to help you," Hamilton says to the empty window.

I slide out of the way to make room for his friends and stand at the front of the cab. She's not in the windshield either, having disappeared completely into the cab.

I don't know what to do. This is beyond me. But damn, this girl needs a friend. Not police officer friends that will put her into the system, but a real friend. Hopefully, she has family somewhere.

I pace back and forth while they continue talking to her. Luckily, one of the other officers is a lady who's currently standing on the truck steps, whispering into the cab. I sigh, the throbbing from my eye is spreading across my head. The heat, even in the shade, is getting to me. Deciding I had better sit before I fall, I walk between the two trucks directly in front of Isla's cab and sit in the shade.

I don't know if it's the two hits to my head, the lack of food, or the exhaust fumes piling up around me, but I drop my head into my hands to not pass out.

"Why do you have blood in the back of your hair? Did you hit your head on the floor?" Hamilton asks, crouching in front of me to pick through my hair.

It hurts under his touch, and I stare at the oil-stained concrete. I debate on how much to tell him about the garage incident. It's unrelated to this and isn't nearly as critical as Isla's situation.

"I head-butted my coworker after he held me down and licked my neck. That's his blood. I broke his nose."

Yep, that pretty much sums it up.

"You're kidding. That was today? Before this?"

The astonishment in his tone is unmistakable.

He stops sorting through my hair, and I lift my head to look at him.

"Yeah. I'm having a bad day."

"I'll say, assaulting two guys, and here I was, letting you off with a warning," he says, and I merely look away. "Listen, we need to get you over to the medic to have a look."

He stands when the female officer hops down, and the cab door creaks open. I jump to my feet, my head swirling, and I latch onto Hamilton's uniform to steady myself.

"Whoa, you okay?" He holds me tight against him, cupping my waist to ensure I don't pass out before he releases me.

"Yep, got up too fast."

I definitely need to see the medic and eat some food.

Isla is balancing on those stupid high heels, looking like she's going to vomit. The lady officer is whispering to her.

The male officer is standing next to them with his hands outstretched as if to catch her at any second should she fall. I don't blame him. Watching her run out of the store on those things was hard enough.

Snuggled deep in her arms is a little dog, no bigger than

two handfuls. Isla clutches it to her chest as if it's more valuable than life itself. Poor kid.

The two officers shuffle beside her as Hamilton and I stand off to the side. She glances up at the rig, way too long for my comfort. I look away, knowing she's saying goodbye to her prison and life as she knows it.

My bloody shoe toes the concrete, catching her eyes, so I stop. She doesn't know that it's her captor's blood on them, but she might have figured it out by now. She stumbles ahead. The officers flank each side, with the female's hand cupping her elbow for support.

No possessions, belongings, or clothes, all left behind as she enters custody in scraps of lingerie. It fills me full of anger and vileness at that fucking bastard. We follow behind in silence. My mind is a mess, thinking about her life.

"Hey, Hamilton." I tug at his sleeve, pulling him to a stop as they continue walking. "Can you buy her a big shirt or something inside? I would, but I don't have my wallet."

"It's still Officer Hamilton. They will give her clean clothes when they get her settled in," he says casually, and I glare at him.

"Dude, she's covered in lingerie. Have the decency to buy her a shirt to cover all that, or I'll walk in and steal one. You can add it to my list of charges," I threatened because, damn, bro, have some common decency.

"Why wouldn't I put it past you to steal in front of an officer?" he mutters, shaking his head.

"Cuz I would. And get her the one with the Rocky Mountains on it. She wanted it earlier."

Isla and the two officers are walking toward a squad car they pulled around back, away from the prying eyes of the tourists. Hamilton puts his hat back on as he strides past them like a man on a mission, or at least on my mission. I head toward Isla when she sobs worse than in the cab.

"What's going on?" I demand, glaring at the officers.

"She can't keep the dog," the male officer answers, causing another shriek to rise out of her skinny frame.

"Why not?"

If she's going back home, then the dog can go too.

"Child Protective Services doesn't take animals. And until we find her guardian, she's going into foster care."

Shit just got fucking real. Leaving that cab and her abuser is necessary, but damn, losing her dog to go into the system.

"Isla, where are your parents?" I ask, and she shakes her head, crouching down on her heels to protect the dog. The female officer gives me a look, and it must be even worse at home. "Can you ask if the foster place will take her and the dog?"

"No, we must take her in. They assign a caseworker and have to figure out if they can even do an emergency placement. If not, she goes to a group home until they find a foster family to take her."

Double damn.

Hamilton is back with the shirt that he shoves into my hand and assesses the scene.

"What's going on?"

"She can't keep the dog," I murmur, all of us watching her cry into its fur. He nods, raising a finger to the other officer, and they walk off together.

"Uh, he got her this," I say, raising the shirt. "To cover up."

"Go ahead." The female officer motions for me to talk to her before walking off to open the back passenger door.

I crouch beside her, balancing my forearms on my thighs and holding the shirt lightly in my hands.

"Isla, Hamilton got you this Colorado shirt. He thought you might feel more comfortable with it on."

Her eyes glance at the blood on my Converse before meeting mine.

"I can't take her," she whispers through tear-clouded eyes. I clear my throat against a weird ball of emotions gathering there. "She's all I have. All I was allowed . . ." Her voice trails off while the dog licks the tears from her cheek.

It's the fucking saddest sight in the world.

"I know."

I don't know what else to say.

"Will you take her?"

I don't think I heard her correctly.

"Um, huh?"

"Will you take her? Just until I get to my new home?" she asks, her stare boring into my soul.

"Oh, wow, Isla—"

I start, standing up because I can't take her pleading look. If that damn dog understood what was happening, it wouldn't want me either.

"Pleeeease! She'll die at the pound. She's a Yorkie. They're not street dogs."

She doesn't have to tell me this Scooby snack isn't a street dog.

"Look, Isla. I've never had a dog before. I couldn't love it as much as you do. Clearly."

I toss the shirt between my two hands, more uncomfortable with this situation than her crying or taking a punch from Rick, her rapist. Big fat tears roll down the mascara tracks crusted on her cheeks, and I pace in front of her. Hamilton and the officer stroll toward us, and the pressure is building.

I need this girl to take the shirt, get in the car, and someone else to take the dog. If only that tourist family with the nice husband were here, he'd take the dog. I'm sure of it because he has kids, and kids love dogs.

"They've got to get going," Hamilton says, looking at the shirt still in my hands.

"She has to take my dog. Tell her, please," Isla begs, shoving her tiny dog in my face.

I need a dog like I need a hole in my head. Plus, Carl kicked me out, so I'm not sure I have a home to return to.

"Hamilton, can you take the dog?" I beg him while she begs me. He frowns and shakes his head.

Dammit.

"Please, you have to. This is all your fault," she says.

That's a kick in the balls.

Technically, I see it as me saving her. I guess she could be right-ish in that my actions caused a chain reaction of losing her dog.

"Yeah, well, give it over," I relent, hating myself the second that fur touches my calloused palm. "Just until you get to a new home, then this thing is back with you."

The dog kicks its tiny legs in midair, clawing at God knows what.

"Not like that. Cuddle her close to your body. Like this." Isla sniffs, shoving the dog against my boobs, and the little thing practically motorboats them.

Not the first time they've been motorboated, but most certainly, the first by a dog.

"This is weird," I blurt out. "Here, put this on, at least."

I hand her the shirt, and she scrambles to put it on, pulling it down as far as it will go. I flash Hamilton an I-told-you-so glance before looking down at the thing trying to bite my pigtail.

"Okay, well. What do I feed it? Does it have a name or leash? I can't carry it around all day. I work."

"Her name is Anna, like in the movie Frozen," she says, wiping her face with nails bitten down to the quick. Okay. Never heard of that movie. "And she has been eating human food. I had to share mine. He wouldn't buy dog food or a leash."

"Is she potty trained, at least?" I sigh, wondering how long this commitment is going to last.

"Yes, put her in the grass and tell her to tee-tee. She'll go."

"Anna. Human food. Tee-tee. Got it," I echo, glaring at Hamilton. "How do I give her dog back to her? How will I know when she's got a home?"

"I'll keep track," he replies.

The male officer pounds on the car's hood, signifying it's time to go.

Then she does something unexpected. Isla grabs me, hugs me as if her life depends on it, and whispers, "Thank you" in my ear.

I stiffen, not expecting this, and not exactly sure how I feel about getting her hauled off to Child Protective Services while taking care of her dog.

This is too much.

"All right, all right, that's enough." I shrug out of her hug. "You heard Hamilton promise that we'll stay in touch."

"Okay."

She slowly walks to the open back door with a lingering look at her little dog licking my neck.

Damn if I don't feel sorrier for that girl. She climbs inside, and the male officer shuts the door. When she looks out the window, she lays her palm against the glass to say goodbye, leaving her most precious possession in my care.

Well, shit.

10

"Damn Hamilton, I need a beer, a cigarette, a coffee, and a lay after this." I sigh, looking up at his surprised face. "Let's go see about that medic."

I walk around to the front of the store. The ambulance is still there with his squad car, but Rick, the rapist, and the other patrol car are gone. It's business as usual as if none of this happened. It makes me furious. Reaching for my phone, the screen shows it's coming up on noon. I snap a shot of my shiner with the dog plastered under my chin and send it to Kylie.

She'll be shocked when I tell her this story.

Hamilton touches my elbow, drawing me away from my phone, and I stuff it back into my pocket. We walk silently to the back of the ambulance, where the female medic is waiting for us.

"If you will take a seat up there," she says, pointing to the gurney.

I hesitate because this looks expensive.

"Um, I can't afford this," I blurt out, staying with my feet planted on the concrete outside the truck. I know the moment I step in the sucker, they will start charging my ass.

Her eyes flash to Hamilton. He sits on the ledge of the tail-gate, blocking access to the inside of the unit.

"Please check her out. She might be riding with me and not you."

My gaze flies from her to him, unsure if he's kidding about being arrested or not.

"You had better be joking, Hamilton."

He merely shrugs as she pulls out a clicky thing and steps into my personal space.

"I'm going to check for signs of a concussion. Do you have a headache?"

"Yes, but it's because I need coffee and food. It's why I came here."

I tug my pigtail out of the dog's mouth and shove her in Hamilton's face.

"Hold the dog, Hamilton. It's obsessed with my hair."

"Officer Hamilton," he corrects for the billionth time.

I couldn't care less because both creatures are annoying me now. Begrudgingly, he takes the dog and isn't an animal lover by the look of irritation on his face. She fits in his one hand as it rests against his muscular thigh.

The medic shines her light across one eye and then the next, humming to herself as if she found something important. Her gloved hands press against the shiner and turns my head in different directions to get a better look. I wince from the tenderness.

"Your cheekbone seems intact, although an MRI could detect any hairline fractures or other damage," she says. I shake my head no, causing her to turn my chin even farther. "You have blood in your hair. Did your head hit the floor when he struck you?"

She's more delicate with the back of my head, pressing different spots that hurt less than others.

"No, I broke a guy's nose earlier today. Do I have a cut back there? I feel like I may have hit his teeth."

She rubs a spot, and I hiss.

"Yes, you have a small gash that could use a stitch or two. Again, an MRI could—"

"If I can't afford your fancy ambulance ride, there's no way I can't afford an MRI. Can you slather some ointment on it and call it a day?"

I move my chin out of her hands. She nods, climbing around Hamilton's planted ass to get some crap out of the rig.

"I understand, and yes, I have something I can put on now and give you to take home."

She raises her voice as she's opening boxes to pull out gauze and an ointment tube. Hamilton is rubbing the dog's side with his thumb, calming it down.

Maybe he's a dog person after all.

"You should take it."

If he does, then I can put this mess behind me and deal with Carl and Judd's stupid asses.

"I already told you. I can't."

The medic comes to the front of the truck, puts a hand on Hamilton's shoulder for balance, and jumps out with a tube of stuff in her hand.

"Put this on twice daily and keep the area clean and dry the best you can. Turn around, please."

I comply and hiss when the ointment stings the cut. It's better than stitches, which I can't afford either.

"Is that your blood on your knee and shoes?"

Looking down, I know he bled on my Converse, but I didn't see his blood on my knee until now.

"His."

"Okay, that's all I can do if you're formally refusing treatment," she says, handing me the medicine tube.

"Yes, I am. Thank you."

I take a step back, thinking if I take a few more, I can bolt for my car over there and barrel out of here. On three, I run.

One.

She faces Hamilton. "We're done. If you don't need us for anything else, then we'll take off."

I take two steps backward. He can keep the dog. He never gave me a reason why he couldn't.

Two.

"Thanks, Amy. I owe you one."

He stands, holding the dog against his uniform, which makes him cuter than he already is. I take three more steps backward. When he turns his back to shut the ambulance door, I bolt.

"Stop right there, Louise. You and I are not done here," Hamilton yells across the parking lot, causing me to skid to a stop.

Damn, so close.

I groan as I turn around, refusing to walk back to him since, technically, he said to stop, and that's exactly what I'm doing. He pounds on the back doors as the other cop did on the roof. That must be cop code for let's get out of here. He saunters over to me, his eyes getting lost in the shade of his hat.

"Where do you think you're going?" he asks, shoving the dog toward me. I glance at it before crossing my arms over my chest, which shoves my boobs higher.

He's welcome for that little present.

"Back to work, and I'm not taking that dog. You can't make me, *Officer Hamilton*."

"Not so fast. Didn't you assault someone before coming here? Not to mention speeding and lying to a peace officer."

"I wouldn't call it an assault, just a reckoning. You know, like the old westerns where they harass the guy, and he finally blows their heads off? Like that," I defend because it was my reckoning, and I don't regret it. Felt damn good busting his nose and shattering that window.

"In that case, you'll have to come with me."

He steps toward me and shoves the dog in my face. I release a long groan to convey my frustration with him.

"Am I under arrest?"

"Can you produce a license?"

"I have one, just not here."

"Then you can't drive, and if you try, you will be arrested. Either way, you're coming with me, and we're returning to where the assault happened," he explains, motioning for me to get into his squad car.

"So, I'm not under arrest?" I clarify, not moving.

"Not yet."

His hand moves to unbutton the handcuffs from his belt, and I roll my eyes.

"Fine, Hamilton. I'll go with you, but I don't see why you're giving me such a hard time. I saved a girl and am babysitting her dog because of you. It seems you owe me twice," I complain, pulling my hair out of the dog's small mouth on my way to his car.

"Officer Hamilton."

I'm not calling him that unless I absolutely have to because I don't give a shit. He's Alexander Hamilton to me, dude on the twenty-dollar bill. I'll have to check that when we get back to the shop. He opens the back driver's door, and I stop in my tracks.

"I'm not sitting in the shit and vomit seats. It's bad enough that I have to ride in your pig rig."

I walk around to the front of the car and yank open the passenger side door. It's loaded with papers, empty energy drinks, and old fast food bags.

"Damn, Hamilton, you been on a stakeout or something?

Stalking your ex-wife? This literally is a pigsty in a pig rig. See what I did there?"

"You're not sitting up there. All suspects must sit in the back," he yells through the cab.

I don't care. I shove everything on the floorboard before plopping my ass in the seat. Then I dig out a straw that's poking my thigh to toss on the trash heap.

"Louise, get back here."

"Not a chance, Hamilton. If I'm not under arrest, then I'm a law-abiding citizen sitting in the front. Look, I'll even wear a seat belt." I make a grand gesture of putting it on, careful not to smash the dog with it, and close my door. "I'm all ready, *Officer*."

I throw that in to make him feel like he's in charge. Ignoring him while he deliberates with himself, I flip down the visor to gaze in the mirror at how big my shiner is. Not too bad yet, so long as the swelling stays in my cheek and temple. I'll have to see what it looks like in a few hours when the blood settles.

The back door slams with enough force to shake the car. I smother my smile, loving that I'm getting under his skin. It makes us sort of even.

Damn, if this day hasn't sucked. If I can make his day worse, then I'm happy to do it. He drops into his seat with a huff, putting his hat on a hook attached to the glass shield.

"By the way, I don't go by Louise. Call me Dani," I say, fixing my pigtails in the mirror since they got all messed up in the fight and are crusted with dog slobber.

"Is anything you say actually true?" he asks with a sigh.

I tilt my head, wrapping the band at the bottom, and start on the other side. "I think so. In my mind, it sounds true."

His eyes bore into the side of my head, but I refuse to look and continue fussing with my hair. He gives up talking to me when he pushes buttons on his computer. After several long minutes, I hold the dog in the air and drag my phone out of my back pocket to see Kylie's missed phone call. She probably wants details, but I'll call her later when I have more privacy.

My knee bobs up and down, waiting for him to take off, which seems to be forever since I have fixed my hair, examined my eye, crunched down the mountain of trash into a manageable pile on his floorboard, and stuffed Anna into the neckline of my tank top because she won't stop shaking.

"Can we go already?" I groan, tapping my nails on the door handle in time with my bouncing knee.

He shoots me a dirty look and radios back about a potential assault that he's investigating before we finally pull out of the truck stop. I thought waiting in the parking lot was bad, but it's his driving. It's so much worse.

"Can't we go faster? You drive like a grandma."

"I'm driving the speed limit," he says, sliding on his sunglasses, which brings out his jawline now that I'm closer to him.

"You look kinda hot in those, Hamilton. Does it help you pick up chicks? Does the uniform help? Do you know male strippers make more money wearing the cop costume? Can you put on some music? Driving this slowly will take forever, and I need something to distract me from all the silence in the car."

"No, I don't pick up women while on duty," he replies in a condescending tone. "I also don't know anything about male strippers. My particular unit doesn't regulate the enforcement of those business establishments. And I don't listen to music. It distracts from incoming emergency calls."

"You're a real fun killer."

I glare out the window as we creep down the highway. I swear, I could run faster than we're going. The dog snuggles deeper into my boobs.

Again, she's not the first to use my fun bags as pillows, although she's the lightest.

"Is that dog sleeping against your . . . in your shirt?" He clears his throat.

"Yup, apparently, she's a lesbian, but don't tell Isla. She might not have come out to her yet, and it's not my place to tell," I mumble, watching a flock of birds land on a power line.

"Dogs can't be gay."

"Damn Hamilton, it's a joke. Do they teach you not to have a sense of humor at cop school because you must have gotten an A+ in the class seeing how by the book you are?"

He doesn't respond to my insult, so I continue, "The dog was cold, so I thought skin-to-skin or some shit like that would help."

"That's for babies."

"Whatever."

We ride in silence for a good while, finally getting back into town when he asks, "What's the address of the assault?"

"Carl's Timeless Classics off 123."

Anger flares within when I think about this morning.

"Tell me what happened."

When I glance at him, he's staring straight at the road, his hands positioned at ten and two. Such a rule follower.

"Not much to tell. This dick prick harasses me all the time, had me pinned against the car, licked my neck, and so I reared my head back and broke his nose. Basic self-defense."

His eyes never leave the road, when he asks, "Is that the entire story, or am I going to find out the truth when we get there?"

Fair enough. I deserve that since I haven't been completely truthful with him.

"Fine, the owner took dick prick's side, so I threw a wrench at his window. It might have shattered, and he might have kicked me out."

Yup, that's it in a nutshell.

"Dick prick?"

"Yeah, dick prick is the neck licker and no, he didn't throw me out. Carl, the owner, did."

"Got it."

I resume looking out the window, anger turning into a rage when Hamilton turns onto Highway 123. My hands roll into fists, and I stop bouncing my knee. The second this car rolls to a stop, I'm going to race upstairs, pack a bag, and crash at Kylie's place.

I'm done with Carl and Judd.

11

The drive down the winding road takes entirely too long with his grandma ass behind the wheel, causing me to sweat with anticipation at this pending confrontation. I'm going to lose my shit, and I don't care if Hamilton sees it or not.

Hell, I still might go to jail for all this bullshit. Hamilton puts on his signal, waiting for a car to pass when I spot the black Porsche parked out front.

What the hell is he doing here?

It's been a month, and he picks today of all the days to come back. Yeah, I'll be arrested for assault if he chimes in on this situation, possibly murder if I get hold of Hamilton's gun.

Shit's going down.

"Can you put on the lights and siren? Make it seem like you're responding to a crime in progress?"

That would be icing on this crappy cake.

"Absolutely not. You'll get your ID so I can run it for priors while I talk to the victim," he says.

I look at him like he's crazy.

"You're talking to the victim. Right here."

I point to myself, and he crosses the road to pull in next to the asshole. I wish he parked on my side because I'd slam the biggest dent in that Porsche for fun.

"We'll see."

He puts the car in park and gets out, leaving his hat and me behind.

"Dammit."

Anna's snoozing. Lulled to sleep by his grandma driving. I brace my hand under her body to hold her in place when I get out of the car.

Hamilton throws open the door, the bell chiming wildly, and stops. Carl's lazy ass couldn't have cleaned it up by now.

Damn, man.

I was pulled over by a cop, assaulted by a rapist, saved a girl, rescued her dog, and crawled along the highway to get here. Those lazy fuckers could have swept it up and replaced the glass in that amount of time.

He waits for me, and I realize he's been chivalrous. Well, isn't that nice of our past president? I stride toward the open door and Anna's head pops up to see where we are going. The asshole jumps to his feet. His hand covers his mouth as his worried eyes scan me up and down.

Carl is red-faced behind the counter, having straightened up when I traipse through the door. If I didn't know better, I'd say they are both surprised to see us. Hamilton's fingertips graze my back.

"Louise, er, Dani, have a seat where I can see you," he says in a deep, authoritarian voice.

I'm kind of impressed that his balls dropped around these other dudes. Okay, I'll play along. My rage descends a notch to anger.

Chunks of glass shards crunch under my bloody shoes as I carefully step across the lobby to the bank of seats mounted on the wall. I select the one closest to the door in case I need to make a run for it.

"What is going on here? Dani?"

The asshole looks at me, and Hamilton steps in front of him, blocking my view. This is too interesting not to watch, so I peek around his gun belt.

"Sir, I'm going to have to ask you to step back," Hamilton says, pointing at the asshole.

It's a perfect match in height, but not in size. Hamilton is bulkier, but I've seen what karate moves the asshole has. I'm not sure who would win in a street fight, probably Hamilton, if he can bring his gun.

"I'm Carl Menkey, the owner." He waddles around the counter and shoves his hand out to Hamilton, who ignores it. "What's this all about?"

"And you are?" Hamilton asks the asshole, pulling a notepad out of his front pocket.

"My name is Tomlin Takahashi. I'm a customer of Dani's," he lies.

I open my mouth to object when Carl's wide eyes flash to mine. I can't make out if it's fear or rage.

"What happened to her? Why does she have a black eye? Why is she covered in blood?"

The asshole's questions fall one after another, and it's intriguing. His concern is a curious thing considering how we left things. Maybe I should back off calling him an asshole all the time. Perhaps just reserve it for when he's acting like one, which isn't now. He's actually worried and demanding answers, which sounds like he's taking my side.

Okay, let's see where this goes.

"Mr. Takahashi, I appreciate your concern, but I'm here to find out what happened this morning. If you will, please take a seat."

Hamilton motions to the row of chairs, and Tomlin starts toward me. Hamilton puts a hand on his shoulder to stop him.

"Away from the assailant."

"Assailant?"

Tomlin's forehead wrinkles in confusion. Obviously, Carl didn't tell him what happened this morning.

"Don't you mean victim? Look at her. Isn't it obvious someone beat her? Any why does she have a dog?" He looks from Hamilton to me. "Why do you have a dog in your shirt?"

Anna's head twirls to face him. Her furry ear tickles my skin, but I don't say a word.

"Mr. Takahashi," Hamilton warns.

I wish I had popcorn because this is better than expected. He plops down a few seats away, his eyes boring into me while I glare at that portly ass that took penis breath's side over mine.

Carl doesn't know what to make of this. I think it's fear as he wipes the corners of his mouth with his thumb.

"Mr. Menkey, tell me what happened this morning."

Hamilton preps his pad to take notes and I can't wait to hear his version of events. Carl's eyes dart to mine, and I can tell he's deliberating between taking Judd's side or taking mine. Roll the dice, old man.

"Er, Dani was already here when I walked in. Her music was too loud. It vibrated the pictures on the wall, so I told her to turn it down. She was already in a foul mood," he says, getting an unnecessary dig in. "She hates when I ask her to turn it down, but it's unprofessional when customers are here."

"Does she usually arrive before you? Is this a common occurrence?" Hamilton interjects. "Were customers here? Mr. Takahashi?"

He motions to Tomlin and then raises his hand to stop Tomlin as he starts to stand.

"Stay put, please," Hamilton commands to a grumbling Tomlin, who's struggling with not being in charge. It's humorous watching him agree with someone else. I kind of like it.

"Yes, Dani lives here and—"

"Dani lives here?" Hamilton questions, looking back at me. I neither confirm nor deny it. He'll see it on my driver's license. "Dani lives at Carl's Timeless Classics?"

"Yes, there's an apartment above the garage." Carl's eyes lift toward the ceiling.

"How long has she lived here?"

Carl looks at me, but I still won't help him out.

"Well, since her mom left. I'd say fifteen to twenty years." Sixteen, but who's counting?

I glance at Tomlin. His eyebrows raise in surprise and then his head tilts in silent inquiry. Yeah, a long fucking time. Too long now that I think about it.

"She lived here alone? As a child?" Hamilton continues, drawing my gaze to Carl's wide eyes.

"No, no. Her dad raised her here. He worked for me. We grew up together. He passed a few years back. She had to quit high school because there was no one to take care of her. I let her stay and gave her a job. Her dad showed her how to fix cars. She's better than him," Carl admits.

I hate hearing him talk so casually about Dad. I hate it even more when he says I'm better than my old man. Fuck you, Carl. That man worked his ass off for a pittance.

Tomlin clears his throat to get my attention. I hate the look on his face. Sympathy. Fucking worse than pity.

"Got it. She lives and works here, which makes sense that she would get here before you. She turns down the music, then what?" Hamilton prods Carl, who looks past me when the sound of a crotch rocket throttles into the parking lot.

Karma lobbed one in my favor.

I smile. Judd has no idea what he's walking into.

I take Anna out of my tank top, cross my legs to make a

better lap for her, and rake my fingers through her soft fur, waiting for the door's bell to jingle. When it does, my head jolts up to see a surprised Judd. His expression of shock and worry is priceless.

"What the hell . . ."

His voice tapers off, and his eyes become slits when they fall on me. I smirk at my handiwork when I see a butterfly bandage over the part of his swollen, red nose that I split.

"You brought the police into this? You fucking bitch."

Bitch?

Fine, he's now known as penis breath.

"You had something to do with this?" Tomlin growls, launching out of his seat to charge at Judd so fast that I scoop up Anna to hold her safely against my chest.

Hamilton drops his pad, sliding on the glass to sandwich himself between the two snarling fighters.

Penis breath's ready to beat my ass. Tomlin's ready to beat penis breath.

Good thing Hamilton is a big dude. His muscles are popping out of his shirt sleeves to shove Tomlin across the shards while using his wide back to push penis breath nearly out the front door. It's kinda hot watching all this male testosterone.

"Get back, Mr. Takahashi. Don't do it, or you'll be facing assault charges yourself," Hamilton yells, gaining leverage on Tomlin.

I twist to the side to further protect Anna. One flying shard could kill this tiny creature, and I'd have no way to explain that to a devastated girl. Tomlin shrugs off Hamilton's grip to straighten his dress shirt while looking murderously at penis breath.

"I didn't do anything. That crazy bitch broke my nose," penis breath defends, and I grin at him. "See? Did you see that?"

He points his filthy, oil-laden finger at me. Hamilton's eyes follow. I blink as innocently as possible, cooing at the tiny dog plastered to my skin.

"You're scaring Anna," I state so matter-of-factly that I think penis breath would kill me now if Tomlin wasn't lording over me.

"Who the fuck is Anna?" he roars, taking a step toward me.

Tomlin takes a step toward him, and Hamilton stands ready for another round between the two of them.

"The dog," Hamilton and I say in unison.

"Carl, you're shitting me with this, right?" In frustration, penis breath throws his hand toward Carl. "You threw her out. What's she doing back?"

His accusation flies over to a stunned Carl, dragging a paper towel down his face to collect the sweat. All eyes are on him, waiting for a response.

"Well, now, I wouldn't say that's exactly what happened." Carl shifts on his feet, probably because this is the longest he's ever had to stand.

"That's exactly what happened. You told her to get out of your garage," penis breath says, his voice rising in disbelief.

He's not wrong. That's exactly what happened.

"You kicked Dani out? Why?" Tomlin unbuttons the sleeves of his dress shirt. "Surely there has to be some misunderstanding here?" he continues, rolling up one sleeve.

I'm not sure if it's because it's hot as hell in here with the broken window, letting in all the heat from the open garage bays, or if he's preparing himself to wipe the floor clean with penis breath's face. I hope it's the latter.

"Okay, I need everyone to calm down and take a seat. Mr. Takahashi."

Hamilton points to the bank of chairs again. Tomlin reluctantly sits, his thigh pressing against mine, and it's strangely comforting. Hamilton nods, satisfied with Tomlin's following instructions, before turning around to face penis breath.

"And who are you?"

Penis breath shoots me a dirty look and then stares at Hamilton with contempt. "My name is Judd Wilson."

He lifts his chin as if challenging the law. Smug bastard. I got to hand it to Hamilton. I would have beaten his ass by now and radioed it in as attacking a police officer.

"Mr. Wilson, please go stand behind the counter," Hamilton motions to where Carl is grabbing the old stool to plop his wide ass down.

He pauses, glaring at me, and then slowly complies. Tomlin leans forward, ready to lunge at any second. When penis breath passes behind Carl, he claps him on the back, which makes my blood boil. As if they literally have each other's back.

Hamilton stoops to pluck his pad and pen from the shards to face Carl.

"Now, where were we? Ah yes, she turned the music down, and ..."

"I heard screaming. These two are always at each other's throats, but this morning, I see Judd holding his nose with blood everywhere and Dani screaming like a banshee. When I tried to reprimand her, she picked up a tool and threw it at my window." He left out the most important part, of course. I roll my eyes, and he wags his crooked finger at me. "That's coming out of your paycheck, Dani."

Yeah, I expected that.

"You reprimanded her? For what?" Hamilton scribbles on his pad, stops his pen, and waits for the answer. Carl looks at me, then Tomlin, before answering.

"She broke his nose."

Hamilton hesitates to write it down, and my curiosity piques.

"Dani walked up to Mr. Wilson and assaulted him, without cause, is what you are saying? Do I have that right?"

Sort of, I got a tight uppercut on penis breath before I broke his nose. I hurt my knuckles, but it was worth it.

Carl's face is getting redder by the minute, with little beads of sweat dotting the fringe of hair circling his head.

"I wasn't there, so I don't know exactly what happened."

"Yet you asked her to leave the premises?"

"Yes, she attacked Judd and broke my window. I thought it best she leaves, cool off and stuff."

Carl drags the crumbled napkin down his cheeks and neck while penis breath sprawls against the back counter with a smug expression.

"Did you allow Ms. Winters time to explain?"

"Er, well, no. I asked her to leave instead. I tried to call her, but she wouldn't take my calls."

"You didn't bother to get her side of the story. And I assume she didn't take your calls because she was with me," Hamilton justifies on my behalf, which is true. I was occupied getting my ass beat and finding Isla. "Did you know about him attempting to sexually assault her?"

The blood drains from Carl's face.

Chaos erupts.

Tomlin's up and out of the chair in a flash, clearing the counter to charge after penis breath but he sprints into the garage for fear of getting his ass beat. Dammit, I'd pay good money to see that happen.

Carl backs in the corner to get out of the way. Hamilton blocks Tomlin, going shoulder to shoulder to hold him back and using his weight advantage against Tomlin.

I stand, set Anna on the chair, and put two fingers to my mouth to let out an ear-piercing whistle.

"Everyone stop!" They all freeze to look at me. "Hamilton, do I need to stay for this?"

"Yes, now both of you sit down. Mr. Takahashi, if you try that again, you'll be sitting in the back of my patrol car."

Anger tinges Hamilton's cheeks as he adjusts his police belt loaded with all that junk.

"Come on. You don't want to sit in the piss and vomit seats of his car."

I wave Tomlin over to me to sit back down. Hamilton glares at me over my comment. I'm not wrong though. If I don't want to sit on them, Tomlin definitely wouldn't want to.

"Dani, if any of that's true, you're filing charges," Tomlin threatens.

I understand that's what rich people do, but I'm poor and poor people take it.

"If everyone can settle down." Hamilton's eyes cut to Tomlin.

I pluck the dog off the chair to place her on my lap. He picks up his pad and pen a second time and focuses on Carl again.

"Mr. Menkey, did you know what your male employee was trying to do to your female employee?"

"No." Carl's face is awash in guilt. His eyes are everywhere but mine. Rotten bastard.

"And when she tried to tell you, you didn't listen, correct? You retaliated by requesting she leaves not only her place of work but her home as well."

He unfolds the wadded napkin to refold it and dab his blotchy skin.

"I wasn't retaliating. I was trying to separate them. She broke his nose, after all, so who was the one hurt?"

Tomlin jumps to his feet, Hamilton positioning his body to block him from jumping over the counter.

Tomlin paces, switching between glaring at Carl hiding behind the counter and penis breath, watching from the other side of the shattered window.

"I see. Because her injuries were not seen by you, then they didn't exist. Is that what you're saying?" Hamilton's drilling him into the ground with this line of questioning.

I lay my legs across the seats for a better view, catching Tomlin's attention for a second before he scowls at Carl. It's interesting to see Hamilton maintain his composure, although he's super pissed. Tomlin's hands curl in and out of fists, ready to murder both.

Penis breath cautiously watches with the wall between him and everyone else. Carl is clearly on the defense, no match for Hamilton. I swear this is better than any reality television that Kylie watches.

"No, but she wasn't the one bleeding all over my floor," Carl says.

He can't think beyond Judd not being the victim. It's unreal to listen to him repeat himself.

"You're missing the point," Hamilton says, resting his arm against the butt of his gun holstered at his side. He's right, Carl couldn't get the point if it kicked his ass.

"When you kicked her off your premises, did you allow her time to collect her purse and identification?"

Oh, good one, Hamilton.

"No, I told her to get out of here. I didn't think about that at the time." His beady little eyes fall on me and then the tiny dog curled in my lap. "I expected her to come back eventually, but not with an animal."

Disdain drips from his words.

Hamilton doesn't miss a beat when he says, "That dog will remain in her possession for the foreseeable future."

Dammit, man. Take this dog.

My head is pounding from lack of food, Carl going round and round to weasel out of his responsibility and smashing my head with two other guys. I wince when I lean it against the wall to close my eyes for a moment.

"Look, Officer?" Tomlin stops when he realizes Hamilton never introduced himself.

"Hamilton."

"Dani has been through a lot and is in obvious pain. While you're investigating down here, can she at least go upstairs and get cleaned up?"

His request has me opening my eyes. Even though he's crossing all sorts of lines as Judd's customer, I appreciate him asking because I'd really like a couple of aspirin and a hot shower.

Hamilton glances over his shoulder at Tomlin and then at me. I'd turn on that southern charm again if I knew it would work since I'm desperate to escape this mess.

"She's a flight risk."

Yup, he's going to be a hard ass. I slide farther down to lie across the chairs and Anna climbs over my boobs to become a turtleneck sweater on my throat.

"I'll stay with her," Tomlin offers, which is nice.

I want a nap more than anything and lying across these chairs isn't very comfortable. All eyes fall on me while mine bore into Hamilton's, hoping he'll have mercy on my pathetic self and allow me to go upstairs.

"After everything she has been through, I'm sure she's exhausted and wants to rest," Tomlin says, stating the obvious since I'm basically laid out for a nap already.

"She was struck twice in the head, and even though she refused medical treatment, I don't think it's wise for her to sleep," he explains as his gaze falls on me. "If you want to get cleaned up, I'll allow it, but no napping and no slipping out the back door, Dani."

"Aye, aye, Captain." I shoot to my feet to salute him, forgetting about the glass, and my legs splay in different directions. "Shit!"

I smash Anna against my body, and brace myself with my

hand, ready to break my fall when the Tomlin catches me under my arms. Good thing I shaved my armpits this morning. He doesn't immediately let go when I scoot the shards to the side with my foot to make sure my Converse is flat on the linoleum floor.

"All right, all right, get off."

I shrug him off and catch the amusement on Hamilton's face, which is the opposite of the frown on Tomlin's.

"I don't need a babysitter, but I'd kill to wash this blood off me," I say to no one in particular.

Penis breath cranes his neck to survey me from head to toe before quirking an eyebrow as a question. Wouldn't you like to know, motherfucker?

I scowl at him. His crusted blood in my hair doesn't bother me, but Rick the Rapist's blood on my knee and shoes is starting to.

"I'll need to get her statement after theirs. If you can guarantee she stays, I'll head upstairs when I'm done here," Hamilton says.

A compromise, with Tomlin hanging out in my place. Meh, it could be worse. I want to ask why he lied about being my customer when he clearly isn't. I'll remind him of that.

"I will."

Tomlin's hand hovers under my elbow, and even though I shoot him a dirty look, he doesn't take the hint.

"Everyone move, so I don't break my neck," I say, mostly to Tomlin. It's Hamilton who steps back, more glass crunching under his black boots.

I tuck the dog between my armpit and my boob, so I have one hand free to steady myself as I make my way across the shattered shards.

"And someone should clean this up."

I look directly at penis breath, and then at Carl when I pass him mute in the corner. Tomlin sails across the glass in his fancy dress shoes with no problem and is practically breathing down my neck in the narrow hallway leading to my staircase.

"Mr. Menkey . . ." Hamilton starts, and I'm glad for the reprieve from all that back there.

Sic 'em, Officer Hamilton.

12

"Well, thanks for getting me out of that," I say over my shoulder to Tomlin as we climb the stairs.

"Christ, you have blood in the back of your hair."

Astonishment coats his words.

"Yup."

"Will you tell me what happened?"

His footsteps pound on my creaky stairs. I'd usually be irritated with him for being too close and loud, but at this point, I don't care. I need a break from all the fighting this day has brought.

"Sure."

When we are standing at the landing by my door, I stop him.

"Hey, when you get in there . . . don't judge. I don't live in a fancy museum like you do."

I don't know why my messy apartment suddenly bothers me when it hasn't before. Maybe it's because of the pity I saw on his face when he heard I've lived above an auto shop my whole life.

He reaches out to catch the underside of my forearm, knowing it makes me uneasy, but he does it anyway. It's probably because it looks like I have been through a lot, and hell, I have.

"Dani, I know things weren't the best between us when I left, but I'd like to change that. You said it yourself that I'm going to be around a lot, so I gave it much thought while I was gone, and I'd like us to be friends."

Friends. Interesting.

I mean, I have Kylie. She's been my best friend forever. I have Zach, but he isn't a friend. He's a fuckboy. Okay, maybe having two friends isn't the worst thing in the world.

"Fine, but friends don't stare at each other's boobs."

I shove my finger in his face, and he wraps his around it. Like that church song, I guess he's trying not to let Satan blow it out.

"I'll try my best, but you could at least cover them more. And for Christ's sake, stop putting that dog in them," he says like it's tormenting him.

"Meh, I'll think about it." He releases my finger and I face my door, pause, and then remind him, "Remember, no judgment."

"Got it."

I swing the door open and see it anew. Piles of dusty papers, grease-covered car manuals, and other old books are stacked haphazardly atop the coffee table and end table. The walls still have the faded daisy wallpaper from my youth.

Dad said my mom picked it out, and he always liked it. Said the yellow flowers made her happy. I'm not sure I ever believed it, but it was one of the last remaining things left of her.

Dad's old recliner, draped in his favorite blanket, is stuffed in the corner near the small window with foil at the top to block the unforgiving sun. His eyeglasses sit on the circular table attached to the tall shade lamp near the last newspaper he ever read.

The couch takes up most of the space. A terrible green velour thing that Dad got for free from a customer remodeling their mountain house a decade ago. It's unsightly with bald spots rubbed into the fabric, but comfortable as hell from all the body weight pressed into the cushions over the years.

My apartment is a time capsule to Dad since I'm unable to get rid of anything, even though it appears messy to others. This is all he had to show for his hard work. How can I part with that? I'm both saddened and embarrassed by it.

"What are we waiting for?" Tomlin asks, his expensive cologne wrapping around me like a warm blanket.

"Nothing."

I cross the threshold, uncomfortable with both his proximity and letting him see the tomb of old memories. Kylie has been here a hundred times and complained ninety-nine percent of the time about the state of my apartment. It took me nearly a year to move Dad's clothes out of the closet. However, a few of his favorite shirts are still hanging in the back of it.

"Um . . ." I start and let it die when his gaze wanders over my apartment after he closes the door behind us.

Suddenly, I hate this idea. I wish I had made a different choice downstairs.

"Are you going to go shower?" His eyes slide to mine and then to Anna.

"Yeah, but I don't know what to do with her." When I separate her from my body, she shakes. "I don't want to lose her in all *this*."

My place isn't set up for a dog this size. I'm barely taking care of myself. Now I must keep something else alive.

Dammit.

"It's pretty small. Keep it in the bathroom with you for now."

"Yeah, well, make yourself at home or whatever."

I throw my hand out to the time capsule living room. His gaze travels over it again before I turn on my heel, causing my sneaker to squeak on the floor. I walk down the hallway to Dad's old room, now mine, to pull out some clean clothes. Once I gather what I need, I cross the hallway to the bathroom, glimpsing Tomlin tapping on his phone.

When I close the door and turn on the water to warm up, I put Anna down. She stands on the bath rug trembling, holding up her front paw as if it's hurt.

"I can't keep holding you. You know, I have a life."

I strip, throwing my bloody shoes in my trash can and dropping my clothes on the floor. The hot shower never felt so good. Getting the dried blood out of my hair is taking more than a few washes. The water pooling at my ankles turns from red to clear, and the whole bathroom smells like apricots.

My head is tender from the cut caused by Judd's teeth, and a big bump has formed under it as well. The hot steam makes my swollen eye close almost entirely, which is annoying.

Once I'm done, I step out of the tub, and the dog pops out from behind the toilet to paw at my feet. This needy little thing is going to be the death of me.

Grabbing the towel to dry off, I toss it on the floor when done, and she darts toward it, circling three times to curl in the middle of it. That will work. Note to self, leave towels on the floor for her. Who am I kidding? I already do because I'm lazy.

After I dry off and get dressed, I open the door, and steam billows into the hallway. Deciding I need to train the dog not to be held all the time, I walk out the door and coax her to follow me.

It takes a couple of attempts, but she follows me as I coo down the hall to join Tomlin in the kitchen. He's hunting through the cabinets and stops when he sees me.

"I thought you were going to put on more clothes."

I look down at my white camisole and pink boy shorts and shrug.

"What?"

"You're standing in front of me in your underwear."

"Wrong. According to Victoria, they're sleep shorts. But that's our secret. Get it."

I snort at my joke. I'm clever like that. I braid my wet hair to stop it from dripping onto my boobs and getting my camisole all wet.

"Don't quit your day job," he says and then frowns when he realizes my job is on the line. "I didn't mean—" anything by it. I finish in my head for him. Yeah, I know.

"No offense taken. Anyway, what are you looking for?"

I step into the kitchen, feeling it shrink around us because it's far too tiny for two people. He must feel the same because he shuffles down the counter to stand at the beginning of the alley kitchen.

"Coffee. You look like you could use some."

"Like I told Hamilton, I need a lay, a cigarette, a drink, and a coffee. Now add food and a nap to that list." Wrinkles collect on his forehead while he processes my list. "But I don't have any coffee. I don't buy it because Carl has the coffee pot downstairs. It saves me money."

"You told the police officer you want to have sex with him?" His voice rises, as do his eyebrows, to where they are almost touching the black hair that has fallen forward.

"Shit's true. I want to be face down eating a pillow right now, but we don't always get what we want."

I shrug, opening the fridge and rummaging around for my pint of cottage cheese.

"Christ," he mutters. "You don't say that to him. He might think you are soliciting him, which could be another charge."

I laugh, bending over to shove different jars and containers aside until I find the pint.

"Hamilton would be so lucky to tap this. The dude drives like a grandma. Don't get me wrong, he's pretty, but the pretty ones are lazy lovers. They lie there and expect you to do all the work because they're hot." His eyes are glued to my ass when I look at him. "So, you're probably the worst lay of all. Oh, and friends don't stare at each other's asses, either."

His eyes dart to the ceiling for a moment before meeting mine.

"You always talk this much trash? It's nonstop."

Yeah, I've been told that before.

When guys say I'm too much for them, I call it little dick energy. If they can't handle my mouth, they wouldn't be able to handle the rest. It's cool, though. It helps weed out the wimpy men.

"Can't handle it, then leave. Don't let the door hit you in the ass."

I yank an orange soda from the plastic rings and close the fridge door with my hip before digging for a plastic spoon from my drawer.

"You realize you called me the hottest if I'm the worst lay." He smirks.

I saunter past him, picking up Anna on my way to the couch. He has no choice but to drop next to me since Dad's chair looks occupied. I place the dog on the cushion between us, and she doesn't know what to do, so she stands there and shakes.

"This dog is going to be the death of me," I huff, scooping her up and letting her curl up in my lap as I open the lid of my cottage cheese. "You want some?"

He wrinkles his nose. "That stuff is repulsive."

"Suit yourself. And I didn't say you were the hottest of all, just the worst lay. Some guys are seriously bad at sex. Damn shame if you ask me."

I dig out a heaping pile of the white spongy goodness and

stuff it in my mouth, holding the spoon there while I crack open the tab on my soda.

"As much as I'd love to hear about your bad sex and lazy lovers, tell me what happened today—all of it."

He crosses his ankle over his knee, looking too relaxed in my home.

"And you need to put something on your eye. I was looking for an ice pack or even a baggie for ice, but you don't have any of that either."

"I know. I don't buy that stuff."

I gulp down a ton of the orange liquid and let out a loud belch. When I look back at Tomlin, he's shaking his head.

"What? You know it feels good to get a gas bubble out."

"Unreal. But proceed. I'm not leaving here until I hear what happened to you and why you have a dog."

He points to her.

I look down to see her eyes are closed and she's finally not shaking. I should probably get her a sweater or something. Those celebrity dogs wear clothes on Instagram.

"Fine, but I'm keeping it short and sweet because I have a massive headache, and I'm out of aspirin." I groan, scooping out another heaping bite to eat before launching into the fight with Judd this morning while omitting the part about his car.

Later, I will tell him about that. I need to separate the stories in my head because mine is over. But his story and the swapping out of unnumbered parts are just beginning.

He jumps to his feet, startling Anna and causing her to paw at my arm. I put the pint on the table with my spoon balanced across it to pick her up and smash her between my armpit and my side boob.

"How long has this been going on? The licking, the groping, unwanted sexual advances? It's all against the law and Carl not doing anything about it is a hostile work environment."

"I don't know, Tomlin. It's—"

"You said my name."

His eyes glint with satisfaction, and I purse my lips.

"I must be tired if I let that happen." It's true because downstairs, I made the switch in my mind. "I can return to asshole after I've had coffee."

"No, you said it, and friends don't call each other curse words."

He smiles, looking victorious by this tiny win. Although Kylie and I say, "hey bitch" to each other from time to time.

"Whatever."

"We can get you an employment attorney, get a settlement before you move on from here. Those guys won't know what hit them."

He sounds like he's gloating, and I shut him down.

"Move on? I'm not leaving here. This is my home, my work. Why should I leave all this? Those fuckers were in the wrong, not me."

He casts a long look around the room before returning to me.

"Why wouldn't you? With a settlement, you can get a newer, nicer place. You could get out of this town and start over in Denver. Bigger market, more customers, and eventually have your own garage. I can see it all coming together for you. This could be the best thing that has ever happened to you."

He's getting excited, running down a road I didn't even know existed, much less considered. Leave the only home I've ever known. Leave Dad's memories behind in Cañon City to move to the city that killed him.

"Are you fucking crazy? Is this some sort of sick joke?"

I deposit Anna on the couch before I stand. My temper mounts and I level the playing field by standing, so he's not hovering over me as we talk.

"Is this what you do? Dismantle people's lives with lawsuits and money? Tear down the reputation of an old man to build mine up? That's repulsive. Not my cottage cheese, but you."

I can't help but feel disdain and disgust that he would even think I'd do that to Carl. The old man's a pain in my ass. Yeah, he fucked up when he chose penis breath's side over mine. But he'll apologize after Hamilton's done with him.

"No, Dani, I didn't mean it like that." He holds his hands up, stepping back and bumping into the end table. "I thought that if you got out of here, it would be better for you. Better than putting up with those guys."

"I've had enough fights for the day, so get the hell out and don't bother coming back. I can manage just fine on my own."

"Wait, I'm on your side here." He hobbles around the end table, trying to put space between us. "I'm trying to help."

"Help? I don't need help, nor would I take any help from you." I advance on him, wanting him to retreat right out my door. "Friend? You're not the kind of friend I would ever want. Now get the hell out."

I brush past him, my shoulder slamming into his arm for effect. Damn, I hurt myself in the process because I forgot he's solid muscle under his stupid white dress shirt. He's shadowing me as I walk to the door and yank it open. To my surprise, Hamilton is on the other side with his hand curled into a fist, ready to knock.

"Uh, can I come in?" Hamilton's eyes move in a triangle. From mine to my sleep shorts and Tomlin behind me.

"Yup," I clip, throwing open the door for Tomlin to catch it with his hand. We both step aside to allow him entry. "He's leaving."

I thumb Tomlin.

He shakes his head and nudges the door closed without stepping through it. I glare at him, and he glares back.

"Am I interrupting something?" Hamilton offers. His gaze bounces between us.

"No, but I have a pest problem. Do you know how to get rid of *them?*" I ask, but Hamilton's shoulder radio goes off, causing him to walk down the hall to respond.

"Get out."

"I'm not leaving. I returned to the States and came straight here to see you." He hunches over to whisper in my ear.

That's weird.

Why would he want to see me?

"Why? Where were you?"

He straightens up, glancing at Hamilton, rejoining us in the living room.

"Tokyo."

Tokyo?

Why the hell was he in Tokyo? That's literally the other side of the world.

"Sorry about that," Hamilton says, his elbow resting on his gun belt. "I need to wrap up here and go down to the precinct. They pulled the footage from the truck stop, and I need to deal with the paperwork and charges."

"Okay, does that mean I'm in the clear?"

"Not necessarily. It's up to the district attorney's office to decide to pursue charges, and in that case, self-defense may hold up since he threatened you and then attacked you. Although you delivered the first blow."

"May? The hell you say, Hamilton. It will. Look at my face. I didn't do this to myself," I argue, walking over to flop on the couch. Anna shakes in response. I'm realizing all this dog does is cower.

Hamilton crosses over to stand on the other side of the coffee table while Tomlin hovers behind the couch. I notice Hamilton has difficulty keeping his eyes off my boobs or shorts.

No worries, I'm used to being ogled even by so-called friends.

"It's Officer Hamilton. Now one step at a time," Hamilton

says. "About downstairs, you're both wrong. I talked to Judd and Carl, and neither wants this to go further with the law. I assume the same as you?"

"What charges could Dani file?" Tomlin answers before I even open my mouth. I shoot him a dirty look and then wait because maybe I should find out.

"Harassment, a Class B misdemeanor."

"Not sexual assault," Tomlin asks, and the thought of all this makes me want to vomit.

"Technically, no. Under Colorado law, it is sexual intrusion or penetration, and that's not what we are dealing with here."

"Thank God," I mutter, the cottage cheese sitting like a rock in my stomach.

"Guys, I don't want to pursue any of this. I just want Judd to stop. Carl to back me for once, and have this whole thing go away."

The pounding in my skull is relentless. The thought of criminal charges, attorneys, and the court involved has me holding my head in my hand.

"I'm not inclined to pursue charges for either incident today. But you have got to be careful, Dani. I appreciate what you did for that kid back there and the dog, but another officer might not look so kindly on this. Whatever is going on here between the three of you needs to be worked out civilly, because I'm submitting a report on this, regardless. Another call out here could lead to someone getting arrested and charges filed by the district attorney that you have no control over."

"Thank you, Officer Hamilton, for not filing now, but can that change down the road?" Tomlin says behind me, his hand dropping on my shoulder as if staking his claim.

Friends don't do that either.

I lean forward, forcing it to fall away, which doesn't go unnoticed by Hamilton.

"The D.A. can still file charges on either incident, but it's highly unlikely."

"Good," Tomlin and I say in unison.

Hamilton's eyes narrow for a moment.

"Any chance you'll take her?" I point to Anna, and Hamilton smiles. It's charming, with his dimple popping out on his left cheek.

"None. But I got your number from Carl downstairs. Take my card. It has my cell on it, so we can be in touch when I hear more about Isla."

He digs a card out of his front pocket, looks at the cluttered coffee table, and hands it to me instead. I toss it next to my cottage cheese.

"Oh, what about needing to see my ID? And my car? It's still there." I stand to go grab my purse to ride with him back to the truck stop. "Can I ride with you to go get it?"

"Let's call it even on the ID. I can't take you. The precinct is the opposite way. You'll have to find a ride out there." Hamilton's gaze flickers to Tomlin. I open my mouth to say hell no when he continues, "In the meantime, slow down and follow the speed limit. They're there for a reason."

"Be a law-abiding citizen, got it, Hamilton," I clip, following him through the tightly configured furniture to the door. Tomlin trailing behind me again.

"It was nice meeting you, Mr. Takahashi."

Hamilton leans past me to offer his hand to Tomlin, whose chest bumps my back when he shakes hands. I elbow his stomach, but it doesn't seem to affect him by his lack of response.

"Pleasure is all mine. I'll handle it from here." Tomlin's voice oozes with authority as if he's taking over this situation for me. I scowl over my shoulder at that last comment. Hamilton studies us for a couple of seconds before opening the door.

"Dani, let's talk soon."

"Trust me, I'll be texting you every day so I can return her dog and get back to my life." I lean against the doorframe when he walks out to the landing.

"I'm sure you will," Hamilton mutters, jogging down the stairs that groan under his boots.

"Dani?"

I'm not ready to go another round with Tomlin. I need food and a ride to pick up my car. Not to mention, I have to get dog supplies because I know nothing about dogs.

I lay my head against the door, gazing down the stairwell, with Hamilton's faint cologne lingering in the air.

"Yes?"

"I'll take you."

His tone is soft, and I assume he doesn't want to argue either. In fact, he said he wanted to help. Even if he went too far with the help, he's proposing.

"Fine."

I straighten, close the door, and turn to face him. I'm not sure what to say right now, as I'm used to fighting with him. Trying to be decent feels weird.

"I'll get my purse."

"And put some pants on," he says when stepping aside.

I chuckle because he's right. These aren't made for the streets unless I'm a streetwalker. I click the kitchen light off as I walk down the hallway to my room.

Once inside, I take in the space, as I did in the living room. Dad's bed became my bed, although with a new mattress. The headboard, the dresser, and the old mirror with peeling rose stickers on the top were their wedding set.

Could I leave this all behind? Start over? Start a new life?

I got angry with Tomlin because he thought of a way out of this shitshow that my life is. I got angry because I hadn't thought of it first. I got mad because it felt like a betrayal to Dad to even think of a life different from the one he built for me.

A light tap on the door, and I turn to Tomlin's worried expression.

"Are you okay?"

Am I okay?

I thought I was, but now, I'm not so sure.

"It's been a shitty day."

Deflect.

I'm the master at deflecting because Tomlin stirred up something in me that I don't like. Yet it intrigues me at the same time.

"Yeah."

I don't get why, but his agreement makes me feel heard. For the first time in a long time, I like how that feels.

"What do we do with the dog?" he asks, letting on that he's not a dog person either.

"She comes with, I guess." I shrug and untangle my purse from the doorknob, clustered with a bunch of them. "I'll need to get stuff for her, seeing that Hamilton keeps refusing to take her."

"We can talk about it in the car."

"Can we eat before getting my truck? My head feels like it's splitting in two."

"Of course, but can you put some real clothes on first?"

He makes it a point to look at my shorts, and I was going to put something on over them, but I got tied up thinking about Dad.

I dig around the closet, finding an unused tote bag Kylie gave me three Christmases ago to carry Anna in and my cutoff jean shorts that show off my muscular legs. When I drag them on, he mutters under his breath, and I smile with my back to him.

I don't know why, but him finding me hot after how I look and everything I've been through today is a damn nice compliment.

13

"Where do you want to eat?"

"I don't care. Somewhere that will allow her inside or someplace I can sneak her in." While I finished getting Anna and me ready, Tomlin went downstairs to 'handle things'.

I didn't mind because I was sure Carl would corner me the second he heard me coming down the stairs, and my head was throbbing too much for that nonsense. By the time I got down there, the coast was clear in that penis breath was working in the garage, the glass was swept up, and Carl was nowhere to be found.

I must admit, it was sort of nice to have Tomlin work all that crap out for me. I could sail through the lobby with Anna and get into his car in peace.

"I know of a place."

He makes a U-turn and speeds up. I don't care where we eat. I'm content to let him decide because my head is throbbing so damn badly that it's pulsing against my swollen eye. I snuggle into his comfy leather seat and close my stinging eyes.

Double damn.

"Tell me what happened after Judd."

"Fine, but I'm not opening my eyes because my head is about to explode."

Anna twirls in circles on my lap before finally lying down and I use my arms to block her in before I get settled.

"Lay the seat back if you want to. We'll be there in about fifteen minutes," he offers, and I recline it.

At this rate, I may permanently move into his fancy car with the air-conditioned seats that feel like I peed my pants.

"Comfortable?"

"Yeah, too comfy. I might never get out of your car. So, it really started when Hamilton pulled me over. . ."

I launch into the entire story, from my fake accent to arguing about sitting in the back of the squad car and everything in between. He was very attentive, not asking one question until I'm done blabbering on.

"Wow."

I crack my eyes at his one-word statement. His hands are white, knuckling the steering wheel, and his jaw clenches.

"What?"

"I want to murder the guy just hearing about it," he explains, and now I get his response.

"Yeah, super fucking disgusting. I hope they rape his big ass in prison. Eye for an eye sort of thing."

Anger rises in me when I think back to how he barked at Isla to go and hide and then lied about his truck so we couldn't find her.

"Men are fuckers."

"Present party excluded."

"Yeah, well."

He pulls up to this old-ass diner at the end of a dilapidated shopping center that saw its best days about thirty years ago.

"Uh, we're not eating here."

"Sure, we are."

He shuts off the car, which unlocks the doors, and does other fancy shit in his car, like returning my seat to its original position.

"And they won't mind the dog."

"Oh, I know because they probably catch alley cats to use for meat. I'm not eating here. I've had a crappy day, and I'm not willing to top it off with a case of food poisoning."

"Could you be more dramatic?" He opens his door, and Anna pops up, eagerly dancing around my lap. "Two against one."

He swings out of his car, and Anna lets out a tiny bark, the first one I have heard. Then another. Let's get this food poisoning over with.

"Two against one? Real mature," I grumble, retrieving Anna to put her in the tote and slamming his car door.

"Good thing you can repair car doors when you decide to rip that one off the hinges. Now come on, drama mama, get in here," he mocks, holding open the diner door, complete with a row of jingle bells tied to the middle bar.

I step inside, and it takes me back to the fifties, with a jukebox against the wall playing some cheesy song, the servers in pink and white pinstripes, and even a long checkout counter surrounded by candy and gum that goes on for days. It's charming, and I look up at Tomlin with surprise. Seeing his smug expression isn't a surprise, though. He's been here before.

"Tomlin!"

An older woman sporting white hair in a bob cut rushes toward him with open arms. He hugs her long and hard. I'm fascinated by how friendly they are with one another. Tomlin has friends. That never occurred to me.

"It's been way too long. How long has it been?"

"At least six months," he murmurs, happiness crinkling the corners of his eyes. "My travel has picked up."

"Well, that's too long." Her deep blue eyes slide to mine as she releases him from the bear hug. "And who's this?"

Her hands go on her hips, inspecting me from the ground up and not missing Anna in the process.

"And a dog in my restaurant?"

"She's a friend that I'm helping." Tomlin moves aside while the lady points to Anna. "And that is the dog she is babysitting. Long story, Margaret, but she is having a bad day."

"I'll say, looks like she's been beaten to hell and then dragged in here."

A lovely compliment, as if I'm not standing right between them. This is a mistake.

"Earlier today, she got into a fistfight with a child molester. She saved a fifteen-year-old girl and is taking care of her dog while she is in protective services," Tomlin brags.

I mean, I wouldn't call it a fistfight exactly, but the rest is true.

"Where?"

"The truck stop out on US 50," I say while adjusting the tote's strap to stop it from digging into my arm.

"That old place," she says, and the irony isn't lost on me as this is another old place. "They should have let it burn to the ground when those bikers tore it up some years back. You did a good thing. Come on in."

She turns on her heel and hollers across the crowded diner for water glasses and two setups, whatever that is.

"I guess I passed the test," I mutter to Tomlin over my shoulder as I follow her.

"Guess you did."

She stops at the only booth available in a long row of them. We catch a few curious stares at how my face looks, but nothing I can't handle. In fact, I should make up a better story than the actual one, something more salacious.

Wait till I tell Kylie what happened. She'll probably want

the dog too. Oh, game-changer. Maybe she'll take it in the meantime.

I set Anna's tote in the booth and then slip in beside her. Tomlin slides into the seat opposite me as silverware and water glasses are set on the table. The server hands us the menus and asks for our drink order before leaving.

"Why this place?" I ask, letting my silverware clatter to the table when I unroll the napkin and scaring Anna in the process.

She stands on her hind legs and I pet her head to reassure her. I know she wants out of the bag, but I'd like to eat in peace.

"You've never been here? It's legendary. Margaret started this place over forty years ago. I've been coming here for years."

I'm thankful they serve breakfast all day and take approximately two seconds to decide on a huge breakfast platter.

"Nope, but the food better be good, or else you're taking me somewhere else," I threatened, right before the server appears with our coffees.

He lets me order first. Super chivalrous. I clarify I need toast immediately or else I'll pass out. Her eyes widen, and she swiftly nods before taking Tomlin's more modest order.

"If being your chauffeur around town means we can bury the hatchet between us, consider it done."

He does chemistry with the cream and packets to get his fussy drink just right. I swallow down my black motor oil and moan at the goodness. I needed this about six hours ago.

"I didn't think we had a hatchet to bury. What are you talking about?" I ask, slouching in the booth and accidentally bumping my knees with his.

"After you racked me, I figured you hated me. Then I didn't hear from you while I was gone."

He finally takes a sip and makes a face because something still isn't right with his coffee.

"Well, you said take it, which is super creepy, and the

racking was warranted. So that's resolved. Next up, why would I call you? How would I call you? I don't even have your number."

I'm genuinely puzzled by this one. I told him goodbye as I left to get the parts, which ended up dumping the entire sky's rain on me when I drove back to the shop.

"I figured you'd get it from Carl or the shop records."

"That makes sense, but I didn't think of it. Why would I call you, though?"

I finish drinking my coffee, desperate for another cup, and I flag down some dude walking around refilling patron's cups.

"Wait, you didn't call me. You didn't have my number, but could have called the shop."

"I called the shop for you. Many times, in fact. Didn't Judd tell you?"

"No."

Penis breath didn't mention it at all. Ever.

Now I know why.

He leans forward, resting his elbows on the table.

"How long has this been going on between you two?"

"Basically forever. Look, I know I didn't take your project, and even though I spent several weeks killing myself to get somewhat caught up, I'm still months out."

"Why are you telling me this?"

Wrinkles crease across his forehead, and I hate it. I hate that I have to tell him on the heels of what happened between penis breath and me, but he deserves to know.

"Because Judd is cutting corners on your restoration. That's what started the fight today."

I sit up while he falls against the booth with a thud.

"You're shitting me."

This is really bad if Tomlin is cussing. I can't recall a time that he has.

"Nope, I had been trying to meet my deadline on the Buick,

and then started the Shelby, so I hadn't paid too much attention to yours. But today, when I pulled the light over to look under the hood, I noticed he was swapping parts. I assume he hasn't called you to get your approval on it?"

"Not one call."

I frown because his resto is pretty far in to tear it apart and rebuild it.

"Damn. If I had to put two and two together, I suspect that's why he didn't tell me about your calls. He probably thought I'd tell you, but honest to God, I didn't see it until today."

I hold up my hands as if that proves my honesty or something.

"That son of a bitch."

Tomlin lowers his voice, trying not to yell it out, but I wouldn't blame him if he did. It's thousands of dollars worth of work done and probably paid for.

"The deceit. Does Carl know?"

"I doubt it. He never gets involved in the restores. I'm not sure he would know what I was talking about if I showed him. And I didn't have time to talk to him about it before he threw me out."

My toast arrives, and I dig through the bowl of jellies shoved against the wall to find the kind I like. I smear an obscene amount on my toast and wolf it down. Tomlin's expression goes from fury to thinking and back to fury.

"So, he threatened you when you confronted him?" he finally says, watching me dump more jelly on the next piece.

"Not threatened, but harassed, as Hamilton said. I like that word better when it applies to penis breath."

"Penis breath?"

"Yeah, that's what I decided to call him after he called me a bitch today."

His jaw clenches in and out, trying to harness the fury within while processing everything that has happened.

I tear off a tiny corner of the toast and feed it to Anna. She gently takes it from me and ducks it into her tote to eat it. Once done, she pops up for another piece, and I shred a bunch to toss in with her.

"I'm pulling the car."

"How? Who's going to do it?" I ask, dreading the look he's giving me. "No, I'm still behind, and I can't take on yours."

"Dani, you owe me this. If you had taken it first, none of this would have happened."

He leans forward, resting his elbows on the table.

"Not true and true."

Anna pops her head out of the tote and paws at the inside lining. I grab the small bowl containing all the jelly packets and drop them on the table to pour her some water.

"This doesn't have anything to do with Kylie, does it?"

He taps the table in frustration, and I don't bother looking at him while pushing Anna back so I can get the water bowl in her tote.

"Because you saw us together, and we're fine."

"Maybe it cost me a shit ton in gas to drive to Denver and back. I fucking hate that city."

I glance at Anna, chugging water, then back at him. Annoyance is smeared all over his face.

"Look, you acted like an asshole that day and every day since, well, until today, mostly the last hour or so. Fair is fair."

I grab the third piece of toast when his hand darts across the table to touch mine. Why is he touching me?

"I'm sorry we got off on the wrong foot. I genuinely am."

Super uncomfortable with his sincere tone and the touching, I slide my hand onto my lap.

"Fine, whatever, don't get all sappy and shit. You're blessed or forgiven, whatever nonsense I need to say, but don't be an asshole, got it?"

"Then you'll do it?"

He's so eager that he's halfway across the table and unnecessarily breathing on my precious toast.

"Bro, scoot back. I don't need your germs on my food."

He corrects himself immediately, and I forgot how much he overreacts to correction. I got to pay more attention to that. It may give me an advantage over him.

"And no, I'm not taking your project. You're not jumping the line, and don't even start in on my paint job because that's almost in the bag. One more job, and she's off to the beauty parlor to get all dolled up."

He leans back, his eyebrows furrowed as he watches me pick through the jelly, looking for another grape. I said the exact right thing because he's pouting over there and letting me eat in peace. I could get used to his silence, so long as he drives me around and pays for my grub.

Anna and I polish off the toast at the same time the food arrives, and he still hasn't said anything. They refill my coffee. He covers his cup with his hand because all the chemistry takes a long time to get right.

We eat in silence, which gives me plenty of time to inhale my food. I'm over halfway through my breakfast and he hasn't taken but two bites. I can't take it any longer.

"What gives?" I take a huge bite of my food, forcing him to talk.

"Nothing."

Like a petulant child.

"Uh, Tomlin, I'm not good at this sensitive shit, so if you got something to say, say it. I'm not going to psychotherapy your ass, not after the day I have had. Hell, I should be lying on a couch somewhere yammering on about my feelings."

I refill Anna's water bowl and break off some bacon to toss in her tote. He gazes at me, shoveling food into my mouth, and then passes me a napkin.

"You've had jelly stuck to your cheek for a while."

"Gee, thanks."

"I didn't want to interrupt you."

Dabbing the napkin in my water, I scrub the entire side of my face. What's a little jelly when I have a large shiner?

"Better?"

"Sure."

"Come on, Tomlin, you're terrible company already, so out with it." I burp and then laugh.

"Excuse me."

"Unreal."

He shakes his head.

"You're so stubborn. It is infuriating. If it's not your idea or your way, you won't budge. I can see why Carl threw you out."

I put my fork down, shove the plate away, and start scooting to the edge of the booth, dragging Anna with me.

"Exactly. You don't like what you hear, and you're out. What will you do, hitchhike with your dog back to your car?"

He doesn't move a muscle, and it further pisses me off.

"I'll call an Uber, you nitwit." I stand and pull my phone out to open the app. "Fucking men."

"Put your phone away." He throws a couple of twenties on the table, far too much for even a generous tip, much less the bill, and stands. "I'll drop you off."

My finger hovers over the app. It would be expensive to cart my ass all the way to the truck stop, and moneybags over here likes to burn through money, so what the hell.

"Fine."

I lock my phone and grab Anna's tote without a backward glance when I walk to the front entrance. He's making small talk with Margaret, but that doesn't stop me from pushing through the restaurant door and into the suffocatingly warm heat.

14

Through the large picture window, Tomlin is still talking, twirling his keys in his hands and catching them. A clear sign he wants to get out of there. Good, I hope she's irritating the hell out of him.

Deciding not to cook in the sun waiting by the car, I walk through the aging shopping center and look in the windows of the various businesses until I spot one of particular interest. The moment I open the door, the stench of animals hits me.

"Damn, Anna, I'm glad your shit doesn't smell like this."

The store is small, with a row of fish tanks against the back wall, aisles of products to the left, and a cluster of caged birds to the right.

"Welcome. Is there something I can help you with?"

The guy behind the counter has impossibly perfect hair over flawless skin and an overly tight polo accentuating his slim but muscular frame.

He's excessively chipper, and I can't decide if I'm annoyed or jealous because I can't recall a day that I sounded that upbeat.

"Yeah, I got this dog today, so I need the works." I point to

Anna, who for once isn't popped out of the top and is lying at the bottom against the empty water bowl I accidentally stole. "It's a . . . hell, I don't know what kind of dog she is, but she's tiny."

He walks from behind the counter to greet me, and I open the tote wider for him to see her. Anna pops up like those jack-in-the-box toys and immediately starts barking at him.

That's weird.

"Oh, she's so cute!" His voice goes up several octaves, and so do my eyebrows. "Can I hold her?"

"Um, sure?"

He tries to reach in to lift her out, but she snaps at his fingers.

"It's okay, pretty girl. I just want to hold you. Can I snuggle you?"

He's practically singing to the dog, and I'm fidgeting because this is way over the top. I'd throat-punch a guy if he ever talked to me like that. He tries again, and her tiny growls get shriller.

"Who's a tough girl? Who's a tough girl?"

"Okay, okay, let me get her out."

I break because I'm either going to punch his cartoon voice or leave Anna to live with him forever. I balance the tote on one arm, scoop her up even after she tries to bite me, and hand her over.

Anna doesn't like that but too bad. I didn't exactly start this day thinking I would become a foster dog mom. So, we're both not getting our way.

"You gotta hold her . . ." I don't finish because he's already smashed her to his chest and cooed. Anna decides he's not so bad and soaks up all the pets he's giving her. "Damn, maybe she needs to stay with you."

"Ah, that's sweet, but I already have five dogs at home. My partner would kill me if I brought another home." He looks past me and shifts on his feet, seeming more interested in what's behind me.

"Sir, I'll be with you in a moment."

"I'm with her," Tomlin says.

The guy's face falls for a split second before focusing on me. Technically, he's not with me.

"Of course. Now you said you got her today?"

He straightens, going back to petting her and her eyeballs close as if basking in his love. She's ridiculous.

"Yeah, it's a long story, but I'm sort of taking care of her. I've never had a dog before, so I don't know what I need for her." I close the tote and throw it over my shoulder.

"No worries, I got you covered. How long are you taking care of her?"

"I don't know."

"Like a few days or weeks or months?"

His eyes dart from me to Tomlin, lingering longer on him. I get it. He's handsome but moody as hell.

"I'll kill myself if I have her months or even weeks, but I really don't know."

My response is a little over the top judging by his horrified expression, but I can't even think how disruptive this dog will be to my life.

Where am I going to keep her while I work? Upstairs, I guess. Damn, I have a lot of shit up there that she could get into and possibly hurt herself.

"I got to keep this dog alive long enough to give her back to this kid in foster care."

"Oh, how sad for her, being separated from her precious dog."

He snuggles Anna tighter as if she's the one struggling with the loss of her mom.

"She must be devastated."

"Yeah."

She's devastated over more than just losing her dog, thinking about her being with Rick the Rapist and how his blood ruined my favorite Converse.

Worth it.

"Since this little girl is super important, you'll want to get a collar and tag with your information on it, so if you two are ever separated, whoever finds her can call you. From there, the usual food, leash, treats, toys, and dog bed. Is she potty trained, or do you need a crate and pee pads?"

"I don't know. Get me all the crap you think she needs."

Damn, this is going to be expensive. I already know it.

"Okay, why don't you pick out the tag at the machine over there, and I'll start pulling together some stuff." He points to a big red box by the door before grabbing a cart. "Can I keep this little peanut with me?"

"Sure."

I head to the machine with a silent Tomlin trailing behind me.

"I still can't believe this shit."

I lean against the machine, looking at all the different shapes and colors.

"It's not ideal."

Tomlin's cologne floats around me, and it smells nice compared to the pet store.

"Maybe it happened for a reason."

Bracing my hand on the machine, I glance at him.

"You're kidding, right?"

"No, maybe this is karma catching up to you. Punishing you for all the bad things you do, like turning down my car. Now you must be responsible for something other than yourself."

"You make me sound like a selfish asshole."

Why am I defending myself to him for the umpteenth time?

"If the shoe fits."

I'm strongly thinking of hitting a third man today. Although

Tomlin could pin me against this machine in the second, I would still be deciding to attack him. Granted, he's not the type to do that.

"Obviously, you wanna talk about the car, so spill your guts. Keep this in mind, I'm coming out of working like a dog while you were gallivanting around Tokyo on vacation. If you pull your car from penis breath—"

"I wasn't gallivanting. I was working. And not if. I *am* pulling it from Carl."

I turn to face him and lean against the machine with my arms crossed.

"Okay, you pull it from Carl. You know I've been backlogged for months, and I hate you want to jump the line, but why? What's all this bullshit for? So, you can pick up chicks when you go cruising? I didn't think you were that desperate to get laid."

He sighs, gazes out the window, and gets this faraway look.

"Pebble Beach Concours d'Elegance."

"Damn, man, that's like the Olympics of car shows."

"You've heard of it?"

"Of course, I've heard of it." I wonder if that's where the Buick is going.

Hell, I've drooled over plenty of magazines featuring the cars, their owners, and their restoration team. To get your work submitted into something like that, well, jeez, it's next-level shit.

He blinks and returns to me.

"Yeah."

"Your car isn't antique, vintage, or classic. I guess you could submit in the postwar category, but aren't those dominated by Ferraris and Lambos?"

"Have you been?"

He looks like an excited kid at Christmas.

"No, but I've seen enough about it to know what's there. It's pretty hard to get in. They don't accept any average Joe and his virginity car."

"I have preliminary acceptance, and for your information, I didn't lose my virginity in that car."

His excitement slides into sarcasm. As long as he doesn't tell me how he lost it, we're good.

"You can't submit it with penis breath's work."

I shrug because he can't. Those bunch of rich dicks would look down their nose at the inferior parts, rightfully so.

"Don't you think I know that? It's what angers me the most, and you're a close second."

His eyes bore into mine.

"Me? Why? Is this because I drop-kicked your shit at your museum house or because I racked your junk at my house?"

I scratch my head because I thought we were past all that.

"If you would have taken my car and accepted the paint job in the first place, then all this could have been avoided. Why are you always so combative? It's not healthy."

He throws his hands up to fend me off when I drop my arms and step toward him.

"Stop it. We called a truce. You agreed to it, and yet you want to battle again. I understand you've had a hard life, and I'm sorry. It's not pity, but it makes sense how you feel you must defend yourself all the time. I get all that. Like I said earlier, I'm on your side in this. I was before too, but you didn't want to see it."

I did sort of agree to the truce. That part is true. He did also say he was on my side.

"I know you've been killing yourself. It's all over your face. You looked exhausted coming out of the bathroom after your shower today. Do you think I don't see that? But Dani, what do I do now? I understand you don't want it, but I can't have Judd work on it. So, help me out. Where do I go from here?"

Damn that sincerity again. There must be something wrong

with him. The blood in my swollen eye is throbbing, and the headache that dulled over lunch is ramping back up.

"I don't know, Tomlin. It's a shitshow right now. I don't even know what happens next with Carl."

At this point, I'm surviving minute by minute. Get food, get dog crap, and get my car. Beyond that, I don't know what I'm doing.

"What if I got you a place? A warehouse and apartment above, like you, have now?"

He's looking at me intently, and I stare because I think he said he'd set me up in business, exactly what I told him I didn't want at my apartment.

"I already told you—"

"Not your own business. I understand that now. But a place to work on just my car?"

"So, I quit and drop my clients in the grease? No, no way I'll do that."

I shake my head emphatically because too many customers have waited too long for me to restore their precious babies.

"You're assuming Carl's not firing you and won't let Judd take over your client list?"

Tomlin raises an eyebrow. And sure as shit, I never thought that weasel would do that. He could. He's the owner and well within his right to do so.

"Well, shit."

Tomlin opens his mouth to say something when the store clerk comes over with Anna wearing a rhinestone bow, collar, and a tiny pink sparkly sweater. This dude needs to keep her while Isla awaits her foster placement.

"We went a little crazy in the accessories department. I forgot to ask what kind of food she eats?"

He hoists Anna up, proudly showing off his handiwork, and the look of confusion on Tomlin's face makes me chuckle. Glad we're on the same page about this dog.

"Human."

He blinks, waiting for me to say more, but there isn't anymore, so I shrug.

"Oh dear, so no dog food at all?" The clerk scratches his chin.

"Nope."

I don't know what else to tell him other than the truth.

"Don't you worry. We'll get that turned around in a jiffy." Why do I like that he said 'we' as if he's in this with me?

"I'll put together some things I think she'll like. How's it coming on the tag?" He peers around me to see the silent machine. "Is it done?"

He's way too excited to add more bling to Anna's already blinged-out look.

"No, we haven't decided yet."

"Oh, I can help with that too. We have this cute little pink tag with a clear rhinestone trim."

He breezes past Tomlin to show me the options. I move to the side of the machine, not caring what he picks.

"Oh shoot, it doesn't come in her tiny little size."

"How about the one that says 'Princess' on it? The silver with the pink things." Tomlin's so damn tall, of course, he can see over my head. "Right next to the 'Mama's Boy' tag."

"You have excellent taste. We just got those in. Don't you love the pink rhinestones? It will mix well with the clear rhinestones she already has on."

The guy taps Tomlin's arm when agreeing with him.

"Now, follow the instructions, and I'll be back with the rest. We decided on no kennel, correct? I mean, seriously, she's so small, you could leave her in her dog bed. She doesn't seem very destructive or aggressive other than that little fit earlier."

I didn't think 'we' decided anything.

"Sure, no kennel."

He whisks Anna away, disappearing down another aisle.

"This shit's going to cost me a fortune," I mumble against the glass as I push the buttons for the 'Princess' tag.

The screen pops up, asking for her name, my name, phone, and address. I hesitate to put Carl's address on it because I'm not sure if he's firing me or not after what Tomlin said.

"I know what you are thinking. Put your address on for now, and if it changes, you get a new one."

He's shoulder surfing again. Agreeing with him, I tap all the information and hit submit for the machine to start the engraving. While it's running, I think about everything he said.

Twice he has mentioned going out on my own, but I have only enough money saved for a paint job, not thousands of dollars to rent a place and equipment, and all that crap.

Do I even want to run a business? Do Carl's job too? That would suck ass. I mean, I fill in when the old man needs to go to Colorado Springs to check on his sister, but that's only a day or two.

"This is a fucking mess."

I lie my head against the glass, feeling the vibration in my skull. It's stupid to do with my headache, but I need a break from my life right now.

"I'm sorry you're going through all this," Tomlin says after a while.

I twist my neck to look at him, leaving it against the glass to vibrate the side of my head.

"Tell me I did the right thing today because if I wouldn't have lost my temper with Judd, none of this would have happened."

He reaches for my wrist to pull me off the machine and then lets go.

"If you hadn't lost your temper, a minor would still be captive with her molester."

"Yeah, I wish they'd chop rapists' balls off like they do bulls. That would fix shit."

I sigh, realizing I like the pet store guy's sunny attitude. It's the opposite of my piss-poor, mad-at-the-world one.

"They are called steers after they are castrated."

"That's a fun fact."

My words are coated in sarcasm. The machine stops, and Tomlin squats to get the tag out of the machine. He hands it to me, and I hold it in the air. The charm is small, the writing is tiny, and the design is adorable.

"It's kind of cute, huh?"

"Yes, it is."

Tomlin takes it from me to hold in his palm. It looks like a shiny nickel compared to his large hand.

"If you'll take our little princess, I'll package all this up for you," the guy says from behind the counter when we turn around. He points to all the food and then kisses Anna a few times.

Tomlin reaches the counter first, inspecting different trinkets and toys hanging from the knobs that are far too large for this dog. I collect Anna and then stand silently beside him, sweating the cost of all this stuff.

"Do you have the tag?" The guy extends his palm, and Tomlin hands it over. "I'll put it on her collar if you can slip it off."

I fiddle with the buckle while holding her, and when Tomlin sees it's not working, he helps get it off her neck.

"You two make a cute couple," the guy says, side-eyeing Tomlin.

"We're not together."

I immediately lean forward and touch the counter to emphasize my point, and Tomlin clears his throat.

"We're, well, he's my—"

"Friend is the word she is struggling with. It happens."

Tomlin's smooth delivery makes mine sound even more awkward, and I frown.

"Well, my name is Eli. I'm the owner of this store."

He beams with pride when he says it. I merely nod, not sure if I would ever beam about the place I work. Now the work I perform and the cars I restore, yes, I'd beam.

He makes quick work of the tag and hands the collar back to Tomlin. While we are working on the collar, he's scanning the dog crap, and my eyes are about to fall out of my head as the numbers climb.

Bye, bye sweet paint job.

"Will that be cash or charge?"

I suddenly hate Eli's chipper attitude when the amount comes to nearly three hundred dollars.

"Charge," Tomlin says, pulling out a money clip and handing over a black card.

"You're not paying for this." I block Tomlin's hand, only for him to grab mine and hold it. "Let go."

"My momma always said that if a man wants to pay, let him."

Eli snatches that thing out of Tomlin's hand so fast to swipe it down the side of his register that I'm speechless.

Tomlin smiles. "What else does your momma say?"

"If you like it, put a ring on it."

He quips so fast that Tomlin's mouth drops, and he releases my hand. I laugh.

"Smart momma." I elbow Tomlin, and he recovers enough to frown. "But we can't give this thing away."

I toss my thumb at him, and Eli laughs. That's when I decide I really like Eli. He puts everything in a few bags, drops his business card in one of them, and hands them to Tomlin to carry.

"I dropped my card in there, so call me if you need any help." He adjusts Anna's bow one more time and then clasps his hands together to lie on the counter. "Bye, little peanut."

"Thanks for all your help, Eli. It was nice to meet you."

"The pleasure's all mine."

I walk away from the counter, feeling a smidge better for three reasons. Anna has everything she needs, Tomlin paid the entire bill, and I met any animal lover that can answer all my dog questions.

This day is looking up.

15

Tomlin, like the proper gentleman he is, holds open
the door for us to saunter out. I do like his chivalry,
even if the rest of him pisses me off.

"Thanks for paying back there. You didn't have to. I'll pay
you back when I get paid or if I get paid."

He slides on his sunglasses. His hotness going up a few
notches.

"No need, because you're taking over my job." I open my
mouth to argue again when he smiles and says, "I'm kidding,
well, partially."

We walk across the parking lot to his car, where he opens
the trunk and dumps all the dog stuff in. The chivalry
continues when he opens my car door and waits until Anna
and I are settled before closing it. Once he drops into the
driver's seat to start the car, the air conditioning blasts my
cheeks, and I sigh in relief.

"I'm going to tell you something, but I don't want you to get
a big ole head about it."

His arm stretches over the steering wheel with his hand
dangling from his wrist. With those glasses, the air blowing his

hair, and the casual confidence of his long body draped in the bucket seat, he looks like a model. He adjusts the vents before looking at me. I cringe at my reflection in his sunglasses. I look like a prostitute that got into a fight with her pimp over drugs.

"What?"

"You look kinda hot in those."

It takes a second. Then he gives me that dazzling smile again and bops me on the nose.

"I know."

"Conceited much?"

"Hardly."

I toss my braid over my shoulder with all the attitude I can muster before picking up Anna and snuggling her to my side boob.

"That dog's going to try to nurse from you if you keep doing that," he says, putting the car in drive.

"You're just jealous because you want to nurse from them too."

I reach for my seat belt because his fancy car keeps dinging at us. Modern vehicles are so fussy, just like him. He laughs, the sound deep and lighthearted, and I find it strangely soothing.

"So, truck stop next?"

"Yeah, you know the one I'm talking about?"

"Yes, it's been there for decades."

He fiddles with the music stations. I expect him to stop on opera or classical music, so when he lands on classic rock, I'm pleasantly surprised.

"They need to bulldoze that place. It was busted for a prostitution ring a few years back."

"How do you know so much about this area if you don't live here?"

I'm generally curious since he knows more about my hometown than I do.

"Never shit where you eat."

He turns onto the highway, hooks a U-turn, and then accelerates like a bat out of hell. The back of my head hits the headrest and I hiss in pain.

"Sorry, I was trying to get in front of this eighteen-wheeler."

He glances at me rubbing my head, and his mouth flattens into a line.

"What does that mean?"

The roadside blazes by my window. I have to admit, his fancy car has a nice ride to it.

"I date down here."

"Wait, you date here, in Cañon City and not Denver?" I'm confused. "That's like two hours apart."

"Yeah, guarantees they won't pop up at my place when it's over. Except you. You were the first." He chuckles. "That day, I thought it was all an act. I didn't realize you really are a beer-guzzling, shit-talking redneck from the Cañon."

I glare at him for two reasons. That he dates far away so he can love them and leave them as he did to Kylie and that he called me a redneck.

"One day, you and I are gonna go at it. I broke two noses today. Wanna make it three?"

"As tantalizing as that offer is to have you down on the mat under me, I'll pass for now."

He glances at me long enough to pop his eyebrows suggestively over his sunglasses.

"Whatever. Where do you stay? It's too long to drive back at night."

His dating logistics are fascinating.

"If all goes well with her."

He puts on his blinker, the volume of the music decreasing as he switches lanes. Fancy car shit again.

"Who's her?"

"Whomever I'm dating."

"That's disgusting."

I wrinkle my nose because he basically just told me that he fucks for shelter.

"Is it really? If you are hitting it off with someone and he invites you back to his place, you will not go? And if you go, you're not going to cuddle, fall asleep together, and have breakfast the next morning?"

He glances at me several times, and I look out the window.

Zach knows the score.

DTF.

We've never cuddled or pillow talked. As far as breakfast the next day, well, I've never spent the night with him, so he can't make me breakfast. Hell, I haven't even showered with a guy I was having sex with. That's way too intimate.

"No, I haven't."

"Haven't what? Gone home with someone?"

He's hinting at something, and I don't like where this is going.

"I don't want to talk about this anymore."

I hate he struck a chord I didn't even know I had. Didn't even know I wanted that until he described his one-night stand compared to mine. Casual sex is a fix I need because my solo game is lame.

The alcohol and drug-induced sex makes me feel dirty and gross. Been there, done that, and won't do it again. Sleeping with Zach is a step above that, but it sounds like Tomlin's casual sex is several steps above mine, and it bothers me. Bothers me a lot.

We ride in silence, a welcome break from all the nonstop chatter in my ear. I wish I could go home, without a black eye, without a little dog, and sleep until next week.

I rest my head against the seat and close my eyes. The relief to my burning eyeballs is instant. Maybe I need to pick up some eye drops. Anna is nestled between my boob and the center console, so she's content too.

This day sucks ass.

Tomlin is being all nicey-nice because he wants me to take on his car, but what type of client would he be if he's already an asshole? I sigh. This shit is too much.

What would Dad do?

Hell, he'd never have gotten into this situation in the first place. He always warned me about my temper and said it would catch up to me one day. Well, here's the fucking day it did.

Man, it's threatening to kill me.

What Dad didn't understand was having to grow up in a man's world and become masculine myself to survive it. I had to become tough. Guys are tough from the start. No one expects them to change or be any different. Because we have tits and a vagina, we're supposed to be sweet and sensitive, pleasing, and nice. Well, fuck that shit. I am who I am. If people don't like it, then fuck them.

"You okay?" Tomlin says through the silence.

"I fucking hate people."

I don't even bother to open my eyes to look at him. It doesn't matter anyway because once I get my car, I got a bigger fish to fry with Carl.

"I'd imagine you do."

I open my eyes a sliver. "What's that supposed to mean?"

"You're reactive. You wait around. When things happen to you, you pop off with your smart mouth and hot temper." He glances at me, my reflection staring back. "How's it working out for you?"

It's not working for me, and it hasn't been for a long-ass time.

"Save me the psychobabble. You know my life is in the shitter, and you're more than happy to add fuel to the fire. That's the last fucking thing I need right now, okay? Drop me off at the truck stop and I'll figure my shit out."

I close my eyes and turn my face toward the window. The last thing I need is Mr. I'm-rich-and-have-no-problems piling on too. He remains silent, the music the only sound in the car, and that's more than fine with me. The faster I get out of here, the better. I need space to think about what to do next.

We are getting close because the car slows down as he makes a series of turns. I don't bother opening my eyes until he parks.

"Where's your car at?" My eyes fly open to Tomlin's head, looking from side to side. "Did you park in the back with the rigs?"

I even twist in my seat because I don't see it either.

"Son of a bitch!"

I shove Anna onto Tomlin's lap before yanking on the door handle and jumping out of his car.

He parked in the front of the store by the doors, almost exactly where my truck should be.

"Fuck!"

I step away from his car, slam the door, and charge inside the store to the cashier.

"Where's your manager?"

I'm trying not to go thermonuclear on this poor pimple-faced kid that's stammering while helping a single mom with two wild banshees throwing candy at each other.

"Mr. Tom-Sam is over there, down the line."

The kid points to some dude wearing a short sleeve button-down with a tie too short to reach his belt.

"Tom-Sam?" I question it because that's the weirdest fucking name I've heard. "That's your manager's name?"

"Yes."

"Okay."

I stomp toward his manager.

"Are you Mr. Tom-Sam?"

The guy has the nerve to look me up and down. I know I

look like a train wreck, but didn't he see what happened here a few hours ago?

"I'm Mr. Thompson. Can I help you?"

Thompson, yeah, that makes more sense. I'm about to launch into full bitch mode when I smell that stupid, expensive cologne behind me.

"Mr. Thompson, my name is Tomlin Takahashi. I believe my girlfriend here is looking for her vehicle that was left outside during the altercation that took place earlier today." Girlfriend? Fine, if that gets me what I want. "The one that involved the capture of a felon in your store."

Damn, Tomlin, go for his jugular.

Tomlin extends his hand to the manager, who is currently sizing up the expensive clothes on Mr. Moneybags next to me. He reluctantly shakes hands with Tomlin before going back to clutching his clipboard and looking around to see if any of his customers heard that.

"Perhaps we should talk in my office."

Mr. Thompson points to a narrow hallway before walking ahead of us.

"I had it covered, ya know. I don't need your help," I hiss over my shoulder at him. "And where's the dog?"

He bends over to hiss back at me, "I didn't want you making another scene, so I thought I'd handle it. And you didn't seem too worried about the dog when you threw it in my lap."

Fair, but still.

"I better not find a dead fucking dog when we get out of here, or else you're driving straight to protective services, wherever the hell that is, and telling that kid you murdered her dog."

I shove my finger in his face. He pushes it away as the manager speed walks down the hall to a broom closet of an office.

"The car is running with the air conditioning on," he whispers in my ear before his chest bumps my back.

Accidentally or intentionally, I can't decide.

"You better hope no one steals that fancy car of yours with that damn dog in it, or else you're dead meat," I murmur back because he's breathing down my neck in this godforsaken claustrophobic office.

"Now, where were we?"

Mr. Thompson says as he shuffles behind a desk covered with more paper than that historical mess of my apartment. He picks up a stack, trying to decide where to move it, but it's impossible because there's no space left unless he wants to put it in his chair and sit on it.

"I'm here for my truck. I parked it out front when I got assaulted by your customer. You know, you really need to keep a better eye out for this type of shit, because what if I hadn't caught that guy? Would your employees have noticed him and what he's doing to her? Would you?"

My blood boils at the idiot standing in front of me. I know I live in a shithole, but hell, I'm not managing people. How does he get any work done in an office that looks like this? At least my workstation downstairs is neat and orderly. He stands holding his stack, staring at me in surprise.

"I can assure you, Ms.—"

"No, Ms., call me Dani. You already met him."

I toss my thumb at Tomlin, who's finally listening to me by keeping his trap shut and letting me handle my business.

"Er, Dani, I can assure you that I conduct new hire training with all the employees. But you must understand, we are on a major thoroughfare and service thousands of people a day. We can't see everything."

He sets papers on another stack, and it's teetering dangerously close to the edge.

"That's rich. You service thousands a day but can't see the people you serve. Is that what I heard?"

I slide the guest chair back, grab another stack of his paperwork, and plunk it on his desk. Mr. Tom-Sam is very dismayed by my actions. I know this can't be some sort of filing system. It's a cry for help.

I flop in the chair and gaze up at the manager, waiting for an explanation.

"Well, no, that's not what I meant. If you—"

"Anyway, where's my car?"

I interrupt him because he's full of shit at this point. No wonder they got busted for a prostitution ring if this clown is in charge.

"It's a fully restored 1968, Chevrolet El Camino, with a gray exterior."

"Oh yes, it was towed."

"What?"

I fly out of the chair so fast it catches on the back of my leg. If it weren't for Tomlin standing behind me to catch the thing, it would have clattered to the ground.

"You towed my baby? Are you fucking kidding me?"

My hands curl into fists as I hover over his desk. He backs into the wall and Tomlin holds my arm to keep me from crawling over the damn thing to attack him.

"Dani," Tomlin warns, and when I try to rip my bicep out of his grip, it tightens. "Don't do it."

"Let go! And don't fucking say my name like I'm the problem because I'm not. This dipshit here towed my car in retaliation for making his truck stop look like a Dateline episode, didn't you, Tom-Sam?"

I wrench my arm out of Tomlin's grasp and turn back to the manager.

"If you could calm down and stop with the name-calling." His face is red, probably because of the too-short tie cutting off circulation to his head. "I won't have you talk to me that way."

"Oh, you've got to be shitting me bec—"

I pop my neck, my swollen eye throbbing in time with my splitting-ass headache.

"Dani, take the keys to the car. Go out and check on the dog. I'll handle it from here."

Tomlin's calm voice overrides my threat of violence against this lousy manager in his stupid closet office. He pushes the guest chair to the side, making a clear path for me to exit, and I don't know if I should deck Tomlin or the manager.

Maybe both.

"Go. You don't want him calling your officer friend again."

"And I will!" Mr. Thompson says, stepping forward by borrowing some bravery from Tomlin.

I hate admitting defeat. I might have to give this one to Tomlin, but not without a warning.

"I swear, if there's so much as a scratch on her, I'm reporting this place to my *officer friend* for solicitation and prostitution. I know they busted you a few years back, and since your shitty staff didn't catch that molester, I know that shit goes on right under your nose."

I'm unwavering in my promise to report this place if there is any damage to her. Hell, I should report it just because it's illegal and a poor girl is paying the price for it. His mouth opens and closes like a fish, and his face is getting redder with anger. If Tomlin wasn't kicking me out, I'd stay just to watch this guy blow up.

"Go."

Tomlin slides his fingers down my arm to stuff the key fob in my palm.

"Fine, but I'm warning you."

I stare down Tom-Sam as I pass until he's out of sight. Tomlin apologizes for my behavior, which is bullshit. That apology is on him because I don't feel a damn bit sorry for that crappy manager looking the other way to shit happening in his store.

16

When I walk out of the store, the sweltering heat hits me in the face. His motor is very quiet but running, and Anna is still alive. Good. I click the button, and it unlocks. Anna is dancing in little circles in my seat. The tag that Tomlin picked jingles like Christmas bells.

I scoop her up, place her on Tomlin's seat and close the door to let the air conditioning blast my face. Good thing that little dog now has a sweater, or else she probably would have frozen to death in here. Feeling bad for her, I tuck her between my boob and the console as people stream in and out of that place.

Pulling out my phone, I see Kylie has texted with way too many fucking emojis at her age to use and a million questions that I don't have the patience to answer.

Tomlin heads out of the store, puts his shades on, and gets a look from a couple of girls, whispering to each other as they walk through the doors. Yeah, the man is hot. He opens his driver's side door and drops in with a groan.

"Let me tell you right now. It's not good news. Therefore, if you want to get out of the car and scream like a child or kick the tires, by all means. What I don't want happening is you making a scene inside the store or going charging in after him. Got it?"

He takes off his sunglasses and tosses them on the dash.

"Tell me."

"No, decide your reaction now, because I'm not dealing with it when I'm driving down to the road in two minutes."

He holds out his hand, and I point to the fob that's sitting in his cup holder. He snatches it up and puts it in his pants pocket.

"Come on, I'm not that bad."

He gives me an incredulous look, and I roll my eyes.

"Okay, fine. I might want to bash everyone's head in today, but I didn't choke out Eli or Margaret, or even Hamilton. So, give me a little credit."

"Get out and scream, kick the tires, or have a fit. I don't care which, but once I tell you, I'm pulling out of here, and I'm not pulling over because you can't control yourself."

I take a few deep breaths, which compresses Anna against the console and her head pops up, jingling her charm again. It's the only sound in the car, and as innocent as it sounds, it irritates me.

"Fine, what?"

"Okay," he says, locking the doors and retrieving his sunglasses to put on. "The manager doesn't know where your car is at. He saw it being towed but didn't order it."

"Huh? How can that be?" I'm confused. "He can't look at his cameras and see what wrecker's name is on the truck door?"

"The cameras don't work, no tape since the cops came and took it for evidence." His lips roll into a thin line, obviously irritated at the news.

"That's fucking great. That imbecile doesn't know where my baby is." I rub my temples. "I might not have a job and now I don't even have a car. Can this day get any shittier? Don't answer that because it can't."

I rest my head against the seat, close my eyes, and I count to ten, trying to hold in my murderous rage to not beat that incompetent manager to a pulp.

"Dani."

"Can you give me a minute?"

I know I shouldn't be frustrated with him. Hell, he's carting my ass around and paying for all my shit today.

Tomlin lowers the music and switches it to smooth jazz. It's not bad and a better choice with my pounding headache. At least this guy knows how to set a mood, probably does it with his one-night stands too.

"Officer Hamilton. This is Tomlin Takahashi, Dani's customer from earlier today. Her car got towed from the truck stop, and the manager couldn't tell us where they took it."

I open my eyes and turn my head to see his phone pressed to his ear.

"How did you get his number?" I whisper while he's listening to Hamilton talk.

"Yes, oh yeah, she tried to."

Tomlin holds up his hand to stop my interrupting, then motions at me for a pen and paper.

"Does it look like I carry a diary?" I respond, opening his glove box and looking around his car for a piece of paper or something. Of course, he is neat as can be without a scrap of anything to write on.

"No." He motions for me to take notes on my phone. Got it. "No, she didn't. Luckily. Yeah, will do."

I unlock the screen and open my notes app when Tomlin grabs my phone and starts typing away.

"Repeat that address."

He taps it on my screen while cradling his phone with his shoulder. Even though I'm annoyed he didn't put his phone on speaker, it's nice to have someone take over for once. He also adds Hamilton's number to my contacts, which I admit is something I should have done earlier.

"I will. Yep, of course. Thank you, Officer. Will do."

He ends the call and drops his phone in the cupholder, then hands me my phone.

"What did he say?"

His face is unreadable as if thinking before telling me more bad news, I assume.

"How did you get his number, anyway?"

"I snapped a picture of it back at the apartment," he says in a tone like everyone would think to do that. Whatever. "So apparently, when you left with Officer Hamilton, there were other cops that came out to process the scene and thought it was connected to the case. It's at the police impound lot."

"Well, let's go!"

I yank my seat belt to buckle up and look at Tomlin to move his ass since he's not moving at all.

"You're not getting it today."

"Why the hell not? With your lead foot, we'll make it downtown in no time."

I tap my phone screen to see that it's coming up on 4 p.m., which gives us plenty of time to get there.

"No, they will release it once they clear it as potential evidence."

He punches a button to lower the arctic blast of his air conditioning.

"That's fucking great."

"Yeah."

Do I have anything in my car that can get me arrested? No, but at the same time, do I want a bunch of cops snooping through my shit? Hell no.

"Tell me again that I did the right thing breaking that penis breath's nose?" I press on the top of my swollen eye, trying to relieve some of the pressure collecting there. "Cuz, this domino of events sucks ass."

"You did the right thing, Dani. Sometimes, the high road is the hard road."

This cat spews more philosophical bullshit than anyone I know. It's probably how he gets so many chicks.

"Where to now?"

His mouth twitches when he asks as if knowing the answer before I say it. I look at him, and he looks at me. For the first time in my life, I don't know what to do or where to go. Having to rely on him for transportation is revolting, as I've been able to rely on myself since Dad died.

Where to now?

Zach won't take me in. Nor would I want to go to his place. Kylie would. Easily, in fact, so long as I rehash my day over a bottle of wine. I don't know why, but rehashing with alcohol sounds frustrating and will make me want to beat someone's ass even more.

"I don't know. Drop me at a motel, and I'll figure it out." I sigh, looking away from the pitiful look on his face.

"You don't want to stay with Kylie? She's your best friend." The surprise in his voice is apparent. It would make the most sense to stay with her.

"Don't get me wrong, I love the girl, but I don't have the energy for her. She'll want to dig through all the shit and bitch about Carl and Judd, whose fault it is, and devise a revenge plan. I'm not feeling all that right now. I think I want to be alone."

I glance at him to see a deep frown marring his handsome face.

"Why don't you stay at my place tonight? It's quiet, and I have a guest bedroom that you can use."

There's so much to unpack with his offer. I scratch my head, not knowing where to start.

"I thought you said you fuck for shelter?"

He gasps. "I never said that."

"Not in so many words, but basically, you did. And I don't want to go all the way to Denver tonight, even if you're driving."

"That's disgusting and untrue. And it's not in Denver. I have a place here, more on the outskirts of town, but not far from here."

"I don't know. You're gone for weeks, and now you want to be glued by my side. What gives?"

I probably shouldn't look a gifted horse in the face, or whatever that saying is. Even so, it's weird, and I want to know his angle before I get any deeper.

"Can't a friend help another friend out?"

"Yeah, if it was Kylie, but this is you we are talking about. You broke her heart, and I called you an asshole, so not how friends are."

"We already discussed Kylie, and she's cool. You saw that at the bar. You know I want you to do my car. I've wanted that from the beginning. I've been honest with you from the start. You are carrying on this feud with me, and I don't have the foggiest clue why."

His candor is too much. It hits home because it's all true. I don't know why I want to keep feuding with him. Maybe because he's a mix of badass like myself with a sensitive side that doesn't like to be scolded, which I don't have.

"Fine. But only one night." I hold up my index finger to make my point. "And I'm still not taking your car."

"Always, one step at a time with you, Dani."

He chuckles, putting the car in gear and slowly backing out of the parking spot.

"At least you know what to expect."

I shift in my seat, moving Anna down to my lap to make us both more comfortable.

"Yes, Danielle Louise Winters, I always know where I stand

with you. And if I don't, I can count on you to put me in my place."

He gives me that gorgeous shit-eating grin of his. I swear that's why I carry on the feud because he has the balls to stand up to me repeatedly without caving—something only Dad could do.

17

The drive to his place is straight out of town and into the mountains. I gathered he's never had chicks up here because they would think he's a murderer picking a spot to dump their body by how remote it is.

"Damn, man, where do you live?" I look from the stunning mountain views to his sneaky smile. "I expected you to live in some glass museum here, although those are hard to find in the Cañon."

"Well, look who's full of surprises now. We don't all fit your stereotype."

His sunglasses reflect the amber mountain range and the sun setting above the peaks.

"I never stereotyped you. Is this because you're Asian? Do you have a chip on your shoulder about it? You shouldn't because you know you're hot as fuck."

I turn the car vents toward the ceiling with the sun setting. It's getting too cold with the air blowing directly on me.

"Or were you stereotyping me because I'm blond and supposed to be all prim and proper, like those beauty queens are?"

He laughs, loud and long, genuinely amused.

"Where to start with you? I've never had a chip on my shoulder about my Japanese heritage. Quite the opposite, in fact. You keep calling me hot, so I'm picking up what you're laying down. And—"

"I'm not putting down anything for you to pick up, so forget that. I'm calling a spade a spade. You're hot and you know it. Like I know you like my tits because you stare at them all the time. Then you say Christ or something like that when you get busted. So basically, you think I'm hot, and I know it. Just saying, we both use our looks to our advantage. You probably more than me, but that's because you're vain as hell."

I shrug. It's all straight facts.

"Oh, Dani. You're such a lovable little creature, aren't you?"

He turns his attention back to the road as we climb higher into the mountains until an old cowboy-looking fence appears on his left. He slows the car to turn under a giant wooden cross-beam with antlers mounted on it, held up by other giant wood poles on each side.

It's very un-Tomlin-like.

The gravel road winds around to the right, kicking up rocks that ping under his car. If I had a fancy car like this, I sure as hell wouldn't be driving on this dusty road.

"Someone needs to pave this road or else you'll eventually lose the underplate on your fancy car."

"You know you live in Colorado, right? They won't let you blacktop a road unless it's their highway."

"Fucking granola types. They'd die if they saw how this state allows for the disposal of oils and other car fluids because it's definitely not environmentally friendly. Except in the case of your soup can, where they're all dried up into dust."

I chuckle, thinking back to that rusted-out soup can he delivered to the shop a month ago.

"Hilarious. But seeing as how you are taking my project over, don't laugh too hard."

He flashes me that shit grin of his. I don't know why he's still wearing his glasses when the sun is almost down. Probably to hide behind them.

"Stop with that nonsense. My life is in the shitter, and all you can think about is your precious car. I have bigger problems to deal with."

I look at the crisscross fence that holds back nothing, deciding I'm tired of him pushing his agenda on me. He's got to know shit is super bad for me if I'm playing sleepover at my former nemesis's house. That enough should clue him into my world being turned upside down.

"Dani, the way I see it, you have a prime opportunity running your ass over, but you're either too stupid, too lazy, or too complacent to see it. I haven't been able to put my finger on it yet. But you don't need Carl or his shop. Maybe it's a comfort thing, but you outgrew that place long ago, and you're hanging on for dear life. Why? You could set up shop with my project and move clients over or if you don't want to poach clients, finish my car, take it to Pebble Beach, and you'll get clients there. It's a win-win. A chance to get out of Carl's place and create a name of your own. Eventually, hire guys to work for you and become the new Carl."

I don't miss the earnestness in his voice, but going out on my own has never been my thing. I gave up dreaming dreams when Dad died, and that's basically what he's asking me to do now.

"Stop frowning. It's a good business plan, and I'll back you until you're on your feet. Then we'll be partners from there on out."

At some point in his speech, I turn back to see him taking off his glasses and tucking them into an overhead compartment.

"Are you always like this?"

"Like what?"

"A wistful dreamer."

"I don't have my head in the clouds, if that's what you're saying, Dani. I'm far too strategic and pragmatic for that. You're annoyed because I see through the bullshit you spew regularly. I don't think you're used to being challenged because no one wants to deal with you if I'm being honest. Somewhere past the sailor's mouth and skimpy clothes, you know it, and you don't like it. We all have goals in life. Maybe you gave up on yours, or maybe you never thought about them, but what were you going to do, stay at Carl's forever? If he retired tomorrow, what happens to you?"

His car slows to a halt at a beautiful spot that paints the entire windshield with pink and purple hues coming off the mountain range before us.

"I don't know. I've never thought about it," I say, scratching my head.

What would I do? Be evicted, probably because I don't have any money saved to buy out the place, and the bank wouldn't give a person like me a loan.

That's for sure.

"You have to start thinking about your future and stop living day-to-day."

"That's easy for you to say when you have money and no worries," I spout off in my defense.

"Not even close. It's called making a plan and sticking to it."

Our eyes connect, neither wavering in trying to get our points across to the other.

"Look around, Dani. This is what planning gets you."

He sweeps his hand out at the million-dollar view. If he's driving down a private road at the top of the peak, I can't imagine what his house looks like or how much it costs.

Suddenly, I wish I had called Kylie to stay with her because she isn't trying to push this baby bird out of the nest. Hell, she'd let me build an adjoining nest next to her with a shared bird feeder.

This blows.

Thankfully, he doesn't say anything more while he resumes creeping down the gravel road, allowing me to admire the amazing views. Around the bend comes a stunning house constructed of natural elements.

Wood logs that are so wide, it makes me curious how old the tree was that sacrificed its life for his place. Substantial stone walls meet the wood beams holding massive glass panels to create a wall of endless windows. If car windshields cost hundreds, these windows must cost thousands.

I catch myself with a slack mouth and snap it shut. Damn, if planning gets me this, I'll buy some notebook paper and a pen to start mapping out some goals.

He pulls through the circle driveway and under the porte cochere to align my door with the grand steps leading to the heavy leaded glass doors.

"Damn, Tomlin. What do you do for a living that you can afford this and that museum mansion in Denver?"

I pick up Anna and tuck her into my side boob as I open my car door.

"What?" He gives me the weirdest look. "You don't know who I'm?"

I'm about to get out of the car when I look over my shoulder at him.

"Yeah, duh, you're Tomlin, formerly asshole, who dumped my bestie and now has some angle on me fixing up his virgin car."

My tone drips with sarcasm because I know everything I need to know about him. The rest, well, I don't care about. He sits there dumbfounded while I get out of the car, grab Anna's tote, and bump the door closed with my hip. I put her down on the gravel and walk away from Tomlin, who's recovered enough to get out.

The air is crisp and clean, and my carbon-encrusted lungs love it. I gulp in big breaths of it, my body thanking me. It's stupidly beautiful up here. I can't imagine how much this costs. He's got to be a millionaire to afford this spread.

No wonder money is no object when he wanted that soup can restored to museum quality. He has money to burn, that's for sure.

I walk to the retaining wall, the one that keeps me from tumbling down the side of the mountain to see tree-covered ridges and picture-perfect views in all directions. It's breathtaking, and I take out my phone to snap several pictures. Since I'm only here one night, I want to have these because, with all the planning in the world, I could never obtain this.

"Pretty nice, huh?" He sneaks up behind me, shoving the dog into my camera frame. "Can't do that up here. She'll get eaten by a critter or snatched up by a hawk. Take her."

"Dammit. Hamilton should've taken her."

I stuff my phone in my pocket and take Anna from his hand. She's shaking like a leaf, and I sort of feel bad for dumping her on the ground. I figured she might need to pee, and maybe she did, but I'll be damned if I'm going to have to babysit her even more up here.

"We probably should have gotten her kitty litter instead. Would have been easier with fewer threats," I grumble to his retreating back.

"Oh, watch out for bears. This is their territory, so always keep the doors locked. They have been known to come up on the deck in search of food."

"Damn, man, I'm not a Girl Scout. Are you sure I can't get a motel room with the only threat being bed bugs and roaches?"

He rolls his eyes.

"Come on, let's go in."

I fall in step beside him until I spot a barn-looking structure with several green roll-up doors that match the mansion's emerald metal roof.

"Is that a garage?"

"Of course, you don't think I'd leave her out all night with the bears, do you?"

He sweeps a hand over to his fancy car. I smile at the fact that he called his car her. Now he's learning.

"I wouldn't either. Shit would be destroyed in minutes."

I speed walk over to the garage, curious to check out the inside. Tomlin wordlessly trails behind me. The closer I get, the taller the structure looms over me.

"Is this a two-story?"

It has cute little dormer windows breaking up the metal roof, but I can't tell if it's an elevated garage or living space above.

"You'll see."

He walks ahead, disappearing under the wraparound porch protected by the same green roofline. I follow him to see a large stone hearth with a TV above it, a pizza oven to one side, and a built-in summer kitchen on the other. A smattering of couches and chairs cover the rest of the concrete, making it a welcoming outdoor living room. It's fancy as hell and a great place to entertain all his fancy friends.

"Damn, this is nice."

I could easily sleep out here on chilly nights if it weren't for bears, critters, and whatever else he said.

"Yeah, it's cool to hang out and watch sports. I know you like beer, but do you like pizza?"

The door behind him swings open, and the lights beyond flash on.

"Of course, who doesn't?"

"Good, we'll make some out here tonight. But leave her inside the house."

He motions for me to come over and as soon as I step closer to the door, I stop and stare.

"This is ..."

"Cool, huh?"

"It's a—"

"Diner, like Margaret's, but better. The 1950 red Corvette over there inspired it."

I cross the threshold to take it all in. The entire place is lit with bright, round lights hanging from the ceiling like a soda shop. The shiny epoxy floor reflects the cars parked on it. To the left is a diner with a long white bar, red swirling barstools, and a jukebox.

A giant wall-mounted television hovers above red lounging couches. Opposite the diner is a full garage with several completely restored Corvettes and a parts car shoved under a lift at the far end.

I'm in awe. This is so badass that he went up another notch in my book. Now he's at two. Everywhere I turn, it's perfect. This must have been part of that planning babble from a moment ago.

"This is badass."

He beams with pride when I glance at him. I would, too, if I owned something like this. Hell, I'd never leave if I lived here. Kylie would have to come to me if she ever wanted to see me.

"Thanks. I'm proud of how it turned out."

I walk over to the garage side, my shoes squeaking on the shiny floor.

"Can I put her down?"

He closes the door and locks it, before answering, "Sure."

Anna shakes when I set her down, obviously not happy about having to walk, but I want to check out his cars. Walking over to the 'one that inspired it'. I can't help but admire the workmanship. It's top-notch.

"This is a beautiful car."

My fingertips caress the high gloss cherry red color in contrast to the bright white paint on the fender and doors. The whitewall tires have never been driven, and the vintage chrome hubcaps reflect my legs.

"You don't drive her?"

"No, trailered her up along with the others."

I nod, circling the car and taking in the preservation's quality work—far superior to mine.

"Who did the work?"

I glance across the car at him and find him intently studying me.

"I bought it from Paul Russet. All these were already done, so that's why I brought you that one because I wanted to be part of the process."

My hand rests on the frame of the windshield as I lean in to look at the tight stitches on the upholstered white seat.

"But you're not part of the process. You said penis breath never called you about the modified parts or when he needed a decision from you."

He frowns, leaning against the front fender with his arms crossed.

"Can you stop calling him that? It's disgusting. But yes. Partly my fault. I didn't expect to be out of the country for so long."

I straighten up, walking to the back of the car to unlatch the trunk for a quick look inside.

"Why were you gone so long? And didn't you say you were in Tokyo?"

"Yeah, it's a long story for another night."

His tone is a mix of irritation and anger, probably a story that I don't want to hear after the day I have had. Pizza, beer, and watching a game in his fancy outdoor living room are all I have left in me. Not deep conversations unpacking all his crap.

"Well, Tomlin, this work is superb." Carefully lowering the

trunk and ensuring the latch catches, I give it a light tap to close it entirely. "Far better than anything I could do."

He runs his finger over a spot above the headlamp, probably wiping away imaginary dust as spotless as this garage is.

"Not true."

"What does that mean?"

I join him at the front. He moves off his hip to tower over me.

"A guy at Paul's referred me to you. Imagine my surprise when you were one and the same girl that littered pink paper all over my house."

A partial smile pops up when I shove my finger in his face.

"You deserved everything you got that day." I think about what he just said, then squint at him.

"You're shitting me, right? Because how would a shop like Paul's even know about Carl's place, much less my name? This feels like you're buttering me up to take your car."

He covers my finger again and I let it fall away.

"You'd be surprised. I checked you out, Danielle Louise Winters." Now it's his turn to wag his finger in my face. "You have quite the reputation out there for someone so young."

He whistles as he walks to the diner side of the garage and stoops behind the counter for a moment. I follow him, wondering what exactly he knows about me.

"Quit being so secretive and drawing this out. What do you know about me? Let me rephrase. What do you think you know about me?"

I flop on the barstool by the counter and start spinning, careful not to hit Anna, who seems lost on the ground. He pops up with two frosted glasses and then turns his back to me to fill them with beer from his tap. Hell, if I had that at my house, I'd be three sheets to the wind all the time.

"They say you're the best in Colorado. You've been

mentioned in a couple of magazines, but my favorite was the photo with what's-his-name?"

He turns to look at me with that wily smile.

"You saw that thing? Ugh, kill me now." I fake shoot my brains out with my index finger when he slides the beer under my nose.

"That was for the Denver lifestyle magazine or something. Some dude up there knew some big shot, and they snapped that picture of me smashed between him and Carl. Really nice guy and I'm glad he was happy with the work I did, but to run a story on the car and then put a picture of me in it, that's not why I do it."

Anna's nails clack on the slick floors, and as much as I want to break her from this holding habit, I pick her up to place her on my lap. It's not much space, and she tries to turn in circles to get settled but abandons that when she almost falls, and I catch her by the butt.

"Why do you do it then?"

He takes a swig of his beer, and I look at the foam settling in mine. What answer should I give him? The one I tell everybody? I like to restore the craftsmanship of artists long before me. That's somewhat true. I do think old cars are better.

Or the one I tell no one? Because I'm a high school dropout with no prospects and no future, I do what Dad did to make ends meet.

"What did Paul's place say about me?"

I answer his question with my own.

"Said they want to offer you a job."

"You're shitting me, right?"

I chug my entire beer and set it on the bar top. Damn, I've been needing that. His eyes widen in surprise. Hell, after the day I've had one beer isn't enough and certainly is nothing when I really want to get buzzed.

"You've got to clean up that mouth."

I tap on my mug for a refill. He hesitates, then reluctantly fills it again and pushes it toward me.

"Fuck you. Now, did they really ask about me or not?"

"Yes, Dani." His hands rest on the counter, and he starts tapping out a beat on it. "Why don't you ever believe what I'm telling you?"

I take a swig and then put my mug down. "Because you have an angle. But stop drawing it out. What *exactly* did they say?"

He flicks his wrist to look at his watch and then disappears around the corner while I pet Anna. I gaze out the wall of windows near the fireplace, the golden sunset has dipped behind the peaks.

It makes sense why he likes it up here. The air is fresh, the views are breathtaking, and the only sounds are the occasional birds cawing. I do like my solitude, but this might get a little lonely after a while. He returns with two hunks of white clay covered in plastic and an armful of other stuff.

"What's all that?"

I finish my beer and tap my mug for another.

"Slow down on the alcohol, and we're making pizza. I told you that. So put the dog down and go wash your hands."

He dumps all the stuff on the counter and then spreads out some thin rubbery mat next to where I'm sitting.

"And to answer your question. I called up there asking for a preservationist closer to me. They referred me to you based on some cars you shipped back East that belonged to a few owners in a local car club. Apparently, they don't show the cars you restore but drive them to the events in New England, so word spreads. The owner said he's seen your work and wanted to know how to get in touch with you without calling Carl directly. Mind you, this was after your little stunt in Denver, so imagine my surprise when it turned out to be the same girl that carved a *D* in my front door. I got the guy's number in the house if you are interested. But if you're willing to entertain his offer, then you must consider mine, too."

I don't move off the stool. I'm too busy taking in what he said. I've shipped plenty of cars around the US.

Hell, most are shipped, but I do get a handful of customers who fly in to drive it off the lot when they're complete. Maybe it was the 1940 Lincoln or the 1953 Studebaker Commander. Jeez, I can't remember anymore.

"I'm not moving to Boston. I can barely tolerate Colorado snow. Getting down this mountain in winter must be treacherous."

I hate the hassle of snow tires—a necessary evil in this state.

"Sounds like my competition got a lot smaller. I'll give you his number just in case. You should reach out and network. Keep your options open." His eyes dart from me to the dough he unwrapped and is kneading. "Now, get cleaned up so you can help. I'm not waiting on you hand and foot while you are here."

I smile because he has been waiting on me hand and foot since he showed back up, so sure, I'll give the guy a hand with dinner.

Picking up Anna, I grab the blanket draped over one of the couches, wind it into a circle on the corner cushion and plant her in the middle. She seems content when she yawns and tucks her head into the folds.

When I round the counter, it's nothing like a diner. It's a regular kitchen with cabinetry, drawers, and knobs. It's a complete fake-out and reminds me of what Judd did to his car. If Carl fires me, then I'm out of work and free to do his project. Ugh, kill me now.

"This is pretty badass, with the diner on the outside and kitchen back here. But my favorite part is the soda fountain that pumps beer."

I stand next to him to refill my mug.

"Thanks, I designed it myself. Now stop getting drunk and go wash up so you can do the sauce and stuff."

He bumps my hip with his, never breaking the rhythm of the kneading. I don't know if it's the beers or his awesome garage diner or what, but he's even hotter being all domestic and shit.

"And stop ogling me."

His tongue curls around the side of his teeth, and I immediately look away because my mind snaps to wondering how skilled that tongue is. Probably stupidly skilled with all his hotness and good looks, even if I called him a lazy lover earlier.

"You wish," I huff, rounding the corner to an entire wall of appliances set against a white subway tile backsplash and colossal farm sink. He really did a great job designing this place. If he didn't live here, I'd never leave.

"Why do all the hot ones think everyone wants to screw them?" I holler in his direction since I can't see him.

His soap dispenser is touchless, as is his faucet. I should have figured he'd have thought of that, too, since I get the gist that he's a closet germaphobe.

"I don't know, Dani. Why do you think everyone wants to screw you?"

His breath is warm against my ear, and if I didn't have soap up to my elbows, I would have clocked him for being too close to me. He's not exactly touching me, but it's too damn close for the quasi-friends we are trying to be.

"You need to back your shit up before I lay you out." I hold up a sudsy finger and glance over my shoulder at him.

"There are two things I can always count on with you. One, you threaten violence every time someone says or does something you don't like."

Fair.

It gets people to back off my shit. Carl, Judd, Tomlin, although Hamilton didn't. Then again, I don't recall threatening him because that's a chargeable offense. I mean, I'm not completely stupid.

"And two?"

His cologne wraps around me like a warm, cedar-scented blanket, and I think I may be buzzed after all because when I turn to look at him, his lips are inches from mine.

"And two, you like me."

I stare at them, not hearing what else he's saying, as I dry my hands on a towel. If he's offering me that hot body and talented tongue, then hell, why not? I told Hamilton I needed a beer and to get laid, so yeah, I can one-night stand him.

I shuck the towel on the counter and launch myself at him, my fingers in his hair, pulling him into me. My lips are demanding, hungry against his soft, pillowy ones, and as my eyes are closing, his are widening.

I don't care. I want to taste the beer from his mouth, suck his tongue down my throat, and rub up against him like a horny cat. I do all those things until he shoves me away.

"What are you doing?"

His hair is rumbled, his cheeks are pink, and his lips are swollen. I go at him again, but he grabs my shoulders to hold me back.

"Dani!"

"What? Don't be such a prude. You've wanted this since the first time I called you asshole."

I lick my lips, tasting the remanent of his beer-coated tongue, and want more. His fingertips dig into my shoulder blades, and I attempt to push them off to kiss him again, but he holds me back.

"What the hell, man?"

He immediately releases me and it's confusing as hell.

"Dani, you've got it all wrong."

His words slap me across the face, and I sober up quickly. He's running his fingers through his hair and wiping his mouth with the back of his hand. Damn, did I read the room that wrong? I need a moment—lots of moments.

"You got a toilet in here?" I ask, backing away and into a hallway full of doors.

"First door on your right."

I don't even bother replying as I dash away. The bathroom is quaint, with the vintage diner theme continuing as I splash water on my face and look in the mirror.

"What did I just do?" My reflection drips with cold water. "Did I read his signals wrong, or am I drunk from downing a couple of beers on an empty stomach?"

I grab a soft hand towel to dab the water off my face and stare at myself. My eye looks terrible, my hair is frizzy and coming loose from my braid, and my coloring is pale, other than my bright pink lips. I smell my breath, and it smells like beer. So maybe my appearance isn't the best right now, but what guy has ever turned me down?

This is some weird shit.

Turning on the faucet again, I take a drink, swish it around in my mouth, and spit it out. I straighten my shirt and rebraid my hair to not look like a drunken disaster.

And the eye, well, I should have put ice on it hours ago. It's going to stay swollen until the blood drains. I plop my ass on the toilet lid and pick my nails to waste even more time. The longer I sit there, the more I realize it was a mistake coming here.

I should have sucked it up, gone to Kylie's apartment, and spent the next three hours getting trashed and spilling my guts. Instead, I'm stuck here making passes at a guy that's clearly not interested.

This still blows.

I wait until my patience runs out and then try to wait longer until I can't take it anymore. He's probably thinking I'm taking a dump or intentionally avoiding him. Let's hope it's the former as I sigh and open the door.

In the time I've been in there, he has old football highlights playing on the inside television and a fire going in the pizza oven outside. He's on the patio fiddling with something by the summer kitchen and two pizzas are sitting on the side waiting to go in. Not sure what to do, I mill about at the corner of the prep area.

"Done hiding out?" He quips, walking through the door, and Anna's head pops out of the blanket.

"She likes sports."

"Look, that was embarrassing."

I drum my nails on the counter to release the uncomfortable feeling of both apologizing and being embarrassed. Both are new to me. When he struts over to stand in front of me, I lean against the white marble because his closeness is too much.

"Now you're making it worse. Scoot back." I shoo him, but he doesn't move. It's these types of mixed signals that are messing me up.

"You've had a long day, and I know you think sex might fix it, but it won't. And—"

"Save your lecture. I get it. We're cool." I slip away from him to retrieve my beer and take a sip this time. "I won't do it again."

Partly because my pride hurts, but mostly because I don't want pity sex from anyone in this world, least of all him.

"Can I finish before you get all bent out of shape again?" I can't stop him. It's his house.

"We'd be combustion in the bedroom. Don't roll your eyes at me. You know it. And as much as I'd love to see that smart mouth wrapped around my cock, I need us to maintain a business relationship, so when you do start on my car, it gets finished and in the show on time, and not hijacked by your lovesick feelings for me."

I close my mouth from when it fell open about his cock statement.

"Where I put my mouth is no concern of yours, so no problem keeping it professional. And that's awfully optimistic that I'll be doing your car as I have turned you down several times. Now make me some damn pizza because I'm starving, tired, and buzzed."

With that, I down the rest of my beer and plop my ass on the couch next to Anna. He *can* wait on me hand and foot after that comment. Like I'd go down on my knees in front of him. The apocalypse would happen before that does.

"You're lucky I'm a good host and willing to put up with you while you are here," he says as he heads out the door to put the pizzas into the flames.

Who's waiting on who now? Once he shuts the door, I grab another blanket, fluff my pillow, and lie down with my feet curled behind Anna. Damn, this feels so good that I close my eyes and drift off to sleep.

18

The puddle of drool soaking my cheek awakens me. The television volume is low, a crackling fire is going, and Tomlin's long legs are stretched out on the coffee table in front of me. His head rests against the leather chair, with his eyes closed.

I wipe the side of my face with my hand. The movement causes the leather couch to squeak, and I glance over to see him watching me.

"I kept the pizza warming in the drawer in the kitchen if you're still hungry."

"I thought you were sleeping."

I blink several times, trying to get my eyelashes to stop sticking together.

"I was meditating."

"Oh."

I lower my voice because I'm interrupting his woo-woo time. Come to think of it, I don't think I've ever heard of a guy meditating. I thought that's what influencers blabbered on about, along with manifesting and other nonsense.

"Um . . ." Sitting up, Anna yawns, and the windows all around are jet black. "How long was I out for?"

"A couple of hours."

"And you sat there? Like stayed with me?"

He gives me a baffled look.

"Yes, was I supposed to leave you here by yourself?"

Zach would have. If I ever stayed long enough for that to happen. Kylie would too, for that matter. Staring at the silhouette of trees outside, I recall that the last time someone sat with me while I slept was Dad. It gives me a warm feeling. One I could get used to but probably will never experience again.

"Are you okay? They checked your head when you got hit, right?"

He drags his feet off the table and leans toward me as if looking for something on my head. That nice feeling fades away.

"Yeah, you said something about pizza?" He starts to get up, but I wave him off when I stand. "Nah, I got it. Go back to your woo-woo head stuff."

Anna jumps to her feet, spinning in circles atop the blanket, and she probably needs to go outside to pee. Scooping her up and tucking her under my arm, I open the door, and the cool air caresses my skin, causing goosebumps to break out over my arms. It's refreshing and just the thing to fully wake me up.

I carry her across the patio to a little patch of grass at the edge of the concrete for her to do her business. The call of wildlife surrounds us, and she pees quickly before standing on my foot, wanting to be held again.

I don't blame her. Out here, she's a little jerky treat for the animals that roam this part of the mountain. Picking her up, I walk over to the pizza oven, now cool to the touch, and peer in the windows to see Tomlin watching me.

For someone that wants a professional relationship, he sure throws a lot of mixed signals. I'm going to have to ignore all of them from here on out. I don't want a repeat of what happened earlier.

When I open the door, he points the remote at the fireplace, and the flames die down to a low hum. If this is his garage, I can't imagine what the main house looks like.

"You good?"

I don't know why he's so concerned now. I literally just woke up feeling better than before.

"Yup, do you have a Coke or something? I don't think beer is a good idea."

I should have thought about it before. Even though I don't have a head injury, alcohol is probably the last thing I should have had.

"In the fridge, and the pizza is in the warming drawer to the left of it."

"Want anything?" I offer since it's his house. I should probably have been the one waiting on him hand and foot for all he's done for me today.

"A sparkling water. Thanks."

I hum my response and put Anna on the floor. Her princess charm dangles as she walks behind me into the diner. I should probably get her new food out of the car, but if we are only staying overnight, I don't want to haul it in. Hell, I'll feed her pizza with me and give her water for now.

Rummaging through his cabinets, I hunt for some plastic storage containers but can't find any. He's probably too health-conscious to use plastic, believing it will cause brain tumors or strokes. I barely have a glass bowl in my house, and here in his garage house, he only has glass. We really are from two different worlds.

Deciding on the smallest and lowest bowl I can find, I fill it with water and put it down for Anna. Guilt washes over me when she drinks her weight in water, and I realize I should have offered this to her hours ago.

Dammit, I need to get better at this dog-sitting thing. Her charm chimes against the glass, and Tomlin peeks over the counter in our direction.

"Just giving her water. I should have before," I say, and he's nearly out of his seat before I stop him. "I assume we're not sleeping out here?"

His mouth falls open for a split second before he says, "No, I don't make my guests sleep in the garage."

"Don't be so shocked, this place is more than a garage. Far nicer than my apartment above a real garage."

"I never said that."

"I know, Tomlin. I said it, and it's the truth, so keep your hair on."

I pull a plate down from the shelf and hunt for oven mitts before tugging on the drawer handle. The delicious aroma hits me. He saved me half of each kind of pizza. How gentlemanly.

I remove the tray, close the drawer, and slide both halves onto my plate before putting the mitts back. They look amazing, perfectly charred at the edge and oozing cheesy goodness in the middle. Pulling off a couple of toppings, I drop them on the floor to Anna, still standing next to her water bowl, and she gobbles them right up. How is this dog not fat from only human food?

Looking down at the wall of cabinetry, I don't see a fridge. I turn in a full circle, verifying the wall of windows behind me and the wall of cabinets in front of me. Then I walk down to the second door, open it, and the light flickers on to a lovely bedroom. If guests don't stay out here, why is there a bedroom?

"Uh, Tomlin," I holler down the hallway while closing all the doors again. "Where's your fridge?"

He chuckles and cranes his head to yell, "There's two of them. They both have long vertical handles. The one on the right is the drink refrigerator, the other is for food."

Two fridges that look like cabinets. Who would have

thought it? I barely have one for my food *and* drinks. He has one specifically for drinks. Sure is nice to be rich.

I walk toward the cabinetry and see the two long handles, and when I open the *drink* fridge, I almost choke. He has a better drink selection than the vending machine at Carl's place. There's so much sparkling this and tonic that, that I'm literally reading the labels to figure it out.

Note to self, get rich as hell and have a drink fridge and beer tap. My poor veins would collapse. I already give them a run for their money with all the coffee I pour down my gullet.

Grabbing our drinks and my plate, I carefully step around Anna, who's hunting the floor for more toppings, and walk to the couch. I hand him his drink and set mine on a wooden coaster. Lord only knows how much this coffee table costs and I can't afford to replace it if I get water rings on it.

I grab a stack of napkins from the dispenser on the counter and sit on the floor. Anna comes running from the diner to join me.

"What are you doing?" Tomlin's eyebrows pinch together.

"What?"

"You are not sitting on the floor to eat."

It comes out as a statement when I'm sure he meant it as a question.

"I'm not sitting on your real leather couch eating greasy food and sharing it with the dog, if that's what you're implying."

I crack open my Coke and tear a tiny bit of crust to give to her.

A deep frown cracks his handsome face. "Come on, Dani. Get off the floor and sit on the couch. It's no big deal."

He drags his feet from the coffee table to set on the floor and leans forward, trying to convince me.

"Tomlin, chill. You're making it a big deal, so relax and let me eat in peace." I take a considerable bite, and the pizza is delicious. "Damn, this is good. I wouldn't believe you made it if I didn't see it myself."

I drop more toppings for Anna, who eagerly eats them up and is sitting pretty for more.

"You didn't see it for yourself. You were too busy crying in the bathroom."

"You wish. The last time I cried over a guy was, yeah, never. You guys are a dime a dozen, useful for killing bugs and fucking."

I take a few sips of my Coke, the carbonation burning my throat, and I swear that's the best part.

"Keeping it classy."

He swipes the remote off the side table next to him and starts flipping through the channels.

"Well, since I'm the hostess with the mostest, I'll let you pick what we watch."

He catches me off guard with my mouth full of pizza. What the hell, he's seen me at my worst, and I still don't care.

I shove the food against my cheek and say, "I don't have cable, so I don't care."

His head tilts, and his eyes slide from the television to me. "You don't have cable? What do you watch?" As if the concept is foreign to him.

"Did you see a TV at my place?"

He pauses, looking away for a moment as he thinks, and then gazes back at me.

"No?"

"Nope. I watch porn or Netflix on my phone, so your choice."

I finish one entire pizza with much of the crust going to Anna, then I lick my fingers and wipe it on the napkins.

His mouth opens and closes before murmuring, "Porn and Netflix" and returns to flipping through the channels.

At least twenty go by before he stops on the History channel, showing some war footage. He twists the cap off his fizzy water and settles deeper into his chair as if this show really holds his interest. I dig into the other half, sharing regularly with her when I catch Tomlin watching us.

"What?"

"Nothing."

He shakes his head but doesn't look away, so I start a staring contest to see if he will break.

"Duuuuuuude." I roll my eyes. "Stop staring or tell me what you're thinking already. I barely got rid of my headache with that nap, I don't need it back again."

"Fine, I'm wondering why you are so opposed to taking my car. I really can't figure it out."

This guy has a one-track mind. Got to give him that.

He probably obsesses over every little thing in his life. I bet he drove the builder of this diner crazy with all the details and crap.

"You gotta wrestle it away from Carl, and that won't be easy."

There, that should hold him off and buy me time.

"I already spoke to him."

His eyes flicker between the black-and-white bomb footage on TV and back to me when I choke on my bite and hammer my fist into my chest to dislodge it.

"When?"

My voice is hoarse from the crust scraping a line down the back of my throat.

"When you were asleep. He understands, and the car is being brought up here tomorrow," Tomlin says casually. "He asked if he could talk to you, but I said you were indisposed. I suspect he thought I was bluffing, but . . ."

He shuffles his eyes back to the television in blatant indifference. As if he didn't cause my heart to leap from my chest to my throat, where the crust is still stuck. I pound on my chest a couple more times and clear my throat a bunch before guzzling down some Coke.

"So, let me get this straight. You called Carl while I was asleep, and he's letting you pull your car? No questions asked?"

My brain can't comprehend how easy he's making this sound. Does money really buy easiness as well as a drink fridge and a diner garage?

"Yes. He apologized profusely for Judd's work and, well, for you too."

If my mouth wasn't already open, it would have fallen open. Did Carl apologize for me to Tomlin? That's all sorts of wrong.

"Then there's the matter of settling the final bill since he'll have to deduct for inferior and unauthorized work, which he didn't seem too happy about, but he should have managed his employees better. I think he's slipping, and now that he got caught, he doesn't like the position he's put in."

I touch my swollen eyebrow while processing Tomlin's cavalier attitude about all this. I'm mad at Carl, and Tomlin makes some good points, but he seems to be going at Carl's jugular on this, and that doesn't sit right with me.

"Hey, Carl's not entirely bad. Lazy, yes. Greedy, definitely, but I don't think he did it intentionally or anything. Just trusted the wrong one too much."

Like trusting that motherfucker Judd over me.

"Don't defend him to me, Dani. It's a business, not a hobby shop. Run your business well, or it will run you."

He takes a sip of his drink, balances it on the arm of his leather lounge chair, and tucks his hands behind his head. Suddenly, I witness a side of Tomlin that I don't like. If I were to take his car, this is how he'd be with me. I'm used to the harmless nagging of an old man riding my ass, knowing I'm never going to listen because it all turns out fine in the end.

But if I worked on his project, here with him, every day, it would be bloodshed between us. I need to get back to Carl's place fast and apologize so I can put all this behind me. Keep your enemies close, they say. At least at Carl's, I know the enemy very well and how he operates, but with Tomlin, he'd be tyrannical and my worst nightmare.

"I think I'd like to turn in now, if you don't mind."

I stand, collecting my plate and drink, to head to the kitchen. I don't even give him a backward glance when he jumps up and stomps after me.

"Why? What happened? It's because I mentioned Carl, huh?"

Tomlin plucks the drink from my hand to pour the rest in the sink, along with his, and rinses them out. He places them in the recycler and takes my plate from me. With nothing more for me to do, I pick up Anna's water bowl and hand that to him as well.

"No, it's been a long day and I'm tired."

"Dani, you slept like a log for hours and were snoring like a freight train. What did I say that upset you?" He stops fiddling with the faucet water to look at me. His gaze is piercing, and I sigh.

I wish I had a redo on this day because I would have let Judd lick me, not broken his nose, and been settled in my bed at home rather than being here with a newly identified tyrannical so-called friend.

"It's not all about you, Tomlin. How many times do I have to tell you that? My life's in the shitter, and you want to nag on about that car. Get someone out of school, they can do it, or hell, tow it to Paul's. They do better work than me. Just lay off. In fact, take me back to Carl's tomorrow morning, and we can forget this whole day. So, no deal." I exhale, the longest sigh to represent I'm done with him, this place, and his stupid-ass car.

It's obvious he bullies everyone to do things for him or wears them down, so they finally give up in frustration. The only thing I'm giving up is my pride when I walk back into Carl's and ask for my job back.

I don't even bother waiting for him when I walk out of the kitchen, pick up Anna and leave the diner by slamming the door so hard that the windows rattle. The cooler air feels good on my flushed cheeks.

I walk past his outdoor living room to put Anna down to pee one last time before we go to bed. Hell, at this point, I shouldn't have let her down and hoped she would have peed in his house. Once she's done her business, I pick her up, stow her under my arm, and head to the trunk of his Porsche to get her dog stuff out for tonight.

I don't have any clothes to sleep in or a way to charge my phone, which sucks. But I'll sleep naked with the door locked and pick up my backpack of problems in the morning. They'll certainly be waiting for me.

19

His footsteps crunch on the gravel and the trunk lifts for me to start shoving bags on my arm that isn't holding Anna. I don't bother to look at him when he joins me to lift the dog food and bedding out.

"I know you don't have any clothes, but if you want, you can borrow some of mine."

His tone has a smidge of sincerity in it. If this is him waving the white flag, then forget it. I've seen what I needed to see, and it's a hard pass. Carl may have let the place run him, but he trusted us not to take advantage, and Judd broke his trust. I didn't. The fact that Tomlin smirks at it is sickening.

"I sleep naked."

"Christ."

I leave the rest of the bags for him to carry into the house. He's all strong and ripped. This shouldn't be anything he can't handle. Turning on my heel, I cross the driveway in a hurry and hustle to the wraparound porch to stare through the long windows framing his front door.

Dude, this is some shit. I'd never have massive-ass windows where people could see me walking around in my underwear. I know he's vain as hell but safety first, man. He must have some super spy button somewhere because the front door slides open all on its own, like in one of those futuristic movies.

"Uh..."

I point inside and look behind as he's jogging up the stairs, loaded down with dog stuff.

"I'm not going in there. You first."

"Scared someone is waiting inside to murder you?" He taunts as he saunters past me to cross the threshold.

"Yup, they can kill your ass first."

His chuckle echoes through the vast place when I step inside. Immediately, I stop and stare at the wall of floor-to-ceiling windows across the back of his house, with a silhouette of the mountain range beyond. This place is far fancier than that museum house in Denver.

It looks like a log cabin on the outside with its quaint green metal roof, but inside, it's what I'd imagine LeBron James's house looks like.

White and creams are all over the walls, furniture, and flooring. Absolutely no color at all, except some weird artwork, by the door, tucked into a long niche with its special lighting above it.

"If I were to be murdered here, it would definitely upset your interior designer because she must hate color."

The inside of the house illuminates with soft lighting, making it easy on the eyes compared to my dangling light bulb on a pull chain in my bedroom. At least I have privacy living above the garage. This place, with its wall of windows and lights, everyone could see in. It's like being on stage, and you can't see out. It makes my skin crawl.

"I do like color, but I prefer coordinating neutrals. The home's intention is to rise and greet me with peace and harmony," he explains, dumping the armful of stuff on an oversized modern sectional that could easily seat ten people.

The front door quietly closes on its own, propelling me past the massive dark library to my left and down the wide marble floor that makes up the foyer. When I get to the end of the marble, it opens into a humongous kitchen to my right and a massive living room to the left. The house is insane, with its size and furnishings.

"That sounds like the hippiest, dippiest bullshit I have ever heard. But if I lived here, I'd probably believe it too, especially with that automatic door trick. Does Rosie from the Jetsons live here too? Will a robot be coming out to take my packages and serve me a martini?"

"Sarcasm is the lowest form of wit."

He picks up a tablet from a dark wood table beside the couch and pushes buttons that descend cream-colored shades to cover the windows at the same time, including the ones by the front door. It's kind of cool and a lot eerie.

"Your designer lady says that too?"

I look at his white carpet and then at my beat-up old sneakers and hesitate. There's no way in hell I'm getting this place dirty because when I leave here tomorrow, I don't want to give him a reason to make me come back. He stops pushing buttons and casts me a disapproving look.

"It's Oscar Wilde."

I drop my bags on the floor before sitting on it to take off my shoes. Debating on putting Anna down, I look at the cream marble with gold veins running through it and at the white living room carpet and decide the marble is best. In case she tinkles, and I have to clean it up.

When I put her down, she lifts her front paw and holds it like she's injured. I know the marble is cold. Hell, the chill is seeping through my shorts to my ass. She's going to have to deal with it for a second. She also has a sweater on, so she's fine.

"Tomlin, I don't need to know the name of your designer. I'll never meet him, anyway."

I take off one shoe and set it against the wall, out of the way, so neither of us trips over it.

"He's not a designer. He's a famous play—never mind. What are you doing?"

He points at me in exasperation and pushes another button to start a fire in this low marble fireplace that's barely off the ground.

"What does it look like I'm doing? Taking off my shoes. Duh."

"You don't have to do that. It's not required in my home."

I'm pulling off my second shoe and freeing my toes when I stop to look at him.

"Why would it be required in the first place?"

I can't help giving him a weird look because he uses the oddest word choices at times.

"Because of my culture."

"What?"

I scratch my head because I have no idea what his culture has to do with me taking off my shoes. But I also don't want him to launch into another explanation because I want to go to bed and forget this day ever happened.

"I'm taking off my shoes because I'm not about to track dirty shoe prints all over your white fucking carpet. Who has white carpet in the first place? Beside the White House and maybe the Queen of England?"

He wipes his hand down his face, and I suspect I'm getting on his nerves. Well, he's been on mine ever since he showed up in my life, so call us even.

"Unbelievable."

"Tell ya what, point me toward my room, and we'll call it a day, good?"

He releases a long sigh.

"Yeah."

I stand, leaving my shoes on the marble and then scooping

up Anna to step barefoot onto the carpet. Damn, if it isn't plush as hell when I wiggle my toes in it. He sets the tablet back on the table before rounding the couch.

"The guest wing is down that way." He points to his right, which is past the fireplace on the other side of the room. "And my quarters are this way."

He points to the left, which is a dark hallway beyond his super fancy kitchen.

"Got it."

I walk over to pluck Anna's dog bed off his humongous couch. It would be a shame not to lounge on it once before I leave, but that'll have to be tomorrow. I'm done with Tomlin, and he's obviously done with me.

He leads the way to the guest wing, which has the same marble flooring as the foyer. The lighting softly changes from dark to light as he walks. I never knew lights could be motioned censored inside a house.

Of course, we had motion-censored spotlights mounted on the outside of the garage, but that was to catch thieves. Tomlin's are way more badass. Honestly, what in this house isn't badass, other than that damn white carpet.

"Damn, how many bedrooms you got over here?"

I stop to turn around, counting the doors, and we have passed four already. He glances over his shoulder and sees that I have stopped, forcing him to stop as well. He doesn't close the distance between us, which I appreciate because I don't need to make the mistake of kissing him again. I don't know what I was thinking. Blame it on the day I've had, and the alcohol. Mainly the alcohol.

"They're not all bedrooms. The first two are my office and studio, then the trophy and gear rooms. The rest of these are bedrooms."

He waves his hand casually down the hallway as if he didn't just say he has extra rooms designated for hobbies. Note to self, get rich so I can have hobbies and not work myself to death. Then have rooms for said hobbies.

"Don't tell me you have a room of dead animals? Like laying out food for starving animals and then blasting their ass for sport, or some fucked up shit like that. And sticking their carcasses to the walls."

He tilts his head, his eyes slitting for a moment, and then he chuckles.

"Dani, you're certainly one of a kind."

With that, he turns around and continues down the hallway, passing a couple more doors before opening one.

I stand at the threshold, counting how many doors from the beginning of the hallway because they all look alike, and I don't want to accidentally end up in his carcass room.

"There are fresh linens on the bed. The tablet on the nightstand controls the drapes, television, fireplace, and lighting. The bathroom is through that door. It's fully stocked with towels, toiletries, and the like, so you should have everything you need."

When I look inside the room, it's something out of a magazine. His neutral designer must have done this room too because it's more of the same with that soft lighting and warm neutrals.

Even the chandelier hanging over the bed doesn't seem overdone. It sends glowing sparkles into the crown molding at the top of the walls. Tomlin walks over to the nightstand and touches the screen to turn on the lamps on either side of the queen-size bed. It's everything I can do to not launch myself in the middle of it to see how comfortable the mattress is.

"This room is insane."

Tomlin's head darts up from the screen with a smile.

"You like it?"

I don't miss the eagerness in his tone, and now I'm the one tilting my head and squinting my eyes.

"Of course. Who wouldn't? It's fit for a queen." His asking for my opinion is odd. "Why do you ask?"

"Because you're my first guest. This is like taking it for a test drive."

Something in the way he looks, the boyish excitement and seeking my approval, makes me forgive him for his asshole-ish behavior about the car.

Not about Carl, though. That still crosses a line.

"It looks like one of those hotels you see in magazines."

"Which one? Like the Waldorf Astoria or The Ritz?" His eagerness continues, but I don't know what to say because I have never stayed in a hotel, much less heard of those. Vacations are for the rich people that ask me to restore their cars, not for people like me that work on them.

"Uh, yeah, those," I murmur, looking around the room at some of the expensive artwork hanging on the walls.

"Thanks."

The pride in his voice is unmistakable and leaves me puzzled. He has a shit ton of expensive stuff, starting with this entire house, the custom diner garage, and even the Porsche he drives and the Rolex he wears. Yet complimenting this room makes him proud.

Weird.

Sometimes, I can't figure this guy out. He has everything a person could want, more than a person could need, but praise and correction seem to trip him up. If I cared, I'd ask him about it.

"I'd prefer the dog not be on the bed."

He makes it a point to look at the dog bed, and I toss it on the floor at the end of the bed and deposit Anna in it. She takes her time sniffing the entire thing before curling up in the corner.

"Done." I dump my purse on the bed and wait for him to leave. "You know, I tried to get Hamilton to take her, but he wouldn't. So having this dog was not my idea, but what can I do about it?"

"I know."

He sets the tablet down and hovers by the side of the bed.

"Well, if you need anything, I'll be up for a while. This is early for me. I'm more of a night owl."

He runs his hand through his hair, leaving it clasped behind his neck and massaging the tension that must be there.

"I won't need anything, but thanks for putting me up tonight."

I remember my manners when I really want to tell him to get out already. He doesn't move, just lingers by the bed looking at me.

"Of course, we're friends, Dani. I mean that. Make yourself at home, as long as you need."

"Okay."

I cross my arms, unintentionally pushing my boobs up as I wait for him to leave, but his eyes drop to them instead. Meh, whatever.

Get out, I chant in my mind.

His hand falls away from his tight neck and he smiles sheepishly when our eyes meet, knowing I busted him for looking. To say it's getting awkward as fuck is an understatement. When he finally walks to the door, I'm relieved.

"Night, Dani."

"Good night."

I wave. I don't know why I waved at him, but he needs to get out before this gets weirder. He taps on the doorframe and meanders through the doorway before finally leaving.

I cross the room, shut the door, and lock it in good measure because I haven't slept over at a man's house, so this is uncharted territory for me. At least I'm not as weird and awkward about it as he is.

20

I lean against the locked door, glad to finally be alone. Anna's nose is buried in the corner of the bed. She looks like a speck on that thing.I don't know if I'm supposed to take off her collar and sweater or keep them on. How long does she wear it until it needs washing? I swear I'm going to have to look all this shit up online.

When I walk by her, she shakes and looks up at me. I'm beginning to think the shaking means many things. This shaking looks more cold than scary since it's quiet as can be in his mansion on the mountain.

I cross the room and open the door to the bathroom, and the lights rise too. It's even nicer than the bedroom, with a claw-foot tub in the center of the room, a chandelier above it, and a wood tray over the center of the tub. It's picture-ready for a designer magazine.

The marble floors are the same ones in the foyer. The countertops have gold swirls in them to match all the gold fixtures. There are loads of cabinets, with unseen lights at the bottom to further illuminate the stone floor. Two tall cupboards flank the double sinks, and when I open the first one, it has more cream towels in various sizes than Walmart.

Grabbing one, I'm surprised at how plush it is and rub it against my skin. It's soft as can be, and I'm further convinced it's pretty fucking awesome to be rich. They say money doesn't buy happiness, but I would be happy as hell living like Tomlin.

"All right, Anna, I don't know about you, but I'd sure like to be snuggled under a towel like this, so hopefully you do too."

I exit the bathroom and the lights fade behind me. It probably helps on his light bill. Her head pops out of the corner long enough for me to cover her in the oversized towel. I double it over since it's so big, and she doesn't move a muscle. Which I assume is a good thing, since she's not shaking anymore.

"Okay, you're good, so I'm going to ..."

Why am I talking to the dog like she's a person? If this is what dog people do, I need to cut it out.

Walking back into the bathroom, the lights rise as I open the first door on the left to see two toilets. That's weird. One is a normal toilet, and the other is an open bowl with a faucet on the end. Maybe it's to wash my hands as I'm pooping? With this fancy-ass house, who knows?

The next door is a humongous closet with tons more cabinetry and a line of cream robes hanging from plush cream hangers. Is this what staying at a hotel looks like? I run my thumb over a monogram of his initials on the left breast pocket stitched in the same color of the fabric. His designer dude thinks of everything.

Closing the door to the closet, I round the corner and see the biggest glass shower I have ever seen. It has shower heads and faucets for two people, but four more could easily fit. He could have orgies in here. He has enough robes for it.

Going back to the cupboard, I sort through the towels and grab the ones I need for my shower. I quickly unbraid my hair and leave the tie on the counter for tomorrow. Peeling off my clothes and leaving them on the plush rug at the entrance of the shower, I walk through the opening.

The shower heads are so far back, the water couldn't possibly reach the exit. Unlike mine where I have to plaster my shower curtain to the walls because the shower head shoots water everywhere.

I stand naked under the first shower head, trying to figure out how to turn it on. It has a waterproof tablet mounted on the wall, and when I touch it, a chick appears on the screen asking me what type of shower I want to take.

This is weird as fuck.

It's a robot face, but the British accent sounds like a real person. All I want is a long, hot shower, and this seems like a lot of hassle. She rattles off different showers based on places around the world, so I chose the Iceland one and then wait.

The body jets start first, and they remind me of a drive-thru car wash by the sheer force of the spray. The temperature is freezing. Duh, I should have known. I'm screaming Bali by the time the shower head dumps Iceland water on my head.

The Bali shower is warm, and the pressure drops to a light mist. I don't know how I'm going to get the shampoo out of my hair with this trickle of water. She asks if I like the shower, and I tell her no, I need more pressure, and she changes it to Amazon.

It's odd having an Alexa in the shower with me. It's finally right when fat drops hit my head, and the pressure can remove the soap from my body. This experience is a trip. There are wall-mounted containers filled with everything I need, from shampoo to lotion. I get started since I'm getting on my nerves playing with robot lady over shower types.

Once I'm cleaned up, I concede it's the best shower of my life. After finding his drugstore supply of toiletries, I brush my teeth and hair and wash my face. Then I grab my underwear from the floor and wash them in the sink, laying them out to dry to wear tomorrow.

It's not ideal, but it wouldn't be the first time I've done it. By the time I hit his cloud bed, I'm as refreshed as one of my finished cars. Anna is snoring contentedly under her towel when my phone lights up on the bedside table. I grab it to see Kylie asking if I'm up to talk.

I text her back that I'm in bed but will hit her up tomorrow. By then, I'll have escaped my new bestie, Tomlin, and have gotten back to my shitty little life in town.

I stare into the dark room. His blackout drapes legit work in making it pitch black. It's weird sleeping in absolute darkness and silence. I'm used to the highway sounds lulling me to sleep and the light from Carl's sign blinking into my room. But this kind of peace and quiet at night would take some getting used to.

I should text Hamilton about Isla. Something about that girl being snatched out of a horrible situation with her molester and into child protective services is nagging at me.

I shoved it out of my mind all day, but lying here alone with my thoughts is giving me too much time to think. Opening the app on my phone, I search for his contact and am glad Tomlin saved it in my phone earlier.

> Hey Hamilton. How's Isla?

I don't expect a response right away. It's not like we are friends or dating and stuff, so when the three dots appear at the bottom of my screen, I wait.

> Danielle Louise Winters, I assume?

Something in the way he texts makes me smile. Unlike Tomlin, who seems to say it in a condescending tone.

> Yup.

> She's as good as can be expected.

> Well duh, dude. Give me the real stuff. Where is she? How does this foster care crap work?

The three dots circle and then fade. Dude types like he drives. I'm nearly asleep before he types back what should be a paragraph after how long he has me waiting, but it's only one sentence.

> Technically, I can't tell you, as she's a minor, and the legal system protects her privacy.

> Bro, I literally am the reason she's in the legal system. Did you forget I'm taking care of her dog? The dog you should have taken!

He sends a laughing emoji. Like that answers anything at all. I wait for more, and after a few seconds too many, I open TikTok and start mindlessly scrolling.

He finally responds after five minutes. Jeez, this dude would drive me nuts if I dated him. Not that I need constant communication, but I can't handle his grandma texting skills.

> It's going to be tough to place her in a home with a family because of her age. She's in a group facility for now. Hopefully, she'll tell us where she's from, and they can get in touch with her family.

> A group facility? Like a nursing home for teenagers?

That doesn't sound too bad. If I could have partied with teenagers instead of living with Dad, wait, that sounds kind of reckless. Is it like Hunger Games? Where kids fight kids to survive because Isla is a stick figure and without a temper, they'd kick her ass. Hamilton's grandma timing hits five minutes later.

> Not really. It's more of a facility where she will have a rigid schedule that she must follow and employees to ensure she goes to classes and such.

> > Sounds like jail. Do they lock the doors? Sleep on bunk beds?

I scroll through more videos while he takes his sweet time responding. I check the messaging app in between videos.

> > Dude, you text like you drive. Why are you so slow? I want to rip my hair out waiting.

Legit, I do. He's losing points on being considered for my friend list with how slowly he texts.

> Sorry, working rn.

> > Just tell me. Then you can go back to work.

> Yes, they have locked doors for their safety. And bunk beds. It's not a jail.

> > Whatever bro. Sounds like a prison. Poor girl.

> It's not.

Whatever. Sounds like it is and he's covering it up because he works for the same system.

> > Sounds pretty crappy, Hamilton. How did she end up with Rick the Rapist?

> Runaway.

She ran away to escape, and the rapist was the better option. Damn shame. My fingers hover over the buttons, not knowing what exactly to say or how to put it, so I get close enough.

> Shit. Can I visit her or something? Bring her dog to see her? Is that allowed in prison?

Grandma Hamilton takes a long time again, which irritates me because we were going back and forth steadily, and now I'm back to scrolling videos. It's almost ten minutes before he responds.

> I doubt it. It's not prison either.

> Bro, don't take ten minutes to respond and then tell me no. It probably is a prison, and she's wearing a jumpsuit and eating shitty-ass food. Get me in. You can do it, OFFICER HAMILTON.

I don't know what I'm doing. I can't get involved in this girl's life. My life is a shitshow and now I'm trying to add more crap to it. Well, hell. The kid's got no one and I have her dog. It's the least I can do.

> Get me in tomorrow. And what's the deal with my car? If there's a scratch on her, your ass is grass.

He sends me another fucking laughing emotion. Who does that? Grandmas and peace officers, apparently.

> Are you threatening an officer? Because that's a misdemeanor to a felony, six months to two years.

> I don't give a shit. Just tell me and don't take ten minutes to do it.

I almost, and I mean almost, send an eye-rolling emoji. But I'm not old or lame like him, so I don't.

> I'll find out. Text me in the AM.

>> K. Get me into both. I want my sweet ride back, and I want to see her. She needs a friend, Hamilton, so make it happen!

> Or my ass is grass?

He literally sends three laughing emojis, and I'm done. He's so nerdy, it makes me cringe lying in Tomlin's feather bed.

>> Something like that. Be safe out there.

Bro sends me a fist bump. To think I was nervous when he first pulled me over. That dude is a dork. I click my phone off before putting it on the nightstand.

It's still early, compared to the late nights I was keeping at the garage to get the Buick done. I know I should be exhausted from this shitty-ass day, but that two-hour nap did me right. I resume staring into the dark, listening to Anna snore and thinking about Dad. What would he do? Dad wouldn't have lost his temper. He was a mild-mannered guy and always looked for the best in people. His quiet confidence made him trustworthy and very well-liked by his customers.

But I'm not like him. Where he let things go, I hold grudges. Grudges over the unfairness of life robbing me of him and forcing me to take care of myself are the backbone of my life. If I'm not angry and resentful, then who am I?

Although Dad would be disappointed in my behavior, for sure. He always had trouble disciplining me. Growing up, I think he hoped I'd self-regulate at some point to relieve him from the pressures of parenting. I don't blame him. I was hell on wheels most of the time.

His wanting to let off the gas as a parent didn't bother me because I could handle my own business. He taught me how to fight behind the shop one summer. He was so worried my mouth would get me into a bad situation, and it had a time or two, that he thought it best to show me how to protect myself.

Today, my temper finally caught up with me. Now I'm going back hat-in-fucking-hand to Carl to smooth things over and get my life back. It's not all on me, though. That fucker, Judd, is the problem, and Carl, looking the other way, is the other.

It makes my blood boil when I think about it. I was so pleased with how fast I whipped the Buick into shape, and then the dominoes fell when I noticed Tomlin's car.

Dammit, I should have kept my trap shut today. I need a reminder, something to keep me from opening my mouth and sticking my foot in it. Yeah, I'm going to think about that. I burrow deeper under the piles of thick bedding and wait for sleep to come.

21

I wake with a start. My heart pounding as I get my bearings. Tomlin's place. That's right. I flip to my back, enjoying the deepest sleep I've had in months. It's his expensive cloud bed. The reality of yesterday hits me, and I groan. Dread knots in my stomach as I stare at the ceiling, knowing what I need to do today.

Get my life back.

Pushing the layers of bedding down, I pad into the bathroom to go pee and splash some water on my face. Anna's charm jingles as she comes looking for me.

I quickly shut the door to the toilet because we are not snuggling while I'm on it. She probably needs to pee herself. I hope she didn't go on his fancy floors because I don't know how to get urine out of the white carpet.

Once I finish in here, I wash my hands and inspect my eye, which is more swollen than yesterday. The sleep did me good, but it allowed plenty of time for the blood to pool in my eye socket. My cheek is super tender as well, and again, I regret not putting ice on it. Granted, it was the furthest thing from my mind yesterday.

I shrug into one of those plush white robes from the closet and carry Anna out of the bathroom with me. I don't bother opening the heavy drapes because I'd have to figure out the controls and I don't have that kind of energy this morning. It's got to be like 5 a.m. with how achy my body is.

When I open the bedroom door, the quietness of the house greets me, and I sigh in relief that I don't have to deal with him yet. We pass the first few doors when I get curious about the other one.

His trophy room.

Suddenly, I'm curious about his carcass collection. He doesn't strike me as a hunter, but then again, I don't know much about him. Testing the handle on the door, it's unlocked, and I swing it open to stop dead in my tracks. It's not carcasses.

It's him. Covering the walls of the enormous room are framed pictures of him on various podiums holding medals and flowers.

He's a champion.

There are rows of trophies, medals hanging neatly under each podium picture, and sometimes framed newspaper clippings. I circle the room, glancing at the captions and titles. World Judo Champion, All Japan Champion, Gold Medalist at two different Olympic Games, and a Silver Medalist at another.

It's beyond impressive. Everywhere I look is him, winning with a cool judo move. It's a trophy room of his achievements. How did I not know this about him? Did Kylie know?

As I'm reading the last display on the wall, his damn expensive cologne wafts under my nose, and I whirl around. Dammit, if he doesn't look hot.

He's shirtless, his pectoral muscles are carved far out from his eight-pack of abdominal muscles, and that tiny waist drops to a hard *V* shape that might as well be a direct arrow to his junk. His athletic shorts hang low on his cut hip bones. If I have to admit it, he's even more sculpted than when I drop-kicked his shit a couple of months back.

"Tomlin!"

I wave my hand at the whole room, wanting an explanation. His eyes flicker from mine down to Anna for a moment and then back before frowning.

"Yeah."

Resignation is in his voice, and I don't get it. He has an ego the size of Texas, but it's justified. If I won all this shit, I'd probably walk around with my dick hanging out because I could.

"What the hell do you mean 'yeah'? This is awesome. Here, I thought you cut down the guys in Denver from a self-defense class you learned at the mall."

I can't keep the astonishment out of my tone, especially when I point to his most recent Olympic gold medal. It's beautiful behind the protective glass. The design shines in the sliver of sunlight streaming through the side of the blinds.

"You're like a big deal and stuff."

"*Was* a big deal," he mutters, stepping around me to linger by the very picture I'm pointing at.

It's probably the best one of him doing that scissor kick to his opponent's chest. The same one he did in Denver that day.

"Was?" My eyebrows bunch together. "This room doesn't say was. It says am."

Bro is nuts if he thinks he's all washed up or whatnot. He sighs, like the longest sigh humanly possible, and plants his hands on his hips. His eyes shift, uncomfortable being in here, and I'm seeing a side of him that I've never seen before.

Dejected.

It's weird and very un-Tomlin-like.

"You gotta tell me what this is all about. How do I not know this about you? It's like you have a double life or something. This room, hell, this house, that garage, the reason you're even in this city when you have that modern museum in Denver."

"You never ask about me. You don't ask questions about my life, hobbies, or even what I do for a living. So not really hidden, Dani."

Well, shit.

His statement sucker punches me. Is that true? Have I never asked about his life?

I look away.

Yeah, I sort of made up this narrative of him being another rich guy that gets their way when they throw extra dollars at Carl and break Kylie's heart.

I guess if I'm going to give this friendship thing a try, I need to ask about his life and stuff. Aren't friendships two-way streets and I have been parked at the dead end of my sad cul-de-sac?

"Okay, then why 'was'?"

I turn to ask him, but he's wandering over to the doorway, content to watch me watch his trophies.

"Long story," he says with another exhalation, which lets me know he will not spill his guts right now. "I was coming to ask if you wanted breakfast or lunch since it's so late."

My head jerks up. "What time is it?"

"After noon, maybe 12:30 p.m."

"What?" I stomp to the window and shove the covering aside to see an endless sunny day outside with another stunning view of the mountains. "Well, shit."

"I figured you needed the rest considering your day yesterday, but when it started creeping up on twelve, I thought I should check on you, considering your shiner and getting hit in the head. I'm sorry I didn't check earlier. I got sidetracked by something."

He looks down the hall, his hand squeezing the back of his neck as if he's had a stressful day already. It never occurred to me that he'd need to work, and carting my ass around on a workday was taking him away from it.

I don't know which to address first. He's worried about me,

but I guess friends do that, so maybe not too weird. Or do I try again to pry into the 'was' a long story or discuss the fact that I slept over fourteen hours straight?

"I thought . . ." it's 5 a.m. "Never mind. I need to take her outside."

"Sure, but I must warn you—"

He moves aside, waiting for me to exit his trophy room before he closes the door firmly behind me. Did I cross a line going in there? As a host, he shouldn't have told me about it if he didn't want me to check it out.

"Warn me what?"

As we walk down the hallway, he lurks like a shadow behind me, which is basically riding my ass too closely. I'm about to turn around and erupt on him when a distinguished-looking gentleman looking at the view out of the floor-to-ceiling windows in the living room turns in our direction.

I stop in the middle of the hallway. Tomlin bumps into me and whispers apologies before passing on my right to divide the space between me and the mystery man.

The man is an older and equally hot version of Tomlin, but not as tall. Gray wisps the sides of his black hair, his eyes are more angular, and his jawline is narrower. His dark eyes bore into me as he straightens his tie.

Well, this is both intriguing and embarrassing.

"Who's this?"

His words come out as a bark at Tomlin after those glaring orbs rake me up and down. And his tone. I'm not exactly sure I like it. It sounds a lot accusatory and very unfriendly.

Granted, this man is my elder, and that warrants a level of respect, but if he doesn't change his tone. We're going to have words. Tomlin remains planted between us. His face is tense, with his jaw muscle popping out from clenching his teeth.

"She's a friend of mine," Tomlin says, his voice low and tight.

Friend.

Okay, I agreed with that.

"We talked about this. No more women and . . ."

His eyes return to me, taking in every detail from my bare feet to the robe to my bedhead. Couple that with Tomlin's bare chest and it being later than I thought, and yeah, this looks like what he thinks it is.

"Let me save you the trouble. I'm Dani Winters. I'm a *guest* of Tomlin's. I can see how this looks, but we aren't like that. In fact, your son, I assume he's that because he's a carbon copy of you."

Tomlin frowns and his dad glowers at my comment. Interestingly, they don't like to be compared to each other.

"He helped me out yesterday with a bad situation. I'm actually working on his car."

In the most indiscernible shake of his head, Tomlin lets me know I said the wrong thing.

"Another car?" His dad's voice rises in anger while Tomlin's chest heaves.

"You're wasting more money on another car? First, it's the women, now it's cars. What's wrong with you? Your mother—"

"Don't say a word about her. You don't get that right," Tomlin grits between his clenched teeth while taking a couple of steps toward his dad.

I fly down the steps and into the living room to stand between them. We don't need to shed blood on this white carpet. How would he get it out?

"Look, I don't know what's going on here." I point to his dad. "You have all the wrong ideas. Tomlin and I are not fuck buddies, so stop with that. Also, he's a big boy, so if he wants to fill up his kick-ass garage with cars and stuff, it's on him. Not you. And if you want to trash talk people that aren't here to defend themselves, well, that's pathetic."

I raise my chin because this is going in a direction I don't think is fair to either of us. His eyes glint with venom, and he steps closer to me, which puts Tomlin pressing against my back, and easily within punching range of his dad.

"You don't know my son. You're another one of his *women*." His dramatic pause after his inflection is impressive. He deserves an Oscar for his delivery.

"He doesn't need any distractions right now because he lost in Tokyo. Did he tell you that?"

I glance over my shoulder at Tomlin, his frown deepening, but his eyes never leave his dad. When I turn, the older Takahashi smirks as if he busted his son on something big. Hell, I didn't even know what Tomlin did fifteen minutes before this, so the joke's on his dad.

"I didn't think so," he gloats as if he let some big secret out.

"Who cares? It's one loss. We all have them."

I shrug, switching Anna to my other boob since I am getting a cramp in my arm from holding her against my body for so long.

"No. My son doesn't lose. And if he doesn't get back to Denver to train, he'll continue losing and disgrace the family name."

His dad's eyes flicker from mine to Tomlin's, where they remain for several seconds before he walks toward the front door. I stay rooted to the floor because I'm not following him to the front yard to let Anna go pee. She can pee on this white carpet for all I care.

"Tomlin, I expect you at the facility this week. No more playing games with your *friend*."

He doesn't even look at me. The sole focus of his contempt and rage is on his silent son, still touching my back with his chest. Yeah, his closeness doesn't sell the 'not fuck buddies' bit. He slams the front door as hard as he can, which I'm surprised didn't open itself like last night.

"Well, nice to make your acquaintance too," I say sarcastically and move away from Tomlin to put a respectable amount of space between us. "I don't even know what that was, but damn, does he do that to you all the time?"

His shoulders slump, and his jaw muscle pulses. It's not like he's in a full trance, but something similar because he stands there gazing at the front door. His mind is either processing what just happened or going back to something in his past. Not sure which, but I got to get this dog outside before she wets my hand.

"Okay, stop brooding and come outside with me." I graze his bicep to get his attention and he ducks his head in agreement. "You can explain what that was all about while she goes pee."

I adjust her bow and follow him as he weaves us through the kitchen, past a dining room fit for a queen. He leads us out to a large deck that wraps around the back of the house with various levels to get to the yard below. Past a native rock waterfall is a built-in hot tub, putting green, and sundeck. It looks like a freaking resort back here.

"Wow, this is amazing."

Once the soles of my feet hit the ground, I put Anna down to do her business. Tomlin lingers several steps up above, still lost in thought. I sit on the wooden step and pat the space next to me for him to join me.

"Spill your guts."

I cup my hand over my eyes because it's bright as hell out here and I still can't believe I wasted the morning sleeping when I have a ton of shit to do. Like get my car back, visit Isla, and crawl back to Carl with an apology.

He steps lightly down the stairs while I scoot toward the railing. The look on his face is concerning, not the usual smirking or condescending Tomlin that I've come to know and sometimes dislike. This look is bothered and seems far away, not present with me and for once, I realize that maybe I'm not the only one with problems.

"I don't have all day, so say your piece or forever hold it."

"I lost, Dani."

"So?"

I shrug. I lose all the time.

Hell, I lost my entire life yesterday and I'm not moping around, letting an old man get in my head. Well, half true. I have a cranky old man in my life, but he's not in my head yet. That comes while I'm apologizing later today.

"So? I've never lost. Sure, I didn't place as high when I won that silver medal, but the rest were gold."

For the first time since he sat, his eyes flicker to me and they practically burn into mine looking for something. Answers or solace?

No idea.

"You're literally sitting on this step crying over losing one competition when you have a crap ton of other medals. What the hell is wrong with you? I'm not good at statistics and shit, but I'm pretty sure a small percentage of the world can't even qualify for the Olympics, then an even smaller percentage of that wins medals. You're talking about being number one all the time at all matches over all the years you've been doing that judo stuff. That's insane to expect you would never lose. It's statistically impossible."

I'm not a magician or mathematician, but even I know it's not possible.

I shake my head, not even understanding what this dude is thinking. He has a room full of gold medals and gold trophies, famous to some people, maybe not me, so isn't that enough?

"You don't understand, Dani. It affects my ranking. Going into my next competition, I might not be number one."

He runs a hand through his damp hair and gazes off again.

"You're right. I don't understand. Tomlin, you have it all.

You're great-looking, stupid fit, and rich as hell. You lost once, in Tokyo, or twice, if your stupid ass considers a silver medal a loss, and you're having a midlife crisis because your old man is an ass to you."

Anna stands at the bottom step, her eyes level with it and she lets out a little whimper to come up. I swear, she held this dog way too much, so what do I do? Pick her ass up and cuddle her on the lap of my robe.

"He's not wrong though," Tomlin mutters, reaching over to touch her bow with his index finger. "I should get back to training. I used that loss as an excuse to leave and hang out here. Or rather, hide out here."

He drags his foot up one step to drape his elbow on his knee, seeming more dejected the longer we talk.

"Don't let one loss fuck with your head. Win or lose, it doesn't change the fact that you have two amazing houses, some fancy cars, and hell, you have a huge-ass room dedicated to your victories. That's cool as shit. And I'm pretty sure you can bang any chick you want. What guy wouldn't want to be you?"

I lean against the staircase, planting my elbows on the steps behind me to give Anna more room. She crawls higher up my lap, circling three times, and then lies down. He mimics my actions, his body so much longer than mine.

"It's not enough."

I jerk my head to look at him and when our eyes meet, he looks like he's about to cry.

"How is all this not enough?"

I can't believe my ears. He's got to be the envy of every dude everywhere. Hell, I'm even envious of parts of his life.

Like I said earlier, if I was him, my dick would be out twenty-four-seven.

"Do you ever get lonely?"

His dark chocolate eyes never leave mine, imploring me to

crawl into his loneliness with him. Drown in it as he seems to be doing now.

I blow out a breath and look at the mountains.

When Dad died, I was painfully lonely. Like my soul hurt by the quietness of the apartment at night. It's why I had my hoe phase. I went on a bender and mistook sex for companionship. Without a doubt, it was the darkest and loneliness time of my life.

Then I stumbled on Zach and our text booty calls. It filled the void of needing a physical release, but beyond that, I've never allowed myself to feel emotionally lonely again because it hurt too much. It still hurts if I'm one hundred percent honest with myself. But I'm not going to admit that to Tomlin, especially after that kiss mishap last night.

"I think everyone feels lonely at times," I say, returning my gaze to his solemn face.

Good general statement to keep him out of my business.

"Not everyone. But you, specifically."

Dammit, Tomlin, for digging around where your nose doesn't belong.

I debate how much of this new friendship thing I really want to try out with him because I don't want him using this shit against me.

"How do you mean?" I ask, watching a hawk soar in the sky behind him and making a mental note to never leave this dog alone outside, or else she'll be a hawk treat.

He hesitates, his gaze drifting down to my lips and lingering there before returning to my eyes.

"Finding the one."

"I don't believe in that crap."

"You don't want someone for you? Someone, to be at your side cheering you on and pushing you to be your best? Someone to walk through this life together with common goals and to build a haven where only two people exist? No asshole dads and no asshole bosses."

He's searching my face, my eyes, everything to draw it out of me. To bring me to the place where his desolation and despair reside, so he's no longer alone in his place of emptiness.

I can't explain the lump forming in the back of my throat and the sudden sting in my eyes, but somehow, he struck an abandonment so deep within me, I had forgotten about it.

What would it be like to have someone stand up to Carl or Judd? Someone who had my back. Who would stand up for my rights and what I believed to be fair without always having to fistfight for it?

To have a real man, like my dad, who wouldn't put up with any of their bullshit or mine. That would call a spade a spade and put me in my place or rein me in when I'm the wrong one. A yin to my yang, a cool balm to my hot temper.

Damn Tomlin for opening my mind to things I hadn't thought possible after losing the only man that did this for me.

"I don't know," I murmur, frowning like him.

"I don't know either, Dani." He cups his hands behind his head and closes his eyes. "It sounds good in theory, but I don't think I will ever find that in another."

Out of the corner of my eye, he looks relaxed, stretched out, and sunbathing on his back deck. Like that song lyric, his river runs deep. Deeper than I initially thought. And I agree. I don't think I'll ever find someone that will accept me as Dad did.

22

"Well, on that depressing note. I need you to drive me into town to see about my car, and my job, for that matter." I sit up, cupping Anna as I reach for the handrail. His eyes flutter open.

"Carl said don't bother coming back if you're going to steal his customers," Tomlin says so flippantly that I jump to my feet.

"Come again?"

"He assumes you are working on my car since it got towed up here. I assured him that you are not, but he didn't believe me."

I snap my mouth closed, waiting for him to crack a smile and say, "Gotcha" like it's April Fool's Day or something. But the longer I wait, the less likely that is, and reality starts to sink in. I hold up my hand and roll it into a fist, wanting to knock Carl out. But Tomlin will do because he's literally right here and can hold his own.

"Wait a minute." I take in a deep breath, trying to calm down because I don't think I heard him correctly. "So, I'm fired and homeless?"

He drags his body from the stairs to stand beside me.

"I'm not sure about your apartment, but he was fairly stern about terminating your employment."

I climb the rest of the stairs and set Anna down on the deck to lean over the railing because I feel like I'm going to vomit. The robe is too hot, my skin is getting sticky, and my stomach is cramping all sorts of bad right now.

This can't be true. There is no way I'm suddenly unemployed. Like I woke up this morning feeling fine with the hope of returning and now I have no job and no way to pay my bills.

It's fucking scary.

I hate the way this feels. I hate the betrayal stirring in my gut from all the years I worked like a dog in that shop being sexually harassed. One day, I put my foot down and take a stand, and I'm fired. It's always a boy's club with those fuckers.

And what about my home? The place I grew up and shared with Dad. His old chair and the newspaper that sat beside it waiting for him to come home. I know it doesn't look like much to anyone else, but that place is mine. It's the very essence of who I am.

"Dani."

Tomlin touches my elbow, and I wrench it away. It's not his fault, but I want it to be.

"Why didn't you tell me this before? Or come get me when you were on the phone with him? This is all your fault, Tomlin. Don't you see that?"

Anger surges through my body. I have to blame him. He can handle the guilt. Hell, pile it onto that shit, his dad said.

"This is my life we're talking about. Are you happy? Did you get what you want?"

I'm so mad and shocked, I can't even look at him. Snatching up Anna, I storm off the deck, through the house, and into the bedroom, where I slam the door as hard as I can. I dump Anna on her bed, much to her dismay, to grab my phone from the nightstand. It's nearly out of power, and I'm about to call Carl, but then stop.

"What do I even say?"

My thumb hovers over his name when there's a knock on the bedroom door. Tomlin slowly opens it. The face he has when scolded is the same one he has now, and I roll my eyes before sitting on the edge of the bed.

"Dani, I'm sor—"

"Don't even start."

I tap the side of my phone with my fingernail, and surprisingly, he sits next to me on the bed. It's weird because no one I yell at seeks me out afterward. They usually leave me the hell alone to ruminate on how much I hate them. Tomlin dives right into the conflict, which is a first for me.

"Yesterday, I was so proud of myself for working day and night to get that Buick done. That fucker, Carl, should have been glad, but instead, I'm out. Just like that? Judd can lick my neck and stick his pin dick in my butt crack, and I'm fired for defending myself."

I adjust, scooting farther away on the bed to face Tomlin.

"It's a boy's club. It's been blood, sweat, and tears all these years for me. I gave him everything I had and then some. He used me up and spit me out when he was done with me. Now that piece of shit Judd gets rewarded for all my hard work. Like all the credit will go to him. How's that fair? I was never going to be one of them, was I? If I was older or had a dick swinging between my legs, then maybe I would have been worthy enough to stay. It's always the men that get away with all the immoral and illegal shit. Fuck being a strong woman in that fucking place. Those motherfuckers, I hope bad shit happens to them. Like they die a horrible death in the most painful way possible."

Tomlin listens to me rant. Slowly his hand inches forward,

requesting to hold mine. Hell, I don't know why I consider it, but I drop mine into his palm for his long fingers to curl around my knuckles. His hand is calloused and cool, opposite to my hot and sweaty one.

"Can I say something?" he asks in the calmest voice I have ever heard from him.

"Sure, what?" I shrug one shoulder.

"I'm sorry this happened. It was never my intention when I pulled the car. Maybe I should have thought about the repercussions of my actions on you."

His confession makes me pull my hand away because even though I blamed him, it's not his fault at all. Tomlin was right last night in the garage when he said it's a business to run, not an emotional therapy session. Carl, letting his emotions get involved in making business decisions, is on him, not Tomlin.

Yet, I defended Carl in my mind and took his side against Tomlin. But who's in here now trying to hold my hand to comfort me through the second worst thing that has ever happened in my life?

"No, this has nothing to do with you. Trust me, Carl has been looking for a reason to stop putting up with my shit, and this is the perfect one. Bringing Hamilton there didn't help because he probably thought I went and got the police involved."

I fling my phone on the bed to stand and pace, scratching my forehead as I think. The room is quiet for several minutes. Tomlin grabs the tablet to press some buttons for the heavy drapes to slide back to let the bright sunlight in.

"You can stay here," he murmurs as I stand near the glass. "Until you have everything figured out."

I lay the side of my head against the window. Do I stay with Kylie in the city, closer to everything? Well, what everything? My whole life was in one place and now I can't go there. Or do I stay here, in the remote luxury resort, with my new friend and nothing to do?

"I'll think about it."

I'll need to find a new job, but with my limited skill set and not having my GED, who will hire me? I could take Tomlin's car, somehow get my tools wrestled away from Carl, and pack up my apartment. Possibly, get a storage unit for all my crap.

Damn, this shit sucks.

"Are you hungry? What about the dog?"

Tomlin stands, putting the tablet on the stand.

I lift my head off the glass, glancing down at Anna piled on the towel from last night.

"Shit, I forgot about that. Yeah, I need to feed her."

"I'll find some bowls if you want to get dressed."

"My tote has the bowl from the restaurant if you want to use that." His mouth opens and closes, choosing to lift an eyebrow at me. "What? Like they're going to miss it?"

"We'll return it next time we are in town."

He crosses the room, nearly out the door when I say, "I need to go back today. I appreciate you taking me in yesterday, but this is my problem that I need to handle."

His large hand splays across the doorframe, gripping it too tightly, judging by the white growing around his knuckles.

The tip of his chin dips low enough to glance over his shoulder and says, "Okay."

It's weird because I thought he'd put up more of a fight. Rattle on about his car or how I can stay here and work on it for him, but today he's different. Very introspective and sort of aloof.

I don't know if it's his dad scolding him for losing and missing training. Or how he basically didn't defend himself at all and only stood up for his mother during said scolding. Or if it was the loneliness conversation on the deck. I can't figure him out. But I don't have time because I have to figure my shit out and I'm itching to get back to the city to do it.

He doesn't say anything else, just pats the frame once before walking out. I grab my phone to check my text messages. Kylie is demanding that I call her ASAP. Hamilton says he's still working on today with Isla, but my car has been cleared for pickup and sends me the address to the impound lot. Zach texted in the middle of the night for a booty call, but nothing from Carl. Not that he even knows how to text, but he did leave a voicemail yesterday. I'm too pissed to listen to it.

I rub my forehead, desperately needing coffee because it's way past my normal time for consuming it. Combining that with the stress from yesterday and knowing I'm fired is contributing to the start of another migraine.

With no more texts to view, I walk into the bathroom to check if my underwear is dry from last night. Thankfully they are. I get dressed, use Tomlin's toiletries again, and cuss when I break my hair tie. Looking worse than yesterday, with the black and blue of my eye setting in deep, I exit the bathroom to scoop up Anna, all my stuff, and her dog bed. I'm determined not to stay here again.

I don't know how or why I decided so fast, but carving out a new life isn't for me. Tomlin would back me and put me up here, but that's too much help coming from the same source. Dad raised me to be independent. I thought I was, but now I realize I depended on Carl for both my livelihood and my housing. Look where it got me.

"What a fucking mess," I whisper, walking down the hallway of closed doors and into the living room to dump all my crap on his humongous sectional before putting her on the floor.

Tomlin's looking stylish in the kitchen, wearing a white T-shirt, black jeans, matching boots, and a silver chain at his throat. He's mixing his fussy cup of coffee with a second cup right next to it.

"Is that for me?"

His head lifts, his body twists, and when he sees me, he smiles. Not his pantry-dropping one, but a sad one.

"Yes, I know how much you like your coffee, so I figured . . ."

His hair is perfectly styled, with a ray of sun cutting through the rectangular window to sparkle against the black ink color. He's as gorgeous as ever. He sort of shrugs, setting the spoon on a linen cloth protecting the white marble countertops to take a sip of his.

"I have nothing to eat other than protein bars?"

His hip leans against the cabinetry while watching Anna tiptoe at my feet. His state-of-the-art kitchen has a wall of gadgets that I have no idea what some even do. I hustle over to the steaming hot liquid gold in a dainty teacup to blow rings and cool it off.

"Hello, lover."

I take a big gulp and practically melt at how great it tastes.

"Christ."

"Shut it. I've earned this coffee. Hell, I've earned coffee for every day of my miserable life." I blow more rings under his watchful gaze to gulp the rest.

"Damn, this is the best coffee I have ever tasted, but why so stingy with this tiny cup? Your ass can afford to give me a whole mug."

He smiles. A real one this time that clears away the fog of emotions hanging over him.

"And she's back. Tits out and sailor mouth engaged. I was beginning to think I lost you to curling up in your bedroom and crying like a girl."

Your bedroom.

Damn shame he thinks I'm staying here.

"There's no such thing as 'crying like a girl.' It's just crying.

Idiot. And I don't cry, certainly not over men." Except for three years ago when one man ripped my heart out and took it with him to Heaven.

"Cussing doesn't bother me. It adds to my charm."

"You have charm?" He chuckles, his gaze sliding down my body with the same appreciative look that I did to him.

Mixed signals, Dani. Mixed signals.

"Anyway, I set the bowls out for her over there."

He points to a little mat on the floor with two matching white china bowls near the windows. Both are already filled and ready for her.

"Thanks."

I pick Anna up to set her in front of them. She guzzles down the water and sniffs at the wet food that sits in a can-shaped clump in the center of the bowl. When her eyes look up at mine, I shake my head.

"I don't know what to tell you. Eli said no more human food."

Tomlin remains planted against the counter, content to watch us.

"What?"

"Nothing."

He doesn't stop staring at me, nor does he move from his spot other than to sip his coffee.

"Out with it. You don't say half the stuff running through your brain. I get it, but you don't have to be all guarded with me. It's impossible to hurt my feelings. And I need more coffee and some of that protein crap you eat to look like this."

I gesture my hand up and down at his perfect physique. I'll eat real food after I get my car back, and we go our separate ways.

"Okay, killer, calm down. I'll get you another one."

He swipes the tiny cup from where I left it to start pushing buttons on a machine built into the wall that makes a bunch of racket.

"It's an espresso machine. That's why you like the coffee so much. It's basically like you're drinking coffee beans."

"No wonder that shit is so good. Why were you staring at me?"

He walks away while the machine spins and grinds out the next perfect cup of coffee. I bet this thing cost more than my car. When he reappears, he has a fistful of bars for me to choose from. I pluck one from his hand, and he tosses the rest onto the counter.

"I was thinking how alike you and I are."

I choke on my spit.

"Come again?"

I pull on my earlobe, sure I didn't hear him correctly.

"You don't think so?"

"No, not at all. You're rich, I'm poor. You've got two homes, and I live above a garage. You have a job, and I was fired today. You have, I don't know how many cars, and mine is at an impound lot. You have chicks, I got no cocks, so excuse me if I don't see it."

The machine stops sputtering, and I carefully remove the scalding hot cup from under the lever. He must have let this sit to cool off, so I switch to opening one of his protein bars. I'm a huge bite in when I decide these are good too.

Does this dude have anything crappy in this perfect place?

"How I see it is we are both fiercely independent. Don't like to be told what to do. Don't always respect others' opinions because we know what to do and how to do it. We're both meticulous about our work and don't like the drama and hassle that comes with people."

I think over what he said while chomping on the bar. "Yeah, that's mostly true, but I don't entirely hate people, only the annoying ones or the ones that fire me."

"That might be everyone at some point because I feel like I annoy you all the time."

I grab my coffee and blow rings into the liquid before sipping from it.

"You do."

My smile is hidden behind the cup, and when our eyes meet over the rim, he winks and smiles back.

"That cup doesn't hide anything." He walks over to his, drinks the rest, and rinses it out before placing it in some cool dishwashing drawer. "Are you ready to go?"

"Yup."

I shove the rest of the bar in my mouth and try to gulp down the drink, but it's way too hot.

"I need to load her stuff in the back."

He stops reaching for his wallet and keys to look at me. "You're not staying here?"

"I appreciate the offer, but no," I say firmly because I don't feel like going into why.

He stuffs his wallet in his back pocket and twirls his keys on his index finger.

"How about this? Take the day to think about it, and if you still don't want to stay, I'll pack up the dog gear and bring it to wherever you are staying."

It's such a waste of his energy and gasoline to drive it down to me, but fine, whatever.

"I'm not leaving her here."

Because hopefully, Hamilton gets me into that prison for visitation later today.

"Agree. But you can't bring the cup in my car," he says, walking out of the kitchen and fumbling with Anna's tote in the living room.

I tilt my head and realize he likes to get the last word in. I guzzle down as much as I can stand, burning my tongue in the process, and snatch another bar off the counter so I can have one in my purse.

When I join Tomlin in the living room, he already has Anna in the tote and is holding the bowl to return to his friend's restaurant. I turn to look at her food bowl, and the clump sits untouched. Hmm, I'm pretty sure I can't feed her protein bars, so maybe Eli can help.

23

Tomlin leads the way to the front door, carrying Anna in her tote while I grab my purse and shove my phone in it. Part of me is glad that I don't have to load all this dog junk because it's starting to feel like I have a toddler with a diaper bag. And that immediately gives me the icks.

On the other hand, I don't want to come back here. His offer to drop all this crap off is generous, although I'm suspicious that he has another agenda.

He waits at the open door, his hand resting on the handle while the other holds the tote with Anna's head popped out of the top. Together they look like a magazine ad. It could be that he's hot as hell, and she's adorable in her pink bow. What am I saying to myself?

Get your shit together, Dani, and stop fangirling over him.

I walk past him without a backward glance to prove to myself he's not that damn attractive. I jog down the steps and race over to his garage. Not caring if Tomlin minds or not, I throw open the side door and his car is sitting in the empty bay.

It's as if this space has been awaiting her arrival. Something about seeing her in his diner garage seems kind of romantic.

Sure, the other cars are more on period with his decor, but this one speaks to me. She'll be stunning when Paul fixes her up.

I can't resist popping the hood, reaching for my phone to turn on the flashlight, and looking at her engine. The hood squeals when I lift it. Nothing a little WD-40 can't fix. And that's when I see it. Judd stripped out all the parts and took her down to the block.

Utter bare bones.

Not exactly at step one, but pretty damn close. I shine my flashlight all over until the overhead lights flood the place. Over my shoulder, I glimpse Tomlin setting Anna and her tote on the floor to join me.

"What happened?"

Why is she stripped? Judd was further along than this. It would have been done by Tomlin's timeline for submission to the show.

"What do you mean?"

His shoulder brushes mine, and there is a haunting look on his face.

"What do you mean, 'what do I mean'? She's stripped. She was seventy percent done. You would have made your deadline."

The lingering smell of motor oil is faint in my nose, meaning he drained her today and not yesterday. My eyes keep wandering the engine, new things popping out everywhere.

"I told Carl to take out everything that didn't match. Turns out it was a lot."

His tone is dejected. I almost feel sorry for him after his dad bitched him out and then, getting her back in almost the same shape, he dropped her off.

He's definitely having a bad day.

"Wow." I purse my lips together, moving my flashlight around to investigate. "This sucks."

My gaze darts from him to the car, unable to make sense of

the wasted time and money, and basically Judd lying to him this whole time. He grips the back of his neck, squeezing it as he does, and I completely understand why. This is very disappointing.

"I won't make it, will I?"

Turning off my flashlight, I shake my head, my eyes still surveying all the lost progress.

"I don't see how."

I hate being honest with him, but damn, I have to because this is so bad. He doesn't say anything else when he wanders between his other cars. I close the hood, the squeal echoing across the silent garage, and then I circle the car.

Judd didn't even start on the bodywork while other parts were left to seal. Tomlin is right, Carl should have had better knowledge of the quality of work Judd was putting out.

If he did this to Tomlin's car, did he do it to others? I never really paid attention, as I had my own heavy workload. I probably should have now that I think about it.

But I wasn't his boss. Maybe Tomlin was right last night. It's not a hobby shop, it's a business that Carl failed to run. When I get to the trunk, there's a big cardboard box sitting on the floor. It's all my tools haphazardly thrown in it.

Seeing a smear of black on my pink-painted handles, I pull one out and see the word "BITCH" in marker across it. I pull out another and another, all tagged by Judd. Tomlin's cologne reaches me before he does. I show him what it says.

"How juvenile," he murmurs, squatting beside me to pick through the box.

"I assume these came with the car?"

I turn my head. His face is inches from mine, and his gaze falls to my lips, as it did on the deck. I abruptly stand and walk to the front fender. If I were to admit, there is an attraction between us. Combustion, he said, but he shut me down last night. Something that has never happened to me.

I'm glad he did, but something about it still bothers me. I can't decide if it's my ego that's bruised for having been rejected or if I'm offended for not being good enough to sleep with him.

"Yeah."

Whatever he's holding clangs against the other tools when he drops it in the box and then stands at the back fender, diagonal from me. The disappointment is clear on his face as he scratches his chin, thinking.

I don't want to take his job. I don't want to live here doing it. So, I say nothing at all, waiting for him to come out of his trance to drive me back to my life in town. I walk over to Anna, pick up her tote, and give her a few pets until I catch his eye.

"Right, let's get going," he mutters, crossing the garage and clicking the lights off to plunge his disappointing car into darkness.

Wordlessly, he trails behind me. The only sound is the call of the birds above and the crunch of the gravel below. I'm almost at my car door when his hand comes out to open it for me.

"Thanks."

I settle into the car, putting Anna in her tote on the floorboard and adjusting the air vent to keep her comfortable. When he drops into the driver's seat beside me, I dig out my phone to get the address.

"I have the address. Do you want—"

He takes my phone out of my hand to punch the address into his navigation system.

"Why are all these lots in the worst part of town?" he mutters almost to himself.

"No idea, but do you know where it is? I don't recognize the address."

"Yep, I know."

I catch something in his tone that says he knows it all too well. The longer I'm around him, the more of a mystery he is.

Yet, I don't want to get too involved because this enemy to friends is already enough of a change. Plus, I have too many other things to worry about than unpacking him.

"Okay, I'm going to text Hamilton."

Tomlin messes with his playlist, putting something chill on as he pulls out of the driveway and starts the winding drive back to the main road leading down the mountain.

"Is it me, or was that officer hitting on you?"

I raise my eyebrows when I gaze at him, but he slid those damn sunglasses on when I wasn't looking. I hate not being able to read his face because it's so expressive.

"Jealous?"

The corner of his mouth pulls into a half smile.

"Another thing we have in common is big egos."

"Let me break this down for you. I get hit on All. The. Time. It's the fun bags effect."

I pull down the visor to check my eye in the mirror, hoping it doesn't look that bad when I get to the impound lot because I don't want any trouble getting my car if they think Tomlin did this to me.

"Fun bags?"

"Fun bags, hooters, knockers, melons, tits, boobs, whatever you want to call them. I've heard them all since this rack ain't new. I've had these suckers since I was fourteen, so I'm used to the ogling." I press against the puffiness surrounding my eye and hiss at how sore it still is. "Hell, I use it to my advantage because you all are really big babies wanting to suckle at the tit again."

Those sunglasses reflect my face for so long that I use them as a mirror to smooth the flyaways at the crown of my head.

"That's not true. Some men like a great ass or thick thighs."

He turns to the road, and I return to the visor mirror to put on my lip balm.

"I don't care what you like, I'm just saying men always look but whatever. Once I get my paint job, these suckers are next."

That paint job is evaporating faster with each bad hit I take. I snap the visor closed and pluck Anna from her tote when she lets out a tiny whine. She circles my lap and then snuggles against my stomach. I lay my head against the headrest and close my eyes, relaxing into the ambiance of the car.

"What does that mean?"

His voice is soft and imploring, sounding closer to my ear than I prefer. I open one eye to ensure he's not leaning toward me before closing it again.

"Gone. I'm getting them chopped off."

He coughs. I open my eyes to see him taking off his glasses to stare at me. Surprise is smeared all over his handsome features.

"Why on God's earth would you do that?"

Boys and boobs are as intertwined as milk and cookies.

"Cuz assholes like you stare at them constantly."

As if on command, his eyes flicker to my boobs.

"Don't. We're not going back to asshole again." The warning in his voice is clear that he graduated from asshole to his proper name. "And you have to admit, they are perfect."

"Duh."

"But there's nothing wrong? Like medically required or cancer?" He sounds genuinely confused and concerned at the same time.

I snort at his question. It's like asking a guy to reduce their dick because it's too large. They couldn't possibly understand.

"No, these fun bags are perfectly fine and dandy."

"That's good, but why cut off something so—"

"Cuz, I want itty-bitty *A*'s and not these damn double *D*'s. So, when I have enough money, they're coming off. End of story."

My temper flares because it's my body to do what I want with it.

He opens his mouth and then snaps it closed. Good, he should know better than to throw his opinion at me. I couldn't care less.

I snatch my phone from my purse and open my messages. I text Kylie to see if she can grab dinner tonight.

Then I text Eli for help with Anna because he picked out her food during their sampling session, so why isn't she eating it?

Tomlin puts his sunglasses back on, and the wall between us goes right back up to where I'm most comfortable having it. It's called, mind your own business, and I'll do the same. I hit on Hamilton's message, the address being the last line.

> Hamilton, will the impound lot give me any trouble? Ya know, with my black eye?

I want to type more, but I don't exactly know what to say. I've never had my car towed, so I don't know what to expect.

> Look, I don't want to get there and have them all up my shit. I want to walk in, get my car, and drive out.

Yeah, I need some assurance that one fucking thing will go right today. I already overslept, which sucks because it puts me behind. Plus, I need to get clothes and get back to my apartment. I tap my fingernail against the side of my phone, knowing he won't text back immediately.

I gaze out the window. The landscaping is changing from isolated mansions to populated commercial shopping strips. The closer we get to town, the more I relax, knowing this will all be over in a matter of hours. I'll have my car, talk to Carl, and be back home.

My phone pings. Tomlin glances at it but doesn't say anything.

> Want me to meet you there?

Hamilton's offer is generous. Do I?

> I don't want to bother you, but if it will make it easier, then yes!

I wait, the three dots circling before the answer comes back.

> Not a bother. What time?

I look at Tomlin's navigation. It doesn't show the time, only the route.

"Do you know how much longer until we're there?"

"Why?"

"Because Hamilton's going to meet us."

His head whips around to look at me, his lips set in a line under his glasses.

"He volunteered?"

"Yes."

Did I say something wrong?

He doesn't say anything as he taps on the navigation screen and points to the time. Once he puts his hand back on the wheel, we return to silence among the chill music floating around the car.

> We'll be there in twenty minutes. Is that too short of notice?

> No, who's we?

> Tomlin, the guy from yesterday, is bringing me.

I wait once again, tapping the side of my phone to the beat of the music.

"Can you stop doing that? It's annoying." Tomlin barks, and I drop my phone in my lap next to Anna to start playing the bongos on his dashboard. "Forget it."

He cuts a curve too fast, jostling me toward him. My phone flies to the floorboard while launching Anna toward the console. Luckily, I catch her before she hits it, but she's shaking as fast as my racing heart.

"What the hell?"

I brace one hand on the door, and the other is smashing Anna against my side boob to calm her down.

"It got you to stop banging on my car."

"You could have hurt the dog, dumbass."

I swear, the faster I'm away from him, the better because he's annoying me as I am him. Leaning forward to retrieve my phone, Hamilton's brief reply is on the screen that he'll be there.

Good. I want this to go as smoothly as possible so I can get away from everyone. I swear, if I didn't have more pressing issues, I'd drive out to the Royal Gorge and spend the day figuring out my life.

We stay silent, neither willing to break the standoff. I'm content to stare out the window and watch the buildings change from commercial business parks to run-down, boarded-up houses.

When Tomlin rolls to a stop, it's in front of this super high steel fence with no openings or way to see inside. Sitting beside the entrance is a pole with a button on it to call. I don't see Hamilton parked outside this walled fortress, so I assume his ass is already inside.

Tomlin's window glides down to press the button. It takes a few moments until a voice cuts through the static to say, "Hello."

"Yes, we are here to retrieve a car. I believe Officer Hamilton arranged for our pickup."

Tomlin's voice is smooth and authoritative. And I think back to what he said about having someone there for you. This is the kind of stuff I'd want to be handled by someone who had my back.

"What's the name?" the female voice cracks over the speaker.

"Danielle Louise Winters. Do you need me to describe the car?"

Tomlin waves me off when I start to list what kind of car it is.

"Hold on."

He settles back in his seat, touching his watch to look at the time.

"This place closes at 3 p.m. Good thing we got here when we did."

What I read as an annoyance for having to take me here is him ensuring we could still get in.

"Yeah, good thing," I mumble.

It takes a few long seconds before the steel gate rolls open to reveal a narrow pathway between dozens and dozens of cars parked haphazardly all over the lot.

"I swear, if they got so much as a scratch on her, I'm going to—"

"What? Fix it yourself?"

"Sarcasm is the lowest form of wit."

I mimic his deep voice, in the same way, he said it to me. He merely shakes his head and rolls up his window.

24

We creep past rows of vehicles until we come upon a small trailer with a deck attached to the front. Without a proper parking lot, Tomlin is left to figure out where to park safely to avoid getting his baby hit by the tow trucks plowing through this place.

Grabbing Anna's tote from the floorboard, I gently place her inside, much to her displeasure. When he finds a spot, I'm up and out of his car at lightning speed with Anna on one arm and my purse on the other. I don't bother waiting for him when I charge up the stairs and fling open the door.

The place reeks of smoke, with the walls crying from the yellow staining. It takes my breath away literally as my lungs seem to constrict by the stench in the air.

The furniture is worn with two guest chairs held together with duct tape and two more smeared with motor oil. This place is as much a dump inside as the area around it. It must be the city trying to save money by owning this cheap piece of land.

"Help you?"

The female from the speaker is sitting at the only desk in

what must have been a living room at one time. How she works in all this smoke is beyond me.

"Yeah, I'm Dani Winters, here to pick up my truck that was towed yesterday."

"Have a seat."

Her flaming red drugstore-colored hair sits in an impossibly tight chiffon at the back of her head. It has to give her a headache by the end of the day. She points to the taped-up seat with long cheetah-patterned nails.

Reluctantly, I sink into the old chair that squeals under my weight while I put Anna's tote in the chair next to me. Tomlin glides through the door, tucking his sunglasses into his shirt breast pocket and joining me.

"You with her?"

She points one of her cheetah nails at him.

"Yes, ma'am."

"Then you can have a seat next to her. I need to pull her file."

She rolls her chair out before picking up her cigarette and stuffing it in her red lipstick-stained mouth.

"I'll stand, thank you," he replies before she walks through a closed brown door. "The smell is pungent."

As if right on cue, Anna sneezes three times in a row, and her little charm clinks against the inside of the tote. She paws her face, trying to stop the smell, but that chance died thousands of cigarettes ago.

"I thought they banned indoor smoking years ago?" I ask as he eyes the peeling walls with disdain.

He's probably never smoked in his life. The thought of putting all those chemicals in that shrine of a body must be horrifying to him.

"They did, but who's going to drive all the way out here and tell her?" he mutters, walking toward the window and dipping a finger through the pee-colored blinds. Anna sneezes three times again and continues pawing her face.

"You need to take her out of here. She's small, and this is probably too much for her tiny lungs."

He doesn't bother turning around to look at us when he says it. I look from him to the brown door, hoping she'll come through it at any minute.

"I don't want to miss her. Can you take her outside?"

That question gets him to turn and face me.

"No, she's your responsibility. Just go, and when she comes back, I'll get you."

His eyes cut me a look as if he doesn't want to talk about it anymore. After how things were in the car, I expected him to stay in it and not come in here.

Maybe he debated with himself about that before he walked in. If the roles were reversed, I'd have dropped his ass at the gate and sped off. Fine, I'll give him this.

My phone buzzes in my purse when I stand. Pulling it out, Hamilton texts he can't come, but wants to talk about Isla when I'm done. Hopefully, I can head there when I get my car out of here.

Deciding that's my next step, I text him my status and that I'll call him when I'm on the road. He thumbs up the message, which is pretty good for his usual grandma texting.

"What's up?"

When I look up, Tomlin is lurking over me, and I step back.

"Not that it's any of your business, but Hamilton's tied up and not coming."

I adjust the strap of my purse on my shoulder to make room to carry Anna's tote. I don't miss the slight change in Tomlin's expression.

"Don't be so smug. It's not like I'm dating the guy or whatnot."

He merely shrugs to appear disinterested, but he doesn't

deny it either. Whatever. Anna sneezes again, and I pick up her tote and walk to the door.

"I'm going to go find my baby and make sure this shithole didn't hurt her, or else I'm coming back in here and ripping some new assholes in these fuckers."

I wag my finger to emphasize my point and amusement rims his eyes.

"Ah, Danielle Louise Winters, I wouldn't expect anything less."

I throw open the door, fresh air caressing my cheeks, and even I breathe better away from that smoke. Feeling sorry for Anna, I pluck her out of the tote as we walk through the row of cars, looking for mine.

"That place was too much, huh, Anna?"

She sneezes another time, her bow flying around her little head. If I were into being responsible, I could see how Isla wanted this little dog. Hopefully, I can hand her over this week and focus on me again.

Weaving through the vehicles, I catch a glimpse of gray in the far corner of the lot where the river runs alongside the barbed wire fence. As I make my way over to my baby, a tall tree of a man stands next to her. He stoops down by the tire, and I bolt over to him.

"What the hell are you doing?"

I dump Anna back in her tote because if this guy is messing with my car, I'm going to have to kick his ass, and I don't want her to get hurt in the process.

He stands when he hears me, and I grossly underestimated his size. He's built like a bear. Tall like Tomlin, but easily fifty or sixty pounds heavier than that judo champ.

"Uh, sorry. I was checking—is she yours?"

His clump of brown hair hangs in his eyes, and some acne dots his face, but his voice is soft, opposite of his intimidating stature.

"Yeah, what's it to you?"

I move Anna into the shade of the adjoining car and plant my hands on my hips.

"I-I was admiring her. You don't see many in this good of condition."

He scratches his curly mop, moving it away from his bright blue eyes, and I realize this guy is around my age.

"Yeah, well, I did the work myself."

Those blue orbs widen into saucers. Yeah, I'm used to that reaction.

"You did this?"

"Yep, I'm a preservationist up at Ca—"

I stop because that's not true anymore. The line I've said for years that falls from my mouth with regularity now feels weird to say. Reality sinks in causing me to frown at this dude.

"You restore?"

His smile is shy, and his eyes dart away from mine while his cheeks burn bright red. His bear paw lingers on top of the hood.

"Used to, in school. But I'm done and looking for a job. It's hard because people want experience, but no one will give me a chance to get that experience, ya know? Like a catch twenty-two."

"You went to school to restore cars?"

His curly mop shakes when he nods.

"I have a bachelor's in restoration technology."

They have a degree for what I have been doing for years. Damn. How easily could I get a degree with all my experience? Shit, I'd have a doctorate by now. Would it even be worth anything? Probably not if this guy can't catch a break even with a degree.

"What's your name?"

The paw that rests on the hood is swinging my way for a handshake.

"Lars Myers."

"Nice to meet you, I'm Dani."

He grips my hand entirely too tight. If I didn't work on cars all day and had a lot of hand strength, he would have crushed it. His cheeks are red as hell.

I'd blame the heat of the day if I didn't see his eyes flutter past mine to something behind me. He jolts his hand out of mine as if he was caught with it in the cookie jar. Glancing over my shoulder, a scowling Tomlin is crossing the lot. I ignore him because I want to learn more about this guy.

"Wanna see under the hood?"

His eyes fall back to mine, and then the biggest crooked grin pops up on his face.

"You don't mind?"

His hands clasp together, flexing and relaxing, and I know what that means. He wants to get his hands dirty. Yep, that's the sign of a grease monkey.

"Show off my baby? Hell no, I don't mind."

I dig through my purse for my keys, and when I'm about to open the driver's door, Tomlin approaches. His keen eyes survey the situation, his mouth opening to say something, but I ignore him to open the door, pop the hood, and start the engine.

Through the windshield, Lars is looking down, and Tomlin is standing in front of him. Once they shake hands, I breathe out because I know Tomlin wouldn't pick a fight as I do. However, this dude's built like a mountain, and seeing Lars as slightly taller than Tomlin and bigger, I'm not too sure. Although, this Lars guy doesn't seem like much of a fighter. He seems uncomfortable in his own skin.

Lars lifts the hood, blocking my view, so I step out to see him already bent over the engine. Tomlin is leaning against the car where Anna's tote is resting in the shade.

"You did all this?"

Lars's eyes are wide again. I like how easy he is to read. It's also not bad that he appreciates the badass work I have done.

"Yup. As I said, she's my baby."

"All original parts?"

It's a statement that comes out as a question. He already knows the answer and the surprise in his voice is evident.

"Yep, took forever. Just waiting for my sweet custom paint job, and then she's done."

That sweet paint job is evaporating now that I have to find a job. Damn shame. Lars ducks under the hood, his fingers brushing across everything as he mutters to himself. I step back to stand beside Tomlin.

"Fellow enthusiast?"

"Something like that." I lean against the car, my elbow brushing his. "You smell like smoke."

"Yeah."

His lips flatten into a line. If I know anything about him, he's taking a shower when he gets home. He'll probably burn those clothes too.

"I guess I need to go in and pay."

I kick off the car when Tomlin touches my shoulder.

"I already did." His hand comes up when I open my mouth. "I wanted to get out of there as fast as possible, so I handled it."

"I can't blame you, but how much do I owe you?"

"It was five hundred."

"Like dollars?"

Wow.

That's a huge chunk of my paint job money.

"Dani, don't worry about it."

Tomlin takes his sunglasses out of his breast pocket and cleans the lenses with a cloth. I know five hundred dollars is probably like a five-dollar bill to him, but it's a lot to me and too much to be owing him. If anything, the stupid police department owes him that money for towing my car into evidence. Idiots.

"I'll pay you back. I have money in savings, so once I leave here, I'll go to the bank."

I squint against the sun and look out at the river flowing with ease. Why do some people have all the luck and poor suckers like me don't have any?

"If you'd like," he murmurs before slipping on his glasses and the wall that goes with them.

I now know he uses those things as an emotional buffer when things get too real, or he doesn't want to talk about it. I swear, I'm jealous because I wish I had thought of that ploy to avoid talking to people.

"You ready to go, Dani?"

"You don't have to wait for me. Go ahead and go."

He slowly shakes his head, dropping his chin to dead stare at me over the rim of his glasses.

"I'm not leaving you alone."

He doesn't even look in the direction of Lars, but the inflection in his voice is unmistakable. He leans over to grab Anna's tote before handing it to me, clearly ready to wrap this up.

"I can handle myself."

"Dani, you are already nursing one black eye. Do you need another?"

I hate saying that Tomlin is right because I don't really know this guy, but his disposition says he wouldn't hurt a fly.

"Hey Lars, I need to take off but give me your number. I know of a place or two that I can call and see if they will give you a shot."

Lars pops his head up too fast and hits it against the raised hood, eliciting a soft curse word. I step forward, about to help, when Tomlin's hand wraps around my bicep to stop me. I guess he's worried about how this guy will react since he hit it pretty hard.

"Sorry," Lars mumbles, rubbing his head, and his cheeks flush with embarrassment. "You don't mind?"

Tomlin's hand drops, concern abated, and I pull out my phone.

"Nah, type it in here, and I'll text you when I hear back."

I hand him my phone. The car fumes are getting a little much with how long I let her idle in the hot sun. Not a good idea on my part or for the environment, but what the hell? I enjoy hearing her rumble. He grabs the phone, using his thumbs to tap it in, before handing it back to me.

"Thanks a lot. I'll do anything. Start at the bottom. I need someone to give me a chance."

"I get it. I'll let you know."

He steps aside, carefully to not get too close to Tomlin when he passes him to wander the lot. When he's out of earshot, I turn to Tomlin.

"You know that guy wouldn't hurt a fly?"

"Can never be too sure. He's built like—"

"A bear. That's what I was thinking."

I nibble my lip, wondering how the hell I'm going to get him a job when I need one too. Maybe Miller has an opening?

"Not what I was going to say, but sure, a bear. Anyway, are you good? You and Anna?"

Tomlin's sudden change from lingering to being in a hurry piques my interest.

"Why, you gotta get somewhere?"

"Something like that."

"All right, well, have fun with her."

I assume it's a chick, seeing how fast he's trying to get this wrapped up. He opens his mouth and then closes it again, his keys hanging from the loop, circling his finger.

"Let me know where to drop the stuff," is all he says.

Now I'm more curious about what he's up to.

"I will. You sure you're okay?"

I give it one more try. I know we're not in the best spot with each other, but something's bothering him aside from my annoying ass.

"I'm fine, Dani."

His voice deepens with finality and I'm familiar with that too. He's definitely not fine, but he also doesn't want to talk about it.

"Okay then."

His jaw muscles clench as I stare at my reflection, then shrug because I have nothing left to say. He gives me a quick nod and rolls back those wide shoulders while I wave away the overpowering exhaust fumes that are threatening to choke us. How Anna's not sneezing from this compared to the smoke inside the trailer is beyond me.

I turn toward my car, opening the door to put Anna on the seat so she can cool off in the cold air conditioning. His back is to me, walking away when I call out to him.

"Hey, Tomlin?"

He half turns, his hand catching the keys that he is twirling.

"Thanks for everything."

"Anytime," he says, leaving me wondering if he really means it before he weaves through the rows of cars to his own.

Usually, I wouldn't dwell on him, but something about how we leave it bothers me.

"Today's shaping up to be another weird day."

25

I plop into my driver's seat, and reality sinks in. It's a regular workday, but I'm not at work. I'm unemployed for the first time in my life. It's surreal.

Thinking one thing and doing another. I used to daydream about days like this. About being free as a bird to set my schedule and possibly have a real life outside of that garage. Now that it's been thrust upon me, it's not right.

It wasn't on my terms. It was an injustice that happened to me, and I'm living with the consequences of others' decisions. My life hangs in the balance, and he doesn't care. Carl is only about himself and the almighty dollar. My feelings from this morning still haven't changed.

I hope he burns in hell.

Judd too.

My hands circle the steering wheel. At least I have my baby back, one thing restored to my life. I look around the inside of my cab and admire my work. I'm meticulous, which shows, and that guy Lars even admired my craftsmanship.

It's nice to be appreciated by someone who knows cars.

Sure, my old clients loved me when I restored their babies, but to be appreciated by someone in the industry is validating.

My phone pings and I grab my purse to pull it out. Kylie can't make dinner because Ryan is coming over, but she can meet now for an early happy hour. For the first time today, I smile. Yeah, I could go for a beer and wings at our place. I text her back, saying I'm on my way.

I toss my phone next to Anna's tote before moving her to the floorboard. Seeing how I'll be taking her everywhere for the foreseeable future, I need to figure out how people drive with dogs and keep them safe since my first priority is keeping this dog alive.

With that thought, I pull out of the parking spot and slowly navigate through the cars that are parked too close together. It takes a few precarious maneuvers to get out of the lot, but when I pass the metal gates, energy surges through me. Cruising in my classic car feels like home.

The drive to the bar is short, and when I pull into the lot, it's mostly empty. I'm unsure if Anna is allowed in, but she's coming. I park at the front, throw my truck in gear, and roll up my window. Debating on waiting in the truck or waiting in the bar, I decide inside is better because that protein bar is long gone in my belly. I need some real food. So does Anna, since she didn't eat her dog food this morning.

Yanking open the door to the bar, my eyes adjust to the darkness, and Anna sneezes. Granted, this place is old and musty, but not the smoke shack at the impound lot. I slide into a booth on the far wall and throw an index finger to greet the bartender. He's not the one that usually serves us, but he nods back, so I know he'll be over to take my order.

Reaching for my phone, I text Kylie that I'm here and ask for her food order. Lord help me if she orders another salad in this dump.

"What can I get for you?"

"Two Coors and two glasses of water. A basket of tenders and fries, ten pieces of sriracha wings, and hold on—" I glance at my phone, waiting for her text, but nothing. "I'll let you know about the rest."

"Got it."

He casts a questioning eye at Anna, standing on her hind legs, scratching to get out of the bag, but he doesn't say anything. I pretend to be arranging the silverware he set on the table with a clump of napkins.

I can't imagine the dog being a problem in this dive since I doubt the health department ever visits. If they did, it would be shut down immediately.

My phone chirps with Kylie's order. Cobb salad. Of course, because that girl never learns. I add her order to mine when he comes over with two frosty beers. I take a long swig of mine and savor the taste.

Leaning my head against the back of the booth, I glance around at the bar patrons. It's only Anna and me, except for a businessman making out with a woman at the corner table. They're too engrossed in each other to notice I'm here. Judging from the gold ring on his finger and the lack of one on hers, I'd bet it's a little tryst the wifey doesn't know about.

Reason number one why I won't marry.

Men are cheaters.

Plus, I can't imagine sharing my space and being around someone every day in a row. Reasons number two and three.

The bartender brings the basket of wings and celery, mumbling about the rest coming out soon. My mouth instantly waters when I smell them. Wasting no time, I dive into one and moan obscenely. Anna yips at me, but there's no way I'm giving her this. She'll shit everywhere. I don't have the time and patience for that crap. Literally.

Going back to my wings, I polish the first one off and dump

it back in the basket to reach for another one. I'm three wings in when Kylie breezes into the bar.

"Damn, your eye."

She dumps her sweater and purse on the bench as I touch my eye in response.

"It's not that bad."

I pick up another wing when the bartender brings the rest of our food. His eyes linger on Kylie's ass sticking out while she's bent over the booth, rifling through her purse.

"Kylie."

Her eyes slide to me at the mention of her name, and I glare at him. He mutters something, and she takes the hint by sitting her ass down and rummaging through her crap.

"What are you doing?"

"Oh, I'm looking for my phone because I wanted to show you the flowers Ryan got me today," she explains, coming up empty-handed. "But you're more important, so what happened?"

I roll my eyes. Why she thinks I'd give a damn about flowers is beyond me.

Anna barks, scratching at her tote, and I tear off a tiny piece of a french fry to feed to her.

"OMG, that's the cutest dog ever. Can I hold her?" she gushes.

Kylie has always been maternal. I swear if she found 'the one', she'd be knocked up before I could finish saying knocked up.

"The bartender already scowled at me over her."

"Since when do you care?" Kylie's hands are already in my face, trying to reach Anna, but the booth is too wide. "Gimme that dog, and then explain why you have it."

She's right. Let the guy say something to me. I extract her from the tote, and Kylie's eyes light up. The moment I set Anna in her hands, the baby voice starts, and I want to vomit on my wings. She plasters the dog to her face, smothering Anna in kisses and letting the dog lick her lips. Yup, I'm going to hurl.

"You know their mouths are like cesspools of germs and bacteria?"

"Says the girl with motor oil under her nails," Kylie's retort isn't wrong, except today. I raise all ten fingers to show her and then reduce them to double middle fingers.

"Okay, tell me everything, and don't you dare leave a detail out."

I take another drink of my beer, nearly finishing it before launching into the longest, most annoying thirty-six hours of my life. Kylie listens intently while eating her salad and making out with the dog.

"Don't give her any of that dressing. I don't want her to have the shits in my car."

I wave a french fry in her face, and she snatches it up to tear it into little pieces on the table before putting Anna on it.

"Get that dog off the table."

"She's fine. Let the girl eat in peace."

Kylie tries to stab my hand with her fork when I attempt to snatch Anna off the table.

"So, where's Isla now?"

"In some group home. Hamilton says it's fine, but it sounds like a fucking prison. I'm trying to get in to see her today, but hell, if I know how much more I can help. I mean, I got her dog and keeping that tiny thing alive is a priority. Plus, I got to figure out how I'm going to pay my bills."

I shovel a tender in my mouth while Kylie chews on her lip for a moment.

"I say good riddance to that place. You don't need Carl and you know it. You could open your own place. With your client list, you'd be making money hand over fist."

She shreds another one of my french fries for Anna as she talks.

"I'm not stealing Carl's clients. That's a fucking death sentence in the restoration business. And I still need to get into my apartment, pack it up, and move God knows where."

I motion to the bartender for two more beers, even though Kylie hasn't touched hers yet. Not a problem, I'll drink both of them.

"Easily solved, you can stay with me. You know I only have one bedroom, so sleep on the couch, and when I'm at Ryan's, sleep in my bed."

That's what I expected her to say, except for the part about Ryan.

"You're sleeping over now?"

"Yup, he likes having me over, and I like the breakfast he makes me in the morning." She winks. "If ya know what I mean."

Once again, this entire bar knows what she means, including the bartender that drops the beers off. He is about to say something to Kylie about the dog when she raises her fork as a threat to him, prompting him to shake his head and wander behind the bar.

"That problem is solved. Now employment. I didn't think there was anyone else in town that does car stuff as you do."

She smothers her salad in dressing to the point that it cancels out any health benefits.

"Unless you can do regular cars and not those old geezers' cars."

"There's not. That's the problem."

I wipe the wing sauce from my fingers, debating on if I should tell Kylie about my other offer. The wrinkles between her eyebrows let me know I should since she's deep in thought trying to figure out my problems.

"Tomlin wants to back me."

"Huh?" She stops stabbing at her salad to stare at me. "What does that mean?"

"He pulled his car from Carl's, and it came back stripped of all the inferior work that Judd did. That's what the fight was over."

"Okay, but I'm still not following you."

"Basically, he wants me to finish his car."

"Really?"

Her eyebrows go up and then fall back down as the surprise wears off.

"Well, you could. He's a customer, and you need a job, so it would work. And honey, if you are worried about me, we're good. I moved on with Ryan. Tomlin and I made amends, remember?"

I sigh, dropping my half-eaten wing on the discard pile to extinguish the blaze on my tongue with more beer. I remember. It was not too long ago that he ate my wings, insulted me, and sort of apologized to Kylie.

"But you don't have a shop, and he lives in Denver," she says, her mind cranking through the details that I'm weary of sharing because she might find this to be a good idea after all.

And my I-don't-want-to excuse is just that, an excuse because I really don't want to work for Tomlin. I didn't when he asked the first time and got Judd, nor this time.

"Actually, he has a killer garage at his house in the mountains."

Her mouth falls open as she blinks at me. Anna paws her hand, and Kylie silently shreds another french fry before collecting herself.

"I don't know where to start first. Wait, how do you know this?"

"I stayed there last night."

"You didn't mention that a minute ago when you told me that long-ass story."

She huffs in annoyance, setting her fork in her salad to lean back in the booth.

I groan, deciding to come clean with my bestie because I really need her help.

"Fine. When my car got towed, he took Anna and me in for the night. Even made me brick oven pizza for dinner."

"Wait, I'm still wrapping my head around he has a place here. That bastard made me drive all the way to Denver to see him."

She crosses her arms over her chest, her face turning pink with anger.

"Clearly, you are over him."

I chuckle, breaking off a tiny piece of my chicken tender so Anna can have at least a bit of protein to go with her fast-food diet.

"Anyway, it's a humongous mansion at the top of the mountain, with an epic garage decorated like a 1950s diner. He already has some other classic cars there. He had that rust bucket of his towed out of Carl's and up the hill this morning while I was asleep. It's bad. Judd wasted so much of Tomlin's time and money, it's obscene. I looked it over today."

"So . . ." she starts slowly, leaning forward and putting her elbows on the table. "You would have a job and a place to stay. Is that what I'm hearing? I assume he'll put you up in his mountain mansion if you already stayed the night in a place that I didn't know existed until now, even though I dated him for months."

It's my turn to lean back and cross my arms because this isn't the conclusion I want her to draw with her accusatory tone.

"Do you not hear yourself? Do you not hear what's wrong with that?"

Her head shakes, and she pushes her salad aside to guzzle her beer.

"No, Dani, I don't. It's not grade school, and I'm not calling dibs on him. But he must really want you to restore his car if he's letting you spend the night, and with a dog. That blows my mind because he dislikes kids and animals. Well, kind of like you, something you guys have in common. But anyway, why not? It's like Carl's but better since it sounds like a nicer place to work, and you won't be harassed and felt up. That's huge."

"You're missing the fact that my boss or a business partner, as he said it, would be Tomlin. TOMLIN," I emphasize because she's clearly missing the point.

As she sets her beer down, I pick mine up, needing liquid courage to even think about going into business with him.

"What do you mean?" Her tone is full of skepticism. "A business partner?"

"That's just it. He wants to front me in a new business venture. Like I'd be the new Carl's Timeless Classics and work on his car as my first one and then get customers from there. But damn, Kylie, I'd be doing double work. Restore the cars and be Carl."

"It sounds amazing."

Awe spreads over her face as if I said I was marrying the man.

"It sounds miserable."

"Dani, this is leveling up. Getting out of that hovel you've hidden in. You said it yourself, there's no competition to Carl's, and you always bitched about how he ran the place. To become your own boss, well, that's wonderful. That old man took advantage of you and worked you like a dog."

She sits back, a dreamy look in her eyes as she plucks Anna from the table to kiss her again. I pick through my wings, finding an uneaten one to chomp on while stuffing my mouth with fries. I must be missing something.

Tomlin thinks he's brilliant over this offer. Kylie is fantasizing about it, and I still don't want to take it. The longer she smooches the dog, the worse the idea sounds.

"Again, do you hear yourself?"

I'm unable to comprehend how both are on the same side, and they don't even know.

"You should have heard him last night. He was cutthroat about how Carl runs his business, like Cut. Throat. I'd be part-nered with that. He'd be a nightmare to work for or with. I don't know which one."

She levels me with her eyes in between Anna's bow and ear.

"Since when do you take shit from anyone? I'd never worry about you. I might actually feel sorry for Tomlin this time."

I drop the chicken bone on my discard pile and slide the basket to the edge of the table. My mouth is on fire, and I need another beer. I point my index finger in the air to get the bartender's attention, indicating one more. When he nods, I return to watching Kylie love all over that animal.

"Why don't you take care of her? You seem to love her already."

"Because I work long hours, today excluded, and you know that. And, you promised that little girl that you'd take care of her." She wags her finger at me, and I look down at the crispy tenders in my basket. "Don't change the subject. You have no good reason to turn down Tomlin's offer, and you know it."

"I have plenty of reasons for turning it down."

I don't have plenty.

I have one. I don't want to.

"You know what I think?"

"No idea."

She waits while the bartender drops off my beer and I immediately pick it up.

"I think you've met your match in him, and you don't like it. Admit it, you're attracted to him."

I choke on the foam, sputtering to get it out of the wrong pipe and into the right pipe. I beat on my chest to swallow and breathe at the same time. My eyes water when I set the mug down to grab my napkin.

"Are you okay?"

She leans forward in concern, setting Anna on the tabletop again to reach a hand out to me.

"Fine."

I cough a bit more and clear my throat until I'm finally able to talk hoarsely.

"Let's get one thing straight. Tomlin can be an asshole, and I called him that for months. Sure, he's hot. Did you know he's a famous judo champion? His trophy room is ridiculous. He was blabbering on about losing his last match, and then I met his dad. It was a mess."

Now, she's the one trying to recover. "Y-you met his dad?"

"Yeah, now I know where Tomlin gets his assholeness from."

She blinks, her mouth hanging open as she processes.

"What?" I ask and shrug at the same time.

"His dad is his coach."

"Okay?"

What am I missing? I'm sure plenty of dads coach their sons. Hell, look at the Manning family.

"He hates him. I never met the guy, but Tomlin and he would get into shouting matches on the phone sometimes. Don't tell him I told you, but his dad used to beat his mom until Tomlin was old enough to intercede."

I drop the chicken tender I'm holding to stare at her. Images from this morning click through my mind. It's why he didn't defend himself. It's why he only defended his mom. It's why every time I scold him, he gets all weird about it.

"Damn."

"Yeah, he told me that in confidence, so don't use it against him." Her index finger shakes at me from across the table.

"I'm not one hundred percent heartless." But it explains a lot. "Where's his mom? Denver?"

"Dead. He wouldn't tell me the details, just said she was gone."

"Like my dad," I echo.

I know what it's like to love a parent and hate another.

"Yep. So cut the guy some slack. I know he can be temperamental and high-strung but underneath all the physical machismo, is a little boy missing his mom."

"No, don't turn this bullshit into a Hallmark moment. He's still famous, rich as hell, in amazing shape, and can get any girl he wants. Trust me, he's not crying in his pillow at night."

I shove half the tender in my mouth, forcing my cheek to ball out with food.

"Why do I ever think you'll be compassionate with people?"

She huffs, breaking up a couple more fries for the dog pawing at her hand.

"Compassion gets you this?" I point at my shiner. "And this." I point at the dog.

"Looks like my girl is finally growing up."

I pick up a french fry and throw it at her. I hate that she's a few years older than me and gets all motherly sometimes. I blame her mom because that woman smothers Kylie more than gravy-covered biscuits with the amount of meddling she does.

"I've got to run. I want to shower and change because Ryan's picking me up for a concert tonight in Colorado Springs." She digs through her purse and throws down two twenty-dollar bills when I object. "Don't. Pick up the next tab. Anyway, I'll hide a key in the flowerpot for tonight, so you have the place all to yourself. Oh, and no inviting Zach over. I don't want his jizz on my sheets."

I wrinkle my nose because I don't even invite Zach over to jizz on my sheets.

"Don't worry, I won't."

She picks up Anna to kiss her about a hundred more times before setting her back on the table.

"Have fun tonight and make good choices."

She laughs as she slides out of the booth to collect all her stuff.

"I'm making only naughty choices from here on out. If you know what I mean."

"Yup."

She winks and hustles across the bar, waving to the bartender looking the other way.

I look at Anna and say, "Well, looks like we have a place to stay."

26

Sitting with my legs propped on the booth bench Kylie vacated, I move Anna to sit beside me and empty the basket to pour water in it. She laps it up and I join her in downing the rest of my water before sharing the last of the fries.

It's nice of Kylie to pay. Something I didn't expect but offering me her couch or room when she's not having a sleepover with Mulvaney is expected.

As my gaze wanders to the lady in the corner table slipping underneath it to give the guy a happy ending, I think about what Kylie said. Or more specifically, why she thinks it's a good idea to work for Tomlin.

Every time I think about it, my answer is an immediate no. I want to return to my old life because this weird unknown that I find myself in is uncomfortable as hell.

My phone pings with a message from Hamilton. He can get me in tomorrow but doesn't know the time yet. Good. The sooner I can see her and show her Anna, the better. Poor kid is probably freaking out in there. I know I would be if all my choices were taken away from me.

Speaking of choices being taken away, I need to get my shit together and go to the shop to talk to Carl. Dropping off my tools with the car definitely means I'm fired. Tomlin confirmed it, but Carl needs to let me into my apartment.

Deciding to get a move on it, I finish my beer, tuck Anna into her tote, and slide out of the booth. I don't bother waiting for the bill. Kylie was too generous with her money, so the dude will get a nice tip. Plus, he's preoccupied with the oral sex couple that he's charging across the bar to handle.

I push open the bar door and blink against the intrusion to my eyeballs. It's not as bright and sunny now that evening is beginning, but compared to the dark bar, it's bright.

I glance at my watch, seeing it's nearing six o'clock, and I'm losing precious time. Unlocking the door, I slide in and set Anna's tote on the floorboard. A passing thought of seeing if I can use the seat belt to buckle her in for better safety floats across my mind, but that's a task for another time.

I need to get over there in a hurry if I want to catch Carl and avoid Judd. I'll beat his ass again if I see his damn face taunting me about getting fired. Throwing the truck in reverse, I peel out of the parking lot and then realize I don't need to take my anger out on my baby since I just got her back.

I also don't need another officer pulling me over for speeding. I might not get lucky as I did with Hamilton's grandma ass. My knee bobs as I drive, trying to release some of the adrenaline coursing through me as I turn down the highway leading to my old life.

It's odd how fast I was ejected from it. A mix of anger and anxiousness nips at my nerves. To say I'm on edge is an understatement. My fingers tighten around the steering wheel when the garage comes into view. Judd's fucking crotch rocket is parked in my fucking spot, and Carl's car is gone.

Dammit to hell.

Just my shitty luck.

As if the universe has my back, the skies blacken around the place, matching the foul mood coming over me. I was going to appeal to Carl's good side when I got here. With that bastard Judd darkening the doorstep with his presence, my anger builds and I'm itching for round two.

My headlights flash across the bay doors and into the dark lobby, where a large sheet of plywood covers the lobby window. That was quick. I guess Carl figured out someone else could pick up stuff and bring it to the shop after years of making me do it. I throw my car in park on the side of the building, out of Judd's sight.

"All right, Anna, remind me that I can't get arrested for murdering a man tonight, or else your little ass will be at the pound while I sit in jail."

Opening the driver's door, I loop my keys on my finger, hoping he didn't change the locks, and shove my phone in my back pocket.

Anna yips in excitement when I clutch her tote handles. Glad one of us is happy to be here. I approach the front door, half wanting Judd to see me coming so I can threaten his ass, but knowing he's probably working at his station. When I slip my key into the lock, I'm surprised it still works.

I fling open the door, forgetting about that damn bell attached to the top. When it jingles throughout the lobby, I yank the door closed, trying to silence it. I'm not fast enough as Judd steps through the glass door leading to the bays.

"What are you doing here?"

His accusation drips of venom, and my hand clenches around Anna's tote.

"I live here, dumbass."

I take a few steps forward, noticing the way the light from the garage falls across his face, making me hate him even more. The scent of motor oil and tires that cling to this place is making me even more homesick to climb those stairs, close the door, and forget this ever happened.

"Question is, what are you doing here? You never work this late."

If we're hurling accusations, I have one of my own. He's such a shady shit, I wonder what's going on.

"None of your fucking business after Carl finally fired your lazy ass." His lip pulls into a sneer.

Lazy ass is hardly an insult. I worked like a fucking dog in this place.

"Do I need to say it again? Why are you here in my garage? You were kicked out and then fired, so leave."

He crosses his arms over his chest, the effect supposed to be intimidating. The fact that he has a white strip across his nose, and it's swollen as hell, makes me smile sweetly at him.

"Or what? You wanna another go at me? I already broke your nose. You want me to break those itty-bitty balls too?"

I step up to his face, glaring at him when a half-naked girl huddling behind a stack of bald tires is in my peripheral. When I turn my head, she darts behind them.

"You sneaky shit. That's why you're here this late."

I step toward her, but Judd blocks the doorway with his body.

"It's none of your business."

"It's none of mine, but I'm sure Carl would be interested in hearing about your hanky-panky."

His face is in the shadow with his back to the garage lights, but I can still make out the flash of panic that crosses over it.

"Go ahead, see if he'll take your call."

Little does he know, his eye candy is peeking out behind him, trying to cover herself while retrieving her clothing from my old workstation.

Disgusting.

As much as I hate him, this isn't my problem anymore. If he

wants to bang chicks in Carl's shop, who am I to care? It's not mine, anyway.

"Maybe I will. But I need to get some stuff, so carry on."

I step back, seeing relief sag his shoulders that I'm not calling Carl just yet. The girl scrambles to use her dress to cover her generous assets.

"Your shit is outside."

I try to process what he means, but I don't understand.

"Huh?"

"Did I stutter? Your shit is outside by the dumpster."

Panic seizes my chest, and sucks the air from my lungs.

The realization of what Judd is bragging about hits me. I nearly miss the counter when I drop Anna's tote on it to race up the back staircase. I try to fling open the door, but it's locked.

When I jingle my keys to find the right one, Judd bellows from below, "He changed the locks."

Rage surges through my whole body and I shake. My pulse is beating a thousand times a second, and there's so much pressure in my head I think it's going to explode. Blood slugs through my ears, and I turn to repeat what he said.

"He ch-changed the locks?"

Now my face is in the shadows, and Judd's is brightly lit when he looks up the narrow stairwell.

"What did you expect, Dani? That he'd let you waltz back in here? You're working on Tomlin's car, which I should kick your ass for, but good riddance to both of you. Pompous prick thought he owned this place."

I close my mouth once I realize it's been hanging open this whole time.

"I'm not working on his car, you nitwit."

"Not what your boy told Carl, and not what Carl told me when I broke it down." He grips the railing, planting his foot on the bottom step. "Doesn't matter, anyway. I get your backlist, so good luck finding a job after these clients find out that you dropped them in the grease."

"I didn't want any of this to happen. It's your fucking fault for all the years of bullshit and harassment. Don't you think I could come after you both? I have the right, you know. I can sue you and him. Hell, I could make this place my own if I wanted to."

"Go right ahead, but no one will come here because your reputation is ruined. You'll never do another job again, so go ahead and take your little boyfriend's car. It will be your last," he taunts and I'm ready to rip his balls off his body as I pound down the stairs.

"Baby, I'm going to go."

Judd mouths, "Fuck you" before disappearing around the corner to handle her.

"Don't go, sweetheart. She's leaving, and then we'll be alone again," he murmurs, with smacking sounds following.

I nearly gag at her loud moaning, and I don't even want to know why.

Stomping back up the steps, I stop on the landing to rattle the lock a jillion more times. The glass door to the shop squeaks, and I know Judd won't risk losing a little pussy to bicker with me.

I pace the small landing, debating what to do. Thankfully, I have my truck bed to load stuff in, but Kylie doesn't have enough space for it all. Plus, if I leave my stuff in the truck bed in her apartment complex, it will get stolen.

Fucking Carl.

After all the years Dad and I worked for him, this is how I'm treated? Cast out with barely a five-minute conversation between us. I fucking hate old men. Now all my belongings are by the dumpster. My hands roll into fists, hoping every bad thing imaginable happens to him.

"Fuck it."

I square up in front of the door and haul off to kick the flimsy thing open. Of course, I can count on him to buy weak-ass locks. When the frame splinters and the door flies open to an empty room, my heart plummets.

I can't believe what I'm seeing.

Nothing.

My entire life is gone.

The walls are bare, the furniture is missing, and the place is even broom-swept. I'm utterly speechless as I stare into my apartment. The one I shared with Dad. Where the couch turned into a sofa bed and became my bed every night. Where Dad would sit in that chair by the window and read his news-paper, sometimes reading to me as I fell asleep. It was our ritual.

I cross the threshold, my hand clutching the splintered frame to brace myself against the shock. The small kitchen where I bitched at Tomlin was the same one Dad would flip pancakes on Sunday mornings.

It was the floorboard in the hallway that squeaked when I had to pee in the middle of the night. It was the place I played trucks on the floor as a kid, did my homework at the kitchen table, got my period in sixth grade, and grew these huge-ass boobs in eighth grade.

It was all the lonely nights, waiting for Dad to come up from the shop to eat TV dinners and share what we did that day. It was all the evenings in middle school that I'd sneak down to bring him a beer and watch him work, hand him tools, and play on the creeper.

So many memories of this place. A time capsule to my childhood, and my soul aches now that it's ripped away. I never got rid of anything because everything meant something. Granted, I turned this apartment into a museum dedicated to him. A place where he didn't exist, and I didn't really live.

Neither of us thrived, and I was comfortable with that. Dad

and I were getting by, living paycheck to paycheck, and it was fine, safe, and known. Now, my future is as wide open and as empty as this apartment. I have no safety net, home, job, livelihood, or idea of where to go from here. I was gone one day, and he threw out my entire life.

Flipping on the hallway light to walk into my bedroom, my stomach feels hard as a rock. Dread settles in deep as each room confirms what Judd's already told me. Seeing it for myself makes it worse, but I have to. I wouldn't have believed him.

My footsteps echo on the bare floors when I leave my bedroom to check the bathroom. I don't know why, but I pull out my phone to take pictures. I never took them when I lived here, and Dad couldn't afford a smartphone, so I'm not even sure I have ones from when he was alive. I guess it's the only thing I have left. That and my stuff sitting at the back of the building.

When I pass the squeaky board in the hallway, I stop and walk across it a couple more times, trying to commit the sound to memory, as this will be the very last time I hear it.

Water clouds my eyes, and I try my fucking hardest not to cry, but damn it if I don't quickly wipe my tears as they fall. Anna's shrilly barking travels up to me. I don't know if Judd's messing with her or not, but I've got to go.

After sniffing in my boogers and drying my eyes, I take a few more pictures before I say goodbye to the only home I have ever known. I'm doing good holding it together when I catch the door handle and lean against the splintered doorframe. My gaze falls to Dad's corner, and my eyes blur with tears once more.

"I'm sorry."

I lick my lips and mash them together, trying to hold back the wave of sadness and regret my actions caused in losing the home he provided for me.

That's when I know I need to take one more picture—his

corner. It doesn't matter that it's empty, and the foil has been removed from the window. I'll never forget what it looks like when I close my eyes. After taking it, I lock my phone and shove it in my pocket to slowly close the door behind me.

Sorrow and loss fill my body as I sag against the wall. I've always been a fighter, not one for crying, but dammit if I want to sit on this step and bawl my eyes out.

Seeing as how it won't do any good, I draw in a ragged breath and force myself down the stairs to hear rhythmic thumping on the other side of the wall.

I'm relieved to see Anna is fine in her tote bag. She must have been lonely down here all by herself. That makes two of us. I'm done with this place. I dig my keyring out of my front pocket and twist the garage keys around the circle until it's free to set on the counter. With one last look around the lobby, I pick up Anna's tote and walk out the door, the bell chiming for the very last time.

The sky is dark, with the clouds lying low and smothering the stars. I get in the truck and set her tote on the passenger seat while pulling around to the back of the building. When my headlights flash across my furniture sitting to the side of the dumpster, I death grip the steering wheel wishing it's Carl's neck.

My blood boils at how inconsiderate Carl is to have thrown my stuff out like the trash. Even after all the years that Dad worked for him. Hate me, that's fine, but damn, this feels like a betrayal to Dad.

That crosses the line.

Leaving the motor running so Anna has air conditioning, I stomp on the parking brake and slowly open my door, careful to avoid knocking over boxes of my possessions.

Dad's chair is the first priority. It's buried under a ton of kitchen crap that can be tossed since I don't have a kitchen. Checking the dumpster to make sure that shithead didn't throw stuff in there, it's mostly empty with none of my stuff. I guess I should be glad about that if I were a grateful person. But I'm not. I heave the crap I don't want into the dumpster, the thud echoing into the surrounding buildings. I load boxes of clothes and other stuff into the truck bed.

Once I have a clear path to Dad's chair, I twist and turn it to get it over to the edge of my truck. I lower the tailgate and wonder how the hell I'm going to lift this heavy-ass chair by myself.

"Fucking Carl," I yell to the night sky as I climb into the truck bed.

Cussing at him doesn't do any good other than pissing me off even more. I grip the top of the chair, wishfully thinking I can lift it onto the edge of the tailgate. That's dumb as hell. I'm not strong enough to pull it straight into the bed. Thinking for a moment, I lean against the chair, trying to figure out what to do as I refuse to ask that bastard Judd for help. Not that he would help me, anyway.

Rummaging through the boxes, I come across more house-hold stuff I don't care about and figure I can use it to hoist the chair onto it. Stacking the chair on boxes cuts the distance in half to the edge of the tailgate, so I'll have to stair step this bad boy up there if I have any hopes of getting it in the bed.

Dragging boxes to the rear of the truck, I nearly choke on the exhaust as I get the left side of the chair wedged on top of the box long enough to do the same with the other side. With its odd shape and dead weight, it's heavy as hell and threatens to blow out my back. One box caves in, but at least it's high enough for me to continue lifting the bottom until the chair falls into the bed. Lying on its back, I huff and puff, shoving the thing all the way to the back. It's probably ripping the fabric, but I can fix that later.

Once I have it wedged under the window, I jump down to sort through the rest of my stuff. I'd love to take my worn green couch for sentimental reasons, but with the sleeper in it, there's no way I can lift it on my own. The memories of it will have to stay with me. I hunt for Dad's table and find it overturned and buried under trash bags filled with my clothes.

It's next to go in the bed, pressing it against the chair to ensure it doesn't slide around. I stuff the clothes-filled bags around the table, trying to pack it tight and keep it in place. Dad's lamp sits neatly next to the dumpster. I'm glad Carl didn't toss that in because it would have been shattered. Even though the shade is creased, I pick it up and open the passenger door to place it on the floorboard.

It's freezing inside the truck and Anna is shaking. Poor thing. I cut off the air conditioning and leave the door open for some of the cold air to escape into the muggy night.

My clothes stick to my skin and sweat collects on the back of my neck, but I press on. Sorting through boxes and bags, I dump some, load a few, and hope to find that one special box filled with all the things that belonged to Dad. The longer I look, the more frantic I become until the very last box sitting closest to the dumpster has it in there, buried with some of his books.

I briefly rifle through Dad's special box to ensure everything is there and then sigh in relief as I put it on the passenger seat. Cracking my back, I'm emotionally exhausted and thoroughly enraged by Carl's betrayal. Judd's crotch rocket fires up, and to avoid him, I take my time locking the tailgate and closing the passenger door.

My phone vibrates my butt. When I pull it out, it's Tomlin asking where I'm staying so he can bring Anna's stuff to me. I stare at the text, my finger tapping the side of my phone as I think about the last two days.

Tomlin's been incredibly generous, but it comes at a cost. Kylie has my back either way, but I'm still surprised she sided with Tomlin. Judd and Carl, those pack of fuckers ruined my life in a matter of minutes.

And my reputation?

Judd said it's ruined.

I can only imagine the lies that Carl is spinning to my clients. The web of deceit to fit his fucking narrative. Could Judd be right? Will I never work in this town again? Never do another preservation project because of a bitter old man? It's my livelihood on the line.

Don't those fuckers know that?

Fuck them.

I'll take Tomlin's deal.

I'll fucking kill it on the restoration. And I'll get his pretty little car into Pebble Beach if it's the last fucking thing I do.

27

With a new fire lit in me, I fling open the driver's door to slip inside, moving Anna over to throw my truck in gear and make the long drive to his house.

The soberness of losing my apartment is replaced with a sliver of gratitude at salvaging Dad's stuff and some of mine. But having a revenge plan to exact on Carl and Judd is even better. Those two won't know what hit them.

I'm almost out of town when the universe decides to hate my guts by opening the sky and pouring rain. I debate on pulling under a gas station awning to wait it out, but I'm already out in the boonies and would have to backtrack.

It's a damn shame my shit is getting wet. The real thing that fucking pisses me off is Dad's chair and table getting ruined by the weather. Another thing to blame on Carl because if he handled it like a man, I could've gotten a moving truck, and my shit wouldn't be ruined. One more log on that revenge fire.

My hands tighten around the wheel as I take the steep mountain road slowly. The last thing I need to do is slide off the side of this thing and die, which would give them the ultimate satisfaction that I lost, and they lived.

"Fuck that."

I'll drive like Grandma Hamilton if it ensures we arrive safely at my new home and workplace. To think forty-eight hours ago, my life was dull and ordinary.

Look at it now.

Unbelievable.

Fat raindrops splatter my windshield. I immediately slow down to glance in the rearview mirror at Dad's cloth chair buried under mounds of stuff. I hope it's somewhat protected from the rain because I don't know what I'll do if it's completely ruined.

A long bolt of lightning streaks across the sky, and a thunderous crack causes me to jump. Driving up this narrow, winding road is already a bitch.

I don't need a scary-ass weather soundtrack to go with it. Another clap of thunder booms, giving me a heart attack, and I stop the car. Anna's whimpering. I don't blame her. This shit's scaring me.

I plaster her to my chest, muttering, "I know, Anna. I don't like this either."

The slick road grinds under my wheels, which are trying to maintain traction when I maneuver a curve in the road. Squinting through the windshield, past my wiper blades, slapping back and forth, I blow out a relieved breath when Tomlin's ridiculous gate entrance comes into view. I ease the truck to the left and onto the gravel road.

It's dark as can be out here. My headlamps can barely cut through the driving rain blowing in sideways. I always loved weather like this when I was snuggled in my apartment. Driving up a treacherous mountain pass in it is another thing.

I loop around his circle drive, grateful for the porte cochere to protect my belongings, even if it might be a lost cause already. Once I'm parked and the engine is off, I strap my purse across my body, ensure my phone is in there, and tuck Anna against my side. The moment I open my door, a wind gust closes it. I shove it back open to make a run for it.

This fucking sucks.

I run toward the wraparound porch, dodging the blowing rain. Before I can find his doorbell, the door swings open to a sweat-glistening Tomlin, only wearing black basketball shorts and a surprised look.

"What are you doing here?"

I probably should have called or at least texted my decision, but I was in too big of a hurry to get out of Carl's back lot and up this damn mountain.

"I'll do your car," I yell, over the rain pounding on the metal roof above us.

"You will?" Confusion mars his face, and then he snaps out of it. "I mean, come in, come in, get out of the rain."

I shake my head because I need to deal with my belongings getting drenched by the monsoon before I step inside.

"Can I park my car in your garage?"

He frowns for a moment. "I don't have another bay."

Now I frown because I don't know what to do.

"Why?" he asks, looking past me to my truck loaded down with my crap. "My car is in the garage, but let's switch. I'll get my keys."

I hadn't thought about where his Porsche is since the circle drive is empty, but that will work for tonight. Now tomorrow, that's a whole different story.

His bare feet slap against the marble floor as he jogs away. I gaze at that damn white carpet. If it rains this hard up here, how does he not get mud and dirt on it? If I lived in a house like this, I'd need black epoxy floors. He jogs back, wearing black Air Forces and his keys are dangling from his index finger. I step aside to make room for him as he pulls the front door closed.

The fact that I'm at eye level with his muscular chest distracts me momentarily, but I catch the end of what he says. Something about waiting till he's out of the garage to pull in.

"Okay," I holler over another boom of thunder.

One of his garage doors rises as he remotely starts his car and then bolts into the sheets of chilly rain. The one thing I've noticed about him is that he has manners all the time, probably to a fault.

"All right, Anna, one more time."

I hoist her between my side boob and arm, trying to shield her as much as I can. It's fruitless because the rain slashes at us when I jog back to my car, careful not to fall on the slick stones.

Once inside my truck, I start her up and carefully ease her into his garage next to his classic Corvette. Because my truck doors are so long, I carefully shimmy out to avoid ramming it into his beautifully restored masterpiece. Tomlin is already inside clicking the lock on his car with a flash of his lights and closing the garage door. When it's completely closed, he surveys the stuff in the back of my truck.

"What is all this?"

He's soaked from head to toe, with droplets dripping from his hair onto his chest and rolling into the sweatband of his shorts. Any other day, I'd imagine following the droplets with my tongue, but this is him, and he turned me down yesterday. Not to mention this is already the second worst day of my life.

"My life."

I lean against the truck, the rain from the vehicle cold against my thin shorts.

"I went back to the shop, and all this was by the dumpster."

Tomlin's mouth slacks when his eyes glimpse mine before returning to my belongings. His finger grazes an open box, peering inside, and then correcting himself as if it's an invasion of my privacy. I guess now that we will be roommates, I can say goodbye to said privacy.

"He cleared out your place?"

"Yup."

He points to the boxes and furniture when looking at me.

"But this isn't all of it, is it?"

I move toward him to see what he sees. It's not much compared to his possessions, but I got most of what I wanted, or rather, what was most important.

"Nah, but what can I do?" I shrug.

"I can't believe he'd do that to you. From what I heard yesterday, you lived there your whole life. He was friends with your dad."

His astonishment matches what I felt when I saw it by the dumpster. Although I agree with him, it makes my stomach hurt even more.

"Can we not talk about it?"

My hand grips the side of the truck bed, curling around the wet metal and trying not to get emotional when I stare at Dad's sodden chair. I shift Anna to my other hand while Tomlin and I stand shoulder to shoulder looking at my life dripping on his fancy floor.

His hand cups my shoulder, pulling me against his side, and I let him. It's not romantic or sexual, more a measure of comfort to a friend having a bad day. He'd know since he's had a front-row seat to the disaster that is my life.

For the first time since Dad died, I relax in the comfort of another. He knows I'm not keen on touching from that time he hugged the life out of me when the car lurched forward. But this side hug is enough comfort to say I understand, and some small part of me wants someone else in this fucking world to feel it too.

I melt into him, letting myself be vulnerable enough to lay my head against the side of his chest. Tomlin hugging me seems to say it's okay to grieve what I'm losing, and for that, he's earned my respect.

What did he say on the deck?

Someone to be at your side cheering you on.

How about someone to hold you when you're having two of the shittiest days of your life? I clear my throat and straighten to lean forward, forcing his hand to fall away.

"That's my dad's chair. You saw we didn't have a TV, so he would read to me. Ya know, at night, after his shift. He'd climb those stairs, his footsteps were always heavy on them from his long days, eat whatever disgusting dinner I could figure out, and then he would read until I fell asleep."

I don't know why I'm sharing this with him. Probably because I don't want him to look at the chair with disdain. He can do that to me or my stuff, but not his chair. It's hideous with its yellow, orange, and brown fabric. A throwback from another era, and free on the curb in front of a house, we drove past. I remember helping him drag that thing all the way upstairs.

"Sounds like he was a good man."

Tomlin's deep voice is low and sincere.

"He was the best."

I sigh and look over at him watching me. We hold each other's gaze for a few long seconds before I look away. I don't trust myself with how emotional I get talking about Dad.

"Will you help me unload it? Until I can get a storage unit tomorrow. I don't want it to sit and mildew overnight."

"Of course."

I bend over to set Anna and my purse on the floor before walking to open the tailgate. Water floods out, spilling all over the floor and creeping toward the Corvette tires.

"Dammit, if you have a push broom, I can sweep this out the garage door."

"I don't."

He joins me at the tailgate to help me safely get into the truck bed without busting my ass.

"If you want to dry out the chair, don't worry about the floor because it will continue dripping overnight. And a little water never hurt concrete."

I look down at him with my hands planted on my hips and a soft smile tugs at his lips. For all his arrogance, he can really be considerate. Maybe I can learn a lesson from him and try being more passive than my normal aggressive.

"What?" He mimics my stance by putting his hands on his hips.

"Why are you being so nice to me?"

I tilt my head, my wet hair sticking to my skin. He's equally drenched and yet he's unbothered, standing here helping me. Maybe we're friends after all.

"Why wouldn't I be?"

I open my mouth to bring up how we originally started, but I'm tired of that old rhetoric.

"No reason."

I shake my head and bend over to stack boxes on top of each other to reach the chair. Coming across the table first, I pull it from the pile, swipe the excess water off the top, and hand it to him. He places it against the far wall, under the air conditioning vents to dry off, before returning to the side of the truck. My soaked shoes squeak against the metal bed and my toes squish with every step. I clear a path through the boxes from the chair to the tailgate.

"What I'm thinking is dragging it to the edge, and then if you could—"

He jumps over the side of the bed, patting the back of his hand against my hip for me to move out of the way. With one fluid motion, he lifts the heavy-ass chair to the edge of the tailgate, hops down, grips each side of the chair, and lifts it out to set it in the puddle of water. His muscles bulge in every direction. It's a beautiful sight showing years and years of dedication to his diet, workouts, and lifestyle choices.

"Well, damn."

He makes it look so easy compared to the struggle I had getting it in. I guess it's harder in than out. Then I snort at the sex joke floating through my mind.

"Go get some towels out of the bathroom so the water doesn't absorb into the wood legs," he directs while moving the chair closer to the door to ensure the tailgate can still close. "And watch out for the dog when you get out. She's right by the tire."

I scoot to the edge to find Anna and then mimic his move of jumping over the side of the bed. When she sees me, she wants to follow, but I run away and nearly slip on the slick floors when my sneaker screeches.

"Be careful," Tomlin hollers as I round the corner of the diner to bolt into the bathroom and grab a stack of white guest towels from the tall cupboard. Always white.

I jog back to Tomlin, sifting through the boxes and bags and pulling out certain ones to stack at the front of his cars. I'm not sure I like him rifling through my things, even if we're friends and partners now. A girl needs her privacy.

"What are you doing?"

I can't keep the accusation out of my tone.

"Pulling out the ones with your clothes, I assume you want to wash them tonight?"

He points to the pile. I blink because I forgot some people don't have to go to the laundromat on Sunday and fight for machines to wash and dry their clothes.

"Yeah, well, that'd be nice."

I wind my hair into a low knot at the back of my neck. The wet strands sticking to me are getting annoying. I join him by the boxes while he rifles through them and suddenly stops.

"If it's too personal, I could leave you—"

"No, no, it's fine."

I'm not used to having help with anything, and here he is, diving in without being asked. It's really becoming a mind fuck with how nice it is to have someone be there for me. Especially a guy that can move shit, considering I almost gave myself a hernia getting the chair into the truck. He shrugs, tilting his head before going back through the boxes, lifting them over the edge to stack with the bags of clothes.

"Well, that's it for clothes. What about the rest?"

"I'll leave it for tonight." I lift the towels in my arms. "Shall we?"

"I'll lift, you spread." I burst out laughing because I immediately think of him fucking me against the wall as I saunter to the chair. "You say that to all the girls?"

We both squat as I double up the towels to shove under the legs while he lifts one side. With our faces inches apart, he gazes into my eyes before dropping to my lips.

"No, Dani, just you."

Damn, that's hot as fuck.

If he hadn't already turned me down, I'd suggest a shower and sex, or probably shower sex. Dammit, if he won't bang me. He breaks the moment by setting the chair on the towels and crossing behind me to lift the other side. Anna tippy taps over to me and stands between my legs as we finish up.

"What about the front seat?"

He's almost yanking on the passenger door before I stop him. Our eyes meet across the hood of the car.

"I'll deal with it tomorrow. I'm so fucking tired."

I put my hands on my flanks and twist, forcing my back to pop in several places—another day of needing to get laid, food, a shower, and a good night's sleep.

"Let's get these into the wash, and we'll figure out the rest."

He already has two boxes stacked in each hand, peering at me.

"Back out in the rain, I suppose?"

I thumb the closed garage door behind me and his eyes crinkle in confusion.

"No. The last door past the bathroom leads to the house. No need to go back outside unless you want to get even wetter." I smile, raising an eyebrow because of that ending, and he chuckles. "Yeah, I hear how that sounds."

Cracking unexpected sex jokes helps lighten my sorrowful mood.

"Go ahead, and I'll follow," I say, grabbing a box and holding it against my hip.

Anna's charm jingles beside me until I get to the last door where he is waiting with full hands. I open it to step into a large mudroom and hold the door as he turns sideways to fit through.

Open shelving runs along the wall to the left, stocked with extra household supplies and gobs of white linens. Marble countertops sit atop the custom cabinetry below, hiding God knows what underneath. I'm beginning to think the carpenter that did all this work is now a retired millionaire.

"Set the box anywhere you want, Dani."

He shoves his armful of boxes on the countertop before walking over to the fanciest washer and dryer I have ever seen. There are far more buttons than the ones at the laundromat.

"Damn man, these are crazy. Why are there so many options?"

I read the buttons, and it's stupid. I shove all my shit in one load to save time and money. Then hope it doesn't shrink.

"Lingerie? You have a lingerie button?" I guess it's sort of like me washing my underwear in the sink last night.

He scoffs. "I've never used that."

"I should hope not, or that's a conversation for another day."

While he's raising the lid to the washer, I attempt to empty my box straight into the machine when he stops me.

"What are you doing? You must sort it first."

The way he worries about my clothes is cute. I'll give him that.

"Calm your tits. This stuff has been washed a hundred times over. My shit won't fade or bleed if that's what you're worried about."

I bumped his hip with mine, getting him to move out of the way so I can dump the rest of my stuff in the washer. He wordlessly grabs the next box and hesitantly dumps it in after mine. We rotate through the boxes, dumping in clothes until he holds up the detergent and fabric softener to measure before pouring them into the machine.

"I really appreciate all your help."

"Of course, Dani. That's what friends are for."

I don't bother looking at him because I can't trust how I feel.

He's the king of mixed signals. I don't want to read anything into what I think he's saying. If this business relationship is going to work, I don't need to mix my sexual feelings with our business. Even if I'm curious as hell about what he'd be like in bed. Fun, I bet.

"Why don't you go ahead and get in the shower? I'll handle the dog since I dumped out the untouched food from this morning."

His offer is generous.

He's the quintessential host, and I'm going to have to be careful not to take advantage of his hospitality. Because knowing my lazy ass, I'll probably try. I walk to the doorway, pause, and peer back at him.

"Tomlin, I don't . . ."

Something in the way he looks at me lets me know he understands words aren't necessary.

"I know, Dani. I know."

His deep brown eyes hold a certain sadness, and something stirs within me. At that moment, I decide I don't want to go to war with Tomlin again. Even though he's arrogant as hell, being around him makes me realize he's more human than I thought. He's flawed and lonely, with his own problems, just like the rest of us.

28

The shower is amazing and exactly what I need to feel better about things. When I step into the living room, the fireplace hums with a low gas flame, and jazz music is coming from the kitchen. Tomlin sure knows a thing or two about ambiance.

Crossing the living room, I can't believe my eyes. Anna is gobbling up her wet dog food. As I enter the kitchen, Tomlin's back is to me. I can't help but stare at those two round globes of his ass in his tight shorts. His shirt is stretched nearly as tight across his chiseled shoulders and drapes loosely at his tiny waist. He makes comments when he sees my tits in a tank top, but I could say the same thing about his leisure wear molded to his body.

"You are already done?"

He glances over his shoulder while standing at the stove, stirring something with steam spewing from it.

"Yup."

"I hope you like spaghetti because it's all I have."

There are a ton of different spices on the counter beside

him, and the noodles are slowly sinking into the bubbling water.

"Need any help?"

Not that I really know how to cook, but it's always nice to offer.

"I have some garlic bread in the freezer if you don't mind getting it out."

He points to the cabinets down the way from him. I cross the kitchen to yank on different handles when he clarifies.

"Two handles down."

Ah, that's helpful since all this cabinetry looks precisely the same. His freezer is full of meat or other things in clear packaging. It's nothing like my freezer chock-full of cardboard pizzas, taquitos, and frozen dinners. I spot a long loaf in clear cling wrap and pull it out.

"This it?"

"Yes, the pans are on the bottom shelf opposite the freezer."

He gestures with his spatula, and I find what I need. Standing beside him at the counter, I catch a whiff of his great-smelling body wash and immediately dismiss it because I want to talk about my concerns with the garage.

"Are you okay?" he asks, his hand tightening around the bottle of seasoning.

"Yeah, why?"

"Really?" He stops seasoning the meat to look at me. "To be honest, I've been waiting for your rage to scorch the earth or for you to break down and cry. And hey, both are acceptable, but this calm demeanor is not like you."

I don't know why but I laugh because he's right about the first one. The second, nah, I did that back at the apartment. That's enough.

"Yeah, well, I think I've accepted my fucking fate. I can't change any of it. It's bullshit what Carl did to my dad's things, but I can't change that either. Maybe a small part of me is tired of my own shit. Ya know?"

I tear open the clear packaging. I need to distract myself with something to do while blabbering on like an idiot about my feelings.

"Maybe I take a page out of calm Tomlin's playbook. That dude has all his shit figured out."

"Hardly. We all have problems, Dani."

He returns to cooking and lets the conversation drop, which I like because I can't keep rehashing how unfair shit is right now. It is what it is, and I need to move on. Plus, I already have my revenge plan in mind, and it starts tomorrow. Grabbing the sheet pan, I walk to his oven and stare at all the buttons. Like the washing machine, there are a million of these too.

"Why is all your shit so complicated? The oven at the apartment had one dial that you turn to the temperature. One dial. Granted, it was old as hell and leaked gas sometimes, but still."

He chuckles, walks over, and presses like five buttons for it to kick on before returning to the stove.

"You have to wait for it to preheat."

"No, you don't." I yank open the door and close it while his mouth falls open. "You stick it in, and it comes out basically the same."

"I'm pretty sure that's not how it works."

"Works for me. Now, I need to talk to you about the car."

I walk over to him, leaning my hip against the counter to study his profile. He stirs the pasta, lowers the heat, and then mixes a bunch of stuff in the meat to start on the sauce.

"Okay."

"It's going to be messy."

His frown is immediate confirmation that this neat freak will hate it.

"I'm trying to figure something out to protect the floor, but I need to look into that. There's also the fact that I need a lift because I can do a lot on the creeper, but most times, I need to get under the car. Lastly, the fluids will go everywhere, and we have to properly dispose of them because of environmental requirements. And because you're a controlling neat freak, I know you want this to be done right."

"I hardly think wanting a job done right makes me a controlling, neat freak. But I appreciate the compliment and will need to take the rest under advisement."

He adjusts the heat on the sauce after stirring in the final round of seasonings and then closes the jars to stow in an overhead cabinet.

"What solutions do you have now that you've laid out all the problems?"

"Well, you can buy a lift and have it delivered. I don't know how fast that'll be, but I can get started on the other things in the meantime. There's also the issue of sound, I don't know how it will resonate up here in the mountains and how your fancy neighbors will feel about it, but when I pound out the metal for the bodywork, it could get quite loud, and you could get complaints. I haven't figured out a solution for the floor yet, but if I can get my phone charged or can get access to a computer, then I can look up some solutions on the Internet. But it would have to be heavy duty for all the liquids to be able to collect, and then we'd have to somehow funnel or siphon them off into a catchall for them to be safely removed."

The more I go through this with him, the more things pop into my mind. I need to get together a list for myself to effectively communicate it to Tomlin, so I don't waste my time and his money.

"Look, I don't know exactly how this is gonna work between us, but you know I like to be honest with my clients every step of the way. It might get to be a little bit too much communication, but I'd rather over communicate than under since it's your money at stake. Let me get a list of everything I need for immediate issues, and then we can discuss them. The biggest thing I'll have to start on first thing in the morning is parts like we discussed before. That will still be a problem. And I know you want to go with the original but seeing as how he broke it down, and some could have included originals, those are gone. So, we'll have to get creative with our solution in trying to find original parts for that model versus using modified parts."

He turns toward me, his face a mask of fury at what I'm telling him. And I get it. I'd be pissed as hell at Judd for all the wasted money, time, and bullshit. At least he has me now, and we're rowing this boat together whether we like it or not.

"I should sue Carl."

"Trust me, I hear you. You don't think I want to exact my revenge on Carl and Judd, also? But at this point, that's not going to get your car rebuilt, and it's not going to get you into Pebble Beach. My revenge is to get that car done, get it into Pebble Beach, put it in magazines, or do whatever the hell you want to do to rub it in their faces. I'll try to keep costs down without cutting corners. But that's how I'm going to get my revenge."

"I like it. Can't keep a good woman down."

"I don't know about all that, but Carl is out there ruining my reputation by spewing lies to my client list. If restoring your car and getting it into Pebble Beach brings back my reputation and restores my livelihood, then that's all I need to show those pack of fuckers who the real winner is."

"What is this about your reputation?"

"Oh yeah, I guess I didn't tell you when I went by the garage. Judd was there having sex with some chick. It was gross."

I shudder, remembering the pitch of her moans when I walked out.

"Anyway, he said that Carl was out there telling lies about my inferior work, and Judd is now getting my client list. Which is fair because Carl owns the place so he can reassign the work to Judd, seeing as how he has no one else. But spinning a web of lies and deceit out in the industry is not cool. It crosses the line, and it's total bullshit by that old bastard. Oh, and did you tell Carl that I was working on your car because that's what Judd said?"

"No, I told you that I didn't. Honestly, I thought you'd never take my project, so the mere fact that you are now still surprises me. Maybe we should let my attorney handle it? Get him to go after Judd and Carl for the use of inferior parts and the expenses for me and the slander and liability for you?"

This is the side of Tomlin I don't like. The venom on his face and voice are the same as last night in the garage. It makes me cautious about wanting to work for him because I don't have the big bucks to go get a lawyer. And if we get sideways, Tomlin could bury me so deep that I'd be destitute. More destitute than I already am.

"Nah, Tomlin. Lawsuits are for rich people like you. Simple people like me take it on the chin. I wanna restore your car. Let that be my revenge and move on."

He doesn't say anything else, just nods his head and goes back to cooking. With nothing to do but watch him, I decide to get Anna out of that damp sweater and bathe her.

"Hey, how long until dinner is ready?"

"About ten to fifteen minutes. Why?"

As good as the food smells, I'm not going to stand here and watch him make the rest. I hate wasting time unless I want to waste time, such as drinks at the bar or going at it with Zach. But this standing around playing house makes me uncomfortable.

"Because I need to give Anna a bath, and I figure you don't really need me in here, right?"

As if right on cue, Anna sneezes, and her little charm jingles as she shakes her head.

"Plus, I want to wash her sweater when I wash the rest of my things."

I scoop her up, press her to my chest and she nuzzles her face in his luxurious robe.

"You're not washing your clothes with the dog's clothes. I won't let that happen."

His lip curls up in disgust. I get it if I were as pristine and perfect as he is. But I'm not, so it's okay.

"Whatever, I'll be back."

I don't bother waiting for his response because I'm going to do what I'm going to do. End of story. The sooner he learns that, the better.

Anna and I exit the kitchen to go back to our room. Once inside the bathroom, I gently remove her sweater and adjust the temperature of the faucet before pumping a bunch of shampoo into my hand from the fancy shower containers.

I place Anna in the sink. She's clearly not enthused by the idea of a bath as she keeps raising her front paws to avoid the water touching them. I assure her that everything is okay as my mind wanders over the restoration project and the amount of time.

Two months is nothing. That includes the paint job needing to cure before putting on the clear coat to seal in the color and protect it from the elements. I'm going to need help. Even if I work night and day, it won't be enough time. I need another set of hands.

Whom do I know that could help? Hell, I don't have a lot of friends since I dropped out of school. The few I had are away at college. It's hard to maintain a friendship when you have nothing in common. Well, that guy today. It's been me and Dad at the shop, and when he passed, Carl hired Judd. I don't know how he got him. I've never seen anyone else ever come in and apply.

But that dude, Lars, is available now. Mr. Moneybags could

easily afford both of us. Which reminds me, I need to figure out how much I charge Tomlin for my work. Hell, I have no clue what that would be. That was all Carl's area. Then again, I'm the new Carl.

Jeez.

I'm definitely overwashing this dog with how lost in my thoughts I am. Rinsing her one last time, I pluck her from the sink and plaster her body against my robe. Poor girl is so skinny I can feel her ribs in her wet fur, and it's kind of grossing me out. Hopefully tomorrow I'll see Isla, and we can figure out when she gets out of that prison to take her dog back. That will be one less hassle while I fix his car.

I roll her in a towel and tuck her into the crook of my arm to retrieve my phone from my purse. There's a message from Kylie asking if I got into her apartment okay. I fire off a quick text that there was a change of plans and that I'm back at Tomlin's but will call her in the morning. I text Hamilton asking about tomorrow and then toss my phone on the bed. I'm not waiting for his grandma ass to respond. That will be forever.

I stride out to the living room and unbundle Anna from her towel to drop it on the floor by the fireplace. Tomlin is angrily texting on his phone when his head lifts.

"Do you want me to dish you up? Or do you prefer to do it yourself?" he asks over the music in the kitchen.

I deposit her on the towel and head to the kitchen, where he has everything on the table waiting for us. I never bothered putting hot food in serving containers. It's too much work and adds to the cleanup. Dad and I served ourselves from the stove, or sometimes he'd eat over the kitchen sink if he was in a hurry or tired from work.

"I'm coming."

I pull out my chair, and he mirrors my actions. It's not until I sit that he sits too, and I get why chicks dig this. It's kind of nice.

"You didn't have to do all this."

My finger taps the plate. It's bone-thin and way too expensive for my tastes. The wine glasses are slender and delicate, and the serving dishes look like they belong at a wedding.

"Do what? I cook all my meals unless I'm out," he defends, lifting the open bottle of wine to pour a small reserve in my glass before doing the same in his. All we're missing are candles, and this would be the nicest date I've ever been on.

"Out getting laid?"

He ignores my comment, choosing to lift his glass and swirl it. God knows why. When I try to grab a piece of garlic bread off the serving tray, he glares.

"That's what the tongs are for."

Jeez, King of England and his fancy manners. He grabs them and moves a slice of bread to my plate before doing the same with his. The fussiness over his coffee makes sense now.

"Are you always this uptight?"

I use his joined silver serving fork and spoon to lift a pile of spaghetti onto my plate before reaching for the sauce ladle.

"It's called manners. And yes, I use them most all the time."

The inflection in his tone is humorous even if it's one hundred percent true.

"Anyway, who were you texting when I came in?" I dump sauce all over my noodles and survey the table looking for parmesan cheese. Seeing none, I pick up my bread instead. "You were frowning."

"My father."

His tone immediately changes from teasing to a hard edge.

"That bad, huh?"

"He was captain of his debate team in college, so he prefers to laminate his points in a Lincoln-Douglas debate and not the abbreviated one."

No idea why he's talking about a dead president's debate. That falls into my I-don't-care category.

"He blabbers on about it, I guess?"

He laughs. A good hearty one that makes me frown because I don't know what he's talking about.

"Dani, that's a good one. Using the word 'blabbering' and my dad together in one sentence is priceless."

He chuckles a little more to himself while picking up a reasonable amount of noodles and then uses the fancy spoon tongs to create a crater in the middle of them.

"Why do I feel like you were raised like the Queen or something? You're fussy about, well, everything."

"Kaizen."

"Kaizen?" I shake my head while twirling spaghetti on my fork. "Am I supposed to know what that means?"

He spoons sauce into his noodle crater before setting the ladle down to gaze at me with a soft smile.

"No, but it's what I operate in or rather how I was raised to operate in."

"Operate in?" I slurp my noodles. "You sound like a robot."

Retrieving a spoon from the side of his plate, he twirls his fork against it to wind the spaghetti around it. I've never seen that before. Now I'm for sure convinced the royal family raised him.

"A philosophy steeped in principle, process, and theory. The ideology is that we should be in a constant state of improvement in all facets of our life. Never settling for who and what you are today, but striving for the version of yourself that you are meant to be every day in the future."

I take a swig of the wine and damn, it's good. Very smooth and a little sweet. I'm going to need more than a quarter of a glass. That stingy bastard.

"Sounds exhausting."

He eats so neatly that I have to stop myself from watching because that's weird.

"You have a little something right here," he says, pointing to my left side and I try to reach it with my tongue.

His forehead wrinkles in disgust as he watches me.

"What are you doing? You're not going to reach it because it's on your cheek. Use your napkin."

I glance down to see a neatly folded white cloth under my knife, which I don't like because my spaghetti mouth will stain it.

"You don't have some paper towels?"

I lean back in my chair to see if he has a paper towel roll on the counter but damn that spotless kitchen. None are in sight.

"No, Dani, I don't have brown bathroom towels either. Just use the napkin like a normal adult."

He points to it with his knife that's adding more butter to the inside of his bread. I'm pretty sure that's against Her Majesty's etiquette to point with a knife.

"Don't insult me. And why is your house white?"

My irritation at his pristine living is bubbling up.

"White carpets, white marble everywhere, white towels and robes." I point to the one I'm wearing and the one on my head for effect. "Even white dishes. It's weird."

His dark brown eyes roam from the wrapped towel on my head to my robe, gaping open, and giving him a nice view of my cleavage before I tug it closed.

"I like white."

His gaze drops to his plate as if that's enough of an explanation. I roll my eyes, reaching for the wine bottle to fill my glass to the brim.

"Dani, come on. You don't need that much."

Challenge accepted.

I drain the entire glass down my gullet to prove a point that he will not control me, especially at the start of this partnership. Then I pour another glass just as full.

"Don't do it. You're going to have a migraine in the morning."

"Don't tell me what to do," I spat, sounding super childish.

Damn if that wine doesn't make my head swim a little, and suddenly Tomlin blurs into two people.

"Okay, that's way too fucking much."

I dig my fingertips into my temples to clear the haze while looking down at my plate full of food. Luckily, Tomlin doesn't rub it in my face for being right. Instead, he eats in silence as I nibble on my bread and let the smooth music float between us.

"You should really stop cussing." His eyes level with mine when he says it. "If this partnership is going to work, you can't keep cussing like a sailor in front of prospective clients."

"If this partnership is going to work, you're going to need to back off my ass. I get that you live this perfectly disciplined life, but I do things my way, so stop trying to change me."

I drop the bread on my plate and grab the wine glass, hovering it below my lips as I wait for his response. He sets his fork aside and sits back in his chair.

"You're right, Dani. We need to set some ground rules, or it's not going to work."

"Fine. Don't boss me around. I know what to do. You don't. I know the deadline I'm under. You don't ride my ass, and I'll cuss as much as I fucking want."

I set my glass down without drinking from it.

"You'll call or text me with any decisions that must be made. I don't want a repeat of Judd."

"Duh." He already knows I won't pull a Judd on him. "What else?"

"I'll pay you twenty percent on top of the cost to restore."

My eyebrows pinch together, my anger flaring.

"You paid that bastard Carl thirty percent."

"Carl isn't living in my house and eating my food," he points out bluntly. I debate on grabbing my knife and stabbing him with it because it sounded a lot like pity, and that's fucking bullshit.

"Don't hold that shit over me. I can go back to town and get my own place if you want to do that. Hell, I could stay with Kylie if you're going to be all high and mighty about this place."

I lean back as well to put more distance between me and that knife.

"I'm not, but cost is cost. Room and board are part of the deal. You can't get the same premium as him." He straightens to retrieve his wine, taking a slow sip as if unaffected by my temper. "And no guys in my home. Handle your needs anywhere but here."

He did not just say that to me.

"Look, asshole, you don't tell me what to do. You know what? Forget it. This isn't going to work."

Hell, I'll turn tricks on the side of the road before I let him control my sex life. I stand up, my chair scraping the floor as I bolt out of the kitchen and into the living room. I'm about to snatch Anna, who's snoozing by the fire when his hand lands on my shoulder. Whirling around to punch him, he dodges my fist and steps back with his hands up in a cautious stance.

"What is wrong with you, Dani? Can't you have one conversation without storming off or wanting to fight? It's like talking to a ticking time bomb. You never know when you're going to explode."

"I don't do that."

"Wrong. The first time I met you. When I dropped my car at Carl's. When you racked me for calling you babe. When you told me to get the hell out of your apartment the day of the altercation. Basically all the time."

His hands drop to his side once mine do, and we're left facing each other.

"Can you understand it from my point of view? I don't want another man naked in my home. That's reasonable."

Dammit, if he didn't flip on his calm and sincere voice, which makes sense.

"Yeah, I get it. I wouldn't want to walk in on you and a chick banging it out."

"Which never happens here, as we talked about already. Can you come back to the table and discuss this rationally while we eat?"

He steps to the side, gesturing for me to lead the way.

"Fine, you're a decent cook."

That's the most apology he'll get out of me. I trudge back into the kitchen with his chuckling echoing behind me. I'm not about to tell him that the food and wine are superb. That big ego doesn't need to get any bigger. He holds out my chair for me, which is weird, but I allow it. I plant my butt on it, and he pushes me in before sitting on his.

"And for the record, I never fuck Zach at my place."

I take that chug of wine I needed a minute ago and watch his face change from amused to curious. Go figure. Tell a guy about my sex life and his mind goes into overdrive. But he shot me down yesterday, so maybe this looks means something else.

"Good to know. What else?"

"Do you remember when I first said ten to twelve months, give or take a month, and you said four?"

He nods while twirling his fork into his spoon. I set down my wineglass.

"Well, now that I'm down to two months, I need help. Even if I work seven days a week, which I plan on doing, it's not enough time for engine and bodywork, plus paint and curing. I need another set of hands to do the body while I do the engine. And if I can't source parts through the usual places, I'll need to drive to junkyards to find parts, and another set of hands will help with that too."

He waits until he has swallowed to say, "Sounds reasonable. What are you proposing?"

Genuine intrigue appears on his face as if he didn't realize this problem himself.

"That guy we met today. He's fresh out of school, but he could do the bodywork with his size. I can show him the engine work as I go, and with the two of us working on it, it will go twice as fast."

I dig back into my spaghetti because it's good, and I'm hungry.

"You don't even know him."

"Yeah, well. I don't have a lot of options, and we need someone now. You'll hire and pay him, but I call the shots in the shop."

"I don't know, Dani. He's a big guy, and I know you think you can hold your own, but he's got to outweigh you by one hundred pounds."

That's kind of sweet that he's worried about my safety, but I weld parts. I could always set the dude on fire if necessary.

"I'm not always going to be here. I need to get back to Denver."

"Is that what he was texting you about?" I ask, before shoveling more food down my gullet. "You were frowning, and kind of seemed like you were angry texting."

"I was. I have another match coming up, and I need to prepare for it. I have been doing some work here, but he accused me of hiding out."

He breaks off a piece of bread to dip in the sauce before plopping it into his mouth. He mentioned that before.

"Are you hiding out?" I ask because that seems very un-Tomlin-like.

"Maybe. I guess all dogs want time to lick their wounds."

He doesn't explain beyond that, just goes back to eating, and I do the same. Several minutes pass, making me realize I need to make some changes. Tomlin doesn't want to fight with me, that's obvious. Then again, he also doesn't shut down or walk away when I do. It's like he heads into the conflict with me to restore peace and balance.

Could I become like him? All white carpet and zen-ish? I chuckle to myself because that's the most ridiculous thought I've ever had.

"What are you laughing at?"

His curious eyes hold mine.

"Me."

I don't bother explaining beyond that because it's my private realization.

"What about Lars? Are we a go? Can I see if he can come up tomorrow to get started?"

"Are you sure?"

He leans back from his clean plate, dragging his nearly empty glass with him.

"No, but I need help. He looks like a bear, but he seems like a decent guy. You could do a background check or something, right? I've seen billboards on the side of the road about that."

He hums an acknowledgment but doesn't answer.

"He might not even be available or might not accept the job, but I want to text him before bed to see. Are you cool with that?"

He downs the smidge of wine left and set his glass on the table.

"Yes, but speak to him about the conditions and such beforehand. If you get an odd feeling, do not hire him. I'm serious about your safety."

"Yeah, yeah, yeah, I get it. You don't want me to have a matching shiner."

I point to the one I already have, trying to make light of the situation, but he doesn't crack a smile.

"Speaking of that, any word on the girl?"

"Hamilton should get me in tomorrow to see her. I feel bad

for the kid. She goes from Rick the Rapist to kid prison and loses her dog in the process. Life's a bitch."

I finish the rest of my bread, and debate if I want more.

"I'm sure the facility isn't that bad, but it's nice of you to visit her. I'm sure she can use a friend right now."

"Yeah, she can."

Something about saying it aloud and acknowledging it deep down sits right with me. It makes me feel good about being there for someone in need, even though I'm usually the one in need.

"Anything else we need to discuss before I leave?" Tomlin asks while stacking his utensils in the middle of his plate and wiping his mouth on his white napkin.

"Leave?"

His comment catches me off guard. Why is he leaving when I just agreed to kill myself by taking on his restoration?

"Yes, for Denver. I'll be up there the rest of the week, maybe longer. It depends on how long I can tolerate my dad. I'll leave you a credit card for car and household expenses since I stock little food here."

He stands, grabbing the dishes from the table as if it's all been decided. My brain is trying to catch up and a wave of dizziness crashes over me when I stand up. Note to self, don't chug expensive wine, even if challenged to do so.

"Um, okay, well, I'll also need to get some equipment. Do you have a computer or something I can use to start looking online?" I ask, collecting things from the table to put on the counter next to him while he scrapes the leftovers into empty glass containers.

"Will you eat the rest of this?" He points to the spaghetti with his silver spoon tongs.

"Yeah, sure."

"Good, and the tablets that control the house are Internet-enabled. Use those. Or I have a home office if you want to use that. I can show you the rest of the house before I go."

I'm sure he is proud of this place. Hell, I would be too if I owned it, but I'm still reeling from the fact that he's leaving without everything being decided and set in order. I know my life appears to be a mess, but I prefer an orderly and structured work environment.

"Sure, but I really need to spend time sourcing the big equipment and lift since we're up against the clock."

Nervousness creeps in as I tick through the list of stuff that needs to be done to his garage to make it work ready. Needing something to do to ease my anxiety, I start rinsing the dishes while he stacks the leftovers in the fridge.

"Not the pots and pans. I hand wash those," he says, patting my hip for me to move out of the way while he loads some dishes in the dishwashing drawer and leaves others on the counter. I slip out of his way when he fills the sink with soap.

"Need help with the dishes?" I ask, hovering by the opposite counter while he moves the pots and pans into the sink.

"No, thank you. I know you need to get started on your equipment search."

He doesn't bother looking at me when he responds. I take that as a sign that he wants to be alone.

"Right."

I clamp my mouth shut, staring at his drawn eyebrows and pulsing jaw muscle. This look, I know. Contemplative, not mad at me, but also not happy for some reason. This is moody Tomlin, and I'm more than happy to give him space.

I tiptoe into the living room, not to disturb a snoring Anna to swipe the tablet from the table and stretch out on his sectional to start searching.

29

With the ambiance of the fire casting a warm hue to my right, and the soft jazz oozing through the sound system above, I relax. For the first time in two days, I'm at ease. Damn, his house is rising up to greet me and sucking me into its cozy abyss.

I tap the screen, looking for the Internet icon to start my search. Parts are accessible to me, but finding the bigger equipment isn't since Carl already had everything we needed. When I stumble upon a website that deals in what I need, I nearly die at the prices listed.

Whoa.

Tomlin's going to need to see these tonight because there's no way I'm randomly putting them on his credit card.

"Tomlin, can you come here? I need to show you these prices because my eyeballs damn near fell out of my head when I saw them."

I peer over the edge of the sectional, but I don't see him in the kitchen. Straining my ears, I gaze at the long wooden beams running along his vaulted ceiling to listen for him.

Deciding he'll come out eventually, I bookmark that page

and go to the next. Before I realize it, it's been over an hour, and several bookmarks later, and still no Tomlin. That's weird. Dropping the tablet on the couch and ensuring Anna is still fine by the fire, I go in search of him.

The kitchen is sparkling with all the dishes washed and put away. The dining room and the back deck are dark when a deep, repetitive bass catches my attention. I follow the sound down an unknown hallway, the lights illuminating as I walk. The electrician must have made a fortune on this feature.

Following the bass, it leads to an open door where Tomlin is squatting, an obscene amount of weight that curves the bar. I step inside. The music is nearly too loud for me. Now I know why Carl used to bitch about the walls vibrating with my music. It's the same with him.

Floor-to-ceiling mirrors coat the walls except to the right, where a wall of windows faces the north. It's impressive to watch the ease and depth of his squats. His shoulder and back muscles ripple under the weight as sweat rolls down his long back. Those round globes of his ass make me flush with heat. Again, I fantasize about what he'd be like pumping into me.

Damn, I got to get laid.

Our eyes meet in the mirror, and he racks the weight like it's no big deal. He waves a hand in the air, and the music shuts off. Cool trick. Grabbing a towel from the black bench sitting in front of two rows of dumbbells, he crosses his weight room to stand in front of me.

"Need something?"

His tone is clipped as if irritated by my intrusion. My typical response would be to say fuck you and walk out, but I'm trying not to do that after what he said at the dinner table.

"You okay?"

He wipes the towel down his face, pausing at his mouth with only his dark brown eyes visible.

"Yes. Why?"

Definitely, a mistake coming in here. I should have peeked inside and then minded my own business by going back to look for parts.

"No reason. The large equipment is expensive. I wanted to review it with you. I'm not getting anything I don't need, but it's a lot of money."

He finishes wiping his face and chest, leaving the white towel to hang from his neck. It's the sexiest shit I have seen in a long time. I swear I'm fantasizing about him tonight when I rub one out.

"I trust you. Get a credit card out of my wallet. It's in the dish on the kitchen bar."

He walks closer. I wait for his body odor to hit me, but it doesn't, which is weird because he's sweaty as shit right now.

"Um, I'd rather not because it's super fucking expensive, and I'm not charging—"

I stop because he's too close, like way up in my personal space. I back up until my shoulder blades touch the mirrored wall.

"What are you doing?"

A smile toys at his lips while his eyes search my face. He continues his descent until we're almost touching. His index finger caresses the hollow between my breasts, and damn if it doesn't send a jolt between my thighs.

"Do you know your robe has been gaping this entire time?"

My hands press against the cold mirror, wanting this and so much more from this fine-ass specimen.

He lowers his chin. His eyes drift down to my lips, where I bite the bottom one to stop myself from devouring him like I did last night. His finger is achingly delicious as it circles the curve of my breasts before dragging up to my throat.

"You told me no," I blurt out.

I don't want to be rejected again. I want to be able to walk away from him this time of my own free will. But fuck if his stroking isn't fanning the flames of my desire. He can take me against this wall. It would be so damn easy.

"I did. I meant it."

I exhale as his finger traces over my collarbone, pulling the robe farther open. I close my eyes when the desire boiling in his becomes too intense. I've never been this desperate for a man. Then again, I've never been rejected. I'm confused by his actions, but horny as hell and curious as to where this is going.

"You flaunt these big, beautiful breasts in my face at dinner," he whispers against the shell of my ear. His palm slides under the robe to cup my boob. It's hot as fucking hell.

"What's a guy to do, Dani?"

I can't answer as I push farther into his hand. His skillful thumb strums back and forth across my nipple while his other hand presses against the side of my neck. I'm barely breathing, waiting for him to devour me as I want to devour him. If only.

My eyes open to stare into those chocolate pools of lust. I move my lips within centimeters of his. I dare him to kiss me, tongue me, eat me alive. Any will do. His head shakes slowly, and I hate it.

"Kiss me, T," I murmur, leaning forward to dust my lips to his except his hand tightens on my neck, holding me in place.

It's hot as fuck being held back. His patience deserves an award that I'm more than happy to get on my knees and give. A smile pulls up at the corner of his full lips. His eyes bore into mine. When his head dips, I exhale.

His hand falls away from my neck to cup my breast. Both are plucking my nipples, which are achingly hard in his fingers. I moan when his mouth covers my collarbone. I haven't had a hickey in years, but with the way he's sucking my tender skin and boiling my insides with want, I'll gladly wear a string of them.

He greedily pushes the robe off my shoulders. His mouth

skims across my skin to hover over my voluminous breast, and I push my nipple toward him.

"Beautiful," he mutters before taking it between his teeth and teasing the hard flesh with his tongue.

Wetness spreads between my legs and drips onto my thighs. Heat surges through my body, causing goosebumps of pleasure to prickle on my skin. My breasts have always been sensitive, but the way he's sucking them is divine.

Fucking him would be an art form.

His hooded eyes gaze up at me. His pupils are blown out with lust, and I pant in his expert hands. Restraining myself from grabbing his face and forcing my tongue down his throat, I loosen my sweaty palms from the mirror to grasp his shoulders.

His smile is wicked when his hands fall away from my breasts to straighten and grab my thighs to hoist me up. My legs wrap around his trim waist, the heat from my mound pressing against his hard shaft. His cologne is faint yet intoxicating when I wind my arms around his neck, knocking the towel to the ground.

"Fuck it," I whisper, pressing my mouth to his.

With wild abandonment on both sides, our kisses are fast and sloppy—a desperate need to consume and be consumed by each other.

His tongue twists and curves with mine, seeking to know my mouth as eagerly as I'm to know his. My robe hikes up my legs as his long fingers knead my ass. They're so fucking close. He could easily slip a finger or two inside and feel how warm and wet I am.

My nipples are rock hard, brushing against his chiseled chest, and I want more, so much more. I want him to fuck me against the wall my back is pressed to. When his mouth leaves mine, we're both heaving, breathing the same air between us.

"Dani."

"Don't say it," I warn, feeling the words of rejection climbing up the back of his throat where my tongue almost was. "Don't fucking say it."

He's slow to lift his head from mine. His words betray him because his lips are swollen, my hands are tangled in his hair, and his cheeks are heated with lust.

"You're killing me," he groans.

A desperate tug of war raging inside of him. His words say one thing, and his body says another. I don't fucking care about his struggle. I know what I want. I pull his mouth back to mine so I can show him what we both urgently need.

It's a battle for dominance between us, giving as good as we're getting. He presses me against the mirror. His mouth expertly devours mine as his fingers crawl closer to my opening.

He grunts when he feels how wet I am for him. Those narrow hips slowly grind against mine to create a delicious friction that continues to flood his fingers. If only two would plunder my insides like he's plundering my mouth, it would be perfect.

How he's restraining himself is beyond me. I rub feverishly against him, trying to get off when he tears his lips from mine. He groans, burying his face in my blistering hot neck. I tilt my head to rest against his. My building orgasm is fading fast as is my hope for him taking me right here, right now.

"That mouth of yours."

His nose presses against my skin, leaving little kisses while breathing me in. It's the hottest action ever.

"That sailor's mouth begs to be kissed, sucked, and fucked."

I want all those things too. To worship and be worshipped. How much fun we'd have together, hours in bed, playing and exploring each other.

Combustion.

Damn fucking shame.

"Damn you, T."

"T, huh? I like it."

His head lifts, and his gaze is intense. I'm entranced by it, and those juice-covered hands are slick when he squeezes my ass.

"Do I get to call you little D?"

"No, because I don't like little d," I smirk, wondering what size he is.

As if reading my mind, he straightens up to adjust his hold on me so I can feel exactly how long he is.

"Not a little d, little D. Just right to leave you sore in the morning."

I rub my mound against his long length, and a tormented growl escapes his throat.

"Fuck you, Tomlin."

One last time, I launch myself at his mouth and take his bottom lip in mine to suck. My breasts rub against his sweaty chest while I return to dry hump the shit out of him through his now wet workout shorts.

Something about that drives me wilder as my teeth nip his lip before twisting my tongue with his. My moans are lost in his mouth as his grunts are lost in mine. He ends it abruptly, holding his lips away from mine, and I pout with displeasure.

"I can't," he rasps.

His eyes drop to my breasts, laid out like a feast waiting to be devoured.

"You can."

"Dani, I'm serious. I want to fuck you against this wall, bend you over that bench, and stuff that smart mouth."

The pressure of his body smashing me against the mirror lightens a fraction, conveying he won't do it.

"Okay," I whisper, trying to nip at his lips, but he dodges my kiss. My hands cup his nape, trying to force his face to mine, but he holds himself back.

"No."

It's a sharp command, but those lustful eyes are betraying him. They reflect the want within me as it is within him.

"It would be a hell of a lot of fun."

I attempt to convince him, but he tilts his chin down, his gaze boring into me.

"No."

Less harsh but equally final.

"One last kiss?"

I sound pathetic, but I want more, not less.

"Dani."

My name comes out as a plea, and he lowers me to the floor, much to my dislike.

"Can't blame a girl for trying."

I grab the lapels of the robe to shove them together and tug the hem down over my ass. He watches me closely, frowning a little when I cover everything.

"One of us has to have control because if I didn't, you'd let me have my way with you."

"Yes."

Yes, I would.

He could.

I'd probably let him do whatever he wants, repeatedly.

"You're something else," he groans, fighting his decision until he slowly raises his fingers to his mouth to lick them clean.

"And you taste good."

"Damn."

Watching him drink me in, floods my inner thighs with more juices to the point I'm crossing my legs. I have to get out of here and finish what we started in my bedroom. I'm horny enough that I might fall to my knees and beg him, even though I have more pride than that.

"I gotta go. Look over the tabs I bookmarked on the tablet, and I'll see you in the morning."

I rush through my words as wetness clings to the apex of my thighs. He smiles that stupid panty-dropping one.

"Come work out with me anytime, Dani. I think I prefer yours to mine."

He winks, and I bolt from the room. His chuckles chase me down the hall and into the kitchen, where I spot Anna stretching. I scoop her up and race back to my room. Once inside, I place her on the dog bed, not caring if she wets it before I dive into my bed and rub one out.

It's nothing compared to actual sex, but enough to relieve the fire that we started. The last thing I do is text Lars to meet tomorrow, throw my phone on the charger, and fall asleep with visions of Tomlin's mouth on my breasts.

30

Last night was weird. I don't know if it was the wine, or making out with Tomlin, or losing all my stuff, but my sleep was interrupted by some wild dreams. Dreams of living here with Tomlin as his girlfriend, running a shop of my own with employees, and even a home for Isla and Anna.

My brain was working overtime when it should have shut the fuck up and gone to bed. My head is pounding before it's even left the pillow. That damn wine and the gorgeous fucker that served it to me are to blame. How am I supposed to work when the throbbing in my head is like rushing water in my ears? I ease up, my hand clasping my head as I push aside the covers.

I hate Tomlin for the wine. I hate myself for chugging it to prove a point. I hate him for making me prove said point. I hate that he rejected me again in the sexiest fucking way. I hate that I offered myself up and practically begged to be fucked like a desperate hooker. I hate feeling this way and hate him for making me feel this way.

Tiptoeing into the bathroom, I hate the fucking soft lights scorching my eyeballs right now. If I could figure out how to turn off his fancy fucking lights, I would. Damn his luxury resort. I just want to pee and wash my hands in the dark.

Once I'm done with both, I swipe my dirty clothes and Anna's crusty sweater off the bathroom counter to walk through the bedroom toward the laundry room to dry my clothes.

I admit I should have done that last night, but it slipped my mind in all my horniness—damn him for that too. I'm going to make that jerk pay for teasing the shit out of me and giving me the worst fucking hangover ever. I open the bedroom door to complete silence. I guess he's not up yet. Walking down the hall to the mudroom, I crack open the door to find my laundry dried and folded into neat little stacks.

Grateful is what I should feel, but anger brews when I think of his dirty paws handling my underwear. That cheeky bastard probably sniffed them. After mimicking his actions last night to get the washer going, I scoop up the stacks of clothes and leave the room to get dressed in my bedroom. I drop the clothes on the bed to open the dresser drawers and arrange my stuff inside. Anna stands to stretch, shakes out her fur, and yawns. I don't know why she's exhausted. All she does is sleep and get carried around. How hard is that?

Picking out some clothes, I take them into the bathroom for a quick shower. The sooner I get that brown sludge down my throat, the faster I can get rid of this fucking hangover. I race through getting ready. Not bothering with any makeup because I don't need to appear any more gorgeous to Tomlin now that he confirmed he's in love with my tits. In fact, I change out of my tight T-shirt to put on another tank top and adjust them so they're nearly popping out of the top.

Payback for two rejections.

It's going to be all look and don't touch from here on out.

Still needing hair ties, I twist my long hair into a knot at the base of my neck, hoping it will stay until I can stop by the drugstore. Deciding I'm ready to face him and slug down my morning coffee, I open the door and hope Anna follows. I need to stop carrying her. What's the harm of her walking through his house? None.

The living room is empty when I get to the end of the hallway, and I round the kitchen to see he's not there either. Carefully, I open different cabinets to find his tiny little teacups and retrieve one before standing at the machine dumbfounded at what he did to make it produce that liquid gold. I press the start button, but nothing happens. I try the size button and then start, but still nothing.

Ugh, stupid fancy shit.

I press random buttons and nada, zilch, and nothing. I lay my forehead against the machine because the migraine is mighty, and the coffee-making is lacking.

"What are you doing?"

I twist my head to see he's wearing dress pants, a white button-down, and fastening a gold Rolex around his wrist.

"Stop yelling."

I remove the side of my head from the front of the espresso machine to step back and hope he'll have mercy on my soul.

"I'm trying to make coffee, but your stupid piece of shit machine isn't working."

He chuckles, and it's the worst sound in the world. I want to throttle him against that machine.

"I warned you about the wine."

Damn him for sauntering over and pushing buttons to get the dumb thing working.

"The finer it is, the worse the hangover."

"The finer it is, the worse the hangover," I mimic in a blabbering voice because he could've just said I told ya so and been done with it.

"Oh, someone woke up on the wrong side of the bed."

"Shut it."

His smile is dazzling when he walks past me to open a drawer at the end of the kitchen and pulls out a piece of paper. I guess my boobs threatening to spill over aren't working because he's irritating me more than I am him.

"Here's everything for the house that you need to know. I have a housekeeper that comes by once a week. Text her your grocery list, and she'll put it on the house account."

He retrieves a key from the same drawer, along with a key fob.

"These are for the house and garage, remember bears wander up here all the time, so keep everything locked as some are smart enough to open doors."

He already told me that but whatever.

"So, you are leaving?"

The machine stops whirling, and I'm about to step toward my cup when he blocks my way. His eyes glance at my breasts before looking me in the eye.

"I think it's best."

I don't miss the inflection in his tone. Even though I want to taunt him with his attraction to me, I'm finding he's taunting my attraction to him.

"Because of last night?"

I step back to lean against the cabinets. The cold countertop cuts into my back as I take in his damp hair, dark eyes, and stoic face.

"I mean, we're cool. You rejected me again, but whatever."

"Did I?"

He steps forward, his hands palming the marble on either side of my body, trapping me between them.

"Or did we both agree that we can't indulge in whatever this is?"

I stare at his lips, mostly seeing the words versus hearing them.

"Lust, T. Nothing more. Just two smoking-hot people wanting to bang it out. No harm in that."

His face dips dangerously close to mine, and if I didn't have a migraine, I'd launch myself at him. But I can't be pounded while my head is pounding. I tried it once, and I almost threw up.

"See, that is where you are wrong, Dani. I don't bang it out. I date women I see a future with."

His cologne is making my headache worse, or maybe it's the insult of his words. Probably both.

"And you don't see a future with me?"

Wait, did I ask that? Did I basically say I want a future with Tomlin in that way, like in my dream? Damn, that fucking wine has me all messed up.

He leans in, his minty breath caressing my ear, and whispers, "You're my business partner, not my life partner."

Softly spoken, but the message is loud and clear. I'm not good enough for him. I can fix his car and make him money, but I'll never be on his level to be datable. That's fucked up. He straightens, and I duck underneath his arm to retrieve my ridiculous teacup.

"And Dani?"

I turn, trying to keep from hurling this hot liquid all over his triumphant face.

"I ordered all the equipment you need. They have your number to arrange delivery. And my card is here."

He points to the black card on the wet bar before fussing with the button on his sleeve.

"And Lars?"

Keeping it to essential questions only.

"I'll leave that up to you."

"Fine."

"Text me if you need me."

He stops messing with his sleeve to look at me. If my blood wasn't already boiling, it is now with how aloof he's coming off.

Well, fuck him.

The faster I get his car done, the sooner I can afford my own place and won't need to live here. I turn away, not bothering to acknowledge him any longer than I have to. He's a real mind fuck, and I'm not getting trapped in that game. He wants it to be strictly business, then I can easily do that. I'll consider him the new Carl, and that will settle that because I'd never lust after Carl. Now, I'll never lust after Tomlin.

Getting to the back door, I open it for Anna, thankful she's following, and I can save face while he escapes to Denver. I slam the door as hard as I can, causing the windows to shake, and for a glimmer of a moment, I regret it before thinking, screw him.

Crossing the deck, this view is impressive, with the sun coming up in the east and painting the mountains a bright red. I pick Anna up when we get to the steps and carry her down to the grassy patch by the last post. She pees a stream that rolls to the edge of the rocks. I realize Anna has probably developed a strong bladder with having to hold it on those over-the-road long hauls.

My hands roll into a fist when I think of that fucker. I need to ask Hamilton about the court proceedings because I'd love to bring popcorn and sit in that fucking courtroom as they nail his ass to the wall in sentencing. I plop down on the steps to savor my coffee while she kicks the grass and wanders away to sniff a different patch.

I don't get Tomlin.

If I don't have any potential to be a life partner, whatever the fuck that means. I'm either a temptation or I'm not. Since he doesn't bang it out, then why leave?

Last night, he wasn't blabbering life partner shit when he was taking my breast in his mouth or sucking my juices from his fingers. That bastard, I blame him for all this. Maybe that's why his guilty ass finished my laundry for me. Because he knew he'd reject me a third time in the kitchen and insult me on top of it. I swear, I'm wasting too much valuable brainpower on him.

Good riddance.

Denver can have him.

I hope his dad kicks his ass.

I guzzle the rest of my tiny cup of coffee and set it on the step, wishing he showed me how he got that damn espresso machine to work. Anna finishes sniffing around to hightail it back to me, ready to go in. That makes two of us. I collect her and the cup and head straight to my bedroom.

Tomlin would probably die if he saw me bringing the cup into my room, but he's not here and I don't feel like washing it. I set Anna on the unmade bed beside me, and she heads straight to the pillows to burrow against them.

Unlocking my phone, there's a barrage of text messages from Judd and a missed call from Carl's place. I ignore the call and voice mail notifications and delete the texts without reading them. Then I block their numbers.

Good riddance.

Hamilton wants to know if I can make it at 10:30 a.m. today and includes an address. Since that's the most important task of my day, I text him that we will be there. Then I map the address and see it's a cinder block building with no windows.

Not exactly a prison because it's missing the barbed wire fence, but close enough. I save the address and return to my messages. Lars responded late last night and again today, eager to meet up.

If I meet with Lars after Isla, then maybe he can start tomorrow. Hell, if I can get the lift and some of the large equipment delivered tomorrow, he can start on the bodywork. A surge of excitement runs through me because even though I'm unhappy with how this all came together, I always love the start of a new car. They're like putting together a puzzle and then making it pretty.

I text Lars to meet in town around noon at Margaret's diner. He immediately texts that he knows the place and will be there. Yeah, he has way too much time on his hands if he responds in seconds. Poor dude. There are also two messages from Zach, and after last night, I'm not interested in hooking up with him anymore.

Something's changed, and it has everything to do with Tomlin's tongue being down my throat. Even though he toyed with me in the kitchen this morning and I could easily use Zach to get off, the thought disgusts me. If I'm going to be completely honest, I don't want to have casual sex anymore. I want something more with the most unattainable person ever that just escaped to another city to get away from me.

Damn shame.

I lock my phone and pick up my purse and Anna before dashing out to the kitchen to grab the key and fob for the garage door. After double checking the front and back doors are locked, I slip through the mudroom and into the garage. Seeing Dad's chair bathed in sunlight by the window causes me to stop and look around at the rest of my boxes unloaded against the far wall.

As angry and disappointed as I am with Tomlin, he always seems to do nice things for me, and I can't figure out why. The king of mixed signals struck again.

So annoying.

I hit the button on the fob and the garage door behind my truck goes up. When I walk to the passenger door to put Anna inside, I realize he unloaded Dad's special box and panic consumes me. I run to the far wall, flipping through different boxes until I find it sitting neatly inside one of the empty boxes my clothes were in. It doesn't appear that he rummaged through it, and I exhale slowly.

The lid is tight to the box as I lift the edge to ensure everything is there. The cards he signed but never sent, not knowing where she lived. The love letters are full of anguish from his pain over the years. A few pictures of them together. Even one of all three of us when I was a baby. It's all intact.

I clear my throat, trying to stop getting emotional over the contents of the box. It's been many months since I opened it and, for good reason, I didn't want to bawl like a baby. More so now that I'm at Tomlin's place. I secure the lid and set it back in the empty box, vowing to hide it later in my room.

With that crisis averted, I return to my truck, slide behind the wheel, and tuck Anna into her tote on the floorboard. Then I back out into the circle drive, Tomlin's car long gone, and head to meet Hamilton.

Pulling up to the gray building, with gobs of concrete and no landscaping, is depressing enough. Having to give my name to the guard at the shack and wait for him to confirm I'm on the list is downright sad. That picture they used online must have been shot inside the fence because this place has razor wire all around it. Are they trying to keep the kids in or people out? Maybe both.

Hamilton is standing on the sidewalk by the front door, talking on his phone. If I were into men in uniform, I'd jump his bones. He's fine as hell in that cop outfit. As fun as role-playing would be, I'm only attracted to dark-featured men. A moody and aloof one in particular.

His wide-brim hat hides his eyes, but I don't miss the tenseness of his body as he yells during his call. He faces my car when he hears her engine, and I couldn't be prouder of her deep throttle. I cut the truck off, grab my purse and Anna's tote, and get out.

Looking around this depressing campus is making me

anxious. Thank God my new prison is a pristine mountain resort, but this poor kid has to live here.

"Hey, Hamilton."

I throw my chin up to accompany my greeting, and he pushes his brim up a millimeter when he ends his call.

"It's Officer Hamilton. And you can't bring the dog in there."

Those piercing green eyes cut a look to her tote where Anna is lying down like a good dog.

"Well, dammit Hamilton, you tell me this now? I can't leave her in the car. She'll die in this heat. Plus, Isla probably needs some happiness in this fucking kid prison."

He dead stares at me and I do the same. We can stare all the way until noon if he wants to because I have that much time until I meet Lars.

"Dani—"

"You're a big shot. Can't you flash your badge or something? Or use those good looks to con the female guards?"

His face breaks for a moment. Guys are such suckers for compliments.

"You know you're fine as fuck, so use it to our advantage or hell, Isla's advantage. Have a heart, Hamilton."

He shoves his phone into his front shirt pocket.

"Let's give it a try. For *her* sake."

I don't know why he's emphasizing that.

"Of course, for her sake. You won't take this damn dog, so it's the least you can do."

He starts for the door, and I walk beside him. His good cop manners have him opening it for me when we're met with a female guard.

"You sure this isn't a kid's prison?" I murmur beside him, and he gives me an annoyed look to be quiet.

"We're here for Isla Frank," he says to the guard, flashing his credentials through the bulletproof glass. "Give her your license, Danielle Louise Winters."

Now I'm giving him an annoyed look for using my full name. But as a good law-abiding citizen, I dig through my purse for my wallet and remove it to place in the cutout at the bottom of the plexiglass.

"I hate that you know my full name," I whisper to him, and he gives me an easy smile.

"Funny, because I rather like it. It's endearing, like an old southern name."

I roll my eyes at the reference to my accent when I tricked him. At least, it got me out of a ticket. The guard behind the glass punches stuff from my license into a computer and then scans it. I fidget next to him while looking around the small foyer, noticing these cinder block walls are everywhere and adorned with plaques of codes and laws.

"This place is depressing," I mumble, hoping they don't do a bag check when I glimpse the metal detectors in front of a set of double doors leading farther into the building. "Frank, huh? That's her last name? Did you find her family yet?"

Hamilton frowns at my questions but doesn't answer them. The lady's eyes flicker from her computer to me and then to Hamilton. It would help if he hadn't taken a vow of silence next to me. So much for him flirting with the guard to grease the wheels.

"I assume you've been here before, Officer Hamilton," the guard asks, shoving his credentials and my license through the cutout. He picks them up and hands me mine before answering.

"Many times. Through the door and to the right?"

"Yes, don't worry about the detectors. They'll go off, but we know why."

Her eyes linger on me, and she probably is wondering why I'm here in the first place. Probably assumes Isla and I are sisters, coming from a bad situation. Isn't that the case with most of these kids?

I've never been a victim of domestic violence. If a man ever tried, I'd be a prisoner of the state for sure. I'd murder his ass by cutting off his dick and shoving it down his throat. I wish they would do something like that to Isla's molester. That would be justice served.

Hamilton leads. I follow and clutch the top of the tote to prevent Anna's head from popping out. Like she said, the detectors go nuts when Hamilton passes through. When I look back, the guard gives me a dismissive wave to proceed. I'm pretty sure this isn't how it's supposed to go, but who cares? We're in.

"That was easy."

"It helps that she knows me," he smirks, stopping in the middle of a wide corridor.

"It would've helped if you flirted or something."

For all his bravado, he doesn't know how to use it.

"Is she coming or what?"

I look both ways, trying to see which direction she's coming from.

"Through those doors. She should already be at a table."

His face juts to a single door to my right. I push through it to see a tiny girl wearing a navy hoodie over gray sweatpants, both drowning her. When her face turns to me, it's not caked with makeup but is clean with dark bags under her eyes and that still fading shiner.

What's this place doing to her to look like she's gone to hell and back? She bolts to me like a long-lost child and throws her arms around my body in a super tight hug.

"All right, all right, get off," I huff, unprepared for this much of a reaction.

The room is full of round lunch-style tables with matching stools bolted to the floor and a television mounted in the corner. The gray on gray is depressing as hell. Can't some kids in here paint a few rainbows and butterflies on the walls?

Anna pops up like a jack-in-the-box, and Isla screams

before diving into the tote to grab her. She smashes the little dog to her face, instant tears streaming down her cheeks. Anna's tail whips fast and furious as she douses Isla in wet kisses.

"You brought her. You really brought her."

I smirk at Hamilton lingering by the door.

The love these two have for each other and their emotional reunion has me clearing my throat and blinking away my feelings. I've got to figure out a way to get these two reunited because they clearly need each other.

"Yeah, Hamilton may have charmed a few guards to get her in here."

I throw undeserved credit over to him, and he returns it with a bored look.

"Thank you, Officer Hamilton!" she hollers across the room while holding Anna against her neck.

I sit on the hard stool, dumping the tote on the floor and my purse on the table. She joins me, clutching that dog for dear life.

"What's going on? Why are you still here and not with your family?"

Her light brown eyes shift from under that blue and black mess of hair to where Hamilton checks his phone by the door. I know he's trying to appear as though he's not listening, but I suppose the good officer in him is constantly listening for new information and whatnot.

"Uh, don't worry about him. He's hard of hearing. Too many fucking hits to the head when he was young. Go ahead."

When her eyes linger a moment or two longer on him, he taps on his phone to make it look more convincing.

"I ran away."

Her voice is so light I lean across the table to hear her.

"What?"

"I ran away," she repeats a little louder this time.

I soften my voice to match her as best I can. I probably should have looked up some shit to ask her rather than rubbing my horny ass on Tomlin last night. Maybe watch some videos on YouTube about child protective services. It would have helped me now.

"Why?"

"My mom's boyfriend. He . . . uh . . ."

Humongous tears well up in her eyes as she looks over my shoulder to the window beyond. Even the windows have fucking bars on them.

"I get it. You don't have to explain."

My knee bounces because I want to go on a murderous rage on behalf of this girl and all the fuckers that have raped her.

"And your mom? Did she, um, know?"

"Yes," she whispers.

The answer causing her to bawl her eyes out into her sweatshirt sleeve.

What the fuck?

I slide to the empty stool next to her to rub her back. My eyes connect with Hamilton's across the room. His look says he hears this all the fucking time. What's wrong with these fucking women that join up with these fucking men? I swear, I hope they all get what's coming to them.

Anna's tail wags at twice the speed, whipping the side of her throat and clawing her way up Isla's neck to lick her face. I clear my throat again because watching this damn dog provide the only comfort this girl knows is ripping my fucking heart out.

"And your dad?"

Some dick had to be part of the fun because women can't knock themselves up. When she shakes her head, it enrages me because some men will knock it and rocket as if it's not their kid to raise.

Fucking bullshit.

"This shit . . . place, is better? I mean, not as bad as home?"

Home is vile on my tongue as I say it. "It's safe here? None of that fucking bullshit is happening, right?"

I'm asking her hunched head, but my eyes are laser-focused on Hamilton, who's also awaiting the answer. Because I swear, if something is going down here, too, I'll report it to every law enforcement agency I can find in this fucking state.

"No. It's strict. We have to go to class, and people try to steal my toiletries or pencils, but nothing like . . . you know."

Her voice trembles, but the tears stop flowing, and she wipes her face with the cuff of her sweatshirt. Stealing shit is not as bad as the molestation, but dammit if that shouldn't be happening either. I guess it's one problem at a time. But I make a mental note to ask Hamilton about that.

When her eyes glance at mine, I nod and give her a little smile to let her know she's got someone on her side. My hand falls away as Isla places Anna on the table and boxes her in with her elbows on each side. Anna's content to dance in between her arms, rubbing her body against Isla's face and peppering her with kisses.

"Did they tell you what happens now?" I ask, trepidation gripping my insides because I'm almost afraid to know.

Her hair falls forward, creating a curtain to block her face, and it takes everything in me not to push it behind her ear. Instead, I smooth my hand over my hair, tucking in a stray strand.

"I stay here until someone wants me."

That's about the saddest fucking thing she could say. I sort of know how shitty it is to be unwanted by a parent. It's why my mom left us. Left Dad with the burden of raising me. He'd never admit it. But after the last seventy-two hours of having my life turned upside down and caring for her dog, I sort of wonder what his life would have been like if he wasn't saddled with me.

Would he have stayed at the garage, or would he have gone

on to bigger and better things in life? I never thought that way before, but now it weighs on my mind.

"I wish I could figure something out, Isla. This is all new to me."

"Me too, but maybe you can take me? Become my guardian?"

When she turns to me, her eyes are big and imploring, and my knee bobs again with uneasiness. My mouth opens and closes while my eyes wander to Hamilton, who's slowly shaking his head. I agree with him. I'm barely taking care of her dog. How in the world would I raise a teenager?

"Isla, I know you think that any adult can take care of you, but trust me, I can't. I can barely take care of myself. As of yesterday, I was homeless, and now I'm staying with a customer and fixing up his car. I have to because I'm broke. It's not an excuse. I'm barely getting myself fed and clothed each day. I can't imagine being responsible for you too. Taking care of your little dog is hard enough."

"I get it. No one wants me."

Tears flood her eyes again and spill over her cheeks. The little dog dancing in front of her instantly tries to soothe her crying, and I rub her back. It's all I can offer at this point.

"Look, I know this place isn't ideal, but at least you're safe for now. You got me, you got Hamilton, and that's two adults in your corner, watching out for you. Even though we aren't here, we're both working all avenues on the outside."

Like the idiot I am, I'm making promises I'm not sure I can keep. And when I glance back at Hamilton, he's frowning as well.

What can I say? Do I tell her the truth? Dash all hope of her getting out of here and finding a family of her own? A decent family who won't do vile things to her. Yeah, I gotta help this kid. I have no idea how, but I'll figure this shit out.

"You really mean it? You'll help me?"

"Yup, give me some time."

She throws her arms around my neck and squeezes again. This girl has more strength than I give her credit for because she easily trusts me, whereas I easily trust no one. Maybe she's one of those that sees the good in people. I'm one of those that sees the worst in people, relying on them to convince me that they're good. Otherwise, I write them off as dead to me.

"Do you need anything? Something in here that people won't steal. Or that you want, that you're not being provided?"

I don't know what I can give her, but I'll make it a point to visit her at least once or twice a week and keep smuggling in that little dog.

"No. Getting to see Anna is all I need. Do you think she can come back in a few days?"

Her face is hopeful when she turns to look at me. I glance at Hamilton and his head slowly shakes no again. Dammit, if that stupid officer isn't telling me no all the fucking time. Hell, I won't ask for his help if I already know his shitty answer. He should know by now that I'm not going to take no for an answer. Let him keep trying to boss me around. It's his funeral. This child protective services facility is a depressing pile of shit. If she wants to see that little dog, then fuck them all because it's happening every damn time I come.

"Yeah, I think me and Hamilton can come back until I figure out how I can be added as a permanent visitor. Do you have a social worker or someone that I can talk to? Like an adult handling your case, or whatever this is called?"

"I have a bunch of people. There's a therapist that I have to talk to or a counselor, I think they call him, but I haven't seen him yet. There's a nice lady who comes in and talks to me about the court process. I'm not sure if she's an attorney or a social worker. It's all in between classes, so I don't always understand what they're saying to me. Sometimes I'm tired and feel lost and behind because I wasn't in school this last year."

I must have heard that wrong. I stare at her because I think she said she was living with Rick the Rapist for a year. Like she was fourteen when it started with him, even younger with the fucking boyfriend.

"You were with that guy for a year?"

I can't hide the surprise in my tone because I can't wrap my brain around how long she has lived this way. How long these fuckers have used her body like it's a toy?

My knee bobs twice as fast, and I tap the table to release some of the rage burning through my body. When her eyes flicker down to the table with a look of shame marring her face, I already know the answer.

"You know what, Isla? Fuck them. It's over now, and we move on. We hope both get their dicks chopped off and shoved up their asses. We figure this shit out. Get you out of this place. At least take advantage of the counseling so you can start getting past all this shit. That way, when you do finally get out of here, you're not dragging that fucking crap along with you."

Easier said than done. This shit's going to haunt her the rest of her life. Damn fucking shame. Her curious eyes bore into mine as if trying to figure something out.

"Can I ask you a question?" she mumbles, picking up Anna and planting kisses all over her.

"Yeah, shoot."

The little dog's head and bow block her lower face, but when her eyes harden a bit. I know I'm not going to like her question.

"Would you ever lie to me?"

It's a fair thing to ask. I can see that she has trust issues like I have trust issues. Both deserved, but from very different circumstances.

"Look, Isla, I'm not much in this life, and I don't have anything to my name, but I'm my own person. Some people may not like that but fuck them. I'm not a liar. I never have been, and I never will be. You may not like the shit that comes out of my mouth, but at least I'll shoot you straight. That I can guarantee."

She lowers the dog to tuck under her neck, and that's when a tiny smile peers back at me. I guess she liked my answer.

"You curse too much. I like it."

Jeez, that's the last thing this girl needs to take after me.

"Don't even start. It's a nasty habit that I am realizing more and more isn't good for me. And I'm thinking about doing something about it. Like, I'm not into all that self-help, hippie-dippie bullshit, but you definitely need it to heal from all this crap. Trust me, everyone keeps telling me about my cussing, and I don't know, maybe I'll fix it, or maybe everyone can go fuck themselves. I haven't decided."

Her smile grows wider, and it makes me feel good. I'm no motivational speaker, not by a long shot, but if I can help this girl out, then maybe I'll fix my cussing. Hell, can leopards even change their spots?

The door behind Hamilton tries to swing open. Luckily, his big frame blocks whoever tries to get into the room. Isla panics and jumps up to kiss Anna and puts her back in the tote on the floor. By her reaction, dogs are definitely not allowed here.

Hamilton intentionally buys us a few seconds as I stand to pick up Anna's tote and close the top to not get busted. I swing my purse on my other shoulder and lock eyes with him to say we're good.

An indiscernible nod has him stepping to the side and allowing an older woman with her hair in a bun and wearing glasses to step through. She instantly frowns at Hamilton and it makes me smile. He's on our side in his own quiet way.

"Isla, your time is up, and we need to get you to class."

"Yes, ma'am."

Isla turns and wraps me in another suffocating hug to

whisper "Thank you" in my ear and "I love you" toward Anna's tote.

And once again, it's the saddest fucking thing about this place. She slowly crosses the room, looking back at me once and dropping her gaze to Anna's tote before passing Hamilton to follow the older woman out the door. When the door closes behind Hamilton, I walk over to him and say, "This is fucked up."

"Unfortunately, we see this all too much."

"That's even more fucked up."

I realize that all the seriousness of the situation with Isla in this fucking kid prison dissolves my hangover. This kid has had a shitty start to life, and mine has been good in comparison. I need to quit my bitching and get some perspective.

"Damn, it's unbelievable how people treat their children, and these fucking men are pigs."

"Not all men are bad, Dani. Just as not all women are good. I've seen some terrible abuse inflicted by mothers too."

"That's bullshit. Why have a kid if you are going to let your boyfriend rape them? I swear, if I had a kid and someone did something to it, I'd carve him up and watch him die a slow death."

Hamilton opens the door for me, and when I walk through it, he says, "Having just met you, Dani. I wouldn't doubt it."

We walk down the hall together, about to clear the metal detectors, when I respond, "Just bring me fifty bars of soap in prison, so if I drop one, I don't have to bend over. Get it?"

He adjusts his hat and digs out his hot police officer glasses before smiling at me.

"I get it. Where are you headed?"

"Well, Hamilton, unlike you, I have to keep a dog alive. I'm going to get some more dog crap. Because you saw Isla in there. If something happens to this dog, she'll kill herself. So, no pressure."

"That's true. That dog seems to be her only source of comfort right now. You're living with your customer?"

"You seem awfully interested in my living situation, Hamilton. Are you trying to hit on me? I've never dated an officer, but I have been in handcuffs before, and not in a bad way."

I wink, but blonds aren't my type. Apparently, frustrating and arrogant elitists are.

He chuckles. "Why am I not surprised?"

His shoulder radio crackles with a static voice coming through, and he murmurs into it he's on his way.

"Well, I guess lunch is out of the question."

It comes across as more of a statement than a question, making me wonder if he's flirting with me. If yes, he's really terrible at it.

"Guess so. Hey, what's up with them stealing her shit? Can't you arrest someone for that or file a complaint somewhere in this kid prison? It's not right."

His hand pats his front chest pocket. "I noted that and will look into it."

"Look into it better mean fixing it, Hamilton. The last thing this girl needs is more stress."

"I will. Don't worry. And need I remind you again, it's Officer Hamilton."

Why he keeps yammering on about his title is beyond me. Hell, I should call him President or Alex and see how he likes that.

"Yeah, well," I mutter, my mind switching gears to this foster care business and how to break someone out of it. Add that to my list of crap I need to get done.

My problems are small potatoes compared to Isla's. At least I'm of age and can make my own decision, even if they are bad. That poor girl can't.

"Rain check on lunch. Text me when you want to see her next," Hamilton says, drawing me out of my thoughts.

He slides his sunglasses in place and touches the brim of his hat in saying goodbye. I don't bother replying. He knows I'll be up his ass about getting back in here with her. Hamilton goes back through the double doors, the detectors going nuts again, which barely gets a glance from the guard behind the plexiglass. I suck in a deep breath and push through the doors.

Now, on to the rest of my life.

31

I open the door to Eli's place, the smell hitting me anew. I chuckle. There's no way I can let Tomlin's house smell like this. Probably another thing I need to talk to Eli about.

"Welcome, welcome," Eli chimes from behind the counter without looking up.

"Sup, Eli?"

I make a beeline to him because this is the expert I need to talk to.

"You never texted me back, dude."

My tone is harsher than I intend it to be. When his face lifts, he has the biggest, brightest smile with grabby hands for Anna. That's cool. If I get a break from being a dog mom for a moment, I'll take it.

"Oh my gosh, how are my two favorite girls?"

He deposits so many loud kisses on Anna's head that my eyes flicker to his birds chirping at a squirrel on the sidewalk outside.

"What do you mean, not returning your text? I always respond."

Returning my gaze to his, I pull out my phone and open the message to where it was sent to him. He grabs the phone from my hands, looks at it, and then says, "ah," before handing it back.

"The number is wrong, sweetie. You're off by one digit. It should be a five and not a six."

He murmurs, "Momma is wrong", to Anna as if she understands.

I'm not her momma, that's for damn sure. Her momma's bawling her eyes out in kid prison. I pound on my phone to change the number, slightly annoyed by Eli's bright and sunny attitude.

"Okay, now that I got that straightened out. I need your help. She's not eating her food." Although Tomlin got her to, I'm sure as shit not calling him to ask. "Especially after you did all that taste testing in the aisle. I dropped it down, and she wouldn't eat it."

He smacks his lips while thinking about it and then holds Anna away to look into her face.

"Are you not eating your food, little peanut? That's not good. No, that's not good at all. Why—"

His baby voice grates on my nerves, and I cut it short.

"No, she's not. What's wrong with her?"

He steps around the counter to stand next to me.

"Hmm, why don't you walk me through exactly what you did, and we can figure it out from there?"

I take him through the morning and night feedings, a smile playing on his lips before he launches into what I'm doing wrong. It's a lot of things.

"See, this is why I shouldn't have a dog. Are you sure that you can't take her since you know so much about dogs?" He clutches her to his chest and Anna nuzzles her face against his shirt. "See, she likes you better than me."

His eyes dart around the store. No idea what he's looking

for since we are the only ones in here. When he leans forward, his voice is barely above a whisper.

"Okay, I shouldn't be telling you this because my partner would get mad if he knew other people knew, but I'm too excited that I'm having a hard time keeping it in."

That explains why he's in such a good mood, an even better mood than his already happy one from two days ago.

"What?"

"My partner, Ronald, he's so cute, has finally agreed to start with the adoption process."

He lets out a little squeal, and I stare at him as if he's lost his ever-loving mind.

"Wait, are you talking about a kid? Like you want a kid? Like five dogs or whatnot isn't enough? Plus, this place? With all these animals? That's a shit ton of responsibility."

"I know! He wasn't exactly sure that he wants to adopt, you know, after being in the system for all those years, but I finally convinced him."

He gives Anna about twenty more kisses, obviously over-whelmed with love at the thought of his family growing. Maybe this guy does have enough love in him for a kid or wants more responsibility, but I don't get it.

"Wait, did you say the system? As in foster care?"

Did the karma gods just smile on me? I'm not used to this.

His chin tilts down and his face is smeared with sympathy.

"Yes, it's tragic how those kids grow up in the system. Like my Ronnie, he's strong now, but his mom died at the hands of her abuser."

His hand covers his mouth as if letting out the secret is a big mistake. I wouldn't rat him out even if Ronald or Ronnie walked in right now. I'd have to know who he is first to tell him.

"His dad killed his mom?"

I mean, you see it on the news all the time, but to actually think that a dad would do that to a mom, in front of their kid. That's fucked up.

"No, she got pregnant as a teen. I think she was involved in drugs back then too. The abuser was a boyfriend or something."

"Damn, like her mom." I point to Anna.

He switches Anna to his other arm.

"Do you want me to take her?"

I go to reach for Anna, but he shoos me away.

"No, she's light as a feather. But what's going on with her mom? How old is she?"

I sigh, feeling a little guilty for telling him about Isla's business. But I need someone with foster care experience to talk this over with since Hamilton's ass seems numb to the whole experience. I wind up telling him the entire story, from what happened with Judd at the garage all the way to this morning.

He doesn't interrupt, just gasps and mutters, "Oh my" at different parts of the story.

When I'm finally done, he's practically in tears. Yeah, this is a normal person's reaction that hasn't been hardened by life as I have.

"That sweet girl, what she's been through? It's incredibly sad. All that and to lose her little dog . . ."

His voice trails off.

Emotions getting the best of him. He turns away to wipe his eyes while smashing Anna into his shirt.

"Well, from what Ronald tells me, foster care is tough. Very difficult for the child, not only for losing the parent and the house they were in. Which basically uproots their whole life, even if it's for their own good. But also, the jarring effect of dropping them into a new environment where they don't know anyone, can't trust anyone, and must compete for the necessities that you and I take for granted. Have they started her in therapy yet?"

"Not yet, but they will."

"Good, because that girl is going to need a lot of help to process and heal from it. The effects of what she's been through are going to be long term and you don't always know what triggers different things in them. Ronald had to fight and sometimes steal food to get enough, so he loves to walk every aisle of the grocery store to see all the choices available to him. He'll be there for two hours just sampling, shopping, and taking it all in."

"Wow."

I hate going to the grocery store. It's such a pain in the ass. Talk about things I take for granted.

"It's good that she has you to count on. She needs every good person in her corner to survive the system."

I didn't plan on standing here spilling my guts to him, but something about Eli's temperament and cheerful personality draws it out of me. It's like he's a ray of sunshine cutting through the dark clouds of my life.

"I'm trying. I just need to get this dog to eat because toast and french fries are all I can get down her."

"Uh, that's not good. Come with me."

He spins on his heel, murmuring to Anna how she needs to eat her dog food to be a healthy girl for her momma. It's both ridiculous and sweet.

I follow him down an aisle where he starts explaining about adding flavoring and how I need to mix in dry dog food to knock the tartar off her teeth. It's starting to sound a lot like Tomlin's fussy chemistry coffee. I don't have the time or patience for that nonsense. Annoyance and dread coil in my stomach as we stand in front of rows of flavoring packets.

"Are you sure you can't take her? This is getting to be too much work and I have to get my life together."

"Sweetie, you're doing the right thing and it will be fine. I can't bring home another dog when he's finally agreed to adopt.

Especially considering how long it will take that sweet girl to find a home. If she finds one at all."

He's petting Anna so softly that her eyes are closed, and she looks like Tomlin when he was meditating the other night.

"Excuse me? I thought I heard you say that she might not find one. If that's the case, I'll have this dog forever."

His expression freezes. His mouth gapes and his perfect eyebrows are sky high on his forehead.

"What's this look for?" I ask, noticing a colorful tattoo peeking out from under his shirt collar.

Interesting.

"Didn't that handsome police officer tell you about the statistics of foster care? It's not good, Dani. The older they get, the more difficult it is to place them. Some never get placed, and essentially age out of the system. Like what happened with my Ronald."

"Wait, wait, wait. You're telling me that girl has to live in that place for the next three fucking years? After all she's been through?"

He touches my arm. I know it's a sympathetic gesture, but it's making my skin crawl. I can't handle random touching and truth-telling at the same time. Only one or the other, and I prefer truth-telling, or maybe not so much in this case.

"Possibly."

I step back to get his arm off me because this is getting a little too real. No, that handsome fucking officer didn't say a damn word about all this. I swear, the next time I see Hamilton, I'm gonna rip his ass a new one.

"Fuck."

"Can't be saying that up there. That will get you kicked out of the visitation center. They're pretty strict from what Ronald has told me, so best to mind your p's and q's when seeing her."

I've cussed my whole fucking adult life, and it's never been a problem. Now I have more people riding my ass these three days about it than I have my whole twenty-one years.

"What am I gonna do, Eli?"

"You're going to give this dog the best life with my help. And let me talk to Ronald about the situation and see if we can meet for lunch to discuss your options, or rather her options because I don't know how good social workers are in this town. Ronald was in the system in Ohio because he grew up in Cleveland. Never go there. It's gross and depressing."

I know I shouldn't make this all about me, but damn if this doesn't suck. I honestly need to get my head out of my ass if I'm going to figure this shit out.

"I guess I'll wait for you to talk to Ronnie, and I'll talk to Hamilton about this foster care business."

"It's all you can do for the time being."

He showers more kisses on Anna before waving a hand at a display of food packets.

"Now let's see which ones our little peanut likes."

He turns to the display and picks up different ones for Anna to sniff. Some she likes and others she doesn't. Somewhere in the middle of picking out flavorings, it hits me.

"What about Isla?"

I don't know why this didn't click before. He gives me a side glance as he's putting the packet back on the hook and pulls a different one off.

"What about her?"

"You could adopt her. Ronnie knows what sort of hell it is. Surely, he'd sympathize."

I move closer to him, wishing I knew how to make puppy dog eyes because I'd make them now if it would help sell her case. He chews on his lower lip. His eyes roam past me to the store beyond, deep in thought.

"I don't know," he says after a while. "I mean, I had visions of babies and matching Halloween costumes, not teenagers and periods."

I knew it. He'd be one of those parents. One that makes homemade Christmas cookies, takes pictures on the first day of school, and brings snacks to after-school games.

"Like you said, she'll age out. You'll only have her for three years and then you can get a baby. Hell, get all the babies you like after. Just take her first," I beg.

I can't believe I'm doing this, but my hands are clasped in prayer as I try some weak-ass puppy dog eyes on him.

"You realize this is a human being we're talking about, not a puppy that you can return here if you don't like it?"

His gaze returns to mine, picking his words carefully. I get it, I could be more sensitive, but sensitivity isn't my strong suit.

"Yeah, well. Just think about it. When you talk to Ronnie about all this, please mention this option for her sake."

The flavor packet crinkles in his grip.

"Maybe. He works late tonight. I'll have to see."

He sighs, sharing the concern I have for her. Maybe it isn't fair to ask him. Maybe I crossed a line. But if it means finding her a new home with a doting animal lover and a guy that's been in the system before, then it's worth asking.

"I think I figured out what our little peanut likes."

Relieved that he's not upset that I asked or pushed him into asking Ronnie, I exhale a long breath.

"Good. Hey, I have to step outside to make a call, so whatever you decide is good. I'll be back in a minute," I say, adjusting my purse strap to search for my phone in it.

He doesn't say anything, directing all his attention to Anna and another flavor packet. Yeah, this guy would be great with babies, hopefully with Isla too. He wouldn't hurt a fly, and that's precisely the type of person she needs to be around to know not all men are rapists and motherfuckers.

32

I walk past the cluster of birds that have quieted down since the squirrel is gone and push through the glass door. The glare of a car windshield nearly blinds me when I get outside.

Throwing up my hand to block the sunbeam, I walk in the awning's shade to call Hamilton. It rings longer than I'd like. I want him to pick up immediately so I can bitch him out for not telling me the truth.

When his voice mail kicks on, I wait for the beep and then say, "Hamilton, you had better fucking call me back. I don't care if you have cop shit to do. Call me."

My thumb ends the call. I double-check the time to see I have fifteen minutes before meeting Lars. The timing couldn't be better, as I call Miller next. He should know about Tomlin's car from Judd. I can get him hunting down parts in the interim. Scrolling through my contacts, I find his number. He picks up on the third ring.

"Miller, here." His deep voice vibrates through the phone.

"Hey, Mills."

"Well, well, well. Dani, what do I owe this unexpected call for?"

I kick a rock with my shoe, and it pings a car fender before landing in the parking lot.

"I'm calling for parts."

"Really?"

Surprise laces his tone, and I get it. He's heard.

"I heard you were canned. Something about ruining Carl's place."

Yeah, that damn old man would say that. Ruining my good name everywhere he can.

"You heard half the truth, but yeah, I'm going out on my own. Fuck him."

His laugh is gritty from all those cigs hanging from his lips every time I see him.

"It's about damn time, Dani."

I ignore his comment because if one more person tells me I could do better than Carl, I'm going to scream. Why didn't these fools tell me that when I was working for him?

"Anyway, did you work with Judd on that 1972 Gran Torino?"

"Some. Why?" Something crashes in the background, and he muffles the phone when he curses. "Damn it, guys, can't you see I'm on the phone?"

I wait for him to stop bitching at whoever works there and to return to the line.

"Sorry about that, Dani. Training some new kid. You know how it goes. Good help is hard to find."

I think about Lars, and I hope he's good help because I sure as hell need it.

"Don't tell me that you're working on that car. Carl will blow a fucking gasket if he finds out you're stealing customers."

I heed the warning, but Miller doesn't know the truth.

"I hear you, man. The deal is the customer pulled his car

after what happened and had it towed to his home. Carl assumed I was working on it and dumped my tools off there. I wasn't going to work for that guy and fix up his car, but Carl cleaned out my apartment and put Dad's stuff in the dumpster. I had to fish it out in the rain last night."

Anger spikes in me about all those years being Dad's best friend and then tossing his belonging out like he didn't matter at all. It's bullshit.

"I guess you can say I'm working on the car now, mostly out of spite."

"That's not right. I understand being upset with you, but not your old man. They were buddies."

Miller's anger-laced tone matches how I feel inside. It's not right, but there's nothing I can do about it.

"Yeah, well. It turns out Judd was swapping parts and not telling the customer. When I saw the car yesterday, it was stripped bare. I need everything. I can't do original numbers anymore because I don't know what Judd or Carl did with them. Not much of it could be saved, considering the car's condition when we received it."

"Well, he didn't get those inferior parts from me. You know that?"

"I do."

I get why he has a huge attitude when he says it. Reputation is everything in this town. Even more reason why I need to restore mine.

"If that's true, it's good you got out of there."

I walk to the end of the shopping center, staring at the highway traffic going by.

"Yeah, yeah, I heard that already. But I'd appreciate it if you could jump on this if you can. She's going to a show in two months. I promised the owner I'd make his timeline."

His sigh echoes in my chest. I already know what he's going to say because I've said it many times myself.

GIGI MEIER

"Can't be done."

"Yeah, well, it's happening, or I'll kill myself trying, at least."

He grunts, making it clear that he doesn't believe me, but he continues, "Tomorrow. Come by, and I'll have something ready, or I can buy you a beer, and you can cry on my shoulder."

I don't miss the slight incline of his voice, but I gotta shut that hope down quickly.

"I'm good, Mills."

"Damn, Dani, cockblocking me at every shot."

"That's me, always a cockblocker."

My phone buzzes, and when I pull it away from my ear, it's an incoming call from Eli. He must have everything ready for me and is probably wondering where I went. I head back to the pet store.

"You still knocking boots with that prick?" he asks, and it surprises me.

Instant venom fires through me when I shoot back, "How did you know?"

"He brags about it at that bar you like to go to. Seriously, Dani, him over me?"

He sounds insulted and he should be. Zach has always been a lousy decision, but he's my lousy decision. Not for the whole world to know my business. I'll straighten that fucker out next.

"Yeah, I hear ya. But you want more than me. Zach knows the score. He doesn't want anything more than I do."

I go with honesty since I've known Miller forever, not to mention the ten-year age difference.

"Who wouldn't want more? You're a catch, Dani. Get rid of him, and I'll take you out. I'll give you what you want and keep the emotional stuff to myself. That work?"

I gaze across the parking lot because this isn't the first time Miller has offered. How do I tell him that 'more' freaks me out? I hate all this emotional shit. Plus, there's Tomlin. Even if he rejected me, I still can't get last night out of my head.

"I gotta go."

"Think about it, Dani, and for your sake, stop fucking the prick. You deserve better," he lectures.

I imagine those dark green eyes of his narrowing as he says it. It's not that Miller's not good-looking with a decent body. It's that he'll get all lovey-dovey, and I'll hurt his damn feelings. Doesn't he see that?

"And you're better?" I joke, trying to end all this mushy, gushy shit until he sighs.

Who's the prick now?

Me.

"I ain't worse."

I let silence fill the phone line until he clears his throat.

"Think it over, Dani."

I wish he'd stop bringing this up.

"I will."

"Don't patronize me. But come by tomorrow to pick up what parts I have, and we can go over what else you need," he concedes.

Talking shop is a relief, and now I'm the one sighing.

"All right, see ya tomorrow."

He holds the line. I'm sure wanting to say more, so I end it. The last thing I need is to get involved with a nice guy. Zach blabbering about us pisses me off. The angrier I get about it, the faster I stomp back to the pet shop. I throw open the door and charge over to Eli standing behind the counter with Anna in a ridiculous purple sweater with feathers around the neck eating treats on the counter.

"There you are. I looked out the window but didn't see you." He scoops up Anna, hugging her to his face to show off his handiwork. "How adorable does she look?"

"Uh, super?"

I wonder how much this is going to cost because Mr. Moneybags isn't here to foot the bill this time.

"Exactly. That's on the house," he says, adjusting her sweater. "I added the kibble she'll need and her flavoring, so with everything rang up, you're ready to go." He points to a large bag, and I envision the money flying out of my paint job fund. "Here's the total."

Sighing, I reach for my wallet and grab my debit card to drag down the machine.

"Oh, and I texted Ronald. He's amenable to discussing adoption tonight, but I'm not sure about Isla. I'll have to see."

Stuffing my card in my wallet, he dotes on Anna again.

"I appreciate it."

He beams so big, I look away, never recalling a time I felt as happy as he is.

"Of course. Now give me your number, so I can text you to let you know how it goes."

He holds up a finger, finding his phone buried under a stack of mail before I give him my number.

"Ah, just texted you." His notification vibrates my phone in my purse. "Fingers crossed."

I situate the bag on my arm before tearing her away from licking his counter of treat dust.

"Bye, little peanut."

He waves to her.

"Thanks, Eli."

33

After dropping the bag of pet crap in my truck, I toss open the diner door to look for Margaret. I don't think she'd throw out Tomlin's friend over bringing in a dog, but seeing as how she isn't here right now, I sigh in relief.

Lars is waving his big hand in the air to flag me over. As I draw nearer, he tries to shuffle out of the tiny booth, which is a battle given his size. It's a nice gesture, but completely unnecessary. I'm not that formal.

"Hey, Lars. Don't bother getting up, since I'm going to sit right down."

He flushes, his rosacea painting his cheeks bright red.

"Okay, um. Isn't this a weird place for an interview? I mean, I don't mind, but I figured it would be like at your garage or something."

I pick up the menu to look over the options since I'm starving and missed breakfast.

"He's the thing, Lars. I don't have a garage. Actually, I just started a new job in the most unlikely place. I'll go over it with you, and if it's not your jam, then cool. But I have to warn you, it will be a lot of fucking work. Like seven days a week."

His fingers drum the table in repetition, and it's hella annoying. I think he's nervous, which is weird because it's me, and I'm hardly intimidating.

"Okay," he says slowly, about to ask something when the server approaches.

I snap the menu closed and order toast, a cheeseburger, fries, and a chocolate shake before pointing to Lars. He seems even more hesitant to order, but I assure him it's my treat and to order anything he wants. His relief is visible. Maybe this guy is more broke than me if that's even possible.

He orders nearly half the menu. After the server walks away, I lean in, not giving him a chance to turn me down immediately because I need his help to meet my deadline. Two months, or six weeks, if I don't include paint and shipping. Miller said it can't be done. I said it can't be done, but come hell or high water, it will, with the help of this guy.

"Here's the deal, Lars. That guy I was with yesterday, well, he started with another guy, and he got screwed. He's invited to show his car at the Pebble Beach Concours d'Elegance. Have you heard of that show?"

His mop of hair answers yes, and a flash of him wearing a headband while he works flitters across my mind.

"Yeah, well, that show is in two months, like a hard two months, which gives me, or rather us, six weeks to fix this car. And I'll be honest, Lars, it's a rusted-out soup can. Probably one of the worst I have ever seen, but I committed to this guy to get it done. Dammit, I will. With your help, if you agree."

He finally stops drumming the table, thank fuck, and drinks his entire glass of water before responding.

"I don't have any experience like that. I mean, I just got out of mechanic school."

I know.

He said that when we met. He's a big dude, but his personality is so passive that it seems like he's been through some shit to make him this way.

"Yeah, but here's the deal. I've never been to school. I've only learned from my old man or taught myself. I don't care that you don't have any experience. It's probably actually better that you don't because then I can train you my way. Although it will slow me down, and I'm not the nicest person to be around, but I'm the best in this part of the country."

My mind filters back to what Tomlin said about Paul wanting to talk to me about working back East for him. I wait for the server to finish dropping off my toast and refilling his water before I continue.

Knowing Anna needs food too, I tear the buttery toast into little pieces and drop them into her tote. Her bow scraps against the inside of the tote as she gobbles it up. Like last time, I dump out all the jelly and pour some water into the bowl to put in her tote with her. Lars watches me but doesn't say anything until he has my full attention again.

"I appreciate you teaching me, but I also need the money."

His voice is small, and that's the reason for his hesitancy. Yeah, I get it. No one likes to come out and say they are broke, especially men.

"Of course, you'll get paid. I mean, I don't know the going rate because I've only worked at one place. Do you know what it is?"

I grab a grape jelly packet from the table, open it and smear the deliciousness on my toast before wolfing it down.

"I only know what the school said. Starting with no experience, I can expect to make about forty thousand dollars a year."

I choke on my toast, coughing and driving my fist into my chest. He leans forward, his hands flailing, trying to figure out how to help me. Anna stands on her hind legs to whine at me. I cough several more times, tears filling my eyes, and I stroke Anna's head to reassure her that I'm all right.

Clearing my throat, I reach for my water to push away the crust that's scraping against my larynx. Worry cuts lines across Lars's forehead as he hands me napkins from the silver dispenser.

"Are you okay?"

"Yeah."

My voice is hoarse and raspy.

"Did you say forty thousand a year? To start?"

"Um, yes. Is that bad?"

He drags his elbows off the table, leaning back as if he said the wrong thing. He did, but it's not his fault. Disbelief rockets through my brain because I never made over twenty-nine thousand a year with Carl.

That cheap motherfucker.

I have years of experience if I counted the times when I worked underage alongside Dad. Did he screw Dad too? Is that why we couldn't afford anything? My hatred for Carl keeps growing.

"What's the highest?"

Lars looks uncomfortable now. He shifts in the booth, shaking it a bit, and his eyes dart around before leaning onto the table to answer.

"Like, one hundred thousand."

His answer steals the air from my lungs. One hundred thousand dollars. It rattles through my mind everything I could afford if I made that kind of money. It's obscene.I could get my own place, get my paint job, and get my boobs reduced. Hell, I could easily pay for all the shit Anna needs. This is unbelievable how much money that would be—life-changing.

"Uh, Dani, you okay?"

His head tilts, concern lingers in his expression, and I blink to snap out of it. Tomlin said he'd pay twenty percent over parts, which sounded about right. Now, I need to call him and renegotiate this deal if I'm going to kill myself to get this car done. That jerk, he's taking advantage of me too.

My blood boils.

"I'm fine."

"Do you know how much he'll pay? Or is this just a one-time thing because I need a steady paycheck?"

He leans back when the food arrives, and I wait for the server to leave to answer.

"I need one too. Here's what I know. He wants to go into business with me or, rather, be a silent partner."

Although I need to work that out too, because the more questions Lars asks, the more I realize I haven't asked enough of my own.

"We get his car done, he takes it to the Pebble Beach show, and that'll get customers. Although I have a pretty good reputation in these parts, I need to let people know somehow."

I mean, I used to have a good reputation. But if Carl and Judd are out there spewing trash about me, I may not have a reputation to uphold. I need Tomlin's help more than I care to admit when filtering through all the details. I guess I was so wrapped up in trying to get my life back and then moving my shit to his house that I really haven't thought this through. I've been taking it literally hour by hour when I should think bigger picture.

I salt and pepper my food while Lars pours a massive glob of ketchup on his bacon cheeseburger.

"I know it doesn't sound like I know what I'm talking about. Or at least I don't have all the details worked out because it has come together faster than I expected. On Monday, I was working on this dude's Shelby, and then Tuesday, I'm fired, and now today, starting on his Gran Torino. But I can assure you that guy is legit, and he has money for days."

I take a huge bite of my hamburger as Lars is finishing up his bite, saying, "I can tell that guy has money."

"The Porsche?"

"I didn't see his car, but the Rolex, his glasses, his clothes, you can just tell," Lars says with a loosened sigh as if money would solve all his problems. Money is nice, but I don't work for money. I work for the satisfaction of a job well done. I guess I get that from Dad.

Anna scratches at me when she's out of food. I shred a bunch of french fries, drop it in there and find a part of my hamburger that doesn't have any cheese on it to rip off a piece. I'm going to have to wash out that tote with all the greasy food that keeps going in it.

"Well, Lars, what do you think? I know I didn't answer much because I don't know. If you want to see the heap of crap for yourself, I'd be more than happy to show you what you're getting yourself into before you take the job. This isn't going to be a walk in the park. Honestly, I quoted the guy ten to twelve months originally. He wanted it done in four. Having it done in six weeks is going to be twenty-four hours a day, seven days a week, for almost the next two months."

His eyes level me across the table, with only a bite of his first hamburger left in his hand.

"I'm not afraid of hard work. I need to make money as fast as I can."

Red flag.

I can't bring someone to Tomlin's house with a criminal record. I need to get a background check on this guy. Something in the way he says it, or maybe it's his desperate tone, that makes me uneasy. It makes me wonder if I've made the wrong decision inviting him here today.

"Why do you need the money? You're not involved in some shady shit, are you?"

I flash him a suspicious look because I'm not about to mess

up the rest of my life by bringing in some criminal with a rap sheet that will steal from Tomlin or threaten my safety. And this dude's size could do serious damage if he wanted to.

His gaze lowers to stare at the small stack of french fries on his plate. He pushes the last bite of his hamburger into the ketchup and eats it before wiping his hands on his napkin.

"Look, if you're in some sort of trouble, I can't hire you. You gotta figure that shit out on your own. I'm trying to offer you a legit job for the next six weeks, and then we figure the rest of this out as we go, or when we get new clients. So long as your work is satisfactory and you show up on time, you're hired. If you bring trouble to my doorstep, you're fired, no questions asked."

His blue eyes slowly raise under that mop of hair.

"It's none of that. I don't have a rap sheet or anything. I got a family to provide for."

A family? The dude moves fast.

"Damn man, how old are you?"

"Twenty-two," he mumbles, dipping his second burger in the ketchup pile before eating it.

I tear off pieces of my bun and drop to Anna before slurping my milkshake.

"You're twenty-two, and you have a family?"

His gaze shifts from my eyes to my milkshake, and I debate on offering him half.

"It's my mom and sisters. My mom works, but it's not enough, so I'm the man of the house."

"Oh, damn. I'm sorry."

I really am because that was an asshole-ish thing for me to say.

"Don't be. I don't want my sisters to go without. It's not their fault."

"How many sisters?"

"Four. My mom remarried but . . ." He trails off, and I don't blame him. Talking about family business isn't cool, but I basically forced him to answer when I threatened that he wouldn't get the job. Another asshole move on my part.

"No worries, man. If you are on the up and up, then we're cool. We all got shit to deal with, right?"

"Yeah."

He hangs his head, avoiding my eyes, and I get it. Pride is a big deal for me too. I shut my trap and go about finishing my food as he does his. I feed Anna a few more french fries and try to get her to drink some water, but she wants more food.

When the check comes, Lars reaches for his wallet, and I stop him to throw down my debit card.

"I already said I got this. Consider it a company lunch, without the company yet," I say to lighten the frown on his face. He's trying to do the right thing by paying, but it's not necessary.

"Thank you." He leans over to put his wallet away, the booth creaking in protest. "You said I could see it today?"

I said that, but I wanted to run by Zach's place to give him a piece of my mind after what Miller said. And I need to call Tomlin about how much I'm getting paid on this deal, and how much to pay Lars.

"I have a couple of things after this, but could you do this evening? It's about twenty-five minutes from here, up by Sangre De Cristo Range."

I down the rest of my water to get the bowl out of her tote and pour what Anna didn't drink back into it.

"I don't know where that is, but I can only do it today because I have to be home to watch my sisters while my mom works tonight."

Well, damn. I can't blow him off just to bitch out Zach. I gotta put business over my personal matters.

"Okay, let me see if I can move a few things around. Can

you give me five minutes to step outside and make a few phone calls?"

"I don't want to cause any trouble. I could do Saturday if that's better for you?"

He splays his hands on the table. How does he get those bear paws into the tighter spots of the engine?

"Saturday's too late because that takes out two days that we could be working. Give me a second and watch my dog. Anything happens to her and you're dead meat."

I point my finger in his face, and his eyes widen in surprise. He drags the palms of his hand off the table, and they squeak from the sweat underneath them.

"I-I won't hurt your dog."

"Good."

I scoot out of the booth and stand as the server is bringing my card and the receipt. I scribble the tip and leave all the papers on the table.

Taking care of his momma and four sisters, I doubt he'd hurt Anna, but a warning is always a good thing. I text Zach, saying I want to see him tonight. He'll assume it's the usual and I can't wait to burst his fucking bubble.

There is also a text message for a delivery window on the big equipment in a couple of hours. Damn, that was fast. Tomlin must have paid for priority delivery or something. After confirming the time, I call Tomlin. He sends it straight to voice mail, and that fucker is going to be sorry for avoiding my call.

What a pussy.

"Hey asshole, don't send me straight to voice mail. After the shit you pulled this morning, you need to take my calls because if I need a decision or an answer, I need it quickly. I can't wait all day for you to decide whether you will answer your phone. Anyway, I need to know exactly in dollars how much you're gonna pay me. Because twenty percent may not be a good deal, and I'm thinking of renegotiating it. Fucking call me back."

I wanted to leave a longer message, bitching him out, but this old couple is walking by me, already giving me the evil eye. Probably because of my language. Oh well, I don't need the whole five minutes since Tomlin didn't answer, and Zach still hasn't responded.

I stand by the front door, putting my card in my wallet and stuffing my phone in my purse before going back to the booth. I didn't realize Lars's watching me the whole time.

"That didn't take very long."

"Yeah, well, I couldn't get ahold of the people I needed to talk to. If you want to go up to the garage now, we can. In fact, I got a text message that they're delivering some equipment today. You can see that too."

"Okay."

His hands rub together, and I take it as a sign that he's eager to get his hands working on something.

"I'll text you the directions unless you want to follow me up there."

I slide out of the booth and put my bag on one shoulder and Anna on the other while he pushes the table away from him to get out of the booth. When he stands beside me, I forgot how tall he is, and the curious looks we are getting for the family next to us are understandable. He's huge and I'm not.

"I have to get gas. If you can text me the address, I'll meet you there."

"Sure," I say over my shoulder as we walk to the exit.

Once outside, I copy and paste the address from Tomlin's text to Lars's. When his phone pings, he drags it out of his pocket, confirming he got it.

"Waze it because it's in the middle of nowhere. Oh, and you'll know when you get to the place because he has this large antler post across the front. I know, completely tacky, but it runs over the top of his gravel driveway. I think it says something, but I can't remember." I shrug.

"Got it. I'll be right behind you."

"Cool, text me if you have trouble finding it."

He nods, focusing on putting the address in the navigation app while I walk to the car.

I'm proud of how I handled my first interview ever. Although I knew almost immediately that I was going to hire the guy. I need help, and he's the only person I know. Plus, with his enormous size, it'll help get the car on the lift, and fast-track the bodywork.

34

"Is this the Takahashi residence?" asks the guy driving the truck that narrowly missed clipping the driver's side mirror off my door. He looks around the outside of the garage, trying to find the address as Lars climbs out of his truck.

"Yeah, I'm receiving the order on his behalf."

I step from the cool shadow of the garage and into the blistering summer sun. The driver gives me a once over before that bear of a man comes to stand beside me.

"You're Danny Winters?"

The driver looks at Lars. Who, in turn, points to me.

"I'm Dani. Did you bring someone else to unload, or are we helping you?"

I get down to business because the faster I can get this done, the quicker I can show Lars around and go over some things with him.

"Yeah, there's another guy in the truck."

The dude turns and whistles and the passenger door pops open. The glare on the windshield blocks the guy until he jumps out the side. He's not much bigger than the driver. Luckily, Lars is here to help.

"Okay, you see that open bay? Start setting everything up over there."

His gaze follows my finger to the spot that I parked in last night, grateful that Tomlin moved my boxes out of the way. I'm beginning to think that after he approved the orders, he came out here to get it all organized. That and drying my clothes for me, which was kind of nice. But the third rejection and not being good enough for anything beyond business partners stings a lot if I'm being honest with myself.

"I'll help."

Lars looks down at me as if asking for permission and telling the driver simultaneously. I simply nod.

"If you will sign here, we'll start unloading."

He thrusts the handheld device and pen toward me while Lars walks off to meet the other guy at the side of the truck. I have to admit, it's really fucking nice to sit back and watch other people do the work. Carl always had my ass going to Miller's to pick up parts. Tomlin having these delivered with help to unload is a night and day difference. One of many. Maybe this partnership will go well after all.

"How do you want everything set up, Dani?" Lars asks, a large crossbeam for the lift hoisted on his shoulder.

"Well, the lift has to go in the center, as you know. If we can put the bigger equipment against that wall, I'll move the boxes while you guys are bringing in the heavy stuff."

He nods, swinging the heavy metal to clang on the epoxy floor while I go through my waterlogged boxes. With everyone having a job to do, we work in silence. Anna dances beside me. The noise from the guys maneuvering the heavy equipment echoes across the concrete floors and is making her nervous.

Periodically, I glance at Lars, who's bantering with the guys while they assemble the lift and move the large equipment into place. Seeing his expression, he looks like he's enjoying himself.

I pick up Anna and collect Dad's special box to tuck under my arm as I walk through the diner, past the mudroom, and into my bedroom. Once inside, I put the box on the dresser and set her on the floor. She trots over to her dog bed, content to curl up in her favorite corner.

The doorbell chimes throughout the house and I jog out to the garage to Lars waiting for me, with the lifted erected behind them. I smile. Now, this is progress, and progress always makes me happy.

"That looks really good."

Lars's mop of brown curls wiggles when his head snaps in my direction.

"I tested the lift and the other stuff for you, but if you want to test yourself, I get it."

I usually would, as that jackass, Judd would say shit worked when it didn't or deny breaking things when I know he did. But Lars isn't Judd. I trust him, or else it will be his ass later.

"Good, let's get this baby on the lift to see how it holds."

I'm definitely glad that I have Lars here because of his enormous size. I'm grateful to have his strong muscles help get this sucker up on the lift because I couldn't do it alone.

"This it?" His eyes light up when he sees the car, then whistles at how bad of shape it is. "Oh, they need you to sign off on delivery so they can leave."

The delivery guys are milling about by their truck when I walk toward them.

"You already signed for delivery. If you're happy with how things work, then we'll take off," the driver says.

"Yeah, we're cool. And watch my truck when you try to get out of here. I wouldn't want to call your boss because you took the mirror off," I warn, wanting them to know I saw what almost happened.

I don't have the time or patience to deal with any fuckups. I have had enough fuckups in my life. They exchange looks and cross in front of the truck to change places behind the wheel. I don't care who's driving, I don't want any damage to my truck or Lars's.

I move to stand in the shade the metal roof provides, with my hands on my hips, and watch them maneuver their truck around the circle drive. I don't give a shit if I look like a nosy old man watching the neighbors. I want to ensure they leave without damaging Tomlin's fence too.

Screeching metal and burning rubber forces me to whirl around to Lars pushing the car out of the garage by himself.

"Hold on, let me help!" I holler while dashing over to join him at the front bumper. I'm pretty sure he doesn't need me at all, seeing how he's pushing faster than I am, and my sneakers are slipping on the rocks when we get into the gravel.

"I got this, Dani. Guide it onto the rails for me."

He stops pushing, moves to the side of the car, and shoves it away from the garage's supporting beam. I jump out of the way when he rounds the back of the car to get situated at the back bumper.

With his hands splayed across the metal, he hollers, "Ready."

I walk to the lift's foot pedal to lower it while he waits. A large piece of the metal frame hangs down, scraping the gravel when he aligns it with the lift. The sound is heinous, hurting my ears and causing me to squint.

Sweat rolls down his face as he pushes the heavy car into place. Once it's on the lift, I secure chains around the tires to ensure it can't roll in either direction. He joins me inside the garage, and we stand side by side, looking at it.

It's going to be both challenging and fulfilling. Seeing how hard Lars's already working causes me to smile as I look from the tired rust bucket to his beat red face.

"What do you think? You up for it?"

His eyes sparkle at the car.

"This is awesome."

"She will be if we can get her done in six weeks. As I said, she's a rusted-out soup can right now."

His hand caresses the dented roof, following the lines of the tree that destroyed it, and gets sticky sap on his fingers.

"That guy didn't even bother to clean it first?" Lars says in surprise.

"Nah. Now I figure you can get started on the bodywork, like pounding all this out. And as we go through the engine and parts come in, we'll work on those together."

His eyes never leave the car, taking in the exterior work that needs to be done before sticking his head into the cab's interior, which isn't much better off.

"And the upholstery?"

"Well, I usually send that off. Carl had this guy that did great work, but I don't know. I don't know if he'll work with me. I'll have to find that out. I source my stuff through Miller's Auto Parts. I already spoke to Miller today. He's hunting down some parts for us as we speak. Come look at the engine."

I move to the front of the car, running my fingers under the hood to find the latch, and then prop it up with the holder for Lars to see. I don't bother with the overhead lights as I use the flashlight on my phone to show him how bare it is.

"It came like this?" He points to the empty engine block.

"Basically. That's why I'm having Miller go out and find what he can. But we need to work on getting a rundown of parts over to him. Whatever he doesn't have, we'll have to source nationwide, or you and I will look through some junkyards."

His hands roll one over the other, eager to get started.

"Tell you what, how long can you stay today before your mom has to be at work tonight?"

He looks at me and frowns as if disappointed that he has to leave at all.

"I've gotta be home by seven o'clock, which means I have to leave here at 6:15 p.m. since I live on the opposite side of town."

Forty-five minutes away.

Damn, that sucks.

If he's willing to make the drive, I'm willing to take the chance.

"All right, then. Let's get started."

For the next few hours, Lars and I go through every inch of the car, itemizing what I think I'll need from what we can see. During that time, he volunteers that he is good at upholstery because his mom taught him to sew clothes for his sisters and their dollies. Who knew this guy would be so helpful and nice at the same time?

Karma smiled at me that day at the impound lot. I don't want to get all spiritual and shit, but maybe my car was meant to be impounded for a reason. And that reason came in the form of Lars.

Time flies, breaking down the exterior and coming up with an extensive parts list. Lars sketches some ideas about the upholstery after I show him Tomlin's trophy room. He's as impressed as I am and thought a custom design for the seats would hit home. We part ways with me agreeing to talk to Tomlin about the pay and Lars agreeing to meet me at Miller's the next morning.

I breeze through getting ready and feeding Anna. Or rather putting her food down with the flavoring in it and watching her sniff it and walk away. At least she went outside to go pee before I left.

Now to settle a score.

35

H is hazel eyes roam all over my black tank dress before giving me an appreciative smile.

"Hey, Dani, aren't you a sight for sore eyes?"

I barge past him, into the dump he calls an apartment. The coffee table is littered with cigarette butts, beer cans, and junk mail. The stench of stale pizza clings to the place, stoking my already red-hot anger.

"I heard you've been running your fucking mouth up at my bar. Is that true?"

I whirl around to confront him, my purse slapping against my hip. He closes the door softly and leans his bare back against it. Granted, he's a gym rat with defined muscles, but scrawny compared to Tomlin. The wavy brown hair that normally dusts his shoulders is pulled into a manbun at the back of his head. He's caught off guard and I'm fucking relishing it.

"I mean, I might have mentioned it to a few of the regulars over a game of darts," he defends, kicking off the door to pluck clothes off the couch and clearing a spot for me to sit. I shake my head because this isn't a social visit.

"What did I tell you about that? This arrangement we got is private. I don't need you spreading my business around town."

My fingers curl around my purse strap, the tightly woven fabric rough in my callous hands. He balls up the clothes and tosses them into a hamper by the TV stand before answering.

"It's no big deal." He stalks toward me, his hands reaching out to touch the curves of my body. "Take it as a compliment that I'm bragging."

"What the fuck?"

I tilt my head, trying to understand his justification for bragging. He's acting like a horny teenage boy telling his friends at school that he got laid.

"A compliment?"

I'm not all flowers and candy, but a woman's privacy is a woman's privacy.

"Yeah, I wouldn't be doing this if you weren't hot as fuck."

Wrong fucking thing to say.

I release my purse, my hand slithering to his hairy chest, and a groan rumbles in his throat. My fingernails claw into his skin to push him away. He stumbles, completely confused.

"What the hell?"

"You wouldn't fuck me if I wasn't hot?" The toxicity of his words makes me want to choke him out. "That's an asshole thing to say."

My gaze drops to the five indents in his pectoral muscle. Satisfaction takes my anger down a notch. I should have ripped his fucking chest hair out.

"Dani, if you're pissed about the bar, I'm sorry, but don't be a little bitch about it. You know you're hot, and so am I. This is why it works because I don't fuck ugly chicks."

I don't even know where to start. Him calling me a bitch or that he calls women ugly, or that he's blabbering my shit all over town. All three.

"You're a fucking asshole." I wag my finger back and forth. "This is over."

My phone vibrates in my purse, but whoever it is will have to wait. Probably Hamilton since it's been hours since I left him that voice mail.

"Come on, Dani. You're overreacting," he complains, like a little boy losing his favorite toy.

"You're ruining a good thing here."

"Nope, it *was* good until you started spreading my business and calling me a bitch just now." I twist the door handle and yank it open. "And do me a favor, keep your trap shut or I'll take a baseball bat to your precious Camaro."

"You wouldn't," he says, sulking by the side of the door. I pop an eyebrow up. "Fine. I won't."

"Good."

I slam the door with all my strength, and it bounces off the frame. Anger burns through me at his audacity. Satisfaction fires with it at my badass way of handling things.

I dig for my car keys, debating on carving my initials in his car. It was fun when I did it on Tomlin's door and this is even more justified. I'll let it slide this time, but if I hear so much as a peep out of him, I'm carving it up.

Right as I plant my ass behind the steering wheel, my phone vibrates, and I rifle through my purse to get it. It's Tomlin. I'm already in a foul mood, so I'm ready to let him have it over cheating me out of fair pay.

"Tomlin."

It comes out as more of a bark than his actual name.

"Dani? Thank God, you're okay."

His words tumble out in a rush, which confuses me.

"Why wouldn't I be, okay?" I ask, smashing the speaker button and setting my phone on the dash to pull at a hangnail.

"I got your message and called you as soon as I was done in

the training room. When you didn't pick up all those times, I thought maybe something bad had happened to you."

How many times did he call? I pick up my phone and see four missed calls.

"Oh, like Lars murdering me, and your guilty conscience was bothering you about it?"

I'm on a roll with making guys feel like shit, so why not him? Payback for how shitty he made me feel this morning. Sure, I'm not all sweet like Kylie crying over their breakup. But I have feelings too. He didn't have to lead me on in the gym and then drop me. That fucking sucked.

"I know, Dani. I'm sorry for that," he says in a sincere voice that has me staring at my phone. It's silent on his end, with no yelling or judo sounds or whatever noise they make when sparring.

"Where are you?"

Technically, it's none of my business, but a part of me is nosy as hell and wants to know.

"Home, in Denver. I debated on driving to the cabin tonight when I couldn't get a hold of you." He sighs, either trying to sell his concern or it's genuine. I can't decide which, so I probe for more.

"Why would you do that if you are already at home?"

"I was here to grab my stuff and head there to find you."

Hmm, how bad do I make him feel about this? It's very, very tempting because I like having the upper hand with him.

"I can take care of myself, Tomlin. I don't need you to do it and you've made that very fucking clear, *business partner*."

I go with really bad. I want to make him feel like shit. I know I'm being catty as hell, but he deserves it with his life partner bullshit. I mean, did he seriously date Kylie with a life partner in mind?

"Dani—"

"Why the hell are you paying me like shit? Huh? That's what I really want to talk about."

The line is quiet for a few moments. I swear, I can feel him wanting to go back to talking about us, not as business partners, but I'll shut that shit down every chance I get.

"Twenty thousand is not enough?" he finally says.

I stare at the phone, wishing I had FaceTime with him now because I can't tell by his monotone if he's serious or joking.

"You're paying me twenty thousand? To do your car? What the hell were you paying, Carl?"

I'm astonished.

My palms sweat when I think of that kind of money in them. Twenty thousand for six weeks of work, and then coordinate the other two weeks with the paint shop and ship her to Palm Beach. It's almost my entire year's salary from Carl's place. That's dumb as hell.

"One hundred thousand, parts and labor."

Holy shit.

I fall back in my seat, blankly staring out the windshield at the apartment complex. Shock doesn't even cover what I'm feeling.

"Dani, I really would prefer we discuss this in person. I don't like not being there."

I hear him, and yet I don't. My mind is trying to process that kind of money for one car restoration. One hundred thousand dollars.

Damn, there's no way parts and labor add up to that. I mentally tick through the list Lars and I created today and even with buying the large equipment that we'll use on other restorations, I still can't get to one hundred thousand.

There's no way.

I place my elbow against the doorframe to make it easier to hold my phone. This is going to be a longer conversation than I intended.

"Didn't you research how much this should cost you? Like ask Paul and then compare it to Carl?"

"Can this wait until I'm there? I don't feel comfortable talking about this on the phone."

"FaceTime me."

I hit the red button, ending our call, and wait. It doesn't take but a few seconds before he calls. When I accept, he's shirtless, with wet hair.

That little liar.

He's not rushing around to get things ready to leave.

"Doesn't look like you were on your way here."

"I had to take a shower first."

He walks over to the bed to show me a bag lying open with clothes and a laptop nearby.

"Where are you?"

Maybe FaceTime isn't the best idea because now I'm getting the third degree. He doesn't need to know that I'm outside Zach's apartment. That's my business.

"I'm at Kylie's."

Lie.

I adjust the phone to bring it closer and block out more of my surroundings, hoping he buys it.

"Okay, spill."

He sits on the bed, the edge of a towel coming into view over his fine-ass V-shaped hips. It still annoys me that he turned my ass down.

"I wanted you to do the work, so when Carl quoted me that figure, I accepted. I didn't think anything about it."

I have a ton of questions running through my mind that I blurt out all at once.

"Why me? Why didn't you renegotiate when it was Judd? What's so important about this car, anyway?"

His shoulders slump, his mouth flattens, and he glances

away, lost in thought. A few more seconds pass before he clears his throat and looks at me.

"It was my mom's car. It took me a long time to find it, but when I finally did, I only wanted the best to work on it. Then you didn't want to do it. I got angry because you didn't know what I had gone through to find it in the first place. You called it all sorts of names and we bickered about it. I thought screw this, I'll get Judd to do the work and rub it in her face. I know it was juvenile, but in a way, I felt like you were insulting me, and to a lesser extent, my mom."

Damn.

I rub a hand down my face, feeling like a total piece of shit.

"I didn't negotiate the price because I wanted it done. I wanted to show her car, but now, I'm not sure." He shrugs, resigned to the fate of his bad decisions and my assholeness.

"Why didn't you explain all this to me before? I understand how sentimental people get about these cars. It's why I'm picky about my work."

It's not completely my fault. He wasn't entirely upfront with me. His stare bores into me until the corner of his mouth twitches.

"Dani, don't take this the wrong way because I'm not trying to start anything, but you're hard to talk to. I have given it a lot of thought, and you are rarely this open as you are tonight. Most times, it's that crusty exterior and hardheadedness, and there's no reasoning with you. You challenge everything everyone says. Although I'm always up for a challenge, you don't know when to stop."

I listen, trying to continue being open even if his words hit a sore spot within me. He's not the first to say something like this. Probably not the last either. I thought I sort of showed him my vulnerable side when we stood together looking at Dad's chair. I guess that was all about me, though. This is about him.

"You were so defiant that day, and then called me an

asshole, it brought out the worst in me. I was waiting for you to back off and when you wouldn't, I kept going. It's why I'm good at what I do. I won't stop until my opponent has lost."

I prop my phone against the dashboard and lean forward. Mad respect for his candor.

"I guess we both want to win."

It's all I can figure out because everyone breaks before I do. It's what I count on happening so I can get my way. If he won't break, nor will I, then we'll have to compromise.

"I believe so, but we can't keep battling each other if this is going to work. When Paul said you are one of the best, I believed him. I saw how you were with that customer and how emotional he got over your work. It's why I want to back you. If we can take this car to Pebble Beach, then the work is going to flow in. You'll have more work than you'll know what to do with. You could be the next Paul."

He's so damn earnest in cheering me on that it's making me uncomfortable. I glance out the window to see Zach fully dressed for a night out, crossing the grass to his car.

The paradox of one guy believing in my talent so much to not mess it up by fucking me. The other viewing me only as fuck worthy makes me mad and sad at the same time.

"Thanks, T," I mumble when I look back at him.

"I mean it, Dani. I hope you know that."

I clear my throat, not wanting to feel the feelings that are coming up. Someone is finally believing in me like Dad used to. It's hard to take.

"Don't pay me twenty thousand. Your project won't cost one hundred thousand. I don't know where Carl got that figure from, but I'm only at twenty-two thousand, even with the lift, welder, and other equipment. You know they won't be originals. And I have a guy looking for parts now. Lars and I plan on going through junkyards for the rest. I couldn't get to Carl's figure unless I was doing three cars."

"But—"

"No, Tomlin. Worry about getting that money back from Carl's, and we'll settle up later."

I cut him some slack. It's the right thing to do and over-paying me makes me sick to my stomach. I don't have it in my nature to scam good people like Carl apparently does.

"With all due respect, I appreciate it, but I'm still paying you what we agreed. Blame my ignorance, but you're worth that and much more."

He moves up the bed to lean against a bunch of pillows. Damn, if I don't want to be right beside him, crawling under the covers to get it on.

"All right, all right. Stop buttering me up." I pluck the phone from the dashboard, trying to smother my smile.

"And she's back. Glad I got all that off my chest before you went all hardheaded again."

He smiles, and I chuckle. It's kind of nice having someone that gets me. I try not to come off as an ass all the time, but I can't help it.

"Yeah, well, I hired Lars. He was already up at the place, helping with the delivery, and even pushed your car onto the lift for me."

His eyebrows shoot up. I smile because I'm proud of myself for hiring my first quality employee.

"He's up for working seven days a week too."

"Really?"

"Yup, get this. He's helping his mom raise four sisters. It's a long story, but he's eager to learn and needs the money." I fix my hair in the rearview mirror and clean up the outer edge of my lip gloss. "We're starting first thing in the morning."

"Do I need to talk to him about pay or—"

"Nah, I got it."

Twenty thousand is too much. If Lars works as hard as I do, then we can split that. I know it's not the forty thousand he said earlier, but ten thousand for six weeks is still a shit ton of money and will go a long way to helping his family.

He watches me as I fix my makeup.

"You look nice. Are you out and about?"

When I look at the screen, he's lying down with his hand tucked behind his head and looking fine as hell with his bicep muscle bulging near his ear.

"Yeah, something like that. I've got an early morning. I'm out to grab a bite to eat and then back to the house."

I can't say home because it's not. Nor can I tell him the truth of where I'm at, because Zach isn't worth ruining all the nice words Tomlin said about me a moment ago.

"Order some groceries. I left the instructions and my card."

"Yeah, well."

I may or may not depending on how inclined I am to stop eating out. If Lars and I are going to work nonstop, it would be helpful to grab sandwiches and chips from the kitchen.

"And Dani, I'm glad you're safe. I probably won't be back this weekend. My training didn't go well today."

His face is weary. He doesn't need to come back to the cabin to check on me if that's what he's worried about.

"I'm good. Lars is a good guy, and Tomlin, don't worry. We got this. I know I told you before that we wouldn't make it, but I'm telling you now that we will. I'm sure of it. Focus on your high kicks or whatever and visualize your dad as your opponent. That should help with your training."

He chuckles. I hate how good it feels making him laugh. I need to stop crushing on him. It will only lead to my hurt feelings.

"Thanks. Take care, and call or text when you need me."

"Yup. Bye, T."

I click to end the call because he looks so fucking hot lying on the bed that it's making me horny. Oh well, with Zach out of the picture, I'm back to my lame solo game.

36

Sitting here wondering what to do with myself, I tap the side of my phone. I'm glad I start work tomorrow because sitting around with all this free time feels weird.

I guess I'll do what I told Tomlin I would do. Get dinner and drive back to his house. It's funny, he calls it a cabin because that thing is anything but a cabin.

Deciding to go for tacos, I throw my car in reverse and peel out of there as fast as possible.

So long Zach.

It was good while it lasted.

I know exactly where I'm going for tacos—this greasy place downtown by all the tattoo shops. I've always dabbled with the idea of getting a tattoo and I admire the artistry that comes out of those shops but has never dared to get one.

Once I get there, I park along the street, rather than battling it out for parking spots that are way too small for my long truck doors. Plus, it's always interesting to people watch as I walk down the sidewalk.

The place is crowded for a weeknight. I order my tacos from

one truck and wander to a picture window where a dude is getting a huge back tattoo. Two chicks are falling all over each other laughing, probably drunk as hell, and a couple to the left are getting matching tattoos.

I stand there for quite a while, watching the ornate detail of the burly artist with thick gauges through his ears and a septum ring through his nose. He glances up when he wipes the blood and excess ink from the guy's back. I throw my head up as a greeting, and he does the same before returning to his client.

When my name is called from the taco truck, I swipe my order off the counter and walk back to the window. Setting my drink on the ledge, I eat and watch him work on the tattoo.

The artist has clearly been doing this for several years. It's fascinating to watch his speed and accuracy as he freehands a blue-black skull on the dude's expansive back. I marvel at the collaboration that must have taken place for the dude to trust the artist to tattoo his entire back with no pattern or sketch.

It's obvious this is a custom piece, and it reminds me of my cars. I have a vision of what I want them to look like, as does the client. Often, they bring in pictures to have it restored to its former glory. I can't imagine this process being too different from the discussion I've had with my clients. We agree on a shared vision and alter it as needed.

Long after I'm finished, the artist motions for me to come in. Why the hell not? I have nowhere else to be. I yank open the door, and a couple of eyes turn in my direction as I walk over to the bald guy.

"You interested in getting one done?"

His voice is gravely, giving Sam Elliott a run for his money. It's sexy as hell, but I'm more impressed with the tattoo crawling out of his shirt and up the side of his neck to coil into his ear.

"Nah, man. I'm good."

He stops, looks at me, and then points to a chair on the other side of the dude, who doesn't move a muscle.

"Have a seat. Better in here than out there."

I glance at his client, not sure if this is normal or not.

"Ah, he doesn't mind, do ya, pal?"

"Mind what?" the man's muffled voice comes from the pads holding his face and neck in place.

"See, now why don't you want one for yourself?" the artist asks while hunching over the guy to continue his design.

"It's not my thing. Nothing wrong with it, though."

I lean in to watch the ink coming out of the needle and it reminds me of the time I saw my first paint job at the body shop. That's another art form because they have to prep the cars so well and keep a steady hand to apply the paint evenly. That was years ago, now they use machines.

"You're a talented artist," I say, watching the steadiness of his downstroke because there's no room for error on a tat this size.

"You think so?" His eyes catch mine for a second above the guy's back, and then he starts again.

"Why?"

"Well, I restore old cars. I recognize artistry when I see it."

"No shit?"

He stops again, wiping the skin, and the dude stretches his muscles to relieve the pain.

"Stop moving."

"Yeah, my dad did it and I grew up around it, so why not?"

I'm being completely nonchalant because nobody likes a bragger.

"You got pictures of your work?"

"Doesn't every good artist keep a portfolio?"

I dig out my phone, find the album of all my work, and hand it to him. He flips through several of them. His expression shows little other than lingering on certain pictures.

"You did these?"

He points to a 1930 Lincoln that was a son of a bitch job. But it was one of my most rewarding when it finally came together for a collector out of Minnesota.

"Yeah, that project was probably one of the hardest I've ever done. Do you ever get one client that for some reason, the design and the whole process gives you problems?"

He hands me my phone before hunching over to continue the lower jaw of the skull. I swipe through my pics, admiring my work.

"Yes, sometimes it's the design, sometimes it's the quality of the customer's skin and how it absorbs the ink. Other times, it's having a bad day. You work with what you got and hope it turns out."

I hum in acknowledgment, closing my phone, and stowing it away in my purse to focus on watching him. He doesn't say anything more. I don't mind because I'd rather watch the way his tool floats across this dude's back, creating a canvas out of nothing.

Where this guy creates art, I repair and restore art. Like the beginning and the end of the same story with different ways to get there. The longer I sit there, the more enthralled I am watching this scene unfold before me.

When the skull is finished, it's intricate and detailed, with dark shadows and highlighted edges. I'm truly impressed. The massive skull sits on the right side of his back, with flames starting at the edge of the customer's waist. As the orange and red flames lick up his lower back, the emergence of a phoenix rises from them.

He edges the bird in black ink and flicks his finger to click the instrument over to the same blueish black as the skull beside it. The phoenix sits within the same scale as the skull, yet when he adds a deep purple to the body of the bird, and a metallic green to its bluish wings, it's absolutely stunning.

Seeing the entire design come together, I realized how symbolic it is. The skull is the death of something important in this dude's life. The emergence of the phoenix from the flames is a quintessential rebirth.

My eyes water as I draw meaning from witnessing this happenstance tattoo. I'm not religious, but it's no accident that I find myself sitting here with a fellow artist, seeing his work, and witnessing this tattoo. Of all the tattoos in the world this guy could have picked, he picks one that relates so hard to what I'm going through, I can't even believe it.

The skull on his back is the death of my former life. My skull is leaving the only home I've ever known, getting fired from the only job I've ever had, and having to say goodbye to most of Dad's possessions.

The flames that caress the skull are a symbol of the fiery explosion of my temper that started this chain reaction. And yet those same flames are the passion within me that I can't damper, even though almost everybody wants me to.

His phoenix, the one on his back, is the same phoenix of me rising from the flames of scorched earth between Carl and me to be reborn with my own project and in my own garage through my partnership with Tomlin.

I sit back in my chair, absolutely dumbfounded at the synchronicities in what I'm experiencing at this exact moment. I don't know if it's karma or God or the universe or what, but my ass is meant to be planted in this chair for this reason.

And if this isn't confirmation enough that I'm on the right track, doing the right thing, I don't know what the hell is. I need to commemorate this breakthrough in some way. To claim this karmic energy. I never expected to receive these answers eating tacos from a truck, and watching a guy ink a tattoo.

Life's a son of a bitch like that.

One minute I'm homeless, and the next I'm living in some rich dude's mansion at the top of a mountain. It doesn't make sense at all. As the guy finishes the dude's tattoo, I can't help but reach for my phone to snap a picture to commemorate this moment. Staring at the picture doesn't do justice to it.

It doesn't capture the weight of everything I'm feeling in this euphoric spiritual breakthrough. I need something more. I need something life-changing. Something that I can see or feel every single day to remember how transformative this feeling is. I stand and stretch, gazing around the parlor for the answer.

I see it.

Sitting in the display case next to the cash register are barbells of different shapes, sizes, and finishes. I'm not a glitzy girl. Gem-crusted barbells are not my style. The square barbells look too manly, but right in the middle is a small set of round barbells that would be the perfect size for a tongue piercing.

Excitement surges through me, as this is something that'll be a part of me forever. Kept hidden from the world and only visible when I want it to be. It couldn't be a more perfect way to encapsulate this experience.

The artist and his customer walk over to the register, his back wrapped from top to bottom in a bandage, and I move out of the way for them to finish up. Once he's done and gone, the artist turns to me and says, "You interested in getting one?"

"Yeah, what's the pain like, and what's the aftercare?"

He leans over the counter to rest his forearms on top of it and launches into a huge diatribe of the different kinds of tongue piercings and the healing process.

He makes it a point to say no oral sex or kissing for four to six weeks. After ending things with Zach and knowing I don't stand a chance with Tomlin, that's not going to be a problem. After continuing with his speech and my agreeing to do it. He hands me a brochure and a wash to help reduce infection and keep the swelling down.

I hate to admit it, but nervousness mixes with the tacos in my belly. For the first time in so many years that I can't even remember, I find myself a little apprehensive. Maybe I should take the night to think about it, but acting impulsively with little forethought is how I get through life.

"Fuck it, let's do it," I say, hating the way my palms sweat.

"Don't explain any of it to me. I don't want to know. Just fucking do it as fast as you can, so I don't chicken out."

"I can tell you, this piercing will be less painful than how you got that black eye."

I forgot about it. With the swelling down, I don't realize it still looks terrible to other people.

"Yeah, well."

I don't have time to explain that story to him, nor do I want to. I want to get this over with. He collects all the necessary things that he needs while my foot shakes from side to side, sitting in the chair. I've never been good with anticipation leading up to something, and I don't know why I'm nervous about this now, but there's no backing out.

Once he plops his ass on the rolling stool next to me, I close my eyes and listen to his instructions. It takes a matter of minutes, and then it's done. He's right, the pain isn't as bad as getting punched at the truck stop the other day. But damn if my tongue isn't swelling fast as hell. He blabbers on about thrust and infections and yeast something or whatnot, but I don't listen as I get up from the chair and head straight to the mirrors to look at my new piercing.

It's badass.

Something I should have done a long time ago.

I snap a quick pic and send it to Kylie. The weight of the barbell feels weird, but I can't stop opening my mouth and sticking my tongue out to look at how hot it looks. Of course, my naturally naughty mind wonders what it will feel like when I blow a guy. That's going to be sexy as fuck.

Walking back to the artist, I try to thank him, but my words come out all garbled because of the new piercing. He assures me that's normal while he rings me up and I bolt out to the car to stare at it some more. I flip down my visor, still not believing I did it. Honestly, it's a rebirth in my own way. A new energy surrounds me, making me optimistic about the future.

In my former life, I was stuck in a rut. Maybe Kylie was right when she fussed at me to get out of Carl's place. But sometimes we don't know how to leave the nest that's built for us.

I don't know why I'm getting all sentimental and shit, but something is going on that I don't understand. I sort of like it. Snapping the mirror closed, I push the visor to the headliner and start the engine. As I pull away, I contemplate where all this is headed and what it's supposed to mean.

The biggest thing I could change is what Tomlin calls my sailor's mouth. I know it's offensive. I know it bothers people because I've seen it firsthand. Everyone I have ever known has bitched about it. They probably have a point, but I never saw the purpose of changing.

Until tonight, when I saw death and rebirth captured and created on that dude's back. I can't deny there was a reason for my ass being there. Maybe this tongue piercing is a reminder to clean up my sailor's mouth and make something of myself.

Tomorrow will be the first day of my new life.

37

Tomlin never came back that weekend or any of the weeks that flew by. He is as busy as I am. Although every night before bed, we have a standing call to make decisions on the car, catch up on what happened during the day, and exchange little stories.

I hate to admit it, but I look forward to those calls.

Something about lying in the dark in the comfort of my bed with his deep voice in my ear is both soothing and sexy. It's as if the miles away from each other and only being able to communicate on the phone somehow brings us closer together.

The distance doesn't erase my attraction to him. On the contrary, it only grows. On some nights, after the call ends, I wish we were more than business partners. I don't know how it happened, or when, but I am falling for Tomlin.

As the weeks pass, I settle into a routine of making breakfast for Anna, eating on the back deck, and watching the morning sun paint the blue mountains gold. It's a balm over my sore muscles and wary mind that allows me time to think and space to breathe.

I'd never admit this to Tomlin, but I can see the appeal of

this place. The isolation and quiet took some getting used to, but now I don't know how I'd go back to the loudness of town.

I haven't told him about my piercing. I want to show him in person. When he didn't come back, I decided it was foolish of me to get excited over that. I let it fade in importance. He remarks about my cleaned-up language all the time, but I merely laugh. If he were here, I might share the story of the tattoo parlor, but he isn't, so I don't.

Lars and I are good friends. Long days on the road scouring for parts and digging through junkyards, sealed the deal. His easygoing demeanor and stories of his sisters add to his charm. He's a teddy bear of a guy, both inside and out. It makes him endearing. Although he doesn't have time for dating, I know he'd be a great catch.

Finishing the car isn't my only success.

Eli and Ronnie are in the foster care parent application process. Something that takes entirely too long in this stupid state. After Hamilton set up a meeting, they're all in on her.

Isla, on the other hand, is far more uncertain. Given her experience with men, it's understandable. I leave Lars working while I visit her twice a week. Eli and Ronnie visit the other days. To say she has support is an understatement. Ronnie's experience in the system pays off by increasing her therapy appointments ahead of the upcoming trial and getting her extra help with her schoolwork.

She's still living at the facility until the application process is finalized, but she's improving rapidly. I keep smuggling in Anna, almost coming to blows with the guard if it weren't for Hamilton smoothing things over.

I've done my best to keep my temper in check, to stop cussing, and to become the phoenix rising from the ashes. What I didn't see in that tattoo is how lonely the phoenix is.

My life is going places. I have everything I could ever want, living in Tomlin's mountain resort. Yet, night after night, as I sit on the back deck with my microwave dinner, I'm alone.

Loneliness is a sneaky emotion.

Creeping in so slowly and so subtly that I don't realize it until it's sitting next to me like a shadow. An overcast and gloomy shadow that begs for the warmth of the sun to visit it again.

The sun being Tomlin.

Who's poetic now?

Naturally, I have Kylie. We chat on the phone when she isn't busy with Ryan or work. But if I'm being honest with myself, I want more for the first time in my life.

Tomlin's words whisper in my mind.

Someone just for you?

The longer those words haunt my thoughts, the deeper they penetrate, until I am at the same reservoir of loneliness he was at, asking the same question he posed to me.

Someone to walk through this life together with common goals and build a haven where only two people exist?

I got there without even knowing I was on the journey. I have more people in my life than ever before. I should be content or happier, but with all the new relationships, I am lonelier than ever.

Living in his mountain resort, working on his car, and talking to him every night is building a life with him in my mind. I am cocooned in the world of Tomlin, and not my own.

Working at Carl's garage was a tiny little universe. I was a big fish in a microscopic pond. But at least there was a separation between my clients' lives and my own.

Not here.

There's no line and no separation. It all blurs together to center on one fine-ass man. Going back inside, I rinse my cup and deposit it into the dishwashing drawer, before going to my room to shower and get ready.

Replacing my usual camisole for a sweatshirt to go with my cutoff jeans, I quickly tie my shoes, since the trailer should be at the bottom of the mountain at any time.

Hitting the button to raise the garage doors, a cool breeze caresses my thighs. It's a sunny day without a cloud in the sky. I hear tires crunching on the gravel driveway and assume it's Lars, eager to give it one more test drive before letting the car go.

I'm downright shocked to see Tomlin's Porsche clearing the tree line and circling the drive to park under the porte cochere. Standing in the shade of the garage, my pulse quickens and all those nights thinking about being more than business partners is making me flush.

Nervousness seizes my stomach. For the first time in six weeks, I see the gorgeous man who stole my heart and consumes my thoughts.

He's wearing those dang aviators again, but the smile beneath is unmistakable. He has a shadow of a beard gracing that stunning face, making his jawline more pronounced. I guess I'm not the only one making changes as I click the barbell against my teeth.

"What are you doing here?"

I shake my head in disbelief.

My body itches to run to him, to jump into his arms and wrap my legs around him. But we're not like that, so I settle for a small wave. He didn't call or text that he is coming. He must've woken up pretty early in Denver to arrive before 8 a.m.

"Last time I checked, I live here."

His tone is full of humor. He rips his aviators from his face and tucks them in his shirt pocket.

"So, this is it?"

His gaze is blistering as it travels from my Converse, lingering on my bare thighs and finally on my face.

Yes, this is it.

His megawatt smile doesn't falter for a second and I try to calm the excitement surging through my body. Slowly, his gaze falls to his car.

She's done.

It's why he's here. I don't blame him. It's been quite a feat by Lars and me, but we did it.

"Yeah, there's our girl."

An odd look ripples across his face, and I briefly wonder if that's the wrong thing to say.

"You've got to hear her engine. She purrs."

Excited, I skip to the driver's side door. His smile can't get any bigger as his fingertips caress the lines of her body. It's intimate, restoring what is lost. His eyes are everywhere, soaking in every detail, as he saunters toward me until we are inches apart. My eyes communicate everything I can't say.

I miss you.

Why did you leave?

How long will you be staying?

Can we start over?

The familiar scent of his cologne greets me like an old friend. His breath is mine and my fingers itch to caress his new beard. The pull between us isn't imagined when I see his hands clench and unclench at his side. He wants to touch me as I want to touch him.

He settles for gripping the door handle and waiting for me to step back before opening it. He slides behind the wheel, patting the passenger seat for me to join him, and I run around the front of the car to get in.

The upholstery is the star of the show. When Lars first showed me his design, I didn't get it. He explained it was the Kodokan symbol from the founder of judo. It looked like a flower to me.

Lars explained that the red center is forged steel, a fired iron core symbolizing the hard inner self and the surrounding white petals are silk with a toughness of its own. Meaning the harder one forges the iron, the stronger it becomes. It's the foundational principles that judo is built on. Knowing Tomlin's love of white, and after Lars's explanation, I knew Tomlin would love it.

He clears his throat.

His eyes roam past me to the upholstered seats with the flower in the middle, and the white leather running across the bench with matching red stitching.

Even with Lars's big bear paws for hands, his stitching was like a perfect little grandma.

"It's remarkable," he rasps, quickly wiping his eyes. I've seen this response many times over the years, but it's all the sweeter coming from this guy. "It's, uh . . ."

My throat closes, watching him get all choked up. Something that catches me by surprise. But seeing him get emotional and knowing how I feel about him makes me emotional. I sniff my boogers and blink away the sudden sting of tears.

Thankfully, he's taking a few seconds to compose himself and doesn't notice the effect this beautiful moment is having on me.

"Yeah, Lars did an amazing job with these seats," I say, rubbing a hand over the buttery softness of the dashboard which catches his eyes.

"I don't know how to thank you, Dani."

As if mimicking me, his fingertips caress the padded instrument panel with a look of admiration.

I don't know what to say. I normally don't sit in the cars with the customers as they process the emotions of what they're seeing. It feels intrusive, like an unwanted guest. My fingers reach for the chrome handle to give him the privacy he deserves when his hand grazes my wrist.

"Please don't go. Can you just sit with me a little longer?"

Something in the way he asks speaks to that reservoir of

loneliness that I've been carrying all these weeks. I don't know if we're coming from the same depth of emotions, but his plea to not be left alone in this difficult moment twists a knife in my heart and makes me think of how I miss Dad.

I've been lucky enough to sit in Dad's chair as much as I want once I dried it out and cleaned it up. But this is his first time sitting in his mom's car.

All the memories and feelings it's bringing up, and he wants me here to ground him. To not be alone in his grief. I understand that completely. I wish someone was there for me on those quiet nights when I climbed the steps to my empty apartment, lied on that couch, and wished Dad was there to read the newspaper one last time.

"I'll sit with you as long as you need."

I don't say anything else, just watch him as he gazes at the instrumental panel. Even though he's sitting beside me, he drifts away to a place in time before me. To a time when this car was everything to her. Seconds turn into minutes, and I close my eyes, talking to Dad as I assume he's talking to his mom.

It ends up being a long while before he says, "Can I take her for a drive?"

I open my eyes, turn my head, and smile at him.

"Of course."

He doesn't smile, but he doesn't frown as he fires up her throaty engine, rumbling underneath us. A few seconds pass of him appreciating the sound before he buckles up and I do the same thing.

He slowly backs out of the garage, as if scared any action will ruin the restoration. Wordlessly, I roll down my window, letting the crisp breeze blow through my hair while he drives the gravel road to the front of his property.

He pauses for a moment, rolls down his window as well, and rests his left arm on the window frame looking as picture-perfect as *Car and Driver* magazine. I swear he's so good-looking he could be on the cover. But this ride has far more meaning than some car magazines.

Looking both ways, he eases her onto the main road leading down the mountain. When we get to the bottom, I still don't see the transport trailer.

"Can I open her up? Like really test her out?"

Worry rims his eyes.

I smile because I won't tell him this now, but Lars already did to ensure she wouldn't break down. It's part of the testing process to make sure that we rebuilt her correctly.

"Go right ahead. Have fun with her. And if you happen to get pulled over by this hunky officer named Hamilton, let me and my tits do the talking."

I mean it as a joke, but that forced smile lets me know it's not the right thing to say.

"If you take a right at the next street, there's an open road that you can let her fly," I volunteer to smooth over my bad joke.

His fingers wrap tightly around the white woven steering wheel before he guns it. Proudly, the engine doesn't sputter, she roars. He takes the right a little too fast, fishtailing for a second before straightening her out.

Then we're off. Barreling down the two-lane road so fast that I fist my hair from flying around my head. The wind sucks my eyes dry and the mountains to my right fly by in one continuous blur.

Men love these old muscle cars.

The velocity and control in their hands, the vibration of the engine in their body, and the strength in their leg to floor it. It's a testosterone boost. One that gets a guy's rocks off.

When I look at Tomlin, his jaw is clenched, his knuckles are white, and he has a hard expression. I'm taken aback that it's not one of exuberance. This look is hard and stern. A reckoning of sorts, and I don't understand what he's trying to work out.

With the needle hitting over one hundred and twenty miles an hour, I clutch the dashboard. My heart races almost as fast as this car is speeding and I pray we don't crash.

One small rock in the road or an overcorrection on his part could send us careening into the side of the mountain. Guaranteeing certain death. With the wind whipping loudly in the cab, my ears pop but I am too scared to let go of the dashboard and armrest.

In my small action, his eye catches and he throttles off the gas, letting the car coast. Goosebumps sweep down my bare legs, both from the cool wind and the near heart attack he's giving me.

I don't know what that was. I don't know if it's a death wish or not, but judging from the glint in his eyes, it's something. He doesn't look at me or say anything when he guides the car to the side of the road. When he puts it in park, my hand falls from clutching the dashboard to shove my finger straight into his face.

"What the fuck was that? If you have some sort of death wish, don't take me along with you." My blood is boiling and my heart is pounding. "I may not have the best life, but I certainly have one I want to live."

Those dark chocolate eyes turn to me as if seeing me for the first time, and he slowly shakes his head. I wait for words that don't come, and that's not fucking good enough. Hand it to Tomlin to break my non-cussing streak and try to kill me within the first hour of coming back.

"Tomlin, I swear you better fucking tell me what's going on or I'm gonna key this upholstery right here and now."

I reach for the keys to shut off the engine and then press them toward that buttery white leather. The indent on the material is making me cringe, but he's got to know that this is unacceptable.

"I wanted to know what it felt like."

His gaze slips past me to the mountainous terrain. I'm gonna need more than that as an answer for his recklessness.

"You wanted to know what it would be like to go hella fast? Do you know if there was a rock or pothole or any kind of obstruction in the road, you could have flipped her, and we could have died?"

His fingers slowly uncurl from the steering wheel as he collapses into the seat with defeat, cutting wrinkles across his forehead.

"I know. I'm sorry."

My ears must be clogged if that's his only explanation. I think he said he knows he could've killed me, and he's sorry about that. As if that's acceptable. My eyebrows raise into my hairline and if he'd look at me right now, he'd be dead by the daggers in my eyes.

"You're sorry? That's it? You have some death wish and you wanna take me with you and you say I'm sorry and I know? Have you lost your ever-loving mind?"

I remove the keys from the leather, hoping the imprint will come out and it barely gets his attention.

"What's going on, Tomlin? What's happening? Help me understand."

His head rests against his seat. I realize his face is thinner as if he's lost weight he didn't need to lose.

"I wanted to know what it felt like. I wanted to know what she was thinking," he says with such dejection that I stay silent, waiting for him to continue. "I wanted to know what one hundred and twenty miles an hour feels like on a body, on my body, and visualize hitting the back of an eighteen-wheeler."

I freeze.

More chills sweep over my skin.

Did he just confirm he has a death wish? If there was an eighteen-wheeler on this road, would he have put us into the back of it?

That's an immediate and painful death. I shake my head, not comprehending what's happening here, now, all of a sudden.

"I don't understand, Tomlin."

"My mom, they estimated she went that fast when she hit the back of it. There were no brake marks on the road. They ruled it an accident. The officers gave her the benefit of the doubt, but she committed suicide in this car."

The hair on my arms stands up as I stare aghast at him. I reach out to touch his arm, but he moves it away. I understand. When I got the call about Dad, Kylie tried to hug me, but I was so numb I didn't want to be touched. I still don't.

"I'm sorry," he murmurs again, but they are hollow and lack remorse.

He could have killed me, or us. I don't know if he's even realizing it.

"That's how you brought it to me. When they unloaded it in the back lot at Carl's, it was—"

"Yeah."

My hand covers my mouth, remembering how it was. The damage to the front end and what I mistook for a tree collapsing the roof. What I thought was tree sap sticking to my fingers, was it her blood or body fluid?

It certainly wasn't motor oil.

I shiver beside him and suddenly want to vomit.

This cab feels like I'm in the coffin with her, and I'm thoroughly creeped out. I want out. I want to escape, but we are a few miles from his cabin, and it's too far for my lazy ass to walk back.

Damn.

Would I have ever worked on it, and restored it, had I known what happened?

No.

No way.

"We need to get back. Transport is probably waiting," I mutter, handing him the keys to get going.

Any second I'm in this car is a second too long now that I know the truth. I want to be mad at him for not telling me in the beginning, but I didn't really give him the chance.

Yet, he could have told me every day since I agreed to take on the job, and he didn't. He's a bastard for that.

A relieved sigh escapes my lungs when he puts the key back in the engine. My knee bobs the entire way back, even as we pass the trailer on the side of the road waiting for us.

I'll have Lars take this car down. When we get to the house, I need to cleanse my spirit or soul or do whatever voodoo to make sure she's not somehow attached to me. Like, do whatever people do when they go to haunted houses.

Tomlin doesn't say anything. I'm glad because I don't need to hear any more family secrets. He can keep them all to himself from here on out.

Once we round the bend with his place coming into view, my fingers toy with the handle, waiting for the nanosecond when I can throw open the door and bolt out of it. I'm never sitting in this car again. It's barely in park when I snatch open the door and run. Lars is standing behind the counter of the diner with a baffled look on his face.

"Hey, transport is here. Can you take her down? I got to drop some kids off at the pool," I yell as I rush past him.

His expression changes to instant worry for me. I ignore it as I barrel through the mudroom, into my bedroom, and lock the door. I don't care how this looks to Tomlin. I need time to compose myself after his confession that I rebuild his mom's death mobile.

He knocks on my door.

"Dani, can we talk?" His voice floats softly in, and I'm not ready. I may need hours or days to get over this.

"Uh, I have to take a dump."

It's a terrible lie. So obvious, but I don't know what else to say other than go back to Denver until I sort this all out.

"Okay, I'll be waiting."

The uncertainty in his tone matches the uncertainty of how I've fallen for a guy I barely know. This huge omission is evidence of it.

How do I get past this?

It's a big deal.

38

I pace the side of the bed, trying to figure out what to do and what to say while sorting through my feelings. It's messed up. I can't come to any other conclusion. Anna's curled in her dog bed, content to watch me fret.

Why didn't he tell me this before? I know we traded barbs and switched off being assholes to each other, but still. He could have told me every single day that I worked on it. Every single night when we had those deep intimate talks before bed. He could've brought it up then.

"Hey, you know that car you're working on? My mom killed herself in it."

Fuck.

These are things that people should know.

And why now? Why bring this all up the day it's going to transport? I get wanting to take it for a spin. It's an exciting day, but damn. How do I even get in that car again? You know what, I don't. I don't have to because once it goes to the paint shop, it's trailer-bound for California.

In actuality, I'll never have to sit in that car again. And honestly, it'll be too soon. I'd rather hell freeze over first before

I drop my butt in that seat. But none of that, none of how I feel about that car, changes the fact that he lied to me. And that's what makes my veins burn with anger.

I've always been a straight shooter with him. No lies, that's what we agreed on. And this is the biggest lie of all time. Why the hell didn't he tell me? Why did he decide to confess now that it's done?

I know I can't hide in this room forever. It's not fair to Lars and all the hard work he put in. It's his first car. It's a big moment for him to drive her one last time down to transport.

Letting out a long, and frustrated breath, I unlock the door. When I peer into the hallway, it's empty. Thankfully, Tomlin isn't waiting to pounce on me the second I come out.

I proceed through the mudroom and out to the garage, where Lars and Tomlin are talking by the grill. Lars's gesturing with his hands while Tomlin leans against the counter, with a less than enthusiastic face. I know that face has nothing to do with Lars, and everything to do with me, but he doesn't have to be a total jerk to that nice guy.

Tomlin heads toward the door, leaving Lars lifting the lid to the grill. I duck behind the counter to hide from him.

"You know I can see you, right?"

Dang it.

I slowly stand, shoving my hands into the pockets of my cutoffs.

"Whatever, I was tying my shoe."

He stalks down the counter, rounding the corner to stand way too close to me. I hold my hands up to stop him because I'm angry and hurt and still trying to figure this all out.

"Look, I don't want to talk about it, okay? We've basically killed ourselves to make this day happen, so let us enjoy this before you rain on our parade."

It's a low blow, I know.

I honestly don't want to hear any more about what

happened to his mom in that car. Maybe it's insensitive, but I just want to take a moment to relish the fact that we did it. And I proved to myself that I could be a phoenix rising from the ashes. That getting fired and then finishing a job in record time is a glorious feat, even when I doubted it could be done. Part of finishing that car was believing in myself and believing in Lars. Sue me if I want to celebrate it, without him ruining it with his unwanted revelations.

"Fair enough. Enjoy yourselves."

His glaring eyes betray the well-wishing of his words. He bows his head before tapping the counter and walking out the garage door to his Porsche. When the engine starts and the tires crunch on the gravel, I can breathe, knowing he won't be around to sour the mood.

Lars strolls through the door carrying grilling tongs and looking surprised.

"Where's he going? I thought he was staying."

"There's something I gotta tell you."

He crosses the room and sits on a barstool opposite me. His expression changes to worry. I hate to tell him Tomlin's news because it feels like gossiping. But I won't lie to Lars the way I was lied to. Even after I made him drive the car down to transport.

"Sounds bad."

"It is. Let me just start by saying I didn't know. I literally just found this out. And it pisses me off. I'm so freaked out, I don't even know how to start."

I rest my hands on the countertop, looking from Lars's concerned blue eyes to the plume of dust drifting into the garage from Tomlin's car.

"Am I fired?"

I stare at him as if he said he had two heads.

"Heck no! Why would you say that?"

"Well, I figured something happened between you and him

with the way you hustled out of that car and said you had the shits. I didn't know if what he said caused you to have it or if you're feeling sick."

I shake my head and start tapping on the countertop.

"No, and no. I don't have the screen doors. It's just, let me start at the beginning."

Lars shifts, the stool squeaking under his weight. I tell him the events that transpired between us this morning. He doesn't say a word as I pace, rant, and rave, trying not to curse but letting a few slip out. It's only when I get to the end of the story that his eyes fall to the countertop to pick at some spot I can't even see.

"What? What are you doing? What's that look for?"

He continues to rub that spot until I walk over and slap his hand, forcing his eyes to look at mine.

"Tell me what you're thinking. Aren't you pissed too? He should have told us this crap way up front, because I know for certain I wouldn't have worked on his car."

"Dani, I don't really know the relationship between you and that guy, but it seems something is going on that's more than just business."

I open my mouth to object, and he continues, "But the way I see it. Today wasn't about lying to you or even lying to me. Today was a guy trying to reconcile the fact that the very car you restored and brought back to life was the very car that ended his mom's. I got to say, I feel for the man. If my mom did something like that, do you think I'd go to all the trouble of getting it back, paying that old guy Carl to fix it, then paying you and me to redo it?"

He shakes his long mop in need of a haircut.

"I'll tell you now, no. If anything, I'd probably take a sledge-hammer to that car and finish it off before setting it on fire and watching it burn to ashes. I can't begin to know his motivation for getting you to take on his project. Or even enter it into a show, but it's worth hearing him out. Let him tell his side of the story and then let the chips fall where they may."

Lars's take on the situation is so different from what I'm thinking that I'm speechless. I mean, I hear the words. I understand what he's saying, but the angle is so different.

Who restores the car their mom took her own life in?

I wouldn't.

In fact, when I saw a picture of the condition of Dad's truck up in Denver, I would have easily lit the match and watched it burn in the middle of that freeway.

"And one more thing, Dani. You may want to give some thought to why he included you on that ride in the first place. If he was trying to reconcile with the events of his mom, why take you along? You said it yourself that he was white-knuckling it to get to one hundred and twenty miles per hour. To get to her speed, but you stopped him. You were the voice of reason that he listened to. That cut through whatever haze was going on in his mind. Ask yourself that when you think about talking to him. His answer may surprise you."

He rises from the barstool to lean against the counter.

"I won't mention any of this to Tomlin. And for what it's worth, it doesn't bother me that I fixed up her death mobile, as you call it. But I wish I would have known from the start because I could have treated that car with the dignity it deserved rather than seeing it as my first entry point into my career. You told me stories of how people entrust us to restore their babies but isn't restoring his mom's final moments a greater honor, for a greater purpose? It's like when those tombstones get all black, and you can't read the writing anymore and the weeds climb up the stone from neglect. Wouldn't you want someone to pull away the weeds and clean the stone for it to gleam in the sun, knowing someone took care of it?"

I'm even more speechless than I was a few moments ago. Lars blows my mind with his beautiful sentiments and his thoughtful words. His depth runs like a still stream, and it's a pleasant surprise.

"I'm going to start getting things ready, and if you need to take some time to think about this or possibly make it right, by all means. I got this covered."

He nods, leaving me lost in the truth bombs he dropped to go outside and fiddle with the grill. Processing everything, he just said, I gaze out the window at the trees swaying in the cool breeze and realize the truth in his words.

I never had a headstone for Dad. He didn't want one. He didn't understand the fuss of being buried in a box in the dirt, having to pay for that dirt, and then someone coming around and putting flowers on it, just for them to die a week later.

He was cremated. Said he didn't care what I did with the ashes and used to poke fun that I could keep them in a coffee jar on a shelf for all he cared. He had a simple approach to life and an even simpler approach to death.

The day I drove to Denver to pick up his ashes was the second worst day of my life. The first was the day he died. They sat next to me on the seat of my El Camino as I made that long drive home. Somewhere along the highway, I decided Dad deserved more than to sit in a jar on a shelf.

I knew he didn't care what happened to him, but I did. I took the next exit off the freeway and went straight to the Royal Gorge. It was nearly sunset, and the park was closing within an hour. I knew what I had to do.

When we were little, Dad would pack sandwiches and chips, get a couple of cokes out of the vending machine, and we'd head out to the Gorge to sit on the hood of the car and have a picnic.

We didn't do it often, and that's what made it so special. I used to jabber on to Dad, telling him everything that was going on at school, and in my life, which he probably already knew, and everything else that crossed my mind.

He listened.

In his quiet way, he exemplified strength, patience, and understanding. That day, when dusk was setting and the wind was blowing, I said goodbye and hoped he was happy in Heaven when I released his ashes. The moment they scattered in the air, a black butterfly floated through them.

I took it as a sign that he was where he was meant to be. Days later, as that lingered with me, I looked up the meaning, and it said it symbolized a rebirth.

At the time, I took it as woo-woo crap, that didn't mean a damn thing. Now, after everything I've been through, it was a rebirth. I think Dad sent me a black butterfly to say that he was okay in Heaven, and I'd be okay without him.

Just like the phoenix in the tattoo shop, this second change in life is a rebirth. As special as those two moments are, I wonder if Tomlin ever got that with his mom. I got closure. I got signs that I was being reborn.

What did Tomlin get?

I gotta make this right.

Rummaging through my purse, I pull out my phone to search for his name and hit the button. It goes straight to voice mail. I wait for his message to end when I simply say, "Call me."

I probably should have explained more on the voice mail, but I think talking in person would be better. Lars walks back in the door, his gaze falling to my fingernail tapping the side of my phone.

"What's wrong?"

"He sent my call straight to voice mail."

"Well, don't read anything into that. But think about it from his perspective. Today has brought up a lot of memories and emotions about his mom. He's probably off clearing his head."

"I guess."

Lars rounds the corner of the bar and nudges me to the fridge.

"Come help me cook. Tomlin will come back when he wants to come back. Then you can talk to him."

He gives me that crooked smile and I sort of grin back. He's never one to get down. In fact, I've never seen him lose his temper, or even cuss. He's just too good-natured.

"I don't know how to cook, but I can get the chips and dip ready," I offer, grabbing a bag to pull open and munch on a few. He takes the bag from my hands, grabs a paw size out, and hands it back before stuffing his face.

"Your hands had better be clean."

His hand flies to his chest as if offended, then wiggles his fingers.

"Look how sparkly these nails are. I got the motor oil out from underneath them this morning. The meat is already on the grill, so best get going on the sides."

"I will. Now get out of here."

I shoo him away so I can go back to thinking about everything he said. The sides I got are all microwaveable, so I start on those while glancing at the clock and wondering if Tomlin will be back anytime soon.

Lars is right.

He'll come back when he's good and ready. In the meantime, that gives me plenty of opportunities to devise my game plan.

Day bleeds into the night as our little celebratory cookout ends with s'mores by the fire while watching football. Lars's momma is off from work tonight, so he got to stay late and even helped me clean up the kitchen before he headed home with leftovers for his sisters.

Now I wait.

39

It's late when his headlights flash across the walls of the garage and trepidation seeps into my consciousness. I worried about how long he was intentionally away and now I am worrying because he's back. The man gave me all day and night to think about what to say, and I even made Lars practice with me.

I was confident with what I had rehearsed. Now, I'm not so sure. With only the blue light from the television screen on, his silhouette falls against the windows when he unlocks the door and steps through.

"You're still up?"

His tone is curt. Not warm or friendly at all. I guess I deserve that, since I basically hid from him, overacted, and then cut him off.

He locks the door behind him and tosses his keys and wallet on the coffee table in front of me. I had been sitting most of the night, but as the clock crept toward 11 p.m., I slipped under the blanket to lie down.

A lock of his black hair falls forward when he collapses into the chair beside the couch. An exhausted groan eases out of his chest as he adjusts the pillow at his low back.

"I feel you staring, and I don't think you're going to say I'm hot like you usually do."

His eyes catch mine for the first time, plummeting one side of his handsome face into the shadows.

"True and fair. You don't need me to tell you that you're hot again."

Humor, it's a good start, even if this is as awkward as can be between us.

"What's on your mind?"

His voice switches to soft and inquiring, which is better, making it easier for me to bring her up.

"Your mom."

His beard looks so good around the full pink lips now set in a line. His jaw muscle clenches, readying himself. I hate how this feels and I hate how this is starting, but I have to clear the air between us. I've literally had all day and I can't take it any longer.

"What about her?"

"I'm sorry about how I reacted today. I was talking it over with Lars and—"

He leans forward, his hands gripping the arms of the chair so tightly it's leaving indents.

"You told him about my mom?" Anger laces his words, and it immediately sparks irritation in me.

"Don't take that tone with me. He has a right to know. I was pretty pissed at you and needed someone to talk to about it."

"You should have talked to me. I tried to talk to you, but you shut me down. Then you go share my personal family matters with a guy I don't even know. How's that fair, Dani?"

The leather squeals under his palms when he stands at the end of the coffee table. Hating him lording over me, I pull myself up to sit with my back against the arm of the couch.

"I've learned things about you that I'm positive you wouldn't want anyone to know, and I haven't betrayed your trust, have I?"

Venom.

His words are like acid on a wound.

I open my mouth to respond, but he doesn't even allow me a moment to answer.

"No, I haven't, and you already know that. Friends don't betray each other, Dani. And they certainly don't gossip about family tragedies to their employees. I'm beginning to think this whole partnership is a bad idea. If you can't be a proper member of management and know where the boundaries are, then it's never going to work."

I'm stunned.

Where is all this coming from? The anger, the accusations, and the possible ending of what we're starting.

I take a second before saying, "It wasn't like that at all. I wasn't gossiping—"

"Really? You hide from me. Then waited until I left to chat it up behind my back rather than being an adult about it and letting me explain it to you. How juvenile. I expect too much of you. It's probably your age and immaturity in how you handle everything in your life. Just forget it, Dani."

"Forget what?"

My mind is reeling at how fast things are going down in flames. I didn't think I crossed a line telling Lars about the circumstances surrounding the first vehicle he's ever worked on.

I thought it was only fair, and he changed my viewpoint. It's what I am trying to tell him now.

"Tomlin, I apolo—"

"Forget trying to make this work. I appreciate your work on my car, but I'll take it from here."

My heart is beating in my ears, trying to comprehend that I just got fired for the second time in a matter of months.

I search his face, trying to make sense of what is happening, but it's set in stone. I think I'm both unemployed and homeless again and I break out in a cold sweat.

Where will I go?

What will I do?

"I'll be gone tomorrow," I whisper, my throat clogging with panic. Tossing away the blanket, I bolt from the couch and run to my bedroom.

My nose stings as tears collect in my eyes. I refuse to let them fall. Pride and anger have me looking at the ceiling, trying to force them to recede.

Instead, they slide out of the corners of my eyes and into my hairline before I throw open the dresser drawers to unload my belongings and Dad's memory box. Once everything is out, I lean against the dresser and gaze at Anna snuggled into the pillows on my bed, without a care in the world.

Tomlin lied to me.

I can't believe this is happening. I should be the one walking out, walking away from him. Not the other way around.

Betrayal.

That's what this is. But I didn't betray him. Surely, he has to see that if he'd give me a chance to explain. And how fast he's throwing it all away? It's shockingly fast.

Was he using me to get his car done? Was this part of some sick plan to get what he wanted and then toss me out as Carl did?

Tomlin's basically taking a play out of his book.

And to pull the partnership? That seems extreme just because I told Lars. Shaking my head, I can't make sense of it.

My stomach twists with worry and I want to vomit.

What do I tell Lars?

Granted, he has the money from this job, but Tomlin's rash decision affects him too. And his mom and sisters. How's he going to support them with no job?

Sure, I can couch surf at Kylie's with Anna, until I can figure something out, but he goes back to the unemployment line. I could get the number to Paul's from Tomlin. Hell, I'll just call him myself if what Tomlin said is true. I don't want to leave the only town I've ever known, but I already lost my childhood home and some of Dad's stuff. I'd hate to start over again. I just did it. If I have to, I will. I'd hate living on the East Coast where I don't know anyone.

"Fuck," I mumble, toying with my piercing as reality sets in.

Do I text Lars tonight and break the bad news to him? His eyes were rimmed with fear when he asked if I was firing him. That was the furthest thing from my mind. But hours later, it's happening for no good reason other than I needed help. Damn.

Sighing, I push off the dresser to wander into the bathroom I love. This place. His house, which killed me keeping it spotless, as Tomlin liked, ended up making me a better person. Now it's all going away. I rub my forehead, a stress headache building while contemplating a million different things.

Stripping to take one final Bali shower, I take my list of worries into the water with me and go through the motions of getting ready for bed. Tonight will be a sleepless one, I'm sure. When I finally lie in bed, all I can think about is the tasks I need to do in the morning so I can get out of here at first light.

I set my alarm for 6 a.m., hoping to get most of my stuff packed into my truck and out of here before he wakes up. Because after tomorrow, I'll never have to see him again, and that brings the tiniest glimmer of hope I can muster at this bleak hour.

40

It's the middle of the night, and I'm wide awake. Sleep finally came a few hours ago, but a nightmare about dying woke me up. Then reality hits and it's similar to losing my life in my dream but in a different way. Anna is plastered to my side. When I shift to my back, she rolls over and resumes snoring. At least one of us is sleeping.

I stare at the ceiling, needing to pee and wanting some water. I could drink out of the bathroom faucet, but I want one of his stupid sparkling waters I got hooked on living in this mountain resort.

The wind howls outside my window while my mind replays the events leading up to my termination. It's a vicious cycle of betrayal, anger, hurt, and shock, with no new answers found.

I switch to my side, looking at the stacks of clothes on top of the dresser until my protesting bladder forces me from the warm bed. Throwing a robe around my body, I handle my business, wash my hands, and go in search of that damn sparkling water in the kitchen.

My side of the house is dark and quiet as I tiptoe down the hallway and into the living room. I make it into the kitchen and twist the cap off my water to take a refreshing swig when I notice the living room drapes are still open with the moonlight streaking in.

Oddly, he didn't close them.

Not hearing a peep from his side of the house, I leave the kitchen and see his silhouette sitting in the dark living room, with a highball glass pressed to his forehead. He obviously knows I'm here, even though I pretend not to see him when I tiptoe through the living room.

"I'm sorry."

It's so faint, I think I imagine it and continue toward the marble hallway.

"Did you hear me?"

My lips press together. I heard him and wished I didn't. I sort of formulated a loose plan for how this will go down between us. His apologizing in the dark isn't part of it.

"Will you sit with me?"

The sadness in his words stops me and I gaze out the front door. His car is under the porte cochere because mine is in the garage. Beyond the porch, the outline of trees sway, and the brisk wind whistles across the metal roof. The weather would keep me up if I wasn't already up for another reason.

"Please?"

I exhale, not wanting to talk to him, but hearing the desperation in his voice makes my heart twist. Against my better judgment, I cross the living room and sink into the sectional across from him.

I can't even see his face until he flips the fireplace onto a low hum. It provides enough light to see he's very upset. His face is blotchy. His eyes are bloodshot and puffy when he looks at me. Could he have been crying like I was crying?

Probably but not for the same reasons.

I'm not talking first. He's in the wrong, and I'm not

jabbering it up like I normally do to make this right. He owes me a better apology than the one he whispered a minute ago.

The ice cube clinks against the side of the glass as he sips his scotch. My legs are curled underneath, and my robe is tucked in as to not give him any wrong ideas.

"Don't leave."

His index finger and thumb rest against his face as his drink balances on the arm of the couch. He hasn't changed out of his clothes and his long legs are draped on the coffee table as usual.

"I'm—"

"Dani."

He sounds exhausted.

That makes two of us. I'm tired of fighting with him. My new leaf has been nice in that I don't argue anymore unless it's with suppliers over parts. Gone are the days of arguing and fighting with Judd and Carl because Lars is so laid back and patient, he doesn't like to argue. Tomlin waltzes back in and the arguing starts, putting me back into a world I don't want to be a part of.

"Tell me what you told him."

"It's late and what's done is done."

I rise, walking toward the kitchen to pour out my water when he catches my wrist to stop me. His thumb rubs against my skin and his head falls against the back of the couch to gaze at me.

"Please?"

I sigh and frown.

Knowing this could erupt into another fight, I have nothing to lose. I'm already leaving tomorrow. He drags his legs off the coffee table and releases my wrist, making his intentions clear.

I walk by him to set my bottle on the coffee table before curling up on the same sectional as him. He drains the rest of his drink and sets the glass next to mine, then looks at me.

"I was mad. I felt like you were trying to trick me or take advantage of me," I mutter, my voice sounding too loud at this hour of the night.

The low flames from the fireplace dance across his face as he contemplates what I said.

"You always think I have an angle with you. Why?"

I shrug, the robe's soft lapel brushing my ear.

"I don't know. You say one thing and then do another. It makes it hard to trust you. Makes it hard to trust any man. Can you blame me?"

"Your dad sounded like a good man."

A tinge of sadness hits his words. Is it because he has a shithead father, and never got the dad that he deserves?

"Yeah, he was. I miss him in my soul."

Tomlin drags his knee up the cushion and leans his back against the arm of the couch to face me.

"How did he die?"

The fire crackles between us, the mood somber. We both miss the same person, a loving parent. I look away, out the window to the darkness that haunts my memory of that day.

"It was the first snow of the season. I was excited about going sledding with some friends from school. Dad called me and said he had to run an errand for Carl. He didn't want me to know the truth. That was really hard."

I look at Tomlin, his arm lying across the back of the couch, watching me intently.

"He told me to have a good time and that he'd picked up a pot pie at the store for me to have for dinner since he wouldn't be back until late. It was unusual, but I thought nothing of it because I was excited about going to the mountain. We stayed out there till dark and then built a fire until the park ranger busted us."

I smile.

"That was the first night I felt like my life was going somewhere. With graduation in a few months, I was going to leave the Cañon. I hadn't told Dad yet. I wanted to wait because I had applied to the Schools of Mines but hadn't gotten my acceptance letter yet."

"You were eighteen?"

"Seventeen."

He nods but doesn't say anything else, so I continue.

"My friend dropped me off at the garage and there were these cop cars. I thought someone had broken in and stolen one of the cars. Going in they aren't of much value, but coming out they are. When I walked through the door, Carl was standing behind the counter and his face was white as a sheet. I think I knew."

I shake my head as the ache in my chest forms. It's been so long since that day but everything feels raw and broken.

"I remember being on the mountain and looking at the sky. There was a shooting star and when I pointed it out to the guy next to me, he didn't see it. I remember getting a bad feeling as if disappointed that he missed it. I couldn't shake the feeling. It made little sense at the time, but later I would find out that it was the same time my dad had passed. I'm not religious or anything, yet I'd like to think that was him saying goodbye. That probably sounds stupid."

I don't want to tell him about the black butterfly or the phoenix. We are worlds apart and at odds with one another. Those two stories are too special to share under these circumstances.

I purse my lips, trying to hold back the tears that are filling my lower lids. Tomlin moves closer to where our knees touch, and he lays his open hand on top of my clothed thigh. A comforting gesture, letting me know he gets it.

"No, some cultures believe stars represent their passing into the heavens and a sign to those on Earth of where their loved one resides."

For once I love his hippie-dippie stuff and I intertwine my hand in his. He squeezes it while I wipe my tears on the sleeve of my robe.

"Carl was my dad's emergency contact, so he met the officers at the garage to tell me. I remember hearing the words but not believing them. Like going through the motions of acknowledging what had happened but still waiting for Dad to climb the stairs that night. I waited on the couch for him. He never came. It was the loneliest night of my life. Every night after that, I would lie facing the door, hoping and praying that it was all a lie. I begged God to hear his heavy footsteps again, but it was always quiet. The silence echoed in volumes back to me. On the most difficult nights, I'd listen to old voice mails just to hear his voice. I'd sleep with his lamp on, pretend he was working late, and that he'd be up by the time I drifted off to sleep. Then I'd wake up, the apartment would be silent and empty, and the cycle would start all over again."

The tears come fast and furious as Tomlin eases forward to wrap me in a tight hug. I reciprocate, winding my arms around his back and crying into his shoulder.

He holds me the way I should've been held all those years ago. The way I've always wanted to be held. Someone stroking my hair with a gentle touch and kissing the side of my head. My mom should've held me like this, whispered how sorry she was instead of it coming from Tomlin.

Sobs rack my body, causing his arms to tighten. I can't help but soak up the beautiful tenderness of this moment. Where I feel cared for by someone in this damn lonely world.

I turn my face to bury it in his neck, the starchy fabric scraping my cheek as I inhale that expensive cologne I love. He lifts me onto his lap, my tears wetting the collar of his shirt as I continue to grieve what I lost that day. I lost my rock, my world, and the reason for living.

These past three years have been existing as a shell of an

adult when all I want to do is run back to my youth where Dad is alive, and my problems are few.

"I'm so sorry," he whispers, his deep voice vibrating into my chest as his hand continues rubbing my back. It's such a nice feeling that I close my eyes, trying to commit it to memory because I doubt I'll feel anything like this again.

"You are so brave."

Hearing those words breaks a barrier in me as if speaking to the depth of my doubts and failures as a person and saying it's okay to be broken. It's okay to make mistakes and fail because going it alone with no one to help is brutal.

My chest aches with heartbreak and my throat burns from sorrow. I haven't cried like this in years, never trusting anyone beyond Kylie to share my story with. But tonight, seeing Tomlin sad and broken allows me to share it with him.

"I know what this feels like. Our grief is meant to be carried, not resolved. I'm sorry you had to go through it alone," he whispers into the shell of my ear. The scotch is light on his breath and I sink further into him.

We're alike in our grieving. He knows what it's like to lose part of yourself and have it go off to Heaven, never getting it back. Our grief is an invisible string that runs through us to thread together. Both are burdened with carrying it to our graves. He understands how mourning fundamentally changes a person. Very few people my age know the grief I carry with me. That a part of me has died.

Yet, right here, hugging the life out of me is someone who shares this pain. Who has had to bury a parent and then figure out how to live with a shattered heart.

I swallow past the lump in my throat, needing to let him know I was wrong too. I pull away to gaze into his eyes. For all the times he's been vulnerable and sincere with me, I owe it to him to be the same right now.

"I'm sorry I reacted the way I did. I didn't mean to hurt

you when I shared it with Lars. I just needed a different perspective. That's all. I wouldn't ever intentionally hurt you, T."

"I realize that now. At this moment, you would never hurt me in the same way that you have been hurt." His hand seeks mine as if holding me is not enough.

I shake my head. "Never. I know what it's like to live with a broken heart."

The intensity between us is so strong and unexpected. For the first time since Dad died, someone understands me. Understands that anger and rage are a fortress I have built around the pain that lives behind it.

"And you've been on your own ever since?"

I nod. Sympathy, not pity on his face.

"I didn't find out until later, like months later, that Dad was going to see my mom."

"Why?"

"After all those years, he still loved her. So, when she wrote to him, he went to see her. I don't know why. He never made it. He was on the highway when a truck carrying a fruit harvest pulled out in front of him. With nowhere to go and no time to respond, he hit the back of it. They airlifted him out but by then ..."

His thumb caresses my knuckles as more tears stream down my face, and I wipe them with my sleeve again.

"The same as my mom. Dani, I—"

"I know. Just like I'm sorry for your loss."

His smile is gentle as his fingertips graze my cheek to tuck my hair behind my ear.

"Did she come to the funeral? Your mom?"

"No. I don't think she knows or knew of his passing. The notice was in our paper, not Denver, where he died."

"He died in my Denver?" he echoes. "Where I live."

"Yes."

He looks deep in thought, his gaze drifting down to my lips before returning to my eyes.

"She doesn't have closure either."

I cover my hand with my mouth.

Such a simple statement packed with a ton of impact. My mom doesn't have closure either. He never made it. They arranged to meet, and he never showed. What must she have thought?

"I never thought about that." My hand falls away. I stare at him as he stares at me. "She was waiting for him."

"I'd imagine that must have been hard on her. Especially after all those years away. Do you know why she wanted to see him?"

He has no idea what he just did. It's like he opened pandora's box letting all the hatred and hurt out that surrounds my mother.

Do I feel sorry for her for not seeing him before he died? Is this the sweet justice the universe dealt her for walking out on her husband and her little girl? I can't begin to know what to think about all this.

"No. She killed him. It's her fault. If she hadn't written, he would be here with me," I mutter the words that have been my sole truth for nearly four years.

She killed him again.

The first time when she left and the second time when she wrote. There's no other narrative, but now Tomlin hinting at one is freaking me out. When I see his frown, I know. I know what he's going to say, and I don't want to hear it. I don't want to forgive her or make amends. I want to continue to blame her for everything.

"Don't say anything, please," I beg, reaching out to touch his chest, feeling his muscles tighten in response. "I know what you want to say, but I can't hear it. Not yet." Tears bristle at my eyes and I tilt my head, imploring him to remain silent.

"Come here."

He pulls me to him. I willingly collapse into his muscular chest, taking solace in the fact that he understands my need for denial right now. One arm is around my shoulders like a steel grip, the other is at my waist and everything about this is right, even if his words are wrong.

It's her fault. It will always be.

"Don't leave. I lashed out. I pulled a Dani, so you need to pull a Tomlin and forgive me."

I smile and lean against his arm on my shoulder. The orange hues from the fire dance across the room while a sad expression blankets his face.

"Pull a Dani? Is that some sort of phrase for freaking out?"

Proud of himself, he winks. "Freaking out, starting fights, running away without resolving anything, you name it, but yes, I just coined it. I'm glad you like it."

I can't stop smiling at him because he sat with my sadness and swam in it with me. Then made me apologize and insulted me at the same time. Truly an art form.

"You're cracking yourself up now."

He bops me on the nose. The tension from our heavy conversation evaporates, allowing me to breathe again.

"Nope, I made you smile, so I'm cracking you up."

A few long seconds pass with us smiling at each other. It feels like a new understanding between us. I want to reciprocate and give him the graciousness and mercy that he gave me.

"Do you want to talk about your mom? I'll listen this time."

I close my lips, act like I'm turning a key, and throw it over my shoulder. His chin dips and he leans forward to whisper.

"Another time."

With the crackle of the fireplace, the liquor on his breath, and the lack of sex for almost two months, I can't tear my eyes off his lips, inches from mine. I won't lean in and risk getting rejected, but if he does, I won't resist. As if feeling the pull himself, he places a hand at the back of my neck, drawing me toward him to leave a prolonged kiss on my forehead.

When his lips leave my skin, he whispers into my hair, "Thank you for telling me about your dad. I wish I could have known him as you did."

Damn, if that doesn't cause me to grip his wrist and hold him against me. The intimacy of tonight's confessions, his understanding of my grief, and the acceptance of me are healing. I close my eyes to savor how amazing this feels.

"Me too."

His nose nuzzles against my jaw, leaving a light kiss on my ear and murmuring, "Come with me to California."

As perfect as this moment is, I have to see his face. I don't understand where this is coming from or what he's talking about. I lift my head, leaving his warmth and forcing space between us.

"What?"

The intensity of his gaze never falters, even as his hand sweeps down my arm to interlock our fingers.

I love everything about this. Our vulnerability brings us closer than business partners, more intimate than friends, but not quite lovers. I'm willing to see where it leads. Willing to lay myself bare another time, hoping he doesn't reject me.

"I have an exhibition in Los Angeles this week, just ahead of the Concours d'Elegance. It's something my sponsors lined up to showcase the sport to inner city youth."

"Like a charity show?"

His shirt is wet from my tears, with a big spot on his shoulder that I glance at for a moment.

"Sort of. I was hoping you'd come with me. See me in action, kind of thing." He leans in, trying to convince me with his words, but his lips are dangerously close to mine. "Then onto Pebble Beach to show our car."

Our car.

Is this another chance for us? Not business partners and maybe not life partners, but somewhere in between?

"Why?"

"Because I want to share this with you. You stood in my trophy room, and when you looked at me . . ."

His voice is barely a whisper, giving that earnest expression I've come to love about him. His eyes close and he swallows hard. The fire crackles as I wait for him to collect himself.

I love emotional Tomlin, as much as I love arrogant Tomlin. So many sides to him and he's got to be the most complex man I've ever met.

"When you looked at me, you said that I'm a big deal. I said was, and you said am. You basically called me an idiot. Do you remember that?"

I do.

I memorized every word and interaction between us, trying to make sense of his sudden departure. The long time he stayed away and the nightly calls. I analyzed so much of us that I gave myself headaches and vowed to never get involved with him, only to take it all back the second he stepped out of his car today.

"When you stood in that room, you didn't see the losses, you only saw my wins. You called me out on my wallowing, even stood there naked in that robe, and chewed out my father. No one does that. Not for me." Pride fills his words.

I analyzed that day too, fearing I had crossed the line, and that's what pushed him away. That and a hundred other things made him go.

"I want you to see me, at my best. Not here hiding out, but in the zone, winning. You stood in awe looking at those pictures. I want you to stand in awe at the edge of the mat when I win. It's a non-ranking competition, but it's a start."

I don't know what a non-ranking competition is. Nor do I care, because somewhere in him asking, my mouth falls open and I catch myself closing it. I did stand in awe. I was in awe. I still am. He doesn't need to stand on the mat for me to tell him. He's the most successful person I know.

"Tomlin—" I murmur, not knowing how to follow that big speech up with anything profound like him.

He squeezes my hand and inches closer, his knee overlapping my leg.

"Don't say no. Say you'll go. I'll handle everything. Pay for everything."

It's not the cost. I have the money from his car project. It's not the unexpected travel, even though I've never been on an airplane. It's what does this mean?

For us.

If there is an us and if he wants there to be an us.

"Please, Dani."

Those dark chocolate eyes are imploring, practically begging. With anxiety twisting my gut and hope blooming in my chest, I say, "I'll go."

That beautiful smile spreads quickly across his face as he releases my hand to pull me into a crushing hug. I hesitate for a second, wanting him to tell me what this means. What I want it to mean. What I want it to mean to him.

The hell with it.

Surrender and see.

I slide my hand over his rough dress shirt to wrap around his narrow waist, molding my body to his and closing my eyes. The crackle of the fire, the warmth of his embrace, and the hope in my heart has me wishing he truly wants me this time. His arms tighten, his face presses into my hair, and his lips rest against my ear.

"You won't regret it."

The End

BONUS SCENE #1
TOMLIN TAKAHASHI POV

"You're certain this is her car?"

My heart pounds in my chest. It's been years.

Years of combing through police reports, reading first-hand accounts of my mother's death, and shoving aside my grief to recover the very car she loved and died in.

I was overseas when I got the call. Competing in my second Olympics, with my father by my side. Their marriage took a toll on her. The abuse she suffered at my father's hand was intense before I got strong enough to defend her.

At sixteen, I won my first Olympic gold medal and nearly beat my father into a coma. That was the last time he ever laid a hand on my mother. He divorced her shortly thereafter.

It devastated her.

Wanting the man she married, not the monster he had become.

My earnings easily supported her and me. She was free from the abuser, but not from the abuse. The memories raged within her. Until one day, she took the car out for a drive and never came back.

I was twenty years old.

No note. Nothing to explain her decision. I struggled with that for years. Therapy helped. Time did too.

The wins were for her, not him. Never for him, even though he celebrated them more than I did. The room I built in the cabin was for her. Far away from him and the influence he seems to think he has over my life.

He ceased being my father the day I put him in the hospital. He is merely a coach. After these next Olympics, when I retire, he will be dead to me.

It's the promise I hold to her.

"Yes, Mr. Takahashi. The VIN matches, but it's in terrible shape. Not just the original damage from the . . . accident."

He clears his voice, uncomfortable with the circumstance of this search. But I reconciled with the fact long ago that I wanted to restore the vehicle that held my mom's last moments.

I wanted it restored so I could drive it on sunny days, feel the wind in my hair and remember the times she laughed and sang in the seat beside me.

"Can you transport it?"

The extent of the damage didn't matter.

I had bought a few cars from Paul out of Boston, and he was aware of my search. If he couldn't take on the project, he had a couple of referrals for me.

I didn't like moving the project away from him, as I trusted his quality of work. However, he had been on standby for years now, and I couldn't expect him to drop his workload for my car.

His pause doesn't go unnoticed, but I wait him out.

"I'll have to pull it out, possibly crane lift the car, which could cause more damage. With all due respect, sir. Are you sure about this? Sometimes these things are best left where they are."

"Can you transport it, or do I need to get another guy to do it?"

Direct and to the point. I didn't ask his opinion.

He releases a long breath, and I figure this is his way of telling me it will cost more.

"I'll do my best, but I'll need to bring in a couple more guys to help, so the cost might go up."

Exactly what I thought.

"Can you get it on a trailer this week if I send you the destination?"

"Um, yes sir."

"Good. Give me a day or so and I'll be back in touch." Then a thought. "Send me pictures of the car, all angles, and if you intentionally damage the vehicle to up the price, I'll sue."

Not that I have any grounds to sue him, but I figure this will incentivize him to remain honest, as he has done.

"Of course, I was just planning on doing that."

We both know he wasn't, but that is beside the point.

"I'll be back in touch."

I end the call and lean back in my leather chair to watch the flames dance across the glass embers of the fireplace.

He really did it.

I had already reached a dead end with the previous two guys I hired to look for the car. This was Paul's guy. He said this character could find anything, and he did.

A smile blankets my face. I would celebrate with a drink, but I have a competition coming and can't afford to lose focus.

Going through my contacts, I scroll to Paul's number and wait for him to pick up. It's handy to have his cell and not have to deal with the front office anymore.

"Paul, here."

"Paul, it's Tomlin."

"Hey bud, how's it going? You in Tokyo?"

I'm surprised he remembered.

"Not yet, but it's coming up. Your guy did it. He found the car."

"Well, I'll be damned. Feels like Christmas, doesn't it?"

If I celebrated holidays.

"Yes, it does. He's getting it on a trailer this week."

"Well, shit."

That doesn't sound good.

"I hate to do this to you, but I can't take it. I've got too much right now, trying to get a few ready for a show on the East Coast, here by me. Can it wait? I can store it for you here, but it's going to be another next year before I can get to it."

Next year is far too long to wait. He warned me of this. Told me about the cars and the shows and even asked if I wanted to enter my car whenever I found it.

All that's off the table now.

"What if I can't wait?"

What's another year when I have waited years? Too long. I want to feel close to her again and this car is the only way possible.

"I have a couple of names I can give you. You're up against their time commitments as well. I'm not sure if they send any cars to show out there, so that might help ya out," he concedes.

Let's hope he's right.

"Please send me their names so I can call them tonight. See what I can get going."

I lean forward, my elbows resting on the glass desk to log in to my email. Pounding on the keyboard drowns out the soft jazz floating through the speakers in the ceiling.

"You're in Colorado, right?"

"Yes, Denver."

I put the phone on speaker while opening my browser.

"There's a gal out there by you. She's pretty good. Her old man taught her. I've seen two of her cars up here, but I can't get past the owner of the place to talk to her. He must trash my messages. I'd ask her to join my team if I could."

I stare at my phone. "A woman?"

"Yep. Young too. Her work is better than some of my guys."

"How good can she be if she's young and a woman?" I snort, knowing she's not worth my time.

My fingers drum on the desk, waiting to hear about the other guy he has for me.

"I get it, man. She's not for everyone. I've heard she is pretty persnickety, but quality preservationists are scarce, and seeing her work, she can be as picky as she wants. Her name is Dani Winters, out of Cañon City."

"Out of the Cañon?" I chuckle. Paul's got to be pulling my leg. "This just gets better and better."

"Look her up. Dani Winters at Carl's Timeless Classics. I'll send you the other guy since it sounds like you won't be using her."

My fingers are flying across the keyboard. Sure enough, her name is plastered across a couple of prominent car magazines and enthusiasts' websites.

Clicking in and out of a couple of them to scan what they say, she's developed a cult following. It isn't until I see a picture of her smashed between two men with a restored car in the background that I fall back in my chair.

"Well, I'll be damned."

It's her.

The girl that carved a 'D' in my front door.

"What did you say?"

Forgetting Paul was still on the line, I say, "Nothing. Thanks, man, for sending me those names. I'll let you know what they say."

"Give me ten minutes to get them over to you. And you're welcome. I'm glad my guy could help."

I rub my chin. My smile widens as her angry face stares back at me.

"Me too. Talk to you soon, Paul."

What did he say?

It's like Christmas. Yes, it is.

They found my mother's car, and I found the sexy little minx that's going to restore it.

"Let the fun begin, Dani Winters."

Fuck it. Let's have that celebratory drink.

BONUS SCENE # 2
TOMLIN TAKAHASHI POV

Fucking Tokyo. My second career loss. Distracted and frustrated. That's what cost me the win. Over a damn girl that doesn't give a shit who I am. To her, I'm just another customer.

The way those baby blue eyes squinted in the sun when she threw up her hand to explain everything about car restoration.

Didn't she know I am well-studied? Having had all the time in the world to research it on my own while working with Paul and trying to find my mother's car. I let her diatribe continue even throwing in some questions that I already knew the answers to see if I could throw her off.

Paul was right, she knew her stuff. It was fun getting under her skin that first day. Watching her mouth drop when she saw me was the real kicker. Not to mention that ball-busting owner riding her ass at the first meeting.

It was extremely amusing. What I didn't expect was her resolve. I underestimated her stubbornness and that little attitude that she threw at everyone to get her way. I could see right through her and it made it even more enticing.

She was so transparent in trying to act like a man to survive her world. If only she could see that she already stood out and had their respect. She wouldn't have to hiss and scratch at everyone that got close to her.

This girl would not let her guard down for anyone. All I saw was a challenge. The first day when she carved up my door, I thought she was crazy. But the more I am around her, the more I see she's just protecting herself. From what, I don't know, and I intend to find out.

Pressing the highball glass against my forehead, the coolness from the melting ice feels good against my throbbing headache. I raise my index finger at the flight attendant to bring me another one, considering how long this flight is back to the States. Back to her and back to the car she isn't restoring.

That damn defiance got to me. Regardless of my approach, she shut me down every time. That's not something I am used to. The opposite, in fact.

I have girls dropping their panties to be with me. Yet the only one I want to see dropping hers wears zip-up coveralls and smells like grease.

It's why he bested me. My long-time competitor got the advantage over me because all I could think about was getting back to a blue-eyed beauty with braided hair and big breasts.

The thought of it has me chuckling now. Racked by a barely five-foot blonde that I have fantasized about bending over every surface in that garage of hers.

I even tried to relieve my sexual frustration with a female colleague after a practice match. Something I have never done before and will never do again. The frustrating part about it is she hasn't returned my calls. Nor has she messaged me on any of my social media accounts. I hate admitting that I have been watching for that.

She's radio silent with me after all these weeks and seems unbothered by it. Whereas I am borderline obsessive trying to find her on social media and finally decided that she must not have a presence at all.

It's rather refreshing from the Instagram-obsessed types I have dated in the past. Hell, this girl has through my type out the window entirely.

I'm more than intrigued by her. Not to mention how hard I get every time I think about her, which is causing me to shift in my first-class seat right now. The things I'd do to her and that sailor's mouth. I'd have her on her knees in a second if I could. If she were mine, she'd never leave my bed. I down my drink, the burn feeling good in my throat as I close my eyes and fantasize about her once again.

Turn the page to read Chapter One of Dani and Tomlin's trip to California in *Takahashi*.

TAKAHASHI: CHAPTER 1

DANI AND TOMLIN'S STORY CONTINUES

"Get off your knees, Dani."

"Shut up and enjoy the view."

He should. This will be the last time I ever do this. And easy for him to say. He didn't almost die in that tin tube floating in the air over here. If I want to take a moment to thank God that we arrived on the concrete floor in LAX, then I will.

He wasn't the one being jostled around, vomiting his guts out in that coffin-sized bathroom. No, Mr. I-travel-the-world was lounging, reading a book in first class like it was no big deal through the turbulence.

That smug bastard acted like it didn't even bother him, while I was white-knuckling my seat. And the nausea, well, I never sweated so much trying to hold it in since they kept that damn seatbelt sign on the whole fucking time.

I twist my tongue. The piercing clacks against the top of my teeth, desperately needing mouthwash. So much for giving up cussing. That fucking plane ride ruined it.

"That's enough. Now come on so we can collect our baggage and meet the driver."

His calloused palm cups my elbow. If it weren't for needing to pee and hoping I don't shit myself, I would sit here longer. Not to mention, I'll need to burn my shorts from sitting on this disease-infected airport floor.

"You're either going to have to slip my ass a sedative for that return flight home or we're renting a car and you're driving me all the way back to Colorado," I complain, clutching the chrome handle of the row of adjoined seats where a teenager has been watching me the whole time.

"What are you looking at, huh?"

Tomlin shakes his head at the kid and flashes me an annoyed look.

"That's what humbles you? A little turbulence?"

Standing beside him, I sway a little. I don't know if it's my stomach still doing flips or losing its insides for the last half hour.

"A little? That plane was about to fall out of the sky, and you know it."

He chuckles, and it's the worst sound in the world.

"I've experienced worse. Now let's go. It's a walk to baggage claim where we are meeting him."

"I don't feel so good."

His hand slides down my clammy skin to hold my hand. The warmth of his rough fingers seeps into mine. I drop my head and lean it into his chest to peer at his dress shoes. Normally I'd never do this, but the dizziness makes me feel like shit. I know we are in a hurry, but I need a few more seconds for the wave of bile collecting in my throat to go down.

"Did you get up too fast?"

His deep voice rumbles against my head and his muscular arm sits atop my shoulders to comfort me. His clean, woodsy fragrance wraps around me and it's one of many reasons I freaking love this guy.

"Is this a new cologne?" I mumble against the crisply pressed dress shirt digging into my forehead.

Even on vacation, he's all dolled up. I swear he makes all his clothes look good. Especially those damn gray sweatpants he taunted me with last night when he lent me a suitcase.

"I don't think so. I have dozens."

Of course, he does.

This scent differs from the one he wore the night he held me and sat in my pain. He said he pulled a Dani, and I needed to pull a Tomlin. That sealed the deal. He captured my heart without even knowing it.

The last forty-eight hours have been a blur.

He helped me drop off Anna at Eli's house and waited while Eli made the dog introductions. Apparently, you can't just throw them all together and hope for the best.

We visited Isla, who made me promise to buy her a California shirt to go with the Colorado shirt Hamilton bought her at the truck stop. I'm beginning to think she's starting a collection of state-themed T-shirts.

Tomlin even ran me by Hamilton's station and lingered in the lobby while they sized each other up. Hamilton assured me that he'll continue checking on Isla while I'm gone and that things were progressing at that stupid snail's pace in her case.

Tomlin offered some fancy family law attorney in Denver, but Hamilton grumbled he had it covered. I feel like they know each other somehow, but neither will tell me.

"I need to pee."

I lift my head, leaning against his arm to gaze into his warm chocolate eyes. His face softens, a half-smile hanging to one side of his lips when he suddenly tugs on my low ponytail.

"How do you have anything left in there? You were in the bathroom for over thirty minutes. Didn't you hear the attendant knocking?"

"Yeah, but I wasn't going to vomit or have the shits sitting next to you, so fuck them."

"Charming."

He squeezes my hand, conveying his words in touch. Our proximity to each other changed that night. We're standing closer, instigating small touches, and talking entirely too close for business partners.

Whatever happens on this trip happens. I won't initiate. I don't want to be rejected again. But if he leans in and starts something, I'm not stopping, no matter what he says.

"There's a bathroom further ahead on the right."

"Okay."

His arm slides off my shoulder to reposition his carry-on strap across his body before leading us into the stream of people. His fingers tighten over mine as we weave through the crowd of wayward travelers.

This place is insane.

The sheer amount of people is giving me anxiety. Combined with my nausea, I want to throw up or lie down. Neither of which I can do right now. I breathe through my mouth when we pass a food court with its rancid smells.

Tomlin, like the proficient traveler he is, sails through the crowd, garnering curious looks and whispered words behind hand-covered mouths. Yeah, some people know him here, and that makes me more apprehensive.

I never thought about getting all gussied up for him, nor did I think about the photographers that could be here waiting for celebrities like him. It's common on Instagram and I hope we don't get caught in one.

With the way I'm feeling, I'll photograph horribly. Maybe he should pick me up around the corner. That way, they can get the perfect picture of him and all his handsomeness, and I won't tarnish his image.

"I'll wait outside."

Tomlin releases my hand and reaches for his phone as I glance up and see the women's restroom ahead. I don't bother replying because there's already a line forming.

I take my spot in line and keep an eye on him as his fingers fly across the surface of his phone in a texting war with someone. Probably his dad, judging from the look on his face.

As the line creeps forward, a family stops to talk to him. Two boys stand to the side while Tomlin shakes hands with the parents. The older boy suddenly steps forward to bow to him. Tomlin immediately straightens and bows back. The respect is really cool to see. The smaller, younger boy shyly steps forward and Tomlin squats to give him some knuckles. It's the most endearing thing I've ever seen. If I liked kids, I'd want to have boys with that fine-ass man.

Damn, that came out of nowhere.

First things first, Dani. Land the guy and never think about kids again.

They disappear out of sight as I round the corner to an open stall. I hurry to pee, wash my hands, and get out of there because spying on Tomlin with his fans is fascinating. Something I never really thought about, even in his trophy room. By the time I get done, the family is gone, and he is back to angry typing on his phone. Wordlessly, I slide to his side.

"All set?"

He immediately locks his phone and shoves it into his pocket.

"Yep," I say then ask, "You okay?"

"Yes, why?"

He looks puzzled.

"I thought you were angry texting your dad."

A chuckle burst from him. "Angry texting is about right. But no, my agent this time."

Agent?

I never thought about that either. But every elite athlete has one. Why would Tomlin be any different? I don't know as much about him as I thought.

He interlaces our fingers, completely unnecessary, as the crowd has thinned. But I vowed not to turn away any advances he initiates since I'm all chips in now.

We're late by the fast pace his long legs are setting, getting across the concourse. I look like a show pony prancing beside him to keep up. After walking a bazillion miles in my cute wedges, taking an escalator downstairs, and hunting for our suitcases in baggage claim, he finds the man in an all-black suit holding a sign with his name on it. My feet are killing me, my stomach threatens to wage war again, and I'm breathless from jogging.

"Mr. Takahashi, welcome to Los Angeles."

They shake hands and I nod when Tomlin introduces me. I'm not feeling well, and the newness of this place is a little overwhelming.

"I'll collect the luggage."

He whistles to another uniformed guy, who speed walks over with a dolly cart to load our luggage.

"Sir, I must warn you that there are buzzards outside," the driver mutters, leaning toward Tomlin while looking at me.

"I understand. Thank you," Tomlin says before reaching into his crossbody and pulling out those aviator glasses I've stared into countless times. "Dani, put these on."

I'm confused about why I need glasses inside and even more confused about the buzzards outside. How are sunglasses supposed to protect me from birds that prey on roadkill?

"Why?"

Tomlin takes my hand again to follow the chauffeur.

"Just trust me," he utters, moving in front of me and tucking my hand behind his back to ensure I follow.

"This is weird," I grumble to myself before sliding them on.

The overpowering stench of exhaust fumes from the idling cars lined up at the curb blows through the double doors.

My stomach protests.

It doesn't need anything else to upset it.

Tomlin's hand is a vice grip over mine as he walks into a flood of flashing lights. It's chaos. The flash and clicking of cameras, yelling his name and screaming to know who I am.

Coupled with the speed at which Tomlin pushes through the paparazzi to the car makes my dizziness return. My pulse quickens while adrenaline and heat surge through my body. Sweat prickles at the back of my neck and into our joined hands. This is nerve-racking as hell.

The sunglass cut through the blinding lights, and I touch the edge to keep them from sliding down. How Tomlin can see through the flashes to the open car door is a wonder. He steps aside, helping me into the back of the car, before blocking my view for a quick photo op.

Ah, buzzards are the paparazzi.

The photographers are eating it up, calling for him to turn left or right. He indulges them for a few seconds longer while I duck my head between my knees to combat the fumes over-taking the cab of the car. It's entirely too much.

Tomlin slides in next to me, closing the door loudly while the guys load the luggage in the trunk. His hand swirls circles across my back. The leather seat groans when he shifts toward me.

"Try some water."

The crack of the cap is next to my ear. I sit up long enough to press the cold bottle to my forehead and pull his sunglasses from my face. The flashes continue through the blacked-out windows for a few tense moments until the driver and his helper get in the front and roll forward.

"That was—"

"Not too bad."

His hand moves my ponytail over my shoulder, allowing cool air to hit the nape of my neck. The exhaust fumes dissipate with the fresh-smelling air conditioning plowing into the car.

"That's insanity."

I sit up, forcing his hand off my back and drinking almost half the bottle before handing him his glasses.

"Thank you for those."

"Ah, you get used to it."

He tucks them in the open collar of his shirt, looking as relaxed as can be. Of course, calm, cool, and collected over here would say that, after participating in the three Olympics, and who knows how many other judo competitions.

"How are you feeling?" he asks, when the car emerges into the sun and the city opens around us.

With that awful airport experience behind me, I can focus on the real fun of this unexpected vacation. Time off near the beach in LA. Yeah, I can easily lie in the surf for a day or two.

"Getting better."

I down the rest of the water, setting it in a cupholder, before relaxing into the black leather seat. Tomlin's long body sprawls across the back, looking casually relaxed as his finger drums the armrest of the car door.

"Good, since today is a travel day. I figured we'd take it easy and didn't book anything. I wasn't sure how you would do since this is your first time." Those thick black eyebrows pinch in worry. "And it's a good thing I didn't because you look a little pallid."

"I don't even know what that word means," I say, looking out the window at swaying palm trees, a cloudless blue sky, and the cluster of skyscrapers off in the distance. "But I haven't come all this way to park my ass in a hotel room. I'll give you that."

I don't bother looking at him for fear of missing something cool out my window.

"I want to eat corny dogs on the beach, see the car collection at the Petersen, and see the Hollywood sign. Although they better not make me hike that shit because I can hike back home."

He is already watching me when I turn my head.

"Do you hike back home?" His inquiry is soft and relaxed, not the usual aloof or arrogant Tomlin. It's very likable.

"Hell no, all I do is work and . . . well work. You know that."

That's a problem now that I think about it. I'm terrible at work-life balance. Having worked like a dog for Carl and then again for Tomlin. Not that I minded the latter. Getting that Gran Torino show quality ready with Lars was probably the funniest, most grueling, and most rewarding job I've ever done.

"Anyway, I want to go clubbing, drink too much, maybe dance up on some hot NBA players and get propositioned for a threesome."

His eyes widen at that last statement and thank fuck, he stops drumming on the door. When he opens his mouth to speak, I shut it down.

"Not that I would. Been there, done that, and will never do it again."

His mouth snaps shut. A weird look passes over his face before settling into displeasure.

"Don't look at me like that. Hell, with all your fame and good looks, you know your ass has woken up in a hotel room not remembering what happened with two hot bodies next to you."

He stares at me for the longest time before slowly answering. "No, it hasn't. But it sounds like that has happened to you." Not displeasure, concern. "Were *you* roofied and you don't remember, because if that were the case, you could—"

"I don't want to talk about this anymore."

I revert to looking out the window again. He shuffles in his seat beside me, maybe trying to get my attention, but I was wrong for saying that.

What I meant to say is I want to have a great time while I am here.

Who knows if I'll ever come back?

Read the rest of Dani and Tomlin's story
in *Takahashi*.
(Tomlin Takahashi Duet #2, The Cañon Series, Book 2)

HAVING COMPLETED an extensive car restoration in record time, Dani Winters is looking forward to showing off her work and getting new clients at the infamous Pebble Beach car show.

Tomlin Takahashi, the owner of the restored car and new business partner, has more than a car show in mind when he invites her to Los Angeles a week prior to Pebble Beach to watch him compete in a charity Judo match.

Pining after her business partner and taking a trip with him is the last thing her poor heart needs after he's rejected her repeatedly.

Little does she know, his rejection protects him from experiencing more pain and tragedy in his life. Both yearn for love and acceptance, even if they go about it in different ways. Giving it one last shot, Dani Winters agrees to the trip and basks in the newfound love they share until one lie threatens it all.

Takahashi is Book Two of a Duet. It is a single POV, full-length friends-to-lovers, slight age gap, forced proximity romance containing dark themes and a happily ever after. Content warnings are available on the author's website.

Looking for steamy, naughty fun? Turn the page to read *Paolo*, the first book in my Cougars and Cubs Series.

PAOLO: CHAPTER 1

PAOLO AND TAYLOR'S STORY

My fingers dance across the keyboard, basking in the afternoon glow that floods my corner office every Friday. The skyscrapers outside my window stand tall, silent sentinels guarding the bustling financial district below. This view used to fill me with pride, but now it's a constant reminder of the lifestyle that holds me captive. Golden handcuffs are what they call it. Making too much money to walk away and with too much work to feel accomplished at anything.

The clock on my computer marches toward 5 pm. The echoes of colleagues granting well wishes for a joyous weekend fill the halls as they escape out the door to their family and home lives, leaving the corporate grind behind. It's another weekend, another trio of lonely nights in my high-rise apartment, a routine that's become all too familiar since my divorce a year ago.

The moment I opened that bedroom door and saw them entangled on our bed, my world tipped on its axis. My heart shattered into a million pieces, and the pain was excruciating. In the aftermath, I became a different person. I threw myself into my career with an intensity I had never known before, hoping my success would fill the void the betrayal left behind.

There are days when the questions still haunt me. How did I miss the signs? How could I have been so blind in the first place? The painful days are few and far between, but the loneliness is almost daily.

My phone buzzes, interrupting my thoughts. Glancing at the caller ID, I see it's Chloe, my best friend and colleague. I chuckle because she's probably still in the office too.

"Hey, Chloe."

"Taylor, I just heard Williamson's charging down the hall like a dark storm cloud," she whispers through the receiver. "He's looking for you."

By Williamson, she means Theodore R. Williamson III. Firstborn son and current Chairman of the Board of the expansive investment house that bears the moniker of his grandfather. Rarely is he on this floor. Even more rare is that he's looking for me. My heart rate spikes as I furrow my brow.

"What for? He never talks to me, not directly, anyhow."

He goes through my boss, the Chief Executive Officer, who's a stickler for following the chain of command and never stepping outside of it. When I glance across the glass offices, the CEO is already gone for the day, and his secretary is packing her bags to leave.

"I'm buried with the quarterly filing due in two weeks."

Before I can continue complaining to her, Mr. Williamson bursts into my office. His usually impeccable gray hair is in disarray, and his face is a roadmap of bulging veins and angry red splotches.

"Taylor, just the person I wanted to see," he barks with an open collar and his tie hanging askew. "We've got a mess on our hands."

I replace the receiver in its cradle and gesture toward the guest chair on the other side of my desk.

"Please, have a seat."

Mr. Williamson remains standing, slamming a thick folder onto my desk. It hits with a resounding thud, startling me.

"This is Mr. Jacobsen's file, our most lucrative client. He's been with us for over a decade and is threatening to leave."

I blink at the name on the folder. Jacobsen & Associates has been a loyal client for years. They have an extensive real estate holdings company in addition to their oil drilling and mineral rights leases. I can't fathom why they'd want to cut ties now.

"What happened?"

"He's furious about some miscommunication regarding his portfolio. He's been trying to reach Jim all week about some recent trades he took the liberty of making into volatile international stocks, which directly conflicts with Mr. Jacobsen's risk tolerance. And now Jim isn't returning his calls." Mr. Williamson's voice drips with fury.

Fucking Jimothy.

Jimothy is what I call him. It's a disparaging nickname since he doesn't deserve the respect of being called by his proper name, Jim. The man is nearly twenty-five years older than me. He is a narcissistic egomaniac who regularly cheats on his wife with the country club beer cart girls. He broods about the office like he owns the place and treats me as if we are not equals when, in fact, we are. Something I remind my male chauvinistic boss of all the time since he continues to let Jimothy run amuck.

"I'm sorry to hear that, sir."

I'm not. I hope this is the straw that breaks the camel's back in getting him fired since the last three hostile work environment complaints against Jimothy haven't done the trick.

"I knew you would be. Since you're the only one of my senior executives still here, I will need you to get right on it. Familiarize yourself with his portfolio and trades, then be prepared to present your recommendations on Monday on how we save this relationship."

My stomach churns. My inbox is overflowing with emails, and my calendar is a cluster of back-to-back meetings. I don't have the time nor the inclination to handle this just because I'm still here on a Friday afternoon or to save Jimothy's ass yet again.

"Mr. Williamson. With all due respect, I'd love to help. As you know, I'll do anything for the good of the company. However, I have my accounts to handle, and I'm double booked with the quarterly filings due in two weeks. Perhaps another executive . . ." I crane my head to look back to the row of empty glass offices, knowing full well I'm the only one here. "Or perhaps Jim could come in this weekend and work on it. Since he's responsible—"

"Taylor, he's in Mexico on vacation with his wife."

"Oh."

I haven't had a vacation all year, prioritizing work over everything, even my well-being. Now I have to clean up the mess made by this rotten, scheming, and lazy bastard.

"It's settled then." He doesn't look pleased by my objection. That makes two of us. I'm not pleased either. "You'll present first so we can open it up to questions before proceeding with the regular agenda."

I hate Jimothy for this. And right now, I hate Mr. Williamson too. Mostly, I hate my loyalty to this company that goes unacknowledged and unrewarded.

"I'll get right on it and reach out to Mr. Jacobsen." I reach for my phone when his waving hand stops me.

"No need, I already did. Just see what you can find. Then we'll regroup before approaching the client."

He doesn't wait for my reply when he strides out of the office, leaving me alone to grapple with this situation. With an exasperated sigh, I pick up my phone and dial Chloe's number.

She's always the one I turn to when work becomes unbearable, especially since I got her the job here.

She picks up on the first ring. "What happened?"

I lean back in my chair, feeling the weight of the world suddenly on my shoulders.

"You won't believe the mess I'm in right now. Mr. Williamson just dropped this colossal problem on my desk. Jacobsen & Associates is about to jump ship because of some disaster with their portfolio. And guess who's responsible for this disaster?"

"Who?"

"Jimothy."

Chloe lets out an empathetic groan. "Jimothy again? That guy is a menace. I don't know how he keeps getting away with things around here."

I shake my head, my frustration mounting.

"You and me both. I've had it with his antics. The guy must have glossy pictures on someone here because nothing ever happens to him."

As I sift through the mess on my desk, I sigh into the phone.

"I hope this colossal blunder will be the final straw that leads to Jimothy's long-overdue termination from the company. Maybe, just maybe, it's time for him to face the consequences of his actions once and for all."

She grunts in disbelief. "I doubt it. Nothing ever happens to him. Not even when the Head of Human Resources filed a complaint. You know she left because of him."

"I didn't know that," I murmur, flipping open the client folder. "But right now, I must figure out how to salvage this relationship. I am going to have to work late tonight and all weekend to sort through this mess."

"Taylor, you're overworking yourself." Chloe's voice softens with sympathy. "This isn't healthy. When was the last time you went out and had a little fun?"

I can't remember.

"I don't even know, Chloe. It feels like forever. But I can't afford to drop the ball on this."

There's a brief pause on the line before she speaks again.

"I get it. Just promise me you'll take some time for yourself soon. We can plan a weekend getaway or something. Maybe get laid. Oh, wouldn't that be nice? To find two hot guys to wine and dine us, then drill me into the mattress."

I manage a faint smile. I can't remember the last time I had sex either. At least no one since the ex. That's absolutely something that needs to be rectified once I get past these deadlines.

"Yeah, a wild and carefree weekend is long overdue. I'd like that, but after this and after my quarterly filings." I sigh for the third time as if the exhalation will somehow change my reality. "Anyway, I need to order my dinner since security won't let anyone up after 6 pm."

"Okay, call me if you need me."

I put the receiver down, pull the folder closer, and begin poring over the documents.

Fucking Jimothy.

**Read the rest of Paolo and Taylor's story in *Paolo*
(The Cougars and Cubs Series, Book 1)**

When a weekend fling turns into more . . .

In the heart of the bustling city, Taylor Woods, a seasoned executive, finds herself engrossed in an impromptu work project at an enchanting bakery, and her life takes an unexpected turn. There, she meets Paolo Cavallaro, a younger man whose magnetic charm draws her in. With a boldness that takes her by surprise, Paolo asks her to dinner that very night. Intrigued by the novelty of being pursued by a younger man, Taylor agrees, leading to a passionate one-night stand that neither can forget.

But when Paolo surprises her with a text inviting her for breakfast the next morning, their chemistry ignites a weekend fling that defies age and expectations. As their whirlwind romance unfolds, they find themselves caught in a corporate scandal that forces them into an unexpected partnership. Together, they set out to unmask the corrupt executives responsible for a possible company's downfall, all while navigating the complexities of their age-gap romance, meet-cute beginnings, and the irresistible pull of desire.

Embark on an exhilarating journey of forbidden romance, corporate scheming, and the unwavering strength of their connection. Follow Taylor and Paolo as their paths unexpectedly converge at a quaint bakery, setting the stage for a romance of undeniable chemistry and steamy encounters.

Can their blossoming love withstand the turmoil of the corporate world, or will the pressures of their demanding lives extinguish the flame of their fateful encounter?

Paolo is the first book in The Cougars and Cubs Series and is a connected standalone. It is a steamy, reverse age-gap, forced proximity, multicultural couple, office romance.

ACKNOWLEDGMENTS

To my beautiful Elle. Thank you for saying you'll never read my books. It makes the sexy scenes easier to write as your mom.

To my handsome Elkan. Thank you for being my unexpected accountability partner in asking why it's taking me so long to publish my next book.

To my sweet sisters. Tara, thank you for supporting me one thousand percent and taking my calls filled with angst, self-doubt, and wondering if this book would ever come together. Tanya, thank you for putting my Facebook and Instagram posts on blast to your circle of influence.

To my old-fashioned mother. Yes, shirtless men on covers do sell romance books. Thank you for listening to all my crazy story ideas and plot points over countless Sunday lunches.

To my furry colleagues. I lost you, my sweet Molly while editing this book. Your sudden and shocking loss has been incredibly difficult and heartbreaking. I take solace in knowing you are reunited with your brothers and sister in Heaven. To Bully, I'll see you poolside as we write the next book.

To my beta readers. THANK YOU to Emily Beath, Sally Williams, Sarah Cudlipp, and Sarah Hughes. You know this story wouldn't be what it is without your help! The more brutal, the better.

To my readers. THANK YOU. There is no greater honor to be able to write a novel that people lose themselves in. It is especially gratifying when you love the characters as I do. You are whom I write for. 🖤

ABOUT THE AUTHOR

After retiring from a thirty-year career in corporate America, GiGi Meier is delighted to be writing romance novels about strong female characters and their complicated, swoon-worthy men.

She loves telling stories and figuring out why her characters do what they do. With heartbreaking angst, panty-dropping lust, and enviable love, her stories linger long after you close the book.

When GiGi is not eating over her laptop, she likes to spend time in the pool with her children, walk her furry babies, and film videos for Instagram and YouTube. Whether attending a book club or hosting a game night, she loves connecting with new people and making friends.

www.gigimeier.com

Books by GiGi Meier:

Standalone Book
Coyote
Sammie and Carlos's forced proximity
cartel, kidnapped, Military hero, dark romance

The Cañon Series
Tomlin
The start of Dani and Tomlin's
slow burn, enemies-to-almost-lovers
Tomlin Takahashi Duet #1
The Cañon Series, Book #1

Takahashi
The conclusion of Dani and Tomlin's
friends-to-lovers, happily ever after
Tomlin Takahashi Duet #2
The Cañon Series, Book #2

Hamilton
Hamilton and Molli's second chance,
small town, police officer romance
The Cañon Series, Book #3

Isla
Isla and Gabe's opposites attract,
age gap, forbidden love romance
The Cañon Series, Book #4

The Cougars and Cubs Series
Paolo
Taylor and Paolo's reverse age gap,
forced proximity, office romance

The Cougars and Cubs Series, Book #1

Sebastian
Sebastian and Chloe's reverse age gap
Opposites attract, Christmas romance
The Cougars and Cubs Series, Book #2

Giovanni
Giovanni and Kacie's reverse age gap
Protector, Alpha male romance
The Cougars and Cubs Series, Book #3

Kadus
Kadus and Bex's reverse age gap
Best friend's brother, rockstar romance
The Cougars and Cubs Series, Book #4

IF YOU ENJOYED THIS BOOK

Thank you for reading *Tomlin,* the first book in Dani and Tomlin's story. Stick around for the rest of Dani and Tomlin's story in *Takahashi,* the second book in the series.

If you enjoyed it, please consider leaving a review on BookBub, Goodreads, or your favorite retailer to let others know about this cute and feisty couple interracial couple.

Reviews are greatly appreciated!

They help independent authors, such as myself, get our books in front of more readers.

Check out my website for deleted or bonus scenes not found in the book.

https://www.gigimeier.com/freebies

HOTLINES FOR HELP

Help for runaway and homeless youth:
- Call 1-800-RUNAWAY (786-2929)
- Visit: <u>National Runaway Safeline</u>
- Live Chat: <u>www.1800runaway.org</u>

Help for Victims & Survivors of Domestic Violence
- Call 1-800-799-SAFE (1-800-799-7233)
- <u>National Domestic Violence Hotline</u>
- Live Chat: <u>www.thehotline.org</u>

Free and confidential help is available for victims of domestic violence 24 hours a day.

If you need help or just want someone to talk to, please call the National Domestic Violence Hotline at: 1-800-799-SAFE (7233) or TTY 1-800-787-3224. As a survivor of domestic violence, your safety is at high risk when you leave an abusive relationship and right after you make that decision.

It is important to work with a domestic violence advocate to develop a safety plan. Advocates can help you develop a plan for emergencies, connect you to community resources and discuss your options.

For additional information on accessing help and resources, read Getting Help with Family Violence.

National Resource Center on Domestic Violence
· Call 1 (800) 537-2238

National Indigenous Women's Resource Center
· Call 1 (855) 649-7299

Battered Women's Justice Project Criminal and Civil Justice Center & National Clearinghouse for the Defense of Battered Women
· Call 1 (800) 903-0111

National Health Resource Center on Domestic Violence
· Call 1 (888) 792-2873

National Center on Domestic Violence, Trauma & Mental Health
· Call 1 (312) 726-7020

Resource Center on Domestic Violence: Child Protection and Custody
· Call 1 (800) 527-3223

Asian Pacific Institute on Gender-Based Violence
· Call 1 (415) 568-3315

National Latin@ Network of Healthy Families and Communities
- Call 1 (651) 646-5553

Ujima, Inc.: The National Center on Violence Against Women in the Black Community
- Call 1 (844) 77-UJIMA (844-778-5462)

Expanding Services for Children & Youth Exposed DV Technical Assistance Futures Without Violence Children's Program
- Call 1 (617) 426-8667

National LGBTQ Institute on Intimate Partner Violence
- Call 1 (206) 568-7777